A Change of Heart

... and fall in love all over again

Adrienne Vaughan

ISBN 978-0-9573949-5-7

A Change of Heart

Sometimes a heart will tell,
The keeper of the well,
That wishes have come true,
There's nothing left to do.
But though these words are said,
There's something in the head,
That's not all as it seems,
For locked away are dreams,
And further depths to find,
Of heart and soul and mind.
Yet richer veins lie deep,
Within the spirit's keep,
And mining there will show,
There's still more love to grow,
As loyalty and faith,
Humility and grace,
Such solid virtues true,
Will change the rosy hue,
Of love's first lustful charm,
To solid, granite calm,
That forms a bed of rock,
Withstanding every shock,
So nought is torn apart,
Thus turns the change of heart.

Adrienne Vaughan

Praise for A Change of Heart

This book really held my attention, the introduction of new characters linking in with memories of the first book, the way the island is described – I would love to live there. I am definitely recommending this to my friends and I look forward to the next instalment.

Jackie Ratcliffe – Amazon Review

A most enjoyable tale. The characters came to life in such a way that I felt I was living amongst them. Will be looking for more from this author.

Wendy Poole – Amazon Review

This novel is a wonderful way to escape into a world of heartwarming passion and intrigue into an extended family set in rural Ireland. You will experience many types of emotion reading the book ranging from hurt to humour but it is refreshingly genuine and the author really portrays authenticate characters and their stories amazingly well. I couldn't put the either book down and look forward to the next in the series..

Nicola Brown – Amazon Review

Talk about Maeve Binchy meets Jackie Collins – this is another lovely book in the series – just superb – romped through it – couldn't put it down – great story – fabulous writing and so pleased there was a happy ending. Light the fire, get on the sofa, open a nice bottle of something and away you go .... the characters are so wonderful you will be immersed from the outset and won't want to stop for anything at all.

Anna Bergmann, Scotland

It is a very good read that you can get totally lost in and certainly it kept me turning pages wanting to know what happened next. It is a book that had me smiling quite a lot and even crying a little at one point. I have to say this really is a first class read.

Elaine Gall, Goodreads and Amazon Top 50 Reviewer

So many twists and turns to this story. Could not put it down. Kept me on the edge of my seat right up to the end. Suspense, mystery and romance all rolled in to one. An excellent read.

Pam RDH, West Hartland, Connecticut USA

The first two books of the series were both great stories. Each one will stand alone, or should be read in order of publication. No cliff hangers. A satisfying ending, with relationships that can be picked up again in the last book. The Ireland location was fun and interesting. I look forward to the third and final book in the series.

Val, Aurora, Colarado, USA

*This book is dedicated to
my grandmothers,
Molly Wrafter and Alice Houlihan.
Two very different, yet surprisingly similar Irish women, who
influence every word I write, whether I want them to or not!*

Contents

Escape to Ireland...

A Change of Heart

... and fall in love all over again

Prologue

Dear Brian

I don't know where you are, how you are or what has become of you, but I had to put pen to paper to try to communicate with you somehow. I've the most wonderful news.

Our daughter, our beautiful, baby girl, is not dead at all. She's alive and well; what I've always known in my heart of hearts is true. I was lied to, and that lie tore our world apart.

She was stolen by those we trusted to look after her, the nursing sisters who were taking care of her when I was so desperately ill, and while I was fighting for my life, they sold our baby – like a commodity, a by-product. *They told me she died, but they lied.*

She was adopted, educated in Dublin and worked as a journalist in England, and now Brian, and this is what's so utterly amazing, she's on the island, Innishmahon; the gods, fate or whatever, has brought her home! She's living here, and everyone knows I'm her mother and she's my daughter and no-one gives a damn. Don't talk to me about the good old days; times have changed alright and for the better, thank goodness.

So, you have a daughter, our daughter, and guess what? She's called Marianne. They never changed her name, the name we chose for her, and our exquisite, fragile, baby girl, is a feisty, opinionated, warm and loving young woman. She has your eyes and beaming smile, and it breaks my heart a little bit more every time I see her, to think what we could have had, what we've missed.

I still miss you Brian, and I just needed you to know that we're here waiting for you, if you ever did want to come home. But you never will, will you? And that's okay, sort of, you've the right to choose how and where you live your life; we all do. Now I'm having, what did you used to call it? A *philosophical ramble.* You see, I'm still the same, never changed.

How I used to love those long, into the night discussions, particularly when we argued: huge, passionate rows declaring we'd never speak to each other again, with you storming off, me calling you back and then, barely able to keep our hands to ourselves, falling on each other like wild things. Oh, how I loved the making up. *I'm rambling again.*

Anyway Brian, I needed to write it all down, so wherever you are, I'm wishing you could share even just the tiniest fragment of this joy. Having Marianne back in my life has made all the heartache we went through worthwhile.

I may never forgive you, but I will always love you, Kathleen. X

Miss MacReady signed off with a flourish, re-read the cream pages filled with curly writing in green ink and smiled. She folded the letter and taking a matching envelope slid it inside and sealed it. She wrote: *For the personal attention of Dr Brian Maguire* on the front, waited for the ink to dry then placed the document in the small wooden box she kept under lock and key in her desk. The box she kept Marianne's original birth and forged death certificates in, together with the tiny black and white photograph of her daughter as a newborn, the picture which had perfectly matched the photo clipped to the adoption papers Marianne had carried with her all her life – the vital clue that revealed the shocking truth.

Lifting the Martini glass, she drained her drink. It was Monday; Miss MacReady always had cocktails on Mondays. She snuffed out the scented candles between forefinger and thumb, briefly admiring her metallic-blue nails, then wrapping the silk Kimono around her, padded barefoot through the beaded curtain to bed. Like all postmistresses, she had an early start in the morning, and what a morning it was going to be – the first morning of the rest of her life.

Miss MacReady viewed every morning like that. She really was the most unbelievably, annoyingly optimistic person on the planet, a real pain in the arse, particularly when you wanted a good moan!

Chapter One

All At Sea

Marianne stood outside the iron gates of the house. They needed a lick of paint but the place was not in bad condition at all. Renovated to the highest standard, then left empty for years, it had weathered well, standing proud on its hill above the village, looking out across the Atlantic, taking whatever the elements could throw at it on the chin.

Much like herself, the house had a chequered past. She smiled up at the casement windows, cream rendered walls and circular stone pillars either side of the gates. Rumoured to have been a haven for smugglers, a refuge of freedom fighters and a rendezvous for romantic trysts, the house had been home to the island's medical family, the doctors Maguire. When the last of the Maguire's, Brian, a bachelor, packed up and left, it was bought and extravagantly refurbished by a wealthy London stockbroker who had barely graced its pleasant portals before going broke, forcing the bank to put it back on the market.

Now it was hers and her dream could begin. She finally had the perfect property to turn into a holiday home for young carers

– children who did not have a childhood, let alone a holiday. This would be her new and totally absorbing project, this would be her focus, the centre of her world and she would give it all her love, her heart and soul. The project and baby Bridget, what more would she need?

She looked down at the auburn-haired toddler in the buggy beside her and lifted her out. Holding her close, she buried her nose in the little one's freshly washed hair. A clump of sorrow punched her in the chest. Sometimes the child reminded her so much of Oonagh, she could hardly bear to look at her. She missed Oonagh so much. 'As close as sisters', Oonagh used to say they were, and like a sister, she promised Oonagh she would step in and take care of her daughter if needed, laughing at the very idea, never imagining for a moment that Oonagh would be lost at sea and in losing her, a big bright light went out.

Looking out at the ocean, the memories came flooding back. Oonagh secretly admitting she hated being on the water, then laughing, their last meal together, an intimate dinner party aboard the yacht Padar had recklessly purchased to impress his star-struck wife. The guests carefully selected. Oonagh and Padar, playing host to Father Gregory, priest and helmsman; Ryan O'Gorman, movie star and crew member; and herself, award-winning journalist and the island's newest resident. She could hear Oonagh's husky voice begging Ryan to recount all the latest Hollywood gossip, teasing Father Gregory about his vow of celibacy and finally giving strict instructions to Ryan and Marianne, her baby daughter's godparents, to make a go of things, be together, life is too short. And then, as dawn broke and the chilled Atlantic mist swirled about the boat, the awful realisation that somehow Oonagh, who could not swim, had tripped, slipping overboard into the icy sea, and despite Padar and Ryan's desperate attempts at rescue, she was gone; disappeared beneath the black sea, forever.

"There Bridget, do you see? This lovely old house will be filled with fun and laughter and do you know what we're going to call it? We're going to call it Oonagh's Project, after your mother, that way there'll always be something good and solid on the island to remind us, somewhere warm and welcoming like she was, she'll never be forgotten. I'll make sure you know who your mother was, no matter what." She smiled brightly at the child, still too young to understand and then, looking from the house down to the quay, noticed Monty had slipped his lead and was trotting in the direction of the ferry, tail wagging as if he had spotted someone he recognised.

A man was jumping up and down on the quayside, waving at her in desperate welcome. The little dog, running in circles, barked at him joyfully. A couple of passengers were taking photos of the glorious coastline, a sweeping bay, its arms open in welcome. They were trying hard to include the profile of the famous movie star who had shared their passage, hoping he would notice and flash them a Hollywood smile, but he was too distracted.

She started down the hill, Bridget on her hip, pushing the buggy in front of her. The wind whipped her hair around her face; she kept pushing it out of her eyes. Was she seeing things, was it really him? The water sloshed about the boat, sending sparkles into the harbour like diamonds in the sunshine. The noise and bustle blurred her ears, shouts faded to a murmur, calls from the shoreline hushed to a happy hum.

She was close enough to see it *was* him. She tried not to blink in case the image disappeared. Slowing her pace, taking time to breathe, she felt as she always did when she saw him again for the first time: that searing, desperate longing and then the hollowness inside filled to bursting, tears of joy burning behind her eyes.

Praying he could not hear her heart pounding against her chest, she stood before him. The toddler on her hip gurgled, throwing out her arms to greet him. He had stopped jumping up and down and just stood there, grinning at her, one hand on the handle of a baby buggy at his side, the other reaching, stretched out towards her, fingers extended. She looked down at the hand, standing a millimetre from his touch.

"Well, here I am, I'm back," he announced, "me and my son here, we're home." He pushed the child's blue hood back to reveal a beautiful dark-haired boy, sleeping soundly. "Home for good," he gave her a dazzling smile; slate-blue eyes stabbed at her heart.

"Well good for you, Ryan O'Gorman, happy days." She stared straight back at him. He took a step towards her, she took a step back.

"Hey, no welcome, no warm embrace from the woman I love?" he tried a disarming, crooked grin.

"Is she on the island?" she asked him, eyebrows raised.

"Who?" he was confused.

"The woman you love," she replied, icily.

"Come on, Marie, don't give me a hard time. There's a lot to discuss I grant you, things to sort out, but here I am."

"Perhaps you should have done some of that before you and that poor child tipped up here like a couple of waif and strays," she told him.

"Whoa, this isn't…" he took another step towards her.

"How it's meant to be?" she stepped to the side. He caught his foot on the wheel of the buggy and, reaching out, let go of the handle.

"Marie please," the Irish-American lilt was melting, "we need to talk."

She hotched the little one on her hip higher.

"We do, but right now you need to rescue your son," she said anxiously, nodding after the buggy as it rolled gently away. A young man close-by turned his camera on the movie star, his rucksack clipping the handle as it trundled down the jetty, gaining speed, heading towards the sea.

"Ryan!" Marianne yelled.

"Stop!" Ryan roared, tearing after the buggy, dog hot on his heels. The wheels just tipped over the edge as the young man, with only a second to spare, lunged, caught the handle and hauled it back. At the same time, Ryan took a flying leap and, with nothing to break his fall, sailed through the air into the icy Atlantic.

There was a loud splash, cries of alarm, then after a long moment, Ryan surfaced coughing. A flurry of faces looked down from the quayside. One of the men tossed him a lifebelt. He caught it with one hand and, using it as a float, swam back to shore. Remembering his public persona, he stomped boldly up the ferry steps, waving as he reached the top.

"Just keeping in shape," he told them, smiling; he was an all-action hero after all. Cameras and phones flashed.

"Does *he* drink?" he heard one of the female onlookers ask a companion.

"Well, he takes plenty of water with it these days," laughed the man, wheeling luggage to a waiting car.

Pushing the panic from her throat, Marianne stared wide-eyed as Ryan approached them. The now awakened little boy, child on her hip and West Highland terrier all watched him suspiciously. He looked like a two-legged sea monster, dripping and coughing. The little girl started to giggle. She pointed at him. Marianne buried her face in the toddler's hood.

"It's not bloody funny. That buggy could have gone in and we both could have drowned," he said, shaking his head, water flying everywhere.

"What, you, *Thomas Bentley*, the all-action super-spy? No way," she said, referring to his role as the legendary secret agent. "You're fine, you're *both* fine." Her eyes were twinkling with relief, "You're just a bit wet. Come on, let's go, you need a hot shower by the look of you."

He flicked dripping locks out of his eyes, as she turned and pushing the baby boy ahead of her, with the little girl on her hip, walked briskly in the direction of the village. The dog sniffed him briefly and trotted after her. The jetty was emptying. Soon Ryan and his baggage would be all that was left. It was a good walk to the village and Weathervane, Marianne's cosy cottage, and he was very cold; he could die of hyperthermia if he did not get a move on.

The young man with the rucksack was writing in a notebook. Ryan had barely thanked him for saving his son. He watched him as his teeth started to chatter. The man looked up, Ryan raised a hand in acknowledgement, too embarrassed to do more. Muttering to himself, he gathered his expensive luggage, and with shoulders back, squelched after the disappearing cluster: Marianne Coltrane, their goddaughter, baby Bridget, his infant son Joey and Monty the dog. In fact, all he loved in the world.

"Wait for me," he called, pointlessly.

If Marianne was shocked by his arrival, she hid it well. By the time Ryan reached Weathervane, the cottage was warm and welcoming as ever, peat fire in the hearth, lamps lit, cushions and throws everywhere. He dropped his bags in the hall and stood at the kitchen door, taking it all in, feeling as if a very long journey had finally ended and he was home.

Marianne was stirring soup, the children on the rug, gurgling at each other. He shivered.

"Go and shower for heaven's sake, you'll catch your death," she said, barely looking up, "I'll settle these two once they've eaten."

"You seem annoyed with me," he said.

"Ha," she whooshed water into the kettle at full throttle.

"I thought you'd be pleased." He went to stand beside her.

"Did you now?" she moved away from him, heat burning a rash on her chest. She buttoned her shirt to the neck.

"I thought this was what you wanted, me, us, together?" he was bemused. She banged the kettle on the range. "Have I done the wrong thing?" he asked.

She was at the dresser, taking down mugs.

"You most certainly have," she replied, crashing open a cupboard in search of teabags.

"You mean you don't want me here," his voice was harsh in his throat. He laid a hand gently on her shoulder. It branded like an iron. She swallowed. She could smell him. He moved closer, his musky sea-scent filled her nostrils. She could not breathe. She ducked under his arm and found sanctuary by the kitchen door. She opened the top half, letting the breeze cool her. He came to stand beside her, following her gaze out past the little windblown garden, the gate to the lane and the sliver of sea beyond. Grey clouds broiled above the Atlantic.

"Marie," he whispered, "tell me you want me back." She did not answer. He stayed there, looking out to sea. She stole a glance at him as he watched the horizon, the breeze lifting his hair, thumb prints of tiredness stamped beneath his eyes. He caught her looking at him, and moved to block her view, lifting her chin with a finger, eyes burning into her.

"Well?" he lowered his mouth to hover over hers, she tasted his breath. She stepped back, slamming the top of the door closed.

"You're wet. Go and shower, we'll talk later," she dismissed him.

"Did I do the wrong thing?" he asked again.

"Yes, Ryan you did," she replied.

"Don't you love me then?" he spoke quietly.

"Yes, Ryan I do," she told him, avoiding his eyes.

"Gotcha!" he shouted, making them all jump. "Knew I was still in with a chance, can't resist me, mad about me, that's obvious."

She picked a cushion up and threw it at him.

"Don't get carried away, boyo, we've a lot to discuss, things we should have agreed before now, before this." She made a gesture encompassing them all.

He gave an involuntary shudder.

"Shower!" She pointed at the door.

He left, attempting a sort of squishy samba, she rolled her eyes as he sashayed up the stairs.

"God loves a trier," she told Monty, who was waiting patiently for his soup.

Padar Quinn was delighted to see him. He ran from behind the bar and clamped him in a huge hug. Ryan loved Maguire's – it was a proper pub, a real home from home, blazing fire, flagstone floor, glasses polished, brass gleaming.

"It's great to see you. Look at you, you're looking grand

altogether, I have to say," came the burbling diatribe of welcome from the nowadays recalcitrant landlord. Padar had not seen Ryan since Oonagh's memorial service, so long ago, yet raw as yesterday. "Have you seen Marianne? Did you see Bridget? Do they know you're here?" A barrage of questions, from a man who had said less than a sentence in weeks.

"Hold your horses," pleaded Ryan, now in clean, dry clothes and warmed with soup and tea, "how can I discuss anything without a pint of your finest inside me?"

Padar grinned and pushed back behind the bar to draw his friend a pint. It was early, but Padar had never bothered with official opening and closing times.

"You landed off the first ferry then?" he asked, waiting for the two-thirds to settle in the glass.

"Came straight from Dublin after the TV show. Spent last night in Joyce MacReady's bed and breakfast. I thought she'd be dying to see me, thought she'd be pleased."

Padar shrugged.

"Did she not see the show? Is she the only person in Ireland who doesn't watch it? I even asked Miss MacReady to tip her the wink I'd be on it, making an announcement, telling the whole world how I felt. Talk about wearing my heart on my sleeve!" Ryan said glumly.

Padar handed him the pint. He took a grateful slurp.

"I don't understand," he said, wiping his mouth with the back of his hand. Padar guffawed.

"Ah, sure if you understood, well that would make you the only man on the planet who did." He smiled at his friend, "Didn't welcome you with open arms then?"

Ryan's turn to shrug.

"Hardly. She told me to go, sort out my lodgings and she'd see me later. Joey fell asleep once he'd something to eat. She insisted I left him there, shooed me out of the house and here I am. I hope you have somewhere for us to stay, Padar?"

Padar nodded enthusiastically.

"Here, stay here with me. Loads of room, no women, no one telling us what to do and when to do it!" said Padar, grinning.

"I hope I'm included in any bachelor party?" boomed Father Gregory, immediately putting the dampner on Padar's plans, his cassock brushing the stone flags, as he strode up to take a stool. He greeted Ryan warmly, taking his hands in his.

"Welcome home," he smiled, "we're delighted to have you back, for good is it?"

"For good or evil," Ryan grinned back, "but I intend to stay."

"Good man." Father Gregory pumped his hand, as Padar placed a bottle of Budweiser before the priest. It was early for him too, but this was a special occasion.

"Delighted are we?" Sean Grogan slid into the bar. "Yeah, we're desperate for out-of-work actors and their kidnapped offspring here, agog with all the glamour and good fortune your presence will bestow upon the place. Can't wait to see what you and that crazy woman, setting up holiday homes for rapists and vandals all over the shop, are planning to do next."

"Hello Sean," Ryan laughed, "good to see you too."

"Better make mine a large one," Sean told Padar.

Father Gregory scowled at Sean, who was concentrating on his drink, "Not much has changed while you've been away."

"Oh, but it has, there's loads going on," called Miss MacReady from the doorway, hanging up a midnight-blue velvet cape and twirling so they could all get the benefit of her multi-coloured maxi dress and wellingtons painted with flowers. Padar checked his watch. He had not been busy this early since the storm, when the pub had proven sanctuary for half the village. Things were looking up.

Ryan smiled as Miss MacReady approached, news of his arrival had spread like wildfire, no change there then. She threw her arms around him and kissed him lusciously on each cheek, leaving a fuchsia-pink imprint.

"How's my sister Joyce? Did she take good care of you? I told her not to charge you too much, famous film star or no, you're practically my son-in-law and family's family," Miss MacReady gushed at him.

"What?" Ryan exclaimed. The postmistress was famously ebullient, but after a long journey and at this hour of the morning, she had Ryan completely flummoxed.

Father Gregory put a restraining hand on Miss MacReady's shoulder.

"Take it steady Kathleen. He's only off the boat and not even finished his pint yet," Father Gregory said.

Miss MacReady beamed at the priest.

"You're right, Gregory. One thing at a time," she smiled broadly at Ryan. "Did you know I'm Marianne's mother?"

Ryan coughed, splattering her dress with what remained of his drink.

"I probably wouldn't have started with that," Father Gregory reprimanded gently.

"Leave while you still can," Sean advised, giving Ryan a look as he slipped from his stool, "I would."

26

Miss MacReady ignored him. "Now, where shall I begin?" she asked of those gathered.

By the time Miss MacReady recounted the story of a frightened young girl in a home for unmarried mothers, where she had just been told her newborn baby had died, the bar was silent. Miss MacReady explained that the girl, desperately ill and confused, had no choice but to accept her child was lost, yet knew deep down she had not been told the truth. She paused for breath. Ryan grasped her hand.

"The 'Babies for Sale' scam. Marianne's campaign." Ryan was shocked, "No way, it can't have happened to you?"

"The very same," Miss MacReady nodded gravely. "I was one of those unfortunate young women and Marianne is my little girl. The photo of her as a newborn exactly matches the one on my baby's birth certificate, the picture I've treasured all these years. When I showed Marianne the paperwork relating to my baby's death, she realised it was forged, just like those she'd been uncovering throughout her campaign. The pieces started to fit together."

"That's an amazing story," Father Gregory touched her shoulder, "but forgive me, it seems so far-fetched."

Ryan looked into her face. He could see a likeness, he was sure of it.

"Not so far-fetched," Miss MacReady continued, taking a quick sip of her Buck's Fizz. "Marianne was adopted by the Coltranes – a couple who knew the island well, they often came to do research at the Marine Biology Unit. Maybe they heard about the young, unmarried mother, maybe someone knew they wanted a baby, maybe my baby was already earmarked for them."

Padar plonked a glass on the bar, "Ah Kathleen, now that *is* far-fetched, that's like the Dark Ages."

Ryan pushed his glass forward, indicating another pint.

"Padar, you're wrong. I've read some of Marianne's case studies, mothers and babies split up, the babies sold and I'm sorry to say Gregory, the church is often involved," Ryan confirmed.

"I know," Father Gregory agreed, "that's why Marianne's work is so important. But how did you know your baby wasn't dead, Kathleen?"

"I think I've always known in here," Miss MacReady thumped her chest, "but Marianne never researched her own background. A typical journalist, more interested in other people's stories. Strangely enough, it turns out they were *all* her story. She was uncovering precisely what happened to her."

"But why were you sent to that place? Why couldn't you stay and have your baby at home, your home? Who would put a frightened young girl through that?" Ryan was mystified.

"My *own* family," Miss MacReady replied steely eyed.

Chapter Two

Come Fly With Me

New York: seven a.m. Larry dragged the eye-mask off his face and poked about for his ear plugs. Then sitting up, took a sip of water from the glass on the nightstand. His mouth was like a desert. He looked at the clock and checked the phone. The last call logged was his business partner, Lena, who also happened to be his sister. According to the machine she had called six times. This was a lot, even for Lena. Larry, a chronic insomniac, drugged himself so heavily at night he could not hear the phone. There were messages on the answer machine too: it flashed up at him urgently.

Larry hauled himself out of bed and padded to the bathroom. He peed, put the seat back down, washed and dried his hands, then cleaned his teeth. The whir of his electric toothbrush made his head ache. He eyed himself in the mirror: teeth not bad, not good either. He could afford to have them fixed, there was money in the bank, the agency was doing well, successful even, especially as this season's hottest movie star, Ryan O'Gorman was one of their long-standing clients.

Should he call Lena back or shave first? He decided to shave first. Who knew what state he would be in after they spoke. Who could guess what was so *goddamn* urgent it required so many calls in the middle of the night? It was highly likely the impact of her communication would cause his hand to shake, rendering a safe shave impossible. Maybe their conversation would traumatise him so badly he would want to use the razor to end his own life. *I must cut down on the sleeping pills,* he thought, reaching for the bristle brush, hand already shaking.

He dialled her number.

"Larry, *jeez* how can you sleep at a time like this, haven't you heard?" Lena sounded as if she were in the next room, not two and half thousand miles away in Los Angeles.

"Heard what?" Larry tried to keep his voice calm. Lena was excitable at the best of times.

"That friggin' halfwit, O'Gorman, *your* beloved client," she spat the words down the line, "he quit!"

"Quit?" Larry repeated. "What do you mean, as in *resigned?*"

"Yep, right there on TV, in front of millions, he told a chat show host he's giving up his role as *Thomas Bentley* and moving to that godforsaken island he's so friggin' fond of."

"What?" Larry was on his feet now. "He can't do that, it's a three-movie deal, none of us gets our cut until he completes the movies."

"Tell me about it," Lena said. "And the kid, he's got the kid with him."

"I knew he had the kid. I heard Angelique's up to her old tricks, on tour with some young rock star," Larry told her.

"Yeah, I heard that too, but she's gonna hit the roof when she finds out Ryan's taken the kid out of the U.S." Lena confirmed.

"Hell, but you're right," Larry groaned, his head buzzing. "I'm guessing this could get messy."

"It's already messy. So here's what to do, you get your sorry ass on an airplane quick and go bring *Boy Wonder* back *immediately*. I'll do what I can to calm things down here." Lena had clearly been thinking things through.

"What're you gonna tell Rossini?" Larry hissed into the phone.

"Aliens have invaded Ryan's body and infiltrated his brain, is probably the most plausible explanation I can come up with." She hung up. Larry dialled another number.

"Yes Mimi, you heard, a flight. I know it's the weekend but I need you to get me on a flight. Yes, right now," he spoke slowly and calmly into the phone, knowing Mimi would think he had taken leave of his senses. He waited.

"Yes Mimi, that's right, Ireland." He waited again, "Yep, same trip as before." He waited a long time. "Of course it's goddamn urgent, why the heck else would I be ringing you on a weekend to get me on a friggin' airplane!" He screeched, and then pleading, "No Mimi, don't come over, my blood pressure is fine, just fine, okay?"

In less than thirty minutes, Mimi was in his bathroom.

"Please don't touch anything in there, I told you I can manage already," he called to her.

"I can't believe it!" She popped her perfect black bob into the bedroom. "Live on TV, in front of millions, he just quit, said it was over, his contract, his marriage, no explanation, no nothing?"

Larry took his Donegal tweed coat out of the closet, changed his mind and put it back.

"Hey, a publicity stunt is all. Judges on reality TV shows do it all the time, cranks up the ratings, you know that," he told her.

Mimi was sorting through bottles.

"Does he want more money?" Mimi always worried about the pocketbook, one of the reasons Larry liked her.

"Who knows?" he thought for a minute, "nah, not his style, but if he's spoken to Angelique about a divorce, who knows what *she's* demanding?"

"Yeah, I hadn't thought about that," Mimi said. "But surely that was all agreed before they got hitched?"

"Yeah, divorce was always on the cards, everyone knew it was a marriage of convenience, it had to be done at the time." Larry was in a closet looking for his bag, "But whatever about the prenup, Angelique could cut up rough, he should never have taken the boy out of the country without her permission."

"She might know all about it," Mimi tried to soothe.

"No-one knew *anything* about it! That's the whole point. I doubt Ryan knew about it himself until he said it right there on TV," Larry was close to shouting now.

"I'm sure it'll all be fine," she said, placing Larry's plethora of medication on the bed.

"What will you need?" she indicated what looked like the entire contents of a large pharmacy.

"All of it," he said, wrestling with his holdall. He felt nauseous.

"Did you book business class?" he asked.

"Did you tell me to book business class?" she replied.

"Tell me you booked business class?" he said.

"I booked business class," she told him.

"What would I do without you?" he said, with relief.

"Stay home, you can't even book your own airplane ticket." She gave him a smile. Larry admired her straight white teeth; they had been fixed, they looked good. He checked his reflection, he looked dreadful, there was already a line of perspiration on his top lip.

Marianne, still seriously off-kilter following Ryan's surprise arrival, was sipping a glass of wine in Maguire's chaotic kitchen. They sat opposite each other at the large oak table, a child each in their arms: Bridget with Ryan and Joey with Marianne.

"She's amazing," Ryan watched fascinated, as Bridget gurgled at him, gesticulating to Joey.

"She's asking you all about him. Who is he? Where's he from? Is he staying?" Marianne stroked the boy's head.

"You're probably right," Ryan said, as Bridget turned to burble at Joey, stretching out towards him. The boy's lips parted in a near smile. Marianne caught Ryan's anxiety.

"They'll be friends, you'll see," she said. They locked eyes. He looked tired. She tried a smile. "You okay?" she said. He nodded.

"Just a bit of a rough ride," he replied, "and things haven't been so smooth here either, I gather. Miss MacReady told me about the forged death certificate and you and she having matching photos of you as a newborn. Can it be true? Is she really your mother?"

Marianne nodded. "It would seem so, bizarre or what?"

"But in a good way?" Ryan was unsure, so much had happened in such a short space of time.

Marianne's smile warmed. "In a great way really, just going to take some getting used to, for both of us."

Padar pushed open the door.

"I'm desperate for a hand out here," he glanced behind him towards the bar. "Word's gone round yer man's back." He nodded at Ryan. "So the whole island has piled in to see the prodigal son returned for themselves. There's stuff on the telly, you know the showbiz bit, photos of himself sopping wet down at the jetty and you walking off in a huff."

"Great," Ryan groaned. "Smart phones and the internet, nothing's sacred."

"You're hot news at the moment Ryan, what did you expect? We can handle this, we've been through a lot worse." Marianne stood and handed Joey to Ryan, he took the boy in the crook of his arm. "Can you get these guys settled for the night," she indicated the children. "I'll give Padar a hand. If you don't appear they'll soon get bored and drift away."

"I'll have to face my public at some point," Ryan said.

"In your own time, when you're ready," she touched his hand briefly. "It's been a long journey."

He gave her a weary grin, "In more ways than one."

"Right, let's see the whites of their eyes," she laughed, following Padar back out to the bar.

"There'll be questions," Padar warned.

"Yes there will," she said, more to herself. Then, emulating Padar's late wife, her dear friend Oonagh, she painted on a streak of lipstick and her biggest smile.

Larry knew his journey to Innishmahon would take the best part of two days. He hated flying, loathed travelling and usually refused to leave New York full stop, but he had broken all his own rules when Ryan won the blockbusting film role for which he was now famous. When the offer came through, Ryan was nowhere to be seen. His relationship with the actress Angelique de Marcos was over and his career was on the slide. Larry finally found him languishing on the remote isle of Innishmahon, the wild Irish landscape providing the perfect setting for retreat and contemplation. Now Larry was heading there again, to negotiate another deal with his client and hopefully prevent them all from being sued to within an inch of their lives.

Running the past few months' dramatic events through his mind as the cab headed for John F. Kennedy Airport, Larry marvelled at how much mayhem one, very handsome, quite talented, yet totally unpredictable actor could cause. Larry rubbed at his temple, remembering Ryan's initial disbelief at being offered a film part which would make *him* world-famous, and them *all* rich. What was even more unbelievable, Larry had to convince Ryan to take the job.

And now this. Reneging on a contract with Franco Rossini was more than bad form, it was downright stupid. Rossini might be one of the world's most influential film producers, but it was not how the family fortune had been amassed. To say the Rossini's had 'underworld' connections was putting it mildly. Franco Rossini was no pushover, and the fact that Angelique, Ryan's estranged wife, was also Rossini's beloved niece, gave the whole scenario a sinister veneer.

Larry felt the bile rise in his throat. He rummaged in his holdall for his stomach medicine. He may not be looking forward to the journey, but if he did not achieve his objective he would probably decide not to bother with the return trip at all, choosing instead to throw himself off the nearest cliff, helpfully eradicating the need for the movie mogul to commission a hit man.

It was one o'clock in the morning when Padar finally bolted the huge oak door of the pub. The locals, disappointed not to welcome Ryan, their adopted superstar, back into the bosom of the island clan, accepted Marianne's explanation of weariness, resolving to catch up once he and the other new celebrity on the island, his baby son, were rested. In time-honoured Innishmahon style, there had still been a session, with songs and tales, as Marianne and Padar pulled pints until way past midnight.

Finally jaded with tiredness, Marianne wiped the last of the pumps as Padar called from the landing to say the little ones were fast asleep and he was going to his bed. Dragging on her coat, she poked her nose through the kitchen door. Ryan was out cold, stretched the length of the settle, legs dangling over the end with Monty nestled snugly under an arm.

Picking up her scent Monty's black snout appeared. She nodded at him and he leapt over Ryan, trotting towards the door. Ryan stirred, a flop of shiny grey-black hair fell across his forehead and his lips parted in a half-smile. She took a step towards him, longing to push the hair from his eyes and brush his warm mouth with her lips. He moaned, flung himself onto his side and pulled a cushion to his chest in a warm embrace. *Lucky cushion,* she thought, and driving the desire away, swept Monty up and headed for the door leading to the lane and Weathervane's gate. All was still.

"Feels like the quiet before a storm," she said to Monty, wondering if this was indeed the last peaceful night they would enjoy for some time.

Larry was dreading the journey, the memory of his last trip to the Emerald Isle seared on his brain like a brand, the six-hour flight to Shannon, followed by the connection to Knock, a windblown airfield in the middle of nowhere. The stewardess, alternating between heavily accented English and an ancient foreign language, pointing out local attractions: a white sausage made of offal, apparently delicious when fried; a drink allegedly made of red lemons and a nearby miraculous shrine where the Virgin Mary had made an appearance in the late eighteen hundreds. Larry sighed, these people seemed nice enough, but sometimes came across as either insane, inbred, inebriated or all three. By the time they landed, he was badly disgruntled.

Based on his last experience, he also knew he would be so weary from the journey, if he continued straight to Innishmahon, he would make little or no sense and would probably end up bawling out his client and achieving absolutely nothing. So he had Mimi telephone ahead and book him into Joyce MacReady's comfortable bed and breakfast. The guesthouse was a long drive from the airport but only a short distance from the ferry and although Larry hated boats, the bridge to the island had been washed away in a storm, so ferry it had to be. Further proof, if any were needed, that if a person wanted to remain cut off from civilisation for the foreseeable future, Innishmahon was yet again the perfect destination.

Unrolling his raincoat ahead of venturing outside, a shrill voice cut through the hubbub about him.

"Larry, Larry Leeson, yoo-hoo!"

He turned to find Kathleen MacReady, native of Innishmahon and the island's resident postmistress, waving at him enthusiastically from behind the arrivals barrier. Unsure why, he was immediately delighted to see her. They had met before, and as guardian of the island's erratic telephone system had spoken on numerous occasions, usually when Larry was in search of Ryan. Despite her somewhat eccentric dress sense, he found her intelligent and engaging, and right now, her smiling face was a very welcome sight indeed.

He strode towards her, arm extended for the traditional handshake. Miss MacReady threw herself at him in an enthusiastic embrace, kissing him on both cheeks in what she hoped was a suitable greeting for one of the most successful theatrical agents on the planet.

"Great to see you Mr Leeson, how was your journey? Pleased to be on terra firma I shouldn't wonder." She busily helped him into his raincoat, her shrewd eyes taking in the greenish pallor of the far from seasoned traveller.

"A nice surprise Miss MacReady, but surely you're not here to meet me? How the heck did you know I was coming?" Larry asked.

"Well, with all the excitement of Ryan's announcement live on the telly and then his arrival with the little fella yesterday, I had a pretty fair idea you wouldn't be far behind. You're either here to get him back on track or finish with him altogether." She swished towards the exit.

Intrigued, Larry stopped and placed a hand on her arm.

"You surmised all that and came to meet an airplane you were only guessing I would be on?" He was amazed.

"Not at all, Mr Leeson," Miss MacReady laughed, "sure didn't Joyce ring and tell me you were on your way. I'm good but my crystal ball is a little rusty." They swept through the doors.

Larry was dismayed to find Miss MacReady's brother, the taxi driver Pat grinning at them toothlessly from the window of his battered cab. Pat had chauffeured Larry the last time he had travelled from the airport to the bed and breakfast and it had been one of the most harrowing excursions the New Yorker had ever encountered. Realising he had no choice, Larry hoped, with his elder sister on board, Pat might navigate the vehicle in a more considerate fashion. Miss MacReady slid into the rear seat beside him.

"Have there been any improvements to the road since I was last here?" Larry asked anxiously.

"Not at all," said Pat, flicking his cigarette butt out of the window. "Worse if anything," he said smiling at them through the rear-view mirror.

"I tell you what, let's take the scenic route." Miss MacReady was enthusiastic. "It's a little longer, but sure the views make up for it, don't they Pat?" Pat looked quizzically at his sister. There was only one road to the bed and breakfast, the same road which led to the ferry port. There were a couple of 'off the beaten track' pubs along the way, alright.

He nodded. "Scenic route it is, so," he grinned. There might be a pint and bite to eat on the agenda.

Larry looked out at the rain-swept car park, the rolling grey of the hills beyond.

"A spot of lunch and a glass of something will put a whole different complexion on things," she said, squeezing Larry's knee, "you see if I'm not right Mr Leeson."

"Please call me Larry," he said, trying to smile.

"And you must call me Kathleen," she beamed into his face. "We must get to know each other better, you being so close to Ryan and he being almost my son-in-law."

Larry nodded and then, realising what she said, "What?"

"Oh, I've loads to tell you. You wouldn't believe how much has happened on the island while you've been over there in sleepy old New York." She batted her lashes, as Pat lurched the taxi into the oncoming mist. Larry felt his irritable bowel syndrome kick in big time.

Ryan watched the thin streak of dawn stretch to a slice of silver-grey over the eastern cliffs from one of the guest bedrooms at Maguire's public house. He could just make out the sign – Maguire's Purveyors of Game and Quality Victuallers. He craned his neck to look down the lane towards Marianne's cottage but outside was just an inky murk, too early for any lights signalling someone was up and might be willing to share tender words of welcome over hot tea and warm toast. He could hear the gulls rising, calling their sharp cries as dawn broke, the Atlantic cold and blank in this, the last hour between night and day.

The door creaked behind him, he let the curtain fall. Padar stood there, hair on end, blinking into the room. He rubbed his chin and looked at the cot, Joey was fast asleep.

"Go," Padar whispered. "I'll look after things here."

Ryan did not need telling twice. He was already showered and shaved. He pulled his battered leather jacket over his sweatshirt, looked briefly at this sleeping son and touching Padar on the shoulder in thanks, slipped down the stairs and out into the lane.

He knew the spare key hung behind a grinning gargoyle on the terrace. He let himself in quietly, moving swiftly to the terrier's basket under the stairs. Monty opened his eyes and growled softly. Picking up Ryan's scent he wagged his tail. Ryan signalled for him to stay, and, undressing down to his shorts and T-shirt, tiptoed bare foot up the stairs, pushing open the bedroom door at the top.

The light was just beginning to seep into the room, oozing through the gloom it fell on a sheen of satin, edged with velvet thrown across the bed. He stood in the doorway, his gaze sweeping across the sleeping form, her russet mop of hair on the white pillow, the soft curve of her cheek, sweet, slightly smiling mouth. She had pushed the cover away, the strap of her nightdress fallen from her shoulder, the skin glowed smooth and pearlescent.

He held his breath as he watched her, the rise and fall of her chest as she slept, the smooth hollow at her throat. As he leaned against the door frame, he gave his body permission to release all the passion and longing he had been suppressing for so long. He felt it bubble inside him, and as his desire rose to the surface, he could bear it no longer. He wanted her, he needed to make her his once again.

He knelt on the bed, taking the hand she had flung across the covers in his and putting her fingers to his mouth, kissed them playfully, running his nails like butterfly wings along her arm. She murmured and turned towards him, eyes closed, still sleeping. He slipped beneath the covers and slid his hands upwards, under the cool silk of her nightdress to her thighs, stroking her skin until her legs parted. She made a purring sound and turned away from him, pulling her knees together. He smiled, his lust was too strong to be so gently rejected. Gripping her waist he pulled her to him, pressing his erection against her bare buttocks. She murmured again. He brought his hands up to her breasts, cupping them in his palms as he pulled gently at her nipples with his fingers. She moaned. He lifted her hair and nuzzled the back of her neck, nibbling her earlobe, breathing soft, hot breaths at her skin. She threw her arms up, wriggling backwards against him. She stilled, her eyes opened.

"Ryan?"

"It had better be," he said, deep in her hair. She caught her breath, waited and then, turning abruptly, straddled him in one swift movement. Her eyes were laughing. He caught her by the wrists.

"Not so fast my little minx," he said, grinning up at her. "My turn, I think." He pushed her backwards, pressing her flat onto the bed, and holding her hands above her head, was on top of her in an instant. She screamed.

"You bastard," but she was giggling.

He leaned forward, lifting her chin with his fingers, to look directly at her.

"I'm desperate for you, I can't wait another second." He pushed his tongue through her smiling lips. She looked slyly under her eyelids at his face as he kissed her: she wanted to eat him.

"Have me then," she said, relaxing back, guiding him into her. She shuddered with pleasure. He did not move inside her, staying still, savouring the deepness. She wrapped her legs around him; locking them together. "Make love to me," she whispered.

He started to push against her, first slowly and rhythmically, then harder and faster. She clamped him to her, holding him with every fibre of her being, taking him in, bringing him to where he belonged. She filled herself with him, with their lust and their love. She looked up into his flinty eyes, half-closed with desire and she thought she would explode with happiness. He was home.

Chapter Three

The Postmistress Always Rings Twice

Joyce MacReady was delighted to welcome the weary American into her elegant Georgian farmhouse. Having shared the house with a famous ballerina for many years, she still had friends from the world of stage and screen and was hoping to enjoy an interesting evening in his company, as the last time he visited he had been far too tired for conversation. Joyce's life would have been very different if it were not for her guests, the large house empty and isolated without a constant stream of globetrotting visitors.

She pumped his hand firmly, greeting her sister with a brief hug and her brother with a glare. She had prepared a sumptuous dinner of smoked fresh cod with leek sauce to start, slow braised brisket of beef served with colcannon and shallot gravy and then the lightest, most delicious lemon meringue known to man.

Joyce kept a good cellar too. She had always enjoyed the finer things in life and loved hunting, shooting and fishing. Miss MacReady often said her sister should have married gentry, but Joyce had never been the marrying kind.

They talked long into the night, the focus of the conversation being Larry's plight in the light of Ryan's resignation. Joyce considered herself an expert in the legal department, having helped the ballerina disentangle herself from a number of inappropriate fund-draining charitable arrangements. Miss MacReady also considered her knowledge of law extensive and was preoccupied with the rights of her 'adopted grandson', as she referred to Joey. Would the little boy be able to stay in Ireland, where he would receive a proper education and be allowed to lead a normal life?

Larry's head was buzzing. His client's predicament was complicated enough. The abduction of the child, albeit his own, had exacerbated the situation intensely. Pat had been fairly circumspect throughout, for which Larry was grateful. His sisters aired their opinions most vociferously, but Larry could not understand a word Pat said. Add a full mouth of food to the equation and he stood not a chance.

Crumbling some delicious Irish Brie onto a cracker, Joyce forced a small cigar on each of the menfolk, while she went to fetch the port. Larry and Pat stood companionably in the porch, puffing sweet tobacco into the night.

"Better weather than las' time you came, anyway." Pat said, checking his cigar was alight.

Larry nodded. At least it was not raining.

"A lot's happened since that night, that's for sure," Pat continued, "good and bad. Your fella's not much help though, always seems to bring bad luck with him. Well, that's what the locals think."

Larry took his cigar from between his lips. He had not smoked in years, what with his asthma and his allergies but he was really enjoying the cigar.

"He's one guy. Don't lay all the blame at his door. The storm was a force of nature, don't forget," Larry said good-naturedly.

Pat shrugged.

"Some say him and that Marianne-one are the force of nature. A lot of people think there's been nothing but bad news since they turned up," he muttered.

Larry frowned at him under the porch light.

"Hey, that's only bar-room talk. I need Ryan back on my side of the pond right now, but he and Marianne want to make Innishmahon their home, they've made real friends there."

"The problem is he brings too much attention to the island, there's always a spotlight on him, the media and such, people can't go about their business," Pat said, blowing a smoke ring upwards.

"What business? Fishing and tourism is all I see?" Larry tried a laugh.

"There's more to the island than that, much more, the island has always played an important role in the running of the nation, the job's not done yet," Pat eyeballed Larry.

Pat had never been so articulate in his presence: it was clear he had a message to impart. They were quiet for a long moment.

"Are you saying there are people who want him out of the way, want to scare him off?" Larry asked, intrigued.

"That depends on what's needed. We could be talking scare tactics, you know, a type of 'horses head in the bed' warning, or worse." Pat put two fingers to his temple and pulled an imaginary trigger, "Bang...gone."

"Oh, you exaggerate Pat, this isn't *Mafia* country," Larry was dismissive.

"No it's not, but Joyce says some of our lads would leave that crowd standing in the extermination department, if you take my meaning." Pat had finished his cigar, "It would be better if you get him *and* her back to the States and keep them there."

Larry gave a little laugh, these Irish, so dramatic. Unsmiling, Pat ground the cigar underfoot.

"Pick up your stubs," Joyce called from the hallway, bustling into the drawing room, decanter in hand.

Pat slapped Larry on the back, "Do as you're told, there's a good man," he said and went back into the house.

Despite being dog-tired, Larry did not sleep well. He twisted and turned until he woke with a start, sitting bolt upright, sweat trickling from his chest to his stomach. He had been dreaming of the scene in *The Godfather*, a man wakes up covered in blood to find his favourite horse has been decapitated, the severed head placed beneath the sheets.

Larry shuddered, snapping on the bedside light. The reassuring glow cast soft shadows across Joyce's opulent drapes and cushions, helping to calm him. He reached into the drawer for his nebuliser, willing his heart to still as he breathed in the soothing steroid. He could hear the wind howling through the trees, rain beating against the window. No wonder he could not sleep: Mimi had forgotten to pack his ear plugs, and the weather in this country was so damn noisy, it sounded like someone was beating against the pane.

He pulled the covers over his head and closed his eyes. All was still and then another sound: the door opening. Someone entered the room. Larry froze. Footsteps crossed the floor, to the bed. He felt warm breath at his ear. He was terrified, convinced he was going to die, be killed stone dead, right here, right now...

"Are you asleep, Larry?" a voice hissed. He did not answer. Maybe they would go away. "Larry, are you asleep?"

He recognised the voice and drew the covers back slowly. Kathleen MacReady was nose-to-nose. His eyes swept over her, and once assured she was brandishing neither cut-throat razor nor horse's head, he released a breath.

"Not now I'm not," he said, sliding upwards, clasping sheets to his chest. Uninvited, Miss MacReady sat on the bed, her red satin dressing gown splayed out around her, bringing the vividness of his blood-soaked dream to life.

"You called out. I was just checking," she smiled. The poor man was clearly disturbed, his face snow-white, eyes shot with red.

She patted his arm. "Bad dream?"

Larry nodded. Miss MacReady poured water from the jug on the side. She handed it to him. He could smell perfume. She was wearing lipstick. Her ruby nails matched her gown. It slipped from her thigh. He could see stocking-tops. He swallowed.

"Can I get you anything, any medication?" Miss MacReady knew all about these New Yorkers, uppers for this, downers for that.

"No, no," Larry tapped the nebuliser.

"Asthmatic?" she asked.

Larry nodded.

"I wouldn't have thought New York smog and all that air conditioning would be any help at all. A bit of mountain air, some ions off the sea, that's what you need. You do look bit peaky, if you don't mind my saying." Although Larry always welcomed discussion of health-related issues, he was in no mood for even this topic at three in the morning.

"Can I get you a drink – a hot whiskey, milk with a drop of rum in it, Horlicks?" she offered. He shook his head at each suggestion. "Very well," she said, moving around the bed, tucking him in as if he were a child, placing his glass so he could reach it easily. He watched her warily. She knew stuff. He needed to keep her close, on side.

"Thank you, Kathleen," he said, his voice small and tight, "just a dream, I'm not a good traveller."

She tutted, "Sure, I know that. Isn't that why I came to meet you? Silly man, family's family around these parts."

Larry gave her a quizzical look. Surely Miss MacReady had enough family, she seemed related to everyone he met.

"You do seem troubled though, Larry, something more than just the Ryan debacle, maybe?" she asked sweetly.

He shook his head.

"No, that's bad enough. He's no idea how much trouble he's in. We're all in as a matter-of-fact," he said.

"Come, come Larry. It'll all look better in the morning, things always do. And anyway, it's only a film, a bit of nonsense with fast cars, glamorous women and an evil villain."

Larry tried to guffaw, it came out as a snort.

"It's the evil villain I'm worried about," Larry said, half to himself.

Dropping a kiss on his forehead, Miss MacReady shimmered out. As the door closed softly behind her, he was sure he heard a horse whinny in the darkness. He slid quickly beneath the covers. *Get a grip Larry, for Chrissakes. This is the west of Ireland, horses everywhere,* he told himself.

Hoping to ease Larry's passage and warn her loved ones of his impending arrival, Miss MacReady used Joyce's landline to telephone first Maguire's and then Weathervane later that morning, surmising correctly that the newly-reunited lovers might, at the very least, be having a lie-in.

Padar agreed to go and make one of the holiday cottages habitable for the stressed-out American and Miss MacReady assured the landlord she would inform the inhabitants of Weathervane that Larry Leeson, of Leeson & Leeson (New York) Limited was on his way.

"Sounds like trouble," Padar said over the crackly line.

"Well, it's really none of our business. It's something for Ryan and Mr Leeson to sort out." Miss MacReady was snippy.

Padar smiled as he replaced the receiver. Miss MacReady always knew everybody's business and was not beyond interfering, particularly when she considered it was in everyone's best interest. Declaring an issue out of bounds was unusual. It sounded very serious indeed.

"Are you serious?" Ryan exclaimed into the ancient Bakelite telephone, which sat in defiance of the twenty-first century on the polished mahogany table in the hallway of Weathervane cottage. "Already, he's here already?"

"Yes, I was sure he would come, weren't you?" Miss MacReady, asked.

"I knew he'd come, but so soon? He hates flying, travelling of any description, I thought it would take him at least a week to work himself up to the trip," Ryan said.

"He does seem very worried, alright. Far more stressed than last time and that was bad enough," she told him.

"Oh great," Ryan said, "there'll be any amount of pleading, coercing and blackmailing to get me back into that contract. I just wish I'd a bit more time to think things through," he said, more to himself.

"You mean you haven't thought this through?" came a voice from the kitchen.

"Sorry Kathleen, I'll have to go, no doubt see you later," Ryan said, replacing the handset abruptly. Marianne stood in the doorway. She was wearing his sweatshirt, her hair twisted into a pile on top of her head. Arms folded, legs crossed, she was trying not to laugh. Ryan shrugged, giving her his lopsided grin.

"I did wonder if it was all as simple as you made out. I knew it was a three-movie contract, I'd resigned myself to that." She smiled at him. It was so lovely to see him standing there, in her hall, having just left her bed.

"I needed you to know I'd give it all up for you. You and Joey, that's all I care about," he said firmly.

"And baby Bridget and don't forget Monty," she said. Monty looked up from his basket, wagging his tail at the mention of his name.

"Yes, little Bridget and Monty too, I need everyone I love together, in the same place. I need to be putting down roots, getting settled, before it's too late." His eyes were boring into her.

"It's never too late," she kissed him on the nose, "and I'm glad you made the grand gesture to be with us, for us all to be together. I love that you did it so boldly, live on TV. But like so many things that appear easy, the devil's in the detail." She met his gaze full-on.

"You're right," he said, looking across the little garden and beyond to the sliver of Atlantic, barely visible in the swirl of pewter mist.

"Come on then," she said, downing the coffee she was hoping they could linger over, before going back to bed to make uninterrupted love once more, "let's go and see what Padar needs help with ahead of the arrival of Mr Leeson."

Ryan continued to stare out to sea.

"I'm gonna need help too," he said, in a quiet voice, "starting with a good lawyer."

"That's okay, once this starts to rumble there'll be lawyers all over it, I shouldn't wonder," she laughed, pinching his bottom as she left to get dressed. *It'll be fine, we can face anything once we're together,* she thought, still glowing from their lovemaking. *Nothing's going to drive us apart ever again.*

Although Padar had generously offered to take care of the children so Ryan and Marianne could be properly reunited, total chaos greeted them when they arrived back at Maguire's.

Joey was grizzling from the high chair, Bridget was under the table eating cornflakes off the floor and Padar was nowhere to be seen. Marianne set to work sorting out the youngsters, while Ryan ran through the bar, calling for the landlord. Padar emerged from the linen press, piles of sheets and pillowcases strewn about him.

"Your man Leeson is on his way, did you hear? I'm sorting out May Cottage," Padar said.

Ryan started to pick things up.

"Do you know how long he's staying?" Ryan asked.

"No, but Miss MacReady says it's serious and you and he have stuff to sort out," Padar replied.

"Indeed. Need a hand?" Ryan watched as Padar dropped a tangled sheet.

"Please. This was Oonagh's department, one of my cousins gets the holiday cottages ready these days," his eyebrows shot up, "jaysus, the kids." He dumped a pile of towels in Ryan's arms and fled.

"It's okay, Marianne's with them," Ryan called after him.

Bearing a basket piled with linen, Ryan let himself into May Cottage. He just closed the door behind him as Pat MacReady's taxi screeched down Main Street, en route from the ferry. Not five minutes later, he heard heavy footsteps clattering up the stairs and the door to the bedroom swung open. Larry stood there squinting through misted spectacles, as his client pushed a pillow into a crisp, white cover.

"Interesting career move," the New Yorker quipped, "movie star to maid."

Ryan dropped the pillow and strode across the room to greet his long-suffering agent. They embraced affectionately. Larry folded his arms.

"Ryan, we gotta talk. This is serious, this is *real* serious." He looked Ryan in the eye.

"I know, it must be, you came all this way *again,*" Ryan replied.

"Last time it was good news, this time things are far from good," Larry said, grimly.

Ryan nodded but he fixed Larry's bloodshot eyes with a steely look.

"I'm not coming back, Larry. I quit. I've things to do here, I've made my choice," he told him.

Larry was remaking the bed, folding sheets crisply, plumping pillows.

"I've news for you, Ryan," he said, finally throwing a scatter cushion with a flourish, "you ain't got no choice, whatever you think."

"I think you'll find my contract has a compassionate break clause. It's in my terms and conditions, I know that much," Ryan said, emphatically.

Larry sighed.

"Do you think Franco Rossini gives a damn about your terms and conditions? The movie's broken box office records all over the world," Larry made a circle in the air with his hands.

Ryan knew this was true and even though he had an ego, he did not delude himself the film's success was down to his charismatic charm. He was sure Rossini's mighty movie machine could easily find someone to take his place. Any amount of younger, better-looking and more talented actors would be queuing up to audition for the part. *What was all the fuss about?*

"Whether you like it or not, you're a huge hit, you're the *Thomas Bentley* everyone wants, I know there's all the other stuff in the movie and they know they could get any amount of good-looking guys to play the part – hey they could even get one who can act – but you're the brand now, you're the guarantee the next movie will do at least as well as the first. Sorry Ryan, but that's the bald economical truth." Larry walked over to his client. "You can't walk out on this, whatever you think it says in your contract. You have to make the next movie, or there'll be another kind of contract out on you, you see if I ain't telling the truth," Larry hissed.

A loud crack, like gunshot, rang out. Larry lunged at Ryan pulling him to the floor, pushing his face against the carpet. Gasping for air, Ryan wriggled free.

"Jesus, Larry, what's wrong with you?" Ryan struggled up to the window, to watch Pat MacReady's ancient taxi lurch out of Maguire's car park and head back towards the ferry. "That was a car back-firing," he told the trembling bundle, slumped beside the bed.

Chapter Four

A Hopeless Case

As usual, Miss MacReady was first to break the news in Maguire's Bar on a blustery October evening. She wriggled out of her full-length wax coat in the lobby, to reveal a tangerine fading to yellow silk dress, beaded with sparkles as she moved. She whisked a frothy feather boa out of her pocket and wound it around her as she sashayed towards the bar. The outfit perfectly matched the tequila sunrise she ordered. Miss MacReady always had cocktails on Mondays, one of her many personal and fervently upheld traditions.

"Imagine our own lifeboat station at last. I can hardly believe it, it's a triumph and all down to us not giving up on the fight to have the bridge reinstated, it seems they've finally decided we're worth saving after all," she declared.

"How come?" asked Father Gregory, looking up from his *Racing Post*.

"Well, it seems the team building the bridge has also won the contract for the lifeboat station, meaning they may as well stay here and complete both projects," Miss MacReady sipped elegantly through a straw.

"Ah, economies of scale," the priest said, sagely.

"Economies of the back-hander more like!" grumbled Sean Grogan, from his usual stool.

"If it works in our favour for a change, I'm all for it," Padar said, stomping noisily up from the cellar, bearing a crate of bottles.

"We've always needed a lifeboat. I suppose with the rebuilding along the coast since the storm, it's the perfect opportunity to at last give us something we've been promised for so long," he said. It was Miss MacReady's turn to nod.

"And with the Euro-zone finances no better, let's hope what little money people are making they're keeping and spending in *this* country, holidaying here. I've seen a small rise in post office savings accounts, right enough," Miss MacReady confirmed.

"Anyone have enough money to buy a yacht?" Padar asked plaintively, referring to the forty-foot *Moody*, back on the market, after yet another 'sale' fell through.

"Who knows? With the building lads here and some new people coming to manage the lifeboat station, you may be able to hang on to it, might not have to sell it at all." Miss MacReady smiled encouragingly.

"Sure, I could never sail that again," he said quietly.

Father Gregory caught his eye. Padar gave his head a little shake.

"God rest her," the priest said under his breath.

The oak door swung open, as the building boys clattered into the bar, freshly showered and shaved from a long day on site.

"What was on today's agenda lads?" Miss MacReady asked, crossing her legs seductively.

"Erecting the structure for the bridge. The pressure's on if it's to be up by next summer," Shay Shaughnessy told her. "Hiring cranes is an expensive business. We only have a limited window to get the steelwork up."

The lads worked long hours in difficult conditions. Only the day before, huge halogen lights had been hoisted on metal pikes to bathe the whole site in an eerie glow; visibility being often less than perfect on Innishmahon in mid-October.

The headman Shay was a stocky Dubliner with bright-blue eyes, a wicked grin and a fruity turn of phrase. He could not get used to the fact that Father Gregory was often in the pub and apologised incessantly to the priest for his language.

Shay was flirting shamelessly with Miss MacReady.

"God you look fucking gorgeous tonight Kathleen, you really do. I could eat you, you're like a candy floss." Shay raised his glass to her, then noticed Father Gregory reading the paper.

"Oh Jesus, I'm sorry, Father," he said, "ah shite, I'm sorry again."

"I don't think God's that bothered how many times you use the F-word in front of me," Father Gregory smiled, taking a swig of Budweiser.

"I don't want to be disrespectful, Father." Shay turned puce. Father Gregory smiled at the young man, he seemed genuine enough.

"Ah, respect is earned, we all know that. Anyway actions speak louder than words. Tell me Shay, do you think you act in a Christian-like way?" The priest asked, the bar fell silent awaiting the reply.

"I do me best, Father," Shay looked into his pint.

"Sure what more can any man do?" Said the priest. "I'm Gregory, by the way, far too young to be your father." And they all laughed.

Shay spotted Father Gregory's newspaper. "Do you like the gee-gees, Gregory?" he asked, intrigued.

"With a passion. I come from a long line of horse breeders and trainers. Why the 'Big Man' called me to this profession, I sometimes wonder." Father Gregory's eyes turned skywards.

"Must have thought you were a good bet!" laughed Shay. "Mind if I join you?"

They were deep in conversation when Sinead Porter slipped in to the pub, taking a seat in what would have been the 'snug'. Padar had long since removed the walls, erecting a small half-glazed partition, affording privacy off the main bar.

Shay looked up from studying the form.

"Who's that little cracker?" he asked the priest, grinning over at the young blonde, dressed in navy slacks and a pink cashmere sweater wrapped softly around her neat curves. Father Gregory looked up.

"Our lovely midwife," he said.

"Why have I never seen her before?" asked Shay.

"Runs the pharmacy with her husband, Phileas, works part-time at the hospital on the mainland," Father Gregory told him, smiling at Sinead, who was chatting easily with Padar.

"I dunno, why are all the best ones always taken?" Shay asked dourly.

"I'd have thought a good-looking lad like yourself would have a wife, a girlfriend at least," Father Gregory said.

Shay shrugged.

"I did once. But with me working away the whole time, I came home from a job in England and she'd run off with a Polish fella – pregnant, the lot," Shay said flatly. "That's why I'm here, nothing at home for me."

"I'm sorry." Father Gregory went back to his paper.

"Where's her husband? A gorgeous girl like that shouldn't be out on her own," Shay could not take his eyes off her.

"Phileas is not much for the pub. Sometimes Sinead comes in for a quiet glass of wine. Her job is very stressful, I'd imagine," Father Gregory explained. Shay was still staring at her. "I'll just go and check she's okay," said the priest, tapping the newspaper to avert Shay's gaze.

Although whatever Larry and Ryan had to discuss would have serious ramifications on her own life, Marianne thought it wise to leave the men to themselves for a couple of hours. Now with the babies settled, not too far from where Padar was doing his paperwork, she decided to make an appearance at May Cottage.

After greeting Larry warmly, she busied herself arranging the vast quantity of chemicals and concoctions, so lovingly packed by Mimi on the other side of the Atlantic, in the pretty blue bathroom. Oonagh had decorated all three cottages in fresh, gypsy-bright colours and although Marianne totally remodelled Weathervane when she bought it from the Quinns, she delighted in her friend's flamboyant legacy. She missed Oonagh every day, and never more than when she unexpectedly came across little flashes of her ebullient personality. Closing the bathroom cabinet with a sigh, she went back into the room.

Larry, in grey trousers and beige turtle-neck, looked like a character in an old movie shot half in black and white, waiting to turn into colour for the fantasy dance routines. Fidgeting with his spectacles and smoothing his hair, he looked like he was on the wrong set completely.

Despite outward bonhomie, Larry was wary of Marianne. He watched her organise groceries in the yellow kitchen, then taking the cafetière from the dresser he started to make coffee, fussily. Ryan was smoking a cigarette in the garden. He allowed himself one a day, after dinner. It was still mid-morning. Marianne waited for Larry to speak, while he waited for her to say something. They spoke together.

"I er ...you ..."

"No, you first." Marianne watched his hand shake slightly as he put coffee into the pot.

"I'm sorry, Marianne, really I am, but I'm gonna have to take him back. He can't just quit like this. There's too much at stake." Larry avoided her eyes.

She handed him the kettle. As he poured the water, she could see his usually beautifully manicured nails were chewed. She placed a hand on his shoulder. He jumped, splashing the work surface.

"Crikey Larry, relax. You're wound up like a spring." Marianne was careful not to give any hint she knew what was on Ryan's mind. The last thing she wanted was for Ryan to return to America. Now she had him home, they needed to build a life for themselves and their little mismatched family. She had been strong alone for long enough, waiting yet pretending not to wait. Now she had him back, she wanted him to stay.

Larry mopped the work surface with kitchen towel, glancing at her under hooded lids. She was leaning against the sink, arms folded, eyes full of steel. Ryan appeared at the door, still tanned from his sojourn as the world's most famous super-spy, streaky ebony hair swept back, the aroma of exotic tobacco filled the kitchen briefly. He looked like he was in the wrong film too.

"You guys okay?" he asked, feeling the frost.

"Sure," Marianne beamed at him.

"Yeah, I'm making Marianne's day here by telling her you gotta go back and sort this mess out before it goes too far. We still have time to say it was a crazy publicity stunt – you were in Dublin, partying, thought it was funny, a prank," Larry offered.

Marianne blinked at Larry, then looked at Ryan.

"Do you really want to say that?" she asked. "You'd look a bit of a prat." She turned to Larry, "It's not true anyway, he meant it, he has resigned."

Ryan kept his tone light.

"She's right, my friend. It's a decision I had to make, so I've made it, end of."

"*No!*" Larry slammed a mug down, "It's not end of. Act quickly and we can save the situation, continue with this madness and we're all done for."

"Larry, calm down," Ryan said softly. "My contract's with the studio, they deal with this sort of thing all the time. They'll wheel their lawyers out, we'll wheel our lawyers out, they'll haggle a bit, go through the small print and come up with a solution, that's what they're paid for." He gave Larry an encouraging smile.

"Any normal contract, with any normal studio, yes. But your contract is with WonderWorld – Franco Rossini's studio – Rossini, the godfather of the movie industry. No-one says no to Franco, especially when it looks like the franchise you happen to be starring in is going to make him yet another fortune. Get real, Ryan, he ain't gonna let it go," Larry told him.

"He'll have to," Ryan was adamant.

"Your resignation, live on TV, was more than foolish. It made a fool of him – dangerous territory. We need a picture in the press of you two hugging each other like long-lost brothers, saying your differences are resolved and you'll be back working on the next movie in six months' time, as per your contract." Larry was glaring at Ryan.

Marianne looked from one to the other; these men loved each other. She saw fear in Larry's eyes. There was something he was not telling them, something he did not want Marianne to hear.

"Hey, hey," she soothed, "come on, we can work this out, you two just need to talk things through." She took her jacket off the back of a chair, the men were silent. "I'm going to wrap the babies up and take them for a walk around lunchtime, shall I see you both then, or aren't you staying that long, Larry?"

Larry continued to stare grim-faced at his client.

"I'm staying as long as it takes," Larry said.

Marianne pushed the plunger down in the coffee pot.

"Sort it then," she said, flashing Ryan a look as she left.

Ryan was standing on the shore gazing out to sea the next time she saw him, hands shoved in the pockets of his jeans, leather jacket open, flapping wildly in the wind. The mist had lifted and a watery sun bathed the beach in cool, peachy light. Monty charged across the sand to greet him, not having had their usual rough and tumble since Ryan arrived. Ryan bent down and lifted the little dog into his arms, burying his nose in the coarse white fur between his ears. He smelled of the sea. He turned, and placing Monty on the ground, ran with him to greet Marianne and the children.

He bent and kissed both babies, then taking Joey out of the buggy, wrapped him in a huge hug. Marianne smiled, as Bridget raised her arms to him. He handed Joey to Marianne and tucked the little girl under his jacket, jumping up and down in the sand making her laugh. She chortled loudly and Joey turned at the sound, his dark eyes sparkling at his new found-friend. With his free arm, Ryan pulled Marianne to him and kissed her, a hard, dry kiss on the mouth.

"Okay?" he asked.

"We've had a great time. Sinead popped in for a catch-up on the project, promptly fell in love with Joey, so we ended up playing games on the rug, all morning," she laughed. He loved to hear her laugh. She looked younger than he remembered. The grief of losing Oonagh eased away with the joy of Bridget growing and marvelling at every new thing. Now he was spending more time with Joey, he knew what that felt like. It was a wondrous feeling, alright.

"Larry?" she asked.

"Having a lie-down before he has a heart attack," he replied. She raised her eyebrows. "He's exhausted, worked himself into a right state. I worry about that guy."

"He worries about you; he's worried sick," she said.

"I know. I spoke to Lena, she'd just come back from an *emergency* meeting with Rossini's team. Not good," he gave his head a little shake.

They walked along the shore. Monty trotted at the water's edge. The waves seemed to rush suddenly, then stop to whisper into the sand, waiting to hear what was being said.

"Oh dear, was she hysterical?" Marianne asked.

"No, not at all, very consolatory for Lena, quietly spoken, scary in a way," he said.

"Really?" Despite her layers, Marianne shivered.

"Yeah, she said Rossini's seen the tape of the show and while he fully understands I've been under a lot of pressure lately, the announcement was not a good move. I need to get over there, put out the press release and get back on track. No more will be said about it." He put Joey back in the buggy. Marianne was quiet. It took the best part of two years to make and promote one of Rossini's super-spy blockbusters. Even though filming was not scheduled to start for at least six months, the role was a huge commitment. With the third film following the same pattern, they were looking at least five years ahead before they were free. Bridget would be nearly making her First Holy Communion by then, most of her young childhood passed.

"What about Joey?" she asked, eventually.

"She didn't mention him, so neither did I." He pulled the little boy's hood up.

"Does she know he's with you?"

They stopped. Bridget and Monty were digging in the sand.

"Not sure. Why do you ask?" Ryan was smiling at his son.

"He's Rossini's nephew, that's why." She sounded tense.

"Great-nephew," he corrected, "anyway, I have custody, his mother's unfit, you know that." He was dismissive. She took his hands and turned him to face her, looking him straight in the eye.

"I'm just saying be prepared for the worst. He's a rich, powerful man. Joey is the son of his favourite niece. When she finds out what's happened it could get nasty. I can see where Larry's coming from."

Ryan swallowed hard.

"No way, they can't take him away from me, us. They can't." He knelt down, drawing Bridget and Monty into his embrace. "This is where we belong, all of us, together."

"You have filed for divorce and custody of your son haven't

you?" she asked. A wave crashed against a rock. "Haven't you, Ryan?" He sat down in the sand with a bump, head in his hands. The water trickled up to him, wetting the hem of his jeans.

"Come on," she called, grabbing him by the collar of his jacket. "Let's go, sort the paperwork out at least, get something in writing. Honestly Ryan, you're hopeless."

He staggered to his feet as she gathered up the gang.

"I'm an actor. Reckless and impetuous, yes, but surely not hopeless." He gave a quick, swashbuckling move and, twirling an imaginary cape, took her by the waist and drew her to him. Monty rushed to her aid, running between Ryan's legs. He turned, tripped, and they both tumbled, arms and legs flailing, wrestling in a pile of sand. Bridget started to giggle, her tinkling laugh ringing out and then Joey started to chortle too. Marianne stopped wrestling with Ryan. It was the first time she had heard the little boy laugh.

"Hopeless!" She punched Ryan in the chest. He fell backwards laughing, moving his arms to make angel wings in the sand, much to the children's delight.

From his usual vantage point high on the cliff Sean Grogan tutted. *Mad shower of interlopers carrying on as usual*, he thought, *probably on all sorts of drugs. Those poor children, did Padar and the other child's mother know what was going on at all? A disgrace, that's what it was!*

Chapter Five

Rules Of Engagement

Despite Padar's constant fiscal concerns, the destruction of the bridge during the storm had brought some good fortune to the island. When Shay and the building team arrived in September, Padar negotiated with the contractors to provide bed, breakfast and evening meal, offering special rates for those who stayed behind at the weekend to go fishing or play golf on the island's blustery course. So Maguire's, which had never been busy on Mondays, even at the height of summer, was bustling with drinks and meals through to closing time, if there was such a thing.

Marianne was on duty at the pub that evening, so it made sense for Ryan to feed and bathe the children and put them to bed there. Padar had a baby alarm in the bar so they could keep an ear out for any problems. She was putting the finishing touches to a lamb casserole and because a lot of the building team were 'Jackeens' that famous Dublin dish, Coddle, when Ryan announced Larry had arrived.

Hanging his French trench coat next to Father Gregory's wax jacket and Kathleen MacReady's fur stole, Larry walked slowly up to the bar. He was concentrating, he had a job to do and he was damn well going to do it.

Miss MacReady gave him her usual zealous welcome, introducing him to Padar and Father Gregory. She ignored Sean, who was desperately craning his neck towards the gathering, hoping Larry would prove to be an over-generous American and buy the whole bar a drink. He was disappointed when the quietly spoken New Yorker ordered a soda and lime, taking his drink to a table as far away from the bar as possible.Grabbing a pint of stout as he emerged from the kitchen, Ryan joined him.

"Feeling any better?" he asked, as he sat down.

"A little," Larry replied, "I'll feel a lot better when I've talked some sense into you though."

Ryan sighed, "Shall we eat first? I'm starving."

Larry rolled his eyes.

"Eat? How can you think about food at a time like this? The world is falling apart and you want to eat! Nothing has passed my lips since Lena rang me and told me about your TV appearance. I'm fading away." Anxiety had clearly erased the memory of the sumptuous feast Larry enjoyed at Joyce MacReady's. Ryan eyed Larry's portly frame. A bit of fading away would not do any harm, if the truth be told.

"Well, I'm going to finish my pint and have a plateful of Marianne's Moroccan Lamb, with a very large glass of Rioja. Are you going to sit there and watch me eat?" Ryan asked archly.

Larry sipped his soda water.

"I might try a morsel," he said, lips pursed. "Just to keep you company, you understand."

"Good, first we eat, then we talk and then you decide whether you want to stay on for a few days or am I to take you to the airport in the morning and send you on your way." Ryan said sternly.

Larry took another sip of his drink, smiling briefly as Marianne delivered two steaming dishes of the food Ryan had already ordered. She raised her eyebrows at Ryan as she left. They agreed Ryan should speak with Larry alone first. He was his agent, business is business, he owed Larry that. Ryan knew they were discussing the future of her whole world, but it was a conversation she could not be part of at present, she had to trust him to make the right decisions for all of them.

"Have you had a chance to review your contract?" Larry asked, dicing lamb with the side of his fork. Ryan shook his head. "No, I didn't think so," Larry continued.

"That's your department," Ryan told him, helpfully.

"Precisely. That's why I'm here, it's a rolling contract, a three-movie agreement – there's a clue there, Ryan. None of us get the full deal until that which has been contracted is delivered, geddit."

"Money, it's always about money with you," Ryan said, they had this discussion often. It was a joke.

"Ryan, this is more than a dive-in, dive-out mini-series. You can't just walk away. You can have a compassionate break, that's why it's called a 'break clause' but that's all it is. The contract has to be completed, the box office returns filed and then we'll all be paid. Deal done. Then and only then can you walk away."

Ryan put his knife and fork down.

"Are you sure about that? Can't I get out of it?" he asked.

Larry shook his head, dabbing his mouth with his napkin.

"You can, but we'd lose everything, everything we've worked for all these years. Bow out when it's done, go with the world applauding, begging you to stay. Leave at the top of your career," Larry squeezed Ryan's hand, "make us all proud."

"But Marianne, Joey, my life here..." he raised his hands, encompassing the bar.

"They are your life, you've made the grand gesture. We've just got to be pragmatic and work round it. Besides you don't start work on the next movie for six months, plenty of time to put down roots, plan things for the future. And that's what you need to do, look out for everyone's future: you, Joey, Marianne, the whole damn lot."

Ryan sipped his wine, pensively.

"And if I bow out now?" he asked.

"You owe them big time. Not worth it." Larry had finished his lamb and was tucking into cherry pie. Ryan pushed his plate away. Marianne, who had been hovering behind the bar, appeared at his elbow.

"Okay? Lamb not to your liking?" she asked. Ryan's plate was still full; Larry was finishing dessert.

"Delicious, the chef here is amazing," Larry said.

"Thank you," she replied, not sure if Larry realised she was the cook.

"Can I have a few moments of your time?" he asked politely, looking her in the eye. "This is important."

"Of course," she said, relieved. She needed to be part of this conversation, she needed Larry on side. Larry gave Ryan a look. Ryan shrugged and headed for the kitchen, plates and dishes precariously stacked in his arms.

Larry folded his napkin and took another sip of soda water. Marianne pulled her chair up, fists clenched beneath the table.

"Ryan can't just resign Marianne. He can't walk away from the movie deal. Lena went to see our lawyer as soon as she got wind of the TV stunt. The compassionate break clause, to which Ryan so blithely refers, only kicks in if the actor, meaning Ryan, cannot physically or mentally do his job. Now, much as we both love him and know he's slightly off the wall, an untreatable psychotic he ain't!" Larry said.

"I don't get the impression Ryan has ever looked that closely at his contract," Marianne had to concur.

Larry nodded. "True, he's always left that side of things to me, which is fine, that's my job."

"Are you saying there's no getting out of it?" Marianne asked sadly.

Larry felt a pang of guilt. He liked this young woman. He had never seen Ryan happier with anyone in his life. But he had a job to do, he had to deliver.

"It's a rolling contract. Ryan is barely on wages until fees from the box office returns kick in. Even then, money is placed in a client account until all three movies are made and released. If he walks away now, he not only walks with nothing, the film company will sue him for loss of earnings – he'll be broke. It is highly unlikely he'll ever work again. He'll be blacklisted. Not officially, but that's how it works," Larry said.

Marianne looked up at Ryan who was keeping up the pretext of helping Padar behind the bar. He flipped a mixer like a professional cocktail waiter. Padar burst out laughing. Padar did not laugh much these days, tears pricked the corners of her eyes.

"But he doesn't care about the money, it's not important to him, to us," she said.

"That's blatantly obvious, but incredibly naive – there are too many powerful people in this particular food chain. You're an intelligent woman, Marianne, surely you know how these things work?" Larry kept his voice even.

"The main reason he took the role was to sort his finances out, wipe the slate clean. You're saying if he doesn't complete the contract that's not going to happen?" Marianne was also speaking quietly.

"It's not too late, but time's running out. He must go to New York and talk to Rossini. I've no need to tell you how important PR is in this game. We need to get the machine rolling again, assuring everyone, everything is back on track. It's not just about making a movie, it's a multi-national business. There's an awful lot at stake, people have invested a lot of money in the franchise and they have to see a return."

Marianne sat back, watching Larry carefully. "The backers, the money-men you mean."

He nodded.

"*Everyone* Marianne, it's a big deal. Ryan staying with the franchise guarantees the return. He's gone public saying he's chosen you and a life here, so make it happen. Give him a home, something to come back to. Be a family, it's what you both want, but he must do as I ask and I need your support, none of us can do this without you behind him, behind us, take it or leave it, that's the truth of it." Larry looked her in the eye.

Marianne's mouth was set in a grim line. She let out a breath and nodded briefly. Ryan took the fact they stopped talking as his cue to reappear.

"All okay over here?" he gave a slight smile.

"I think we're getting somewhere," Larry said, not taking his eyes off Marianne. "Any bourbon in this place, I could do with a drink?"

"Couldn't we all?" laughed Ryan, trying to gauge the mood, "but you'll have Irish whiskey and be glad of it."

Larry nodded, "Make it a good big one!"

Marianne had been rolling and re-rolling a napkin between her fingers.

"Marie?" Ryan said, bending towards her, brow creased with concern.

"I'll think I'll go and check the children," she said, and left.

Chapter Six

A New Career In A New Town

Dermot Finnegan was classically good-looking: tall, broad-shouldered with slim hips, a mop of sandy blond hair and greenish eyes. He laughed easily, with a robustness about him that left whoever he was talking to with a feeling of confident heartiness. Dermot was a man to be trusted, leaned upon. Dermot got things done and, it had to be said, Dermot had an awful lot of things to do.

He pulled the door of his neo-Georgian south Dublin apartment shut and threw his holdall into the boot of the 4x4. Punching a code into the sat nav, he put his phone on speaker and swung out of the cul-de-sac heading for the motorway going west. He had a good three and a half hour drive ahead of him and as dawn was breaking behind him, he would have a pretty clear run out of the city and on towards Mullingar.

Trying to suppress the bubbling excitement in his stomach, he flicked on the radio to catch the early morning news. He wondered if a large haul of cocaine, recently discovered in a disused warehouse near the airport had made the news yet. It was his dogged thoroughness that uncovered the packets of white powder, hidden in the miniature suitcases of a consignment of dolls dressed as air stewardesses; a clever ploy but Dermot had it sussed. He was keen to know if his boss had managed to keep the story under wraps, holding it in reserve for when the Gardaí needed a PR boost or a minister wanted to give the recession-battered populace of Ireland a little respite.

The clipped vowels of the newsreader rang out. The lead story was a visiting South Asian diplomat promising a new technology factory, followed by a motorway pile-up in the north and the *Lotto* rollover. He smiled to himself, Chief Superintendent McBride was still keeping a lid on it then, buying a bit more time for Dermot to pick up the thread on the far side of the country and see what he could uncover. It was his job to unearth the ringleader, the gangland bigwig co-ordinating shipments in through a number of ports.

Dermot had been integral in the Dublin sting; first in line when they burst upon the gang, bold as brass, loading the consignment into a fleet of illegal taxis, the perfect decoy to speed unchallenged through the city streets and out across the Dublin county border. He was damn good at his job, but he wanted a change, a bit more out of life. He sped along the motorway, making good time; it was still too early for rush-hour traffic to impede his escape.

Dermot's father had been a policeman, but Dermot had railed against the concept of a job for life and 'ran away to join the circus' as his father put it. He became an actor, much to his father's dismay and his mother's quiet pride, but when he returned, out of work and broke, still young enough to join the force, he decided to make a career of it after all, winning his father's approval at last when he was named the force's top marksman. But Dermot wanted to work undercover, using his acting skills to pull off a big job, and now this was his chance. An opportunity to make his mark, go out in a blaze of glory, before finally hanging up his badge.

Musing as he drove, Dermot was looking forward to this new assignment. One of the drug runners had cracked under interrogation, letting slip the next consignment was coming in via an island off the west coast, where a large construction project meant workers coming and going could disguise any extraneous activity. Dermot hit on Innishmahon. It had to be.

Tenacious as ever, Dermot discovered the island had been granted a lifeboat station, and a lifeboat station needed a coxswain, a captain to take the helm and run the show. As a fully qualified yacht master, first aider and serving officer of the Gardaí, Dermot was the perfect candidate.

In no time, Dermot was digging out his sea-boots, defrosting the fridge and kissing a handful of admirers goodbye. Innishmahon beckoned, a friendship needed rekindling, a lifeboat needed launching and a drugs ring needed busting. He switched off the radio and put his foot to the floor. He could almost see himself, scorching a trail across the map of Ireland *Indiana Jones* style.

Marianne drove Ryan to Knock Airport with the two youngsters in car seats behind them and Monty sitting happily on guard in-between. They giggled and gurgled for a while and then dropped off to sleep. Monty curling up into a ball as soon as he was satisfied his wards were slumbering. Marianne remembered Oonagh telling her a run in the car around the village was a sure way to get Bridget off when she was fractious. Marianne was impressed the ploy worked with Joey too.

She told Ryan he should take the trip to New York alone. It was business after all. But he was to be under no illusion, as soon as the agenda was settled, future trips would include all four of them, five if Monty could be accommodated, she wanted him to be clear about that. Initially he had been stubborn, refusing to even discuss going to New York, arguing with Larry that what was done, was done and let the lawyers deal with the fallout. But when Marianne, fully appraised of the situation by Larry, backed up by a lengthy telephone call with Lena, told him he should go and get things straight with the studio, Ryan finally conceded and arranged to meet Franco Rossini in Central Park, two days later.

"They're fast asleep," Ryan said, watching her profile as she drove, turned-up nose, the sprinkle of summer freckles fading, her expression impertinent, even when she was concentrating.

"Good, I'm sure Kathleen wouldn't have minded babysitting but when she told me she was having dinner with Larry, I didn't want to impose," she said.

"I know," Ryan laughed. They were surprised when Larry said he was staying on for a while and would not be joining Ryan on the flight back to Shannon and on to JFK. "What's that all about, surely not a romantic encounter? I mean I love Kathleen but she's years older than Larry, I'd have thought..."

"About the same age difference as us. Are you suggesting he's a toyboy? Why wouldn't he be attracted to a charming, intelligent older woman? She's quite a catch, with all those post office savings accounts at her fingertips." Marianne alluded to the fact Larry was 'careful' with money, one of the reasons Ryan said he never married: too scared a wife would make inroads into his bank account.

"Well, if you put it like that," Ryan smiled, "but has she no love interest of her own. I mean she's still a sexy woman, and definitely sends out all the signals."

Marianne slapped his thigh.

"Ryan, that's my mother you're talking about."

"Well, only just your mother," Ryan replied. He was still getting used to the idea. A strange story of coincidence alright, but one that explained why Marianne felt instantly at home on Innishmahon.

Ryan too, had always felt a strong connection to the island. Brought up by his maternal grandmother nearby, he spent holidays fishing with her brothers, until he won the scholarship to the School of Performing Arts and, after that, hungry for success, joined a rock band, returning two years later to find his grandmother dead and the brothers estranged.

Looking back at the babies and the little bundle of white fur, he squeezed Marianne's knee.

"It'll be alright," she said, sensing his mood of foreboding, Ryan was not looking forward to the trip.

"You're right, I need to eyeball Franco and talk it through with him, face-to-face. Larry's a drama queen, we know that, but Lena's level-headed and she seemed, not stressed exactly, but more, well fearful," Ryan told her.

They picked up the signs for the airport; only a few miles to go and they would be parted again. A sense of sadness hung between them.

"There's a lot at stake. See what he has to say, take it all on board. We can discuss it, chew it over, make the best decision we can, what more can we do?" she said as they turned into the car park.

Sensing they had reached their destination, Monty awoke and placed his paws on the console between the driver and passenger seats. Ryan took him in his arms and cradled him against his jacket, nuzzling the dog's wet snout.

"You take care of the family while I'm away little man," he told him. The sharp dark eyes stared back into Ryan's. Monty knew what his job entailed; he wanted Ryan assured of that.

Realising Monty, their comfort blanket had moved, the two toddlers started to stir.

"Shall you just drop me off? No need to disturb Joey and Bridget, do you think?" he asked her.

"Airports and goodbyes are likely to be a big part of their lives, the sooner they accept that the better," she said, matter-of-factly.

"But we don't want them upset," Ryan offered.

"That's why they have to get used to it. Then they'll know when and what to get upset about," she smiled, trying to ease his concern, "they'll soon love airports as much as I do. They mean someone is going on an adventure or someone's coming home. Who doesn't love an airport?"

He laughed and leaned across to kiss her.

"You're so *Love Actually* sometimes," he said, referring to her favourite film.

"All the time," she grinned.

They arranged the children in their new double buggy, clipping Monty's lead onto the frame, as Ryan slung his bag over his shoulder, taking charge of the steering. Bridget was wide awake and gurgling at Joey, explaining the sights and sounds all around them. Joey sat, white-faced, looking from one adult to the other. Marianne, sensing his anxiety, took him up in her arms and Monty promptly jumped into the spot beside Bridget, who carried on her conversation regardless. Ryan and Marianne laughed. Ryan covered Monty up with a rug as they trundled through the entrance, ignoring the *No Dogs Except Guide Dogs* sign.

"You're nearly boarding," Marianne said, pointing at the screen. The next flight to Shannon boarded in five minutes, ahead of an arrival from Dublin.

"I won't be gone long," he assured her.

"You need as long as it takes," she replied, unnecessarily fixing the collar of his jacket with her spare hand. He touched the necklace at her throat, the exquisite weathervane, studded with diamonds he had commissioned for her, to remind her that wherever he was in the world, she was his world and he would be coming back to her.

"Love you," he said, slate-blue eyes glinting. The doors slid open. A tall, fair-haired man led a small conga of passengers out into the main hall.

"Well, look at that! Ryan O'Gorman and Marianne, all the gang come to meet me. Hello, hello." Arms flung wide, Ryan and Marianne looked up into the beaming face of Dermot Finnegan.

"Sure I was all loaded up and heading across country when the car gave up the ghost. I've fair battered it over the past few months to be honest, so when the recovery man towed it away, I grabbed what I could carry and headed to the nearest airfield. One of my buddies on the force keeps a couple of light aircraft. A quick phone call, slight diversion and here I am," Dermot laid his cup back in the saucer. The crockery looked like a toy tea-set beside his huge hands. Marianne sipped her coffee.

"A happy coincidence then," she smiled back at one of Ryan's oldest friends. "How long have you known about the lifeboat station?"

"Not long. If I'm honest I kind of manipulated the appointment. I fancied a change of scene and you guys seemed so taken with the island and your life there, I thought, what harm, could be a fresh start?" he said.

"I thought you were happy in Dublin, in the guards," she said.

"I am, was. But I've been in the job a long time. Very stressful, and you and Ryan seemed so, well together. I thought, do you know what Dermot, maybe it's not too late for you after all, maybe there's a *happy ever after* for me too," he gave her a half-grin.

Marianne touched the large, calloused fingers.

"No-one special in your life?" she asked, gently.

"There was," Dermot tapped the table, "complicated, wasn't to be, you know how it is." He looked away, nodding at the babies dozing in the buggy beside them. "Little pets, God bless them," he whispered, "Will Ryan be gone long?" he asked, looking towards the doors they had watched Ryan pass through, waving a hurried goodbye, bemused by his friend's appearance but seemingly happy to leave all he loved standing at his side.

"Take care of my gang till I get back then." Ryan's parting shot as he kissed them all farewell, including Dermot. He was an actor, after all.

"As long as it takes," Marianne replied.

"Trouble?" Dermot asked. Marianne was not sure how much Dermot knew about Ryan's situation, or how much Ryan would want him to know.

"Just business," she answered brightly, gathering the wherewithal to get the show on the road. "Would you like a lift? I need to catch the next ferry. I know they would come for us if we were stranded, but I don't want to use all our favours up too quickly."

"Right with you," said Dermot, tucking Monty under his arm as they left the airport's small café and headed out to the windswept car park.

Marianne strapped the youngsters into their seats. Dermot checked his phone.

Clocked and following. The text read. The weather was coming in as they drove carefully away.

Chapter Seven

The Big Apple

Franco Rossini loved New York City. His visits were rare these days, obliged to spend too much time in Los Angeles. He waved the two men away, crossing the little bridge to his favourite bench. It looked down into a small arbour of trees and bushes, beautiful at any time of year but never more stunning than now, as the burnt copper and ruby reds of autumn swayed softly in the breeze, clinging hopefully to each branch before a final, fluttering farewell gave way to the inevitable arrival of winter.

He sat down wearily on the bench, splaying his arms along the back of the seat. He crossed his legs at the ankles, briefly admiring the fine Italian shoes and English silk socks. He let his head fall back, eyes open, relishing the cocoon of towering New York buildings peering over the edge of the park, framing the precious oasis, the whole scene domed in a cobalt, cloudless sky. Franco sighed. The hum of downtown Manhattan just yards away, a world away. This was the stillest and happiest he had been for some time. A good place to be, at the heart of his home.

As if he just remembered something, he felt inside his jacket and took out a delicate, pearlescent box. He flipped it open, popped a small pill under his tongue, closed the box and slipped it back in his pocket. He heard footsteps. The man he was waiting to meet was striding purposefully towards him. Dark aviator glasses, battered leather jacket with the collar turned up, faded jeans, worn deck shoes. Franco sighed. He did wish one of his most high-profile stars would make more of an effort in the style department. *Jeez, he looked like an out-of-work bit player.*

The man gave him a broad grin. Devastatingly handsome though. Franco smiled back, even a full-blooded heterosexual male like him could see, he was still a damn good-looking son of bitch!

"Ryan O'Gorman, as I live and breathe." The men embraced and Franco kissed him on each cheek. "You look like shit," he said, slapping Ryan on the back, beckoning him to sit. Ryan thought Franco did not look too good either, but declined to comment.

"Great to see you Franco, it's been too long," Ryan said, and then the smile disappeared. Slate-blue eyes looked directly into Franco's warm brown gaze, "give it to me straight Franco, how much trouble am I in?"

Franco resumed his splayed arm, crossed-leg position on the bench. He threw his head back and looked at the sky.

"To be honest, O'Gorman," he said, "It is I who is in the trouble my friend, big trouble."

Ryan frowned, sat back on the bench next to his boss, and waited.

For a while Franco said nothing, just continued to gaze at the sky. Ryan knew him well enough, particularly under the circumstances, to wait for his boss to speak first. After a long silence, Franco fished around in his pocket and took out a pack of cigarettes. He gave

Ryan one, put another between his own lips and lit them both with a slim, gold lighter. He took a long drag and blew the smoke out through his nostrils. Ryan did the same.

"They told me to give up," Franco said, rolling the cigarette lovingly between finger and thumb, "I never did do what I was told." He gave Ryan a wry smile.

"Me neither," Ryan smiled back.

Franco looked at the cigarette lighter as it lay glinting in the palm of his hand. He flipped it over and read the inscription out loud.

"'*Mira sempre alla luna, se la manchi, sarai sempre tra le stele.*' My father's saying: '*Always aim for the moon, if you miss it, you'll land on the stars.*' I gave him this when I made my first movie. He treasured it, till the day he died. A lot of people think it refers to ambition, and maybe it does, but ambition takes many forms. Perhaps the greatest ambition is love; the love of a good woman, the chance to be together, share love and grow love, so you have something to hold onto all the days of your life. That's one hell of a moon to aim for."

Ryan nodded. This was the Franco he liked best. The Franco who would seek him out when things were not going well on set; the Franco who would pull up a chair, sit beside him, smooth the troubled waters; the philosopher, the wise old sage, telling of what he has learned of life, what is in his heart.

"Have you landed on your moon, O'Gorman?" Franco asked, looking him straight in the eye.

"I think so," Ryan said.

"Then you must grab it with both hands and hang on. Does she feel the same way?"

"I think so," Ryan repeated. "In fact, I know so. When we're together, it just feels right, know what I mean?"

Franco nodded, puffing gently on the cigarette between his lips. "She stops the churning inside, yes?"

Ryan blinked at him. How did he know about the churning, the incessant whir of butterflies he felt whenever he was alone, without Marianne. He nodded.

"My Sophia, she did that too. Fought like an alley cat with me all our married life, but she stopped the whirring inside, she made everything alright, even when it wasn't. A good woman, my moon and stars."

They fell silent again, companionably smoking their cigarettes.

"Angelique wasn't right." Ryan thought he would seize the opportunity, put the record straight.

Franco raised his hands.

"Hey, I knew that. Thought you were crazy getting mixed up with her. I will take care of her, of course. She's family, but she's real bad news. Sad, but true."

"I'm glad you see it that way. I never meant..." Ryan stopped.

Franco gave Ryan's knee a fatherly pat.

"I know, never meant to hurt anyone, never meant her to get pregnant, have a child, I know. He's with you, the boy, yes?" Franco turned to look intently at Ryan.

"Yes, with Marianne and our godchild, in Ireland. He's fine."

Franco nodded.

"Good, that's good. I like Ireland, nice country, good people. Marianne, she has family there too, her mother close by?"

Ryan was not sure how much Franco knew, probably everything knowing him.

"Yes, some good friends too, we've all been through a lot together."

Franco smiled.

"Okay, now I understand and I am happy for you." The movie mogul went back to gazing at the sky. Hoping he was being dismissed, Ryan stood to go.

"Thanks, Franco. I can't tell you how relieved I am, I've been worried sick, we all have. Thanks a million, Franco, I really appreciate it." Ryan put out his hand, Franco ignored it.

"Now you know I understand you, it's time for you to understand me. We'll go eat and I will explain in words of one syllable why you cannot back out of this contract, why you have to make these movies," Franco stood up. Two men appeared out of nowhere, standing a discreet distance away. Ryan checked them out.

"Does my life depend on it?" he asked, not entirely joking.

"No, mine does," replied Franco. "Now what shall we eat, Italian or Italian?"

Ryan loved the way Franco always gave a guy a choice.

They walked the short distance to Mulberry Street and went through the side entrance Cesare Martinez reserved for his A-list patrons. The Italian restaurant was a favourite New York stop-off for royalty, movie stars and politicians, each afforded the opportunity to dine undisturbed in a private booth or join the hoi polloi in the main restaurant if a higher profile was required. Cesare always had a couple of tame paparazzi on standby, should any of his clientele require a little publicity boost.

He heard his old friend Franco Rossini was in town, so had come on duty early, knowing his fellow countryman could not visit New York without sampling some of the best Italian food in the world. He stood at the entrance waiting to greet him. They hugged and kissed, patting each other on the back. Cesare raised an eyebrow at Ryan.

He heard the star had quit, 'was standing down for personal reasons' the reporter on the celebrity news channel said. *Bullshit,* Cesare thought at the time. Franco extended an arm to Ryan, indicating he was to be welcomed also. Cesare was relieved. He hugged the younger man, crushing him against his solid, little body. He had known Ryan for years, having just opened the restaurant when the young actor hoping to land a part on Broadway, came looking for work, waiting tables between auditions. They went way back.

Recognition rippled through the early lunchtime diners, acknowledging the appearance of one of the world's hottest movie stars and his famous boss. Women turned to gaze at Ryan and smile at Franco, the men checked them out.

"A booth please, my friend," Franco said. "We need privacy today."

Cesare took them to a quiet corner.

"How hungry are you guys?" he asked. He never gave his friends a menu; he knew what they liked to eat. Cesare preferred to create something on the spot, hand-picking the freshest ingredients to produce something seasonal, a mouth-watering delicacy, with the unmistakable twist that made his, one of the most popular eateries in town. He left the men to their discussion, Franco sipping mineral water, Ryan a cold beer.

"This place, eh?" Franco gave a wave, encompassing the restaurant.

Ryan nodded. "I love it, never changes," he said.

"Ah, you may think not, but it does change, subtly, *minimale,* to stay in business, keep ahead of the times, change what needs to be changed, keep the things that make it the best, eh?" Franco popped an olive into his mouth. Ryan noticed the two men who followed them take a table at the edge of the other diners, facing the door. He looked from them to Franco. Franco shrugged.

"Things change, times have been tough, we've lost some major sponsors, I had to refinance the franchise." Franco took another olive from the dish. "The last movie and the next two have been carefully planned to pay for the restructure. That's the deal. It costs in excess of one hundred million dollars to make just one *Thomas Bentley* movie, schedule three and certain aspects come out cheaper, more cost effective as they say these days, but it's an expensive game, you know that."

Ryan's beer remained untouched. Franco continued.

"The restructure is also expensive. Let's just say because a few of my other ventures lost money, the conventional route to finance was not an option."

"Meaning the bank wasn't interested?" Ryan asked. He guessed Franco was referring to a couple of experimental projects that had been critically acclaimed, yet flopped at the movie theatres.

"Precisely," Franco said, "I had to go elsewhere for the money, I got what I needed, but the interest rate, well let's just say it's pretty high."

"Can be extortionate," Ryan agreed.

Franco flashed him a look. "A word I'd prefer you didn't use. The truth is, the movie, *your* movie has broken all records, a huge hit. But one swallow doesn't make a summer. We need all three in the can, and out there earning so we can pay our new backers back, shake hands and walk away, everyone happy." Franco glanced over at the two men, he looked far from happy. "We can't change the leading man at this stage. You being in the next two movies more or less guarantees their success. You can't back out Ryan, even if I let you, they won't."

Ryan watched Franco stab another olive with a cocktail stick, his brow creased in a frown. He was probably fifteen years his senior and today looked every minute of it.

"What about the company assets, you can sell them surely, the cars, the jewellery, the paintings, there's property too isn't there?" Ryan asked in a quiet voice.

"What I *could* sell, I did, but you can't secure a loan without collateral, you know that. The backers need something to guarantee their investment. I've held on to just enough to do that, but things are tight, real tight. Once the box office returns are in, we can start to pay something back, but we need capital to fund the next one and we need to make the movie as soon as we can. Fans are fickle, there's always someone sniping at our heels, trying to steal our crown. We gotta get on with it Ryan, and we can't do it without you."

Ryan pulled his chair up close and leaned across the table.

"Franco, I quit. I get all the reasons why it's not a good idea, and I'm sorry if this is causing a big problem, but I'm still out. I want my life back."

Franco sighed, taking the cocktail stick from between his lips. He laid his hand flat on the table and pushed the stick hard into the skin. He kept his eyes fixed on Ryan. Blood started to ooze where the wood had pierced the flesh.

"What the...?" Ryan tried to pull the stick out, but Franco would not release the pressure, he continued to press the stick into the back of his own hand.

"You're making me bleed, Ryan. I need you to understand, if you have your life back I will lose mine. Everything I've worked for, everything I represent will be gone. I will die a broken man, I will take the shame of failure to my grave, the memory of my family, my beloved Sophia, blackened forever. If I can't pay my backers they'll wipe me out. They're ruthless. I knew that when I accepted the deal and the only way you won't appear in the next movie, is if you can't."

"What do you mean?" Ryan was still staring at the back of Franco's hand.

"You can't make the movie because you'll no longer be around, you'll have been wiped out too." Franco looked unblinking into Ryan's eyes. The blood from his hand was staining the tablecloth, the red turning pink on the white linen.

Cesare appeared carrying two steaming bowls of delicious seafood risotto. Franco took his hand out of sight.

Cesare clapped, "A fresh table cloth, now!"

"Okay," Ryan swallowed, "okay I get it. I'm in, I'm still in."

Franco's expression did not change.

"Cesare, any of those tame *paps* of yours around today?"

"Always," Cesare smiled, arranging cutlery on the fresh cloth.

"Let's have our picture taken then." Franco said wrapping a napkin around his wounded hand, "we're back in business!"

"A compromise, what kind of compromise?" Marianne was speaking into the handset of the landline in the cottage. Ryan sounded every one of the thousands of miles away.

"I'm going to do the next movie and then half of the following one. We're going to work a takeover of the role into the storyline," he told her.

Marianne's heart plummeted. She tried to keep the disappointment from her voice. "Sounds reasonable. Are you okay about it?" she asked.

"Are you? I'm still prepared to tell Franco no deal, if that's what you want," he said. Ryan was a good actor, but Marianne could tell this was bravado.

"Will the compromise tick all the boxes, take the pressure off, satisfy everyone?" she said, running through in her mind *all* the lives this decision affected. "It's a big ask."

"I know, but Franco assures me we can make it work. If you're happy, well as happy as you can be about it, I'll agree."

She thought for a long moment.

He filled the silence.

"I've asked for special conditions too," Ryan continued. "For instance, any long stretches away on location, you and the little ones can come and spend some time; so we're not apart for too long and collaboration, I've asked if there is anything you want to help with, maybe editing or styling, you can get involved with that too."

Although his obvious enthusiasm made Marianne smile, she fleetingly wondered at the wisdom of yet another of Ryan's schemes, but could see what he was trying to do, make the best of things, she appreciated that.

"I'm sure you've done your best. When will you be home?" she asked.

"Fly out tomorrow, home the day after. I'll stay at Joyce MacReady's and take the first ferry back to the island in the morning." He had a smile in his voice now.

"How long till you start filming?" she was anxious.

"Six whole months!" he whooped. "Happy days."

"Good," she laughed. "Get back quickly; we don't want to waste a minute."

"No," he was laughing too. "Knowing you, we won't."

Chapter Eight

The Man From Atlantis

Although he had seen pictures, nothing prepared Innishmahon's newest inhabitant for his first encounter with the savage glory that was the island's landscape. Having grabbed a bite and bed the previous evening in Maguire's, Dermot Finnegan was an early riser and, pulling on jogging bottoms and a sweatshirt, headed out as dawn seeped pearlescent streaks into the dark-grey sky.

He turned right out of the pub's front portal and jogged towards a glittering shard of cliff, blanking off the view of the sea beyond. He ran steadily, following the tract left by holidaymakers as the lane turned to sand and the trail continued right up to the monolith of stone before him. He followed, and just when he thought he reached a dead end, he saw it, a sliver of an opening, so skilfully designed by nature, it was easy to miss, like an optical illusion, he had to concentrate to see it.

Intrigued, he slipped through the crevice into a pitch black cave and holding onto the walls for balance, shivered as his feet sank into cool sand. Standing to catch his breath, he could see light, a slash of grey against the blackness and taking a step forward, pulled himself through the gap. His foot slipped and, terrified he would fall to his death, he threw himself back against the cliff-face, clinging to the rock for dear life. Counting to three, he looked down to find he was perched on a tiny ledge, he saw the ledge stepped down to another track. He was on the side of a cliff alright, but one with a natural stone staircase which trailed and wound through the rock leading to a beach; a perfect horseshoe of golden sand. Magnificent cliffs scaled the skyline on either side of the bay, providing the perfect frame as the rolling Atlantic buffeted the brittle hinterland, before waves, destined for the beach, swished towards the shoreline.

Taking it all in, Dermot allowed himself a soft "Wow!" He was not expecting this. This was perfect, this was heaven. Here was the Ireland of the imagination; the isle of saints and scholars; poets and pirates. Dermot grinned to himself, stepping from the cliff-face onto the pathway, moving stealthily downwards, the stones slippery with dew.

He reached the firm sand of the beach and started to run along the water's edge, the wind slicing his eyes, making them water. At the far side of the bay he stripped quickly, throwing his pants and top behind a rock. Then with a *Tarzan-like* roar, he charged towards the surf, arms outstretched. Running through the shallows, he tried not to scream against the cold as the ground fell away and he went under. He surfaced, gasping and paddling to compose himself, then taking a deep breath started to power-swim around the bay.

Monty spotted him first, and raced down the rocks towards him, cantering into the sea with just a brief backwards glance at his mistress. The little white dog swam boldly out to the man, who waved a greeting as he joined him, turning smoothly in the water to swim another length of the bay together.

Marianne stood anxiously watching this display of bravado, when Dermot scooped Monty onto his back and, taking a lift on a wave, they landed safe and sound a few feet from where she was standing.

"Very impressive," she laughed, as Monty shook himself and galloped off barking.

"That little fella's amazing," said Dermot. "He has the heart of a lion."

"He has," Marianne nodded after the dog, "and brighter than most people I know." She looked at Dermot. "Sometimes, if I take the time to trust his intuitiveness I get very good advice indeed."

Monty bounded back. He wagged up at Dermot. "You've made a friend, anyway," she said.

"I'm honoured, so," Dermot shivered, as he bent to rub Monty's ears.

"You'll catch your death," Marianne said. "Let's find your clothes." She strode off to where the big man's discarded garments lay in a pile by the rocks. Dermot raced after her. She lifted his pants to hand them to him, when something fell from a pocket with a loud clank against a rock.

"Oh sorry!" she said, bending to retrieve the phone, "I hope I've not..."

Without checking the phone Dermot snatched it back and shoved it in his pants pocket.

"No, no, it'll be fine," he assured her.

"Hardly worth bothering with, though," she said. "The island's notoriously bad for telecommunications, no signal unless you're miles out to sea or on top of a cliff." They both glanced upwards. Dermot caught sight of a flash light, high above. He looked again, nothing there.

"That's one of my jobs. The lifeboat station will need first-rate communications. We're already talking to the telephone mast people." He pulled his sweatshirt down and Marianne could not help but notice Dermot was one of those men who looked good in almost anything. And considering the first time she saw him was in uniform, she marvelled not one female in Dublin city, where indeed 'the girls are so pretty', had managed to bag this gorgeous, specimen of manhood.

"Marianne?" Dermot broke her reverie.

She looked away. "I know it's progress, and I'm usually all for it, but the beauty of this place is that you can't be reached by the outside world the whole time. You can be selective." They were strolling along the water's edge now."Have as much or as little of the twenty-first century as you want."

"I get that," Dermot stood for a moment taking in the sweep of the bay. "There's a timelessness about the place alright. I can see how you and Ryan fell for it."

"And each other," she smiled, eyes twinkling, "though the island certainly put us through our paces when we first arrived."

"Yes, the storm. Ryan told me about that, devastating wasn't it?" he said.

"It could have been, but it was like the island wanted us to prove we were worthy of it, like it wanted us to commit to its future." She stopped to admire the view.

"And in doing that, you had to commit to each other?" Dermot asked, skimming a stone into the sea. Monty followed, but only up to the edge, the water was freezing.

"That's right." Marianne slid Dermot a look. There seemed to be a sensitive soul lurking beneath this handsome, hulk of male. Superman or no, Dermot's teeth started to chatter.

"You could do with a nice cup of coffee," Marianne said.

"A tot of whiskey in it wouldn't go amiss," he said cheekily.

"You're a man after my own heart!" Marianne replied.

"I do believe I am," said Dermot grinning, breaking into a run alongside Monty, as they made their way back.

Marianne needed some thinking time before Ryan arrived back on the ferry that morning. If he was returning to his role as the world's most famous super-spy, arrangements needed to be made, and having six whole months together before filming began would give them plenty of time to make plans.

Not only were they going to have their hands full caring for the little ones, Oonagh's Project was forging ahead and things needed to be kept on track to meet the deadline. In fact there was so much on the island striving towards a deadline: the rebuilding of the bridge to the mainland; the new state-of-the-art marina and now the lifeboat station. If she were not careful, the next six months would whizz by in a blur. No sooner would she be welcoming Ryan back from his trip to New York, than she would be waving him goodbye, putting on a brave face and living with that awful, hollow dread she kept buried deep inside whenever they were apart.

She pushed the thought away. Slipping through the ravine leading down to the cove that morning, she had not bargained for Dermot Finnegan doing his *Man from Atlantis* impersonation. She and Monty were used to having the place to themselves, yet who was she to stand in the way of progress, when many of those arriving to make improvements on the island were so 'easy on the eye' as Miss MacReady often said. Marianne smiled to herself, trotting to keep up with Dermot and Monty.

Padar was making his usual hash of things in the breakfast department. Marianne had dropped the youngsters off at the pub ahead of her walk. She steered Dermot towards the coffee pot and exchanging Joey's glass for a plastic beaker, she removed porridge from the microwave and a spoon from Bridget's hair. She was just grabbing her keys when Larry Leeson appeared in the doorway. Marianne had forgotten about Larry. The New Yorker was preened and polished to within an inch of his life, and although he was brandishing a handkerchief, his normal pallor had receded and there was a faint blush of health about his cheeks.

"Morning all," he said, heading straight for the worktop where a pack of baby wipes lurked among the clutter. He proceeded to wipe Bridget's hands.

"Heading to the ferry?" he asked, binning the wipes, checking Joey's highchair was secure.

"Just off," Marianne replied, as Padar passed in search of whiskey for Dermot's coffee.

"Mind if I tag along?" Larry asked, "I need to hear this from the horse's mouth." Marianne hesitated. "I know he's *your* man, but he's my client. Please Marianne?"

She shrugged. "Okay, let's go."

Padar reappeared flustered, "We're out of whiskey."

"The one we use for cooking is in the pantry. Isn't there an order coming on the ferry today?" she said.

"Yes, you're right, well remembered." Padar disappeared. Marianne gave the room a sweeping glance, and, with the children busily breakfasting, pushed Larry ahead and left.

"Has Padar always been like that?" Larry asked as she rattled the 4x4 out of the car park .

"Like what?" she was defensive.

"Flustered, a bit disorganised," he offered.

"He misses Oonagh, they were a good team. We all do, she was amazing." The air suddenly filled with sadness. Larry reached over and touched her hand on the wheel.

"I'm so sorry for your loss," he said.

"So am I," she replied. "Every day."

She drove in silence for a while and then, brightening, "At least I have Ryan coming home. I can't wait to see him and hear all his news."

Larry leaned back, gripping the door for support as the car bounced along.

"You and me both, Marianne, you and me both," he grimaced.

Ryan had an uneventful return trip, flying from Kennedy to Shannon, making the connection to Knock with only one other passenger, who was too preoccupied with his electronic tablet to pay Ryan any attention. There was a time when that would have bothered Ryan. He enjoyed being recognised as a moderately successful actor, hoping for his big break. Now he was an international superstar, anonymity was a luxury, with no need to court the limelight. If a stranger failed to greet him like a long-lost friend, he quite liked it.

After landing, he jumped in a taxi and went straight to Joyce MacReady's guesthouse. He liked the MacReady's – a large, local family with personalities ranging from mildly eccentric to barking mad and was disappointed to find one of the menfolk, Pat, not on the usual taxi run. A ride with Pat was always exciting, his madcap driving almost as legendary as the Holy Shrine.

Joyce was non-committal regarding her brother's whereabouts, as she served Ryan a supper of melt-in-the-mouth boiled bacon and cabbage. In fact, Joyce was quiet throughout the meal, retiring early to leave Ryan alone. He phoned Marianne but the call went straight to voice mail. Disappointed, he guessed she was sleeping: two children, a pub shift and a major project on the go would surely tire anyone, even the super-energetic, workaholic woman he was madly in love with. With no-one to talk to, Ryan too decided on an early night.

"See you tomorrow, my love," he whispered into the phone, before falling into a deep and untroubled sleep, cosseted in Joyce's homely comforts. Which was just as well, because if he knew what was waiting to greet him the following morning, trouble would have been first and foremost on his mind.

Chapter Nine

Guess Who's Coming To Dinner?

Ryan thought he was dreaming as the familiar voice drifted up through the open window. Rubbing his eyes, as bright autumn sunlight poured onto the floral eiderdown, he propped himself up on an elbow, cocking his head. The voices were raised, growing heated, and his spine chilled as every hair on his body rose.

Swinging his legs out of bed, he stepped tentatively across the carpet to the casement window and, standing on tiptoe, peered over lacy curtains into the sweeping drive below. Pat's taxi was not so much parked, as abandoned. A pile of matching luggage was skilfully stacked beside the car and a tall elegant female stood outside the portico, hands on hips, designer sunglasses on head.

"Just tell him I'm here, I mean to see him and I ain't going nowhere till you fetch him *right* down, *right* now."

Joyce bustled passed the woman to the car.

"Pat, who told you to unload all this?" she gesticulated at the luggage. "I've no booking for this person. You know I don't take in passers-by."

Pat shrugged at his sister.

"Sure, how was I to know? She said to come here, she knew your man was here anyway." He scratched his head.

"I haven't said he *is* here. She could be anyone, a reporter, a stalker, anything," she hissed at Pat.

"I thought the Irish were supposed to be hospitable," the woman snapped at them.

"So did I, in fairness." Pat looked glumly at the bags.

"Well, I can't have people just wander in, willy-nilly, asking to see my guests, who may be here incognito or not even here at all." Joyce was indignant.

The front door opened and Ryan, hair awry, appeared squinting in the sunlight.

"Thanks for your concern, Joyce, but I know who this is," he said.

"Am I right then, a stalker, a reporter or some such?" Joyce was intrigued.

The woman spun on her heels to face him.

"And howdy to you too!" she said.

"It's my wife," Ryan said sadly. "Ex-wife actually."

"Jeez," wheezed Pat, spitting his cigarette butt onto the path. The woman sighed dramatically. Joyce looked at her more closely. She had the look of a foreigner alright, a bit too plastic for Joyce's taste.

"Really Ryan, I know this ain't Texas, but these people are downright uncouth." She moved towards the open door, "And where, do tell, is my son? I certainly hope you have not left him in the care of that whore you're shacked-up with. I mean really, where is this all going to end?"

Ryan placed his foot across the threshold, barring her way.

"Any more talk like that, Angelique, and I'll tell you where it will end: here and now and you'll never see *our* son again," he said coldly, glaring back at her, making sure she understood every word.

Angelique threw her shiny hair over her shoulder and eyeballed Ryan.

"Any more of this threatening behaviour, Ryan, and you'll end up with absolutely nothing. No son, no marriage and no career. So don't push it. I've come a long way to reason with you." And suddenly she smiled, "Can't we at least talk?" she said in a little-girl voice.

Joyce was now standing shoulder-to-shoulder with Ryan, arms folded.

"How did you know where I was?" he asked.

She raised her eyes to heaven. "As long as I *want* to know where you are, I'm going to *know* where you are, you should know that by now, Ryan."

He blinked back at her. She was right. Angelique was well-connected; she knew her way round and how to get what she wanted. She always had.

"I only came to talk," she said, using that soft tone again.

"Talking's good," offered Pat. "I'd love a cup of tea myself. We could all have a nice chat over a cup of tea."

"Shut up, Pat," Joyce snapped. Ryan stared at Angelique. Angelique continued to smile back.

"Okay, I apologise for calling, what's-her-name a whore, I take it right back. I'm sure she's a nice person for a *home-wrecker.* But I'm desperate to see Joey, we can't go on like this." She stifled a sob. Ryan looked at Joyce.

"A cup of tea, so," said the mistress of the house, "but anymore foul-mouthing against my kith and kin and you're out the door lady. I don't care how far you've come, or who you think you are!"

"I'm with Joyce on that," said Ryan.

"Thank feck for that," said Pat. "I'm dying of thirst." Joyce stood back to let Angelique inside, as Ryan led the way to the kitchen.

"Isn't she an actress?" Pat asked his sister en route.

"Well if she is, she's not a very good one. Wouldn't trust her as far as I could throw her," retorted Joyce.

But Pat was busy thinking, making the connection between Ryan's estranged wife and the famous movie director Franco Rossini. The taxi rank at Knock Airport was not the busiest in the world, Pat had plenty of time to read the gossip columns, and now some of the conversation he overheard his fare babble into her cellphone made sense.

She was arguing with someone, saying she didn't want to do it anymore, she wanted out, the last time was "too close for comfort", whatever that meant. But as they bumped over a couple of mountains, she lost signal and threw the phone back in her bag.

Pat was intrigued. There seemed any amount of powerful people with money and connections dipping in and out of the island lately, people who would pay for things, information, contraband, whatever. Pat rubbed his hands together. It could be like old times, he might be able to round up some of the team, settle a few scores, earn back a bit of respect.

"Where is your head at, at all Pat? Are you having a piece of toast with that cup of tea?" His sister's voice broke through his thoughts.

"I'd rather have a bacon sandwich," Pat replied.

"You'll never change Pat," said Joyce, slamming the bread in the toaster. "Always over-ambitious, you'll have toast and be glad of it. I suppose your woman from Texas wants eggs over easy?"

"Just coffee," said Ryan, "I'll grab my bag. Pat will you take us to the ferry straight away? The sooner we get the *Clash of the Titans* over the better."

"You mean we're going there now?" asked Angelique, emerging from the cloakroom. She had reapplied her lipstick. "But I'm exhausted, I thought we'd at least stay over, catch up?"

"I thought you were desperate to see Joey?" Ryan looked at her askance. "I'm on my way home *now*, and as you've come this far, you may as well come with me and get this over with."

"Just as you wish, honey?" Cooed Angelique, fixing her hair in the hall mirror, as Ryan took the stairs two at a time.

"Don't call me honey, Angelique. Sometimes you're far too sweet to be wholesome," he called down to her.

"Do you know, I can hardly understand a word you say? Poor Joey, to be this far from home, from his own people, in a foreign land," she drawled.

"We *are* his people and he *is* home," Ryan snapped, heading to his room.

"Only if it's worth it," Angelique told her reflection in the hall mirror.

Kathleen MacReady picked up the handset. It was her elder sister, Joyce.

"What's wrong?" she knew there was a problem, the sisters spoke regularly at an appointed hour; Joyce armed with a cold glass of sherry and Kathleen with her pre-lunchtime whiskey or cocktail if the call was on a Monday. But today's call was unscheduled and too early for alcohol.

"Trouble," Joyce told her, asking if she recognised the name of the tobacco company on the butt she had retrieved from the drive.

"Expensive, American," Miss MacReady confirmed.

"Then it's big, bad, trouble." Joyce said. Miss MacReady was alarmed, Joyce was not one for drama.

"Okay, hold on a minute." Miss MacReady decided she better pour herself a whiskey anyway.

The ferry was just coming into view as Marianne climbed out of the 4x4. The sun had disappeared. Larry pulled his collar up and his hat down against the soft drizzle of the early morning. A couple of vehicles drew up beside them, arriving to meet other passengers. The ferry was small, only able to take half a dozen vehicles and thirty passengers when packed to capacity at the height of summer. In October the ferry was heavily subsidised, bringing only a few tourists, stock for the pub and the odd student destined for the Marine Biology Unit and a long, lonely winter working on a dissertation. Pat MacReady's taxi often made the crossing during the summer, but out of season he left clients at the ferry port on the mainland, rarely able to secure a return fare.

"Is that Pat's taxi?" Larry asked, pointing at a vehicle on the deck. Frowning, Marianne nodded, shoving her hands in the pockets of her cords. She was longing to see Ryan, and felt, as she always did before they were reunited, the soft burning at the base of her chest, yet something was not right. Was it because Larry was with her? Or the dankness of the day dampening her anticipation, her bubble of joy suppressed as she scanned faces of passengers emerging from the salon. No Ryan.

Then she saw him, standing apart, hands on the rails, face set stern. He lifted his hand in stiff salute. She pushed forward, moving faster, Larry jogging to keep up. A woman appeared behind him, glossy hair whipping back, long camel coat flapping in the breeze.

"Oh my God, is that who I think it is?" Larry whispered hoarsely beside her. Marianne felt a rush of blood to her head.

"What the hell is she doing here?" Larry said, catching Marianne by the arm.

Marianne's insides flipped over, she took a breath. "Now that *is* a surprise." She swallowed hard. "It had to be dealt with sooner or later. I guess this is sooner."

"*Jeez-us!*" Larry exclaimed, looking up at the boat, then back at Marianne. "Okay, let me help with this Marianne, I know what we're dealing with here," he said, waving briefly at the wooden figures staring at them from the deck.

"But *we* need to deal with this, Larry, me and Ryan," her voice tight. Larry placed a hand on her shoulder, turning her to face him.

"Please let me help, Marianne," he said. "I know the rules of her game. There ain't none, that's all I'm saying."

She glanced up at the boat, hardly bearing to look.

"Okay Larry." She pulled her shoulders back, striding towards the water's edge, smiling broadly now.

"Hey, hi there, what a surprise, great to see you!" she called above the wind.

Ryan beamed back. *Bloody hell,* he thought, *Marianne should be the actor.* Marianne grinned back at him. *I'm going to kill you for not warning me about this,* her eyes blazed radar-like at her beloved.

"What the hell could I do? I left you a voicemail as soon as she was out of earshot, and yes, she just showed up, just like that." Ryan pulled the door of the 4x4 closed, after ensuring Larry and Angelique were safely on their way in Pat's cab.

"You'd no idea?" Marianne was furious.

"Are you joking, I thought she was still on tour with the boyfriend. We all thought she was. What we didn't know was his tour took him to London, that's how she got here so quickly, how she knew about the TV show, me quitting." Ryan was livid too. "Please don't be angry, Marie, that's playing right into her hands. This is as much a shock to me as it is to you. I thought Angelique would be out of circulation for a long time, long enough to make things legal anyway. I can't believe she just showed up like this."

Marianne put the key in the ignition. "I can, when you think about it, it's only what any mother would do as soon as she heard her husband had absconded with her child."

"Aw, come on she's not 'any mother', she's hardly seen Joey since he was born. He's had a string of nannies and me whenever I could be there. She's been either partying here, there and everywhere or collapsed in a heap." He placed his hand on her arm as she reached for the steering wheel, "That's why I brought him here, that's why I want him with us, you and me, he deserves better." His voice turned to a whisper, "He's only a little boy."

He sounded bereft, desolate. She opened her arms and he threw himself into her embrace, gripping her tightly to him, burying his face in her hair, breathing her in. After a moment he lifted her chin, pressing her mouth firmly with his, and then, because he was hungry for her, a deep warm kiss, sliding his tongue between her lips, lighting the fire inside her, the way he always did. She bit his lip playfully as she pulled away.

"Okay?" she asked, smiling grimly.

"Yep, okay now I'm on solid ground." He looked into her eyes and then straight ahead. "Onwards then, let's get to Maguire's before all hell breaks loose."

"Larry will have things under control. He was very keen to travel with Angelique in the taxi, I got the impression he wanted to get the lie of the land, hear her version of events anyway." Marianne started the engine.

"Larry's a good negotiator, I'll give you that, and he's used to dealing with difficult women, Lena's pretty scary, but I've just spent an hour and a half with Angelique and she's weirder than weird at the moment. She may be out of rehab but she's not okay, not by a long chalk," Ryan said.

Chapter Ten

Call In The Cavalry

The conversation in the back of Pat MacReady's taxi would have been very interesting if Pat could have made head or tail of it. Larry and Angelique were forced to communicate in hushed tones because the elderly cab did not boast the luxury of a glass partition. Under normal circumstances Pat would have no qualms earwigging, but between avoiding potholes in the road, and ensuring the luggage did not land on his head, it was impossible to concentrate on the whispered conversation behind him.

He did overhear Larry ask Angelique to, "Make your visit as brief and as pleasant as possible, for all concerned." He also heard Angelique tell Larry, "I will do as I damn well please." Then it went muted. He heard the actress exclaim that Larry was "Totally wrong", about something and with her new medication she was "completely stable." Larry said he knew why she was there and if she did not do as he asked, he would let the authorities know where she was. Then he heard, without a shadow of a doubt, the Angelique-one exclaim, "You bastard, that's blackmail!" And Larry said, she needed to understand her behaviour could have very serious consequences. She could visit her son, but she had to be nice to everybody and then leave, she was not to make any demands or cause any trouble. "That's the deal, mess up and I'll let the cops know you're here and don't think I won't let your beloved uncle know what's been happening either." Then she snapped back at him to mind his own business.

Looking in the rear-view mirror Pat saw the actress put a hand to the necklace at her throat and then the Larry-fella took her by the shoulders and turned her to face him saying, "There's too much at stake here for you to mess things up, do as I say or it'll be the end of you!" with his face all twisted and nasty.

Then Larry tapped Pat on the shoulder, frightening the shite out of him and told him to "get a move on, there's a good man," so he did, driving like a bat out of hell, leaving Ryan and Marianne in the ancient 4x4 far behind.

And that is precisely how Pat told it to Padar, standing half-in and half-out of Maguire's kitchen, as Angelique swept past them. Padar was fascinated, barely listening to Pat's story. He had never seen such a beautiful creature close up. He watched until she disappeared.

"So the Larry-fella was a bit scary then?" Padar asked, zoning back into Pat's conversation.

"They both were," said Pat. "There's bad blood there, I tell ya."

And before Padar could find out anymore, Angelique asked for the *bathroom,* which threw them into a panic, until Sean Grogan, sitting up at the bar, directed her to the ladies, all smarmy-like.

"And no-one knew she was coming?" Padar asked Pat in a stage whisper. Pat shook his head.

"I picked her up from the taxi rank, she didn't have a clue where she was going, asked a few of the taxi-men did they know where

Ryan O'Gorman was living, and as luck would have it I knew Ryan was heading back from New York, checked he was with Joyce, so took her straight there," Pat confirmed. "Of course, I'd no idea who she was, just a fare as far I was concerned." Padar looked unconvinced.

"Well Joyce must have told Miss MacReady," Sean called over, "because she came in here like a screaming banshee, trawled them all up, the kids, the dog, the lot and took them over to Weathervane. Like a fecking whirlwind that woman is, when the mood takes her."

It was Padar's turn to nod at Pat.

"Sean's right, proper riled, Miss MacReady was, saying, 'No swishy-swashy actress was swooping in here like a pterodactyl interfering with her family, so-called mother or not.' Jaysus, you wouldn't mess with any of them in that humour, talk about protecting their young." Padar's voice was barely a whisper as Angelique reappeared.

"I'm sure that's a great comfort to the whole lot of them," said Sean, joining in the conversation, invited or not. "Miss MacReady would know all about rearing childer. A spinster all her life and then a daughter turns up out of nowhere, reared by another couple. Yes, she knows all about it alright."

"Ah, shut up, Sean," Padar said, turning to smile at Angelique, who looked even more stunning now, freshly powdered with glossy red lips. She stopped before him, hair spilling over her shoulders, eyes dark under her lashes.

"What is this place?" she asked, speaking slowly, hoping he could understand.

"Maguire's, ma'am," Padar answered brightly. She continued to stare at him, arms folded, jaw set. "It's the pub, ma'am." Padar explained.

"You mean this is a bar? I'm to stay in a bar?" her voice grew shrill.

"Well, it's an Inn really. It's the only hotel on the island," Padar offered, dusting a nearby shelf with his elbow. "We do a very nice full Irish breakfast and all the rooms have en suite," he frowned momentarily. "Well, nearly all the rooms."

"In sweet? Is there no bellboy, no maid? My bags have been dumped in the hallway, is this how you treat your guests? Do you even have hot water?" she glared at him.

Larry, who had helped 'dump' said bags, had been to wash his hands. "Okay?" he could see this was far from the case.

"Larry, thank goodness. I can't stay here, it's the pits, book me in with you, wherever you're staying, it will have to do," she waved a hand at him.

Larry raised an eyebrow.

"I'm sorry Angelique, no room at the Inn. Well actually there is room at the Inn, here, but no room at my cottage, there," he pointed through the window.

"You're in a cottage? What is this, *Finnegans Wake*? Christ, this is my worst nightmare." Angelique put her hands to her temples and shook her shiny hair.

"It'll be fine, you see," Larry assured her. "You'll be made most welcome, and what's a little discomfiture, when you've come all this way to see your son and check he's happy and settled in his new home."

"Oh yes," she dropped her hands by her sides, "where is he? Where is my poor baby boy?"

"Up above in Weathervane," Padar told her. She stared at him blankly.

"The cottage a couple of minutes from mine," Larry said.

"He's in a cottage? But why?" Angelique was aghast.

"That's where he lives," Larry explained. "With Ryan, Marianne, Monty and sometimes Bridget, they all live there."

She was incredulous. "And where, do tell, are the help living?"

Larry started to collect her bags, "There ain't no help Angelique, this ain't Manhattan."

"This is worse than I imagined," she said haughtily.

"Remember what I said," Larry told her quietly, "no drama, no trouble."

She ignored him and addressed Padar.

"I'll need at least three rooms, adjoining, two bathrooms also adjoining, and a maid. Can you hire me a maid?" she asked.

"Ma'am, that's no problem, I'll get you a maid. Mary from the supermarket is a grand girl, and she only works there part-time," Pat cut in.

"I'll need her full-time," Angelique told him. "And you, driver, I'll need you here for the duration of my visit, Larry will see to things," she flashed Larry a smile. "Well, I need to be as comfortable as possible, I've been ill, remember." She took a deep breath. "Now, bartender, have you mineral water?"

"I do, ma'am," Padar replied.

"Good, bring a bottle, ice and lime juice to my suite immediately," she swept towards the stairs.

"Suite?" Padar squeaked, following Larry and Pat with the rest of the bags.

Padar had just delivered Angelique's tray when Marianne and Ryan arrived.

"Well, look at that, a grand crowd off the ferry today. Good for business if nothing else. Welcome home, Ryan," Padar said, pointedly to his friend.

"You've met Angelique then?" Ryan replied flatly. Padar rolled his eyes upwards.

"The children?" Marianne asked, keeping the anxiety out of her voice.

"Up above in Weathervane. Miss MacReady and Sinead in charge, all shipshape, as usual," Padar told them, smiling briefly at Marianne. There was a commotion, a clatter of footsteps as Pat and Larry reappeared followed by Angelique. She looked stunning in a cashmere sweater the colour of her eyes, a rope of pearls with diamond clasp at her throat and hair pushed behind her ears, revealing matching earrings. She was carrying a small leather case. She held it out to Padar.

"I'm afraid I can't find the safety deposit box," she said sweetly. "Would you mind taking care of this please?" and dropped it on the bar, turning to beam at those gathered, extending a hand to Marianne.

"At last, to meet properly again after all this time," she smiled. "And now we have so much in common."

"Indeed." It was the first time Marianne had addressed her directly. Angelique gave Marianne's hand the merest squeeze.

"Are you ready? Shall we go?" Marianne asked her. Angelique looked quizzical.

"Go where? I'm here now, aren't I?" Angelique enquired.

"To Weathervane, our home." Marianne let the statement hang in the air. "I'm sure you could use a nice cup of tea or coffee?"

"I did not come here to drink tea, *Miss* Coltrane!" Angelique replied. *Touché,* thought Marianne. "I came to see my son and I intend to take him home, where he belongs."

"Whoa there," Larry interjected, "steady Angelique, one step at a time."

Sean Grogan slid from his stool and was standing beside her, eyes on stalks. Ryan moved swiftly, blocking Sean's view.

"Let's not discuss this here, Angelique. I know you're anxious to see Joey." He swiftly opened the door.

Angelique shrugged his hand from her arm. "Very well, lead the way," she conceded.

Opening the door to Weathervane, Marianne was greeted with the aroma of freshly-baked bread, mingled with beeswax. She could hear laughter and the tinkling, lullaby chimes of Bridget's mobile. She looked back at Ryan. He raised his eyebrows.

The kitchen door opened and *Mary Poppins* appeared, complete with snowy frilled apron and a mop cap plonked on pinned-up hair. Monty trotted into the hall, tail wagging in welcome.

"Oh, there you are and this must be Angelique? Very pleased to meet you, thrilled you came all this way to see us. It's so important for Joey to know how loved and cherished he is, by all of us, *all* his family." Miss MacReady gave them her broadest smile.

"This is my mother," Marianne introduced Miss MacReady to Angelique. Miss MacReady double-kissed the actress and led them into the kitchen, where the scene of perfect, domestic harmony had to be witnessed to be believed. Joey, shiny cheeked in a spotless romper suit was sitting in the playpen, gurgling as he stacked alphabet bricks. Sinead was beside him in the rocking chair, Bridget on her knee. The table was laid with coffee and biscuits, the log burner glowed in the corner, and through the window a line of washing flapped cheerily in the sea breeze.

Sinead was wearing her midwife's uniform, blonde hair

clipped smoothly back, sensible shoes. She exuded calm, capable, confidence.

Angelique flew across the room to where Joey was playing. She bent and lifted him into her arms.

"Darling, darling," she said, covering his face with kisses, "Mama has missed you so much."

Joey's eyes widened with a flicker of recognition, then a curious look, first at Angelique, then Ryan, as he flung his arms towards Marianne. Angelique turned away, but Joey twisted back reaching out to Marianne, dark eyes glittering, mouth pulled down. Ryan stepped into the space between them.

"Okay, gently does it," he said softly to Angelique, "we're just getting this little guy settled. No big shocks, nothing too much too soon, eh?"

"He's my son, Ryan," Angelique snapped, and then, with all eyes on her, started to weep. "I'm desolate without him, it's been so hard for me, alone and worried out of my mind, hard just trying to carry on," her voice trailed off.

"Sit down." Marianne took Joey from her, her cosy kitchen suddenly crowded. Angelique shot her a look through tears. "You're tired, long journey. Let's do as Ryan says, take things gently." Marianne gave her a smile.

Joey started to gurgle down at Bridget, who had wriggled away from Sinead in search of biscuits. Miss MacReady poured coffee. Angelique sat, daintily dabbing her eyes with a tissue.

"I can't believe how much he's grown," she said, giving Joey a watery smile, taking his hand, as he snuggled into Marianne's lap.

"He's still underweight but he's doing well," Sinead said, giving the children half a biscuit each.

"Sinead's a close friend, but also a professional child carer," Miss MacReady explained.

"Has he been so ill, he needs professional help?" Angelique turned to Ryan.

"Not professional help, we're family," Miss MacReady said. Angelique continued to glare at Ryan.

"He needs building up, that's all, good food, fresh air," Ryan said.

"Love and a stress-free environment," Miss MacReady finished his sentence, "Like us all," she laughed, busying herself at the sink. Marianne hid her smile in Joey's hair. Her mother had a habit of saying exactly what she was thinking. Angelique opened her bag, taking three blue pills with her coffee.

"And how are *you* now?" Marianne felt obliged to ask.

"Me? Great, totally fine, completely okay, on the teeniest bit of medication, maintenance, a precaution really and hey, who isn't on something?" she gave the room an all-encompassing wave, "But no, I'm absolutely great, totally *cool*."

"Well, isn't that good news?" said Miss MacReady placing the replenished coffee pot on the table. "It must have been a very good hospital you were at. Which was it now?"

"A private clinic." Angelique's face closed up. "You wouldn't know it." She glanced at Sinead, "Well, you seem to have things under control here, a lot of help for one small child."

"Two actually," Marianne replied. "There's our godchild Bridget. We share childcare with her father, Padar, he's a widower," Angelique had barely acknowledged the other child. She watched her now on Sinead's knees, baby talking to Joey.

"She's beautiful, isn't she?" Ryan said, smiling down at them.

"They both are," Marianne hugged the little boy to her.

Miss MacReady was divesting herself of the nanny outfit in the hallway, exchanging it for a full-length wax, matching hat and wellingtons studded with diamante.

"Well, it's about time for their walk, shall we take charge today, Marianne?" she asked, as Sinead fetched the double buggy. "Or perhaps Angelique would like to do the honours?" Angelique looked bemused. Marianne wondered if she had ever seen one before.

"Would you rather take a nap and catch up with us later?" Marianne suggested.

"I would like to freshen up," Angelique said, looking suddenly exhausted. Ryan fetched her coat, pleased to assist her removal from the cottage.

Marianne took charge of the buggy as Ryan took charge of Angelique. He gave Marianne one of his *I can't believe this is happening* looks. She responded with a *Wallace and Gromit* grimace, as she watched the movie stars heading back to the pub.

Outside the cottage, Sinead gave hurried kisses goodbye. She was long overdue at the pharmacy and Phileas did not like his routine disrupted. Marianne caught her by the sleeve.

"Brilliant work Sinead, what would I do without you?"

"My pleasure sure, I love those two little ones. Sure I'd rather be with them than anyone, they light up my life." Sinead looked adoringly at the babies before striding purposefully towards the main street. Marianne and Miss MacReady watched her go.

"Talk about 'Call in the Cavalry'. What a relief when I saw you both, I was dreading what we would come back to. Padar's great but he's far from organised, and here everywhere calm and gleaming." She gave Miss MacReady a hug.

"Joyce tipped me the wink," Miss MacReady explained, "I don't believe any of that 'desperate to see my son' rubbish. I wonder why she's here really, don't you?"

Marianne pushed the buggy towards the coast road. Monty trotted at the wheels, head cocked to one side. They were all keen to know the answer to that one.

"To try and take him back with her? I can't see how that fits, she's not settled as far as I know, not really based anywhere beyond an apartment in New York and staying with various people wherever she goes, so Ryan says. She's been on tour with the boyfriend, I believe, so I'm not sure what the plan is at all. She's a tricky one I know that." Marianne stopped to pull up the hood.

"And the custody issue, has that been agreed?" Miss MacReady asked, "I can't imagine it would be straightforward."

"Not yet. Ryan hadn't really thought the whole thing through. You know, the divorce, custody of his son, his contract with the studio," Marianne inhaled some salty sea air.

"That's so like him, the grand romantic gesture, hasn't a practical bone in his body." Miss MacReady took the buggy. "You better get on the phone to the lawyers and see what's to be done. I'll take these for a good walk, tire them out, so you, Ryan and Angelique can do some serious talking while she's here. How long is she staying?"

Marianne shrugged.

"Try not to worry, love. She won't stay long, this place won't suit her one bit, nor will motherhood. It doesn't come naturally to everyone you know," she reassured, turning towards the beach. "And remember, we don't even have a GP on the island, she seems to need quite a bit of medical support, if you take my meaning?"

"Well, let's hope what she said is true, and she is on the road to recovery. Any sort of substance dependency is a terrible thing," Marianne said seriously.

"Well, she may have landed in Knock, but there's no miracle cure for what's wrong with that one. She's far from *tootally coooall,* you mark my words," Miss MacReady replied.

Marianne was just about to agree, when a familiar figure appeared, waving from the far end of the beach.

"Larry?" she asked.

Miss MacReady waved back enthusiastically.

"Yes, I said I'd see him here, fill him in on things."

Marianne watched Miss MacReady's face light up.

"Well, here's another question. I wonder how long Larry's staying? He seems to quite like it here at the moment, don't you think?" Marianne bent to kiss the babies farewell.

"Oh, I don't know about that, I wouldn't know about that at all," Miss MacReady laughed, gathering speed as she trundled off towards him.

Marianne was thoughtful, as she and Monty strode back against the wind, to a now thankfully empty Weathervane.

Sinead did not go straight home, where she knew her husband would be impatiently awaiting her return, wittering about how long she had been away, how busy he was and what time would his lunch be ready. Phileas could always find something to complain about, something small and niggly. He never saw the bigger picture, spent his whole life measuring and mixing tiny quantities of this and that, never looking over the top of his reading glasses to see what else was going on in the world. Sometimes Sinead wondered why they moved to Innishmahon. She could not remember the last time she and Phileas had been on the beach, let alone scaled the cliffs or taken a boat out.

Marching up the main street in her sensible shoes, she turned down a lane just before the pharmacy, through a small gate at the back of the churchyard and in the side door. She knew it was open because it was a Friday and Father Gregory would be hearing Confession. She genuflected and took a seat in a pew. A few elderly villagers were mumbling penance. Sinead hoped no-one would come in after her; she wanted to be the last. She checked her watch. She was last, only one person ahead of her. *Hurry up,* she thought, *Phileas will be pacing the floor at this rate.* Finally, the old woman came out and Sinead went in.

"Bless me Father, for I have sinned, and it's been a very long time since my last Confession." Sinead's voice broke. Father Gregory blinked through the grille, flew out of the tiny room and opened the door, where he found her kneeling in floods of tears. The priest took her hand and led her into the now empty church.

"Sinead what is it? What on earth is wrong?" his voice as soft as velvet. She stood, shoulders hunched, head bent. A strand of hair came loose from her clip, it trembled as she sobbed. He pushed the hair back, lightly smoothing her crown with the palm of his hand. She crumbled at his touch and fell into his chest, clutching his cassock, weeping as if her heart would break. The priest was shocked. He had known Sinead ever since the Porters had moved to the island. She came to church occasionally, attended weddings and funerals but she had never come to Confession, and now this. He put his arms around her and led her to a pew. She found a hanky and blew her nose.

"I'm sorry, so sorry," she said between sobs, "I don't know where else to turn."

Father Gregory sat back in the pew, took her hand.

"Take a deep breath, that's right, nice and slow. Now, tell me what the problem is, it can't be that bad, surely?"

Sinead turned huge, cornflower-blue eyes on the priest. "It's bad Gregory, very bad. You see, the thing is, I don't think I can stand it anymore, I'm right on the edge, and if he doesn't stop pushing me, one of two things will happen: I'll either go over the edge or he will."

"What do you mean, Sinead, is it Phileas you're talking about?" Father Gregory asked gently.

She nodded as the tears came again, dripping off her chin onto the large, solid hands holding hers.

"Yes, it's terrible, Father, I used to love him but now I hate him, hate what he's doing to me, to us. And more and more lately I find myself wishing I was free, wishing he was dead and gone out of my life forever."

Father Gregory squeezed her hands briefly.

"I'm at my wits end," she went on. "I even imagine how I could kill him, planning it in my head and there's the truth of it, Gregory. I'm actually planning to murder my husband."

The priest smiled, he wanted to say, "Is that all? Sure, most women want to kill their husbands at one time or another," but he stopped himself and looked deep into those big, baby-blue eyes. Sinead was deadly serious.

Chapter Eleven

A Means To An End

Relieved to have deposited his estranged wife in her suite, barking instructions at her already stressed-out maid, Ryan was sitting outside the pub smoking one of his favourite, French cigarettes, the pint untouched beside him. He was staring blankly at the shop front opposite. It had been the butcher's, doing little business since the supermarket opened not five minutes away and was now just a shell, the building behind the façade washed away in the storm, the remainder crumbling.

"Needs demolishing, that place," Sean Grogan said, taking off his bicycle clips as he wheeled his bike into the entrance of the pub. "Bloody death trap."

"What happened to the Redmonds?" Ryan asked. Colm Redmond was the butcher, he and his wife Joan ran the shop. They had five children and a menagerie of cats, dogs, ponies. Colm had been a stalwart of the makeshift rescue team Ryan had joined at the height of the storm, working together to save lives and homes as the islanders battled against the worst weather in living memory.

"Moved away, back on the mainland. No home, no business, no insurance, sure what had they to stay for?" Sean grunted, eyeing Ryan's cigarette. Taking the hint, Ryan handed him the pack.

"Keep them, I've given up," Ryan said, as he extinguished his. Sean took one, lit it, taking a deep drag. He pulled a face at the taste of the unfamiliar tobacco.

"Shame, nice family, the island needs a bit of young blood." Ryan said. "That was a good property once too."

Sean shook his head. "Not at all. Sure the whole row needs pulling down, barely standing as it is. Isn't a fecking bridge we should be building, it's a new village centre, with a bigger supermarket, an amusement arcade – I love them – and another pub. Sure this place has gone to the dogs since Oonagh fell off that boat."

Ryan's head snapped round, "Hey, enough of that talk."

"What talk?" Padar appeared with a bucket and started cleaning windows.

"Sean was just saying," Ryan said, as Sean glared at him in disbelief, "how the butcher's across the road needs pulling down."

"I agree, something needs doing with it, but there's a lot going on at the moment, what with the bridge and now the lifeboat station." Padar carried on cleaning the glass, "I suppose he wants to knock it down and build another pub."

"Well, he thinks that would be more useful than the bridge," Ryan smiled, watching Sean squirm.

"Ah Sean, you haven't a clue. There's barely enough business here to keep one pub open. Without the new bridge there'll be no trade at all, sure 'tis only the building lads keeping us going at all at the moment." Padar threw the chamois into the bucket and stormed back inside. A yelp and loud clatter meant he had met Sean's bike shin-first. "And get this fecking bike out of here. How many times have I told you? This is a disabled entrance. It has to be kept clear."

"Sure who disabled comes into this pub?" Sean huffed.

"You'll be disabled if you don't move this fecking bike!" Padar called back, slamming the door.

Sean sighed and turned to Ryan. "He didn't mention all the extra business your trouble has brought him, I notice." He gave Ryan a sly look.

"What do you mean?" Ryan asked sharply.

"Well, there's the Larry-fella above renting the holiday cottage, and now your wife, isn't she the actress from Hollywood? She's taken over three rooms because one's not enough and she's paying Pat to stay on as her driver and he's booked into the pub as well, and then there's Mary from the supermarket, taken on as her maid. She must be staying a good while, all the luggage and servants she has around her."

Ryan moved swiftly to face the man. He stood a good head taller than Sean.

"Listen," he said, eyes burning into Sean's face, "She's my *ex-wife* and she's not staying 'a good while' as you put it, and if I were you I'd keep that," he tweaked Sean's nose between his thumb and forefinger, "out of my business!" He took the butt from between Sean's lips, crushed it underfoot and headed off in the direction of Weathervane.

Taking the cigarettes from his pocket, Sean lit another one. As soon as Ryan was out of sight he lifted the untouched pint to his lips. *More money than sense,* Sean thought, as he downed the smooth, cool stout.

Ryan's mood was black, as he entered Weathervane's little hallway. Marianne was playing *Love Cats,* one of their favourite songs, very loudly in the sitting room.

She was in jogging bottoms, pink fluffy top and matching socks, playing the plonk, plonky, plonk piano on top of the desk. He could just make out Snelgrove & Marshall's logo on the computer screen. She was singing and swinging her ponytail from side to side. The happy sound filled the house. Ryan thought his heart would explode with love.

He took his cue from a line to charge into the room, singing at the top of his voice, as she leapt off the chair in fright, laughing as he waltzed her into his arms. Monty joined in, circling their feet and wagging his tail. He loved it when they were silly. But his mistress' 'silliness' often had a deeper purpose. Loud music, mad singing, punishing walks or too much wine usually meant she was thinking something through, giving her brain space to work things out, Monty knew her well enough to know that.

The dancers were developing the technique of waltzing whilst rubbing noses in time with the music, when they heard voices.

"Not sure that'll catch on," Larry said as the music ended, "especially if your partner has a cold."

"Trust you to think of that," Ryan threw back at him, finishing by twirling Marianne and securing her under his arm, "You'd pass a law so everyone wiped their mouths with antiseptic before kissing." Larry nodded, seemed fair enough.

"Anything to report?" Miss MacReady asked, stomping sand off her glamorous wellies.

"I've checked the paperwork and it seems Ryan *does* have a special custody order for Joey if Angelique is incapacitated – for instance in hospital – it's reviewed once she's been discharged and given a clean bill of health by her physician," Marianne told them.

"Anything about being on tour with her boyfriend, abandoning her son and reneging on her responsibilities?" Miss MacReady asked.

"That might count as a *special* special order, it seems that 'incapacitated' covers a multitude, we could be in the clear," Marianne said.

"Okay, let's say she's no longer incapacitated and everything's grand and she's not going to sue Ryan for abduction because he'll countersue for negligence, so then what happens?" Miss MacReady unbuckled Joey and Bridget from the buggy. Larry was frowning over Marianne's shoulder at the screen.

"The legal process to award full custody will commence," Larry said, taking the chair vacated by Marianne, now on the sofa with Ryan and the little ones.

"That shouldn't prove too problematic surely?" Ryan said. "We don't want to prevent Angelique from seeing Joey, far from it, but he needs to grow up in as stable an environment as possible. Angelique with her track record..."

"Health problems," Marianne interjected.

"Okay, health problems," Ryan went on, "is not in a position to provide that."

Larry was scrolling down, reading the document. He turned to face them.

"All well and good, all perfectly logical and reasonable, *but* we are not dealing with perfectly logical and reasonable, we're dealing with Angelique. I'd have been far happier if you'd had the paperwork before you abducted Joey." He smiled at the little boy, softening the impact of his words.

"I didn't abduct..." Ryan exploded.

"Technically you did, no getting round it, and in so doing made the prenuptial agreement invalid. The carefully crafted document you both signed before you married is voided by your action. You didn't apply for this 'special custody order' until after you brought Joey here. Angelique *could* insist on Joey going back to the US and beginning the whole process again, properly," Larry said sternly.

Ryan wrapped his arms around Joey. Bridget lay her head on his lap.

"But that would put us in a very weak position surely, back in the States, with the black mark of abduction against Ryan?" Miss MacReady said in a concerned voice.

"Precisely," Larry agreed, "which is why we need to get to the bottom of why Angelique is really here, see if we can't get things agreed in principle face-to-face. It would save an awful lot of time, money and heartache in my opinion. Marianne?"

Marianne was sitting quietly in the corner of the sofa, twirling one of Bridget's auburn ringlets in her fingers.

"If we can get her to agree, great, but does she want to take him back with her? Is she hopeful for a reconciliation with Ryan?" Marianne shrugged.

"No way," Ryan interjected.

"I'm just talking things through, Ryan. To be frank, I don't think Angelique wants a reconciliation anymore than you do but what her game plan is, I'm still trying to figure out. What is she hoping to achieve?" Marianne said.

Larry scratched his chin.

"A settlement, it has to be!" Miss MacReady exclaimed, "She doesn't want Ryan, or Joey but she does want money. She wants a big fat divorce settlement and a further lump sum for custody. She doesn't want the full-time responsibility of her son. He's a commodity, a means to an end. Ryan's release from the marriage has a price tag and Joey is for sale, part of the package." Her eyes went brittle. The women exchanged a look. Children traded for cash touched a raw nerve in both of them.

Sensing the tension in the room, Joey started to grizzle. Marianne released him from Ryan's grip, smoothing his hair, finding a toy to distract him.

"Shall I make us all a nice cup of tea?" Miss MacReady offered. Ryan looked at Marianne. She knew that look.

"Come on Larry, let's go and visit the viper in its nest." Ryan pulled on his leather jacket. Larry re-tied his scarf.

"Ryan, stay calm, listen to what she has to say, we can sort this out, it'll be fine," Marianne said. As he bent to kiss her, she flashed a look at Larry over his head. Larry nodded, pulling on his gloves.

"I'll see to it, Marianne, but we ain't pulling no punches. Ryan and me have saved her ass on more occasions than I care to remember. Angelique made a pile of money out of the wedding, she ain't due anything in reality. If anything she owes us," Larry growled.

"No tea then?" asked Miss MacReady as they left. "Good, because I'm about ready for a whiskey, what about you Marianne?"

"I think I'm about ready for a fight," Marianne replied, more or less to herself.

Saturday lunchtime mid-October was not usually busy in Maguire's. No more than a couple of tourists and a handful of locals having a sandwich and a couple of drinks. Padar tried to keep the live music sessions going throughout the winter, harking back to when punters came from near and far to enjoy some off-season entertainment, but with no bridge and Oonagh gone, hoolies in Maguire's were scant few. Neighbours on the mainland stayed put. The short trip across the water, a pleasure on a warm summer's evening, was no fun on a black, winter's night.

So the noise and bustle greeting Ryan as he opened the door to the main bar was a surprise. Half a dozen men were at the bar, and by a blazing fire, a cluster of people were chatting and laughing, someone was seated in the midst of them, a woman; Angelique.

Ryan craned his neck. *Oh no,* he thought, *the Hollywood celebrity in a little Irish pub, signing autographs, regaling her fans with anecdotes.*

"Uh-oh," he said, under his breath, as people started to notice they had arrived. The bar grew quiet. Angelique's fans turned to look at Ryan, her estranged husband. He could see their scorn, how could he have abandoned this warm and beautiful person, and so publicly, live on TV, in front of millions of viewers, *the callous bastard.*

"Ryan, darrrling," Angelique, now resplendent in cream silk, suede jeans and cowboy boots, arose, tossing her glossy hair over her shoulder. She extended beautifully manicured hands towards him, cutting through the crowd to take his arm, leaning her head briefly on his shoulder. "You never said how kindly and welcoming these lurvely people are. I mean, we're the oldest friends already. No wonder you love it here. I must confess, I feel right at home, I honestly do." She beamed at him, then back at her fan club. Ryan smiled too, not full-on Hollywood but a good enough effort.

"I'm delighted Angelique, thrilled you've met some of my neighbours and can see how beautiful this place is. You'll come and see us again, next time you need a break from all the razzmatazz of Tinsel Town." He scanned her perfectly made-up face. She pulled her shades down. The pub hushed to silence, waiting for her response to the man who had abandoned her and taken her child.

"Well, I don't know about that, Ryan darlin', coz how I feel at the moment, I could hardly bear to leave, and that's the God's honest truth." She gave his arm an affectionate squeeze, as her fans heaved a sigh of relief and the hubbub resumed.

"What are you playing at?" Ryan hissed. "You're not welcome here, Angelique, so let's organise some time with Joey and you get back on your side of the pond PDQ."

Larry moved to prevent people overhearing. Padar was hovering on the other side of the bar.

"Drinks?" he asked, hopefully.

The door swung open and Dermot Finnegan appeared, windswept and freckled from a day spent on the water. He shrugged off his sailing jacket and hung it up. Angelique lit up at the sight of him, the strikingly handsome blond looked every inch a movie star in his own right. He strode up to the bar. Angelique put her hand on her hip, and turned her voluptuous curves to face him.

"Ryan, where *are* your manners?" she looked at Dermot under her eyelashes, "I have not been introduced to this gentleman."

"Oh, I know who you are," Dermot bowed gallantly, "I'm Dermot Finnegan, an old friend."

"Not that old surely?" Angelique's sassy laughter rang out.

Larry decided to appease Padar and buy drinks. Angelique ordered a pint of stout.

"When in Rome," she fluttered, lifting the glass to a barrage of flashing cameras and phones, as the locals recorded the glamorous, Hollywood actress, tasting her first pint.

Back at Weathervane, Ryan recounted the whole episode.

"And then she did that thing she does – she hones in on someone like a heat-seeking missile, 'Dermot, do tell me this, and Dermot do tell me that.' A vampire sucking every bit of information out of him, flirting and flattering and filling him full of all her usual flannel," Ryan said, stirring soup for his lunch, everyone else replete.

"And Dermot?" Marianne was clearing away.

"Lapping it up, the big eejit, completely beguiled and pretty oblivious to anything or anyone by the time I left. Larry said he'd stay and see if he couldn't persuade her to at least eat something." Ryan took his bowl to the table.

"Oh dear, had a little fix of something, has she?" Marianne sat opposite him, passing him the last of the soda bread.

He looked weary. "What do you think? Of course she has, she's not clean, anyone can see that. She's used that phrase 'freshen-up' for whatever she's doing, forever. Who does she think she's kidding?"

Marianne shrugged. "So how did you leave it with her?"

"Just left, no point in trying to discuss anything when she's like this," Ryan said.

"Like what?" Marianne asked.

"On heat, Dermot doesn't stand a chance," he dipped the bread in the soup.

"No way, not..." Marianne shook her head.

"Don't forget, I've been on the receiving end. She's a vampire, no kidding," Ryan confirmed.

"And what about Joey, when is she coming to spend time with him?" Marianne asked, dismayed.

"Just carry on as normal. She won't even remember she has a son until she's had her wicked way with Dermot, and that's all that's on her mind at the moment, believe me," Ryan told her.

Marianne laughed, "But she's only just met Dermot."

Ryan checked his watch. "Been over an hour now, she'll be shagging him senseless in no time, you mark my words."

"Ryan!" Marianne rebuked, throwing a tea towel at him. "Not in front of the children."

Smiling grimly, Ryan went to help with the dishes. He knew he was right though.

Chapter Twelve

A Deal To Be Done

The following day, Ryan O'Gorman, *world-famous movie star*, was totally absorbed. He had discovered a new and liberating artistic skill – finger painting. He had just coloured his own face bright red, sending Bridget and Joey into fits of giggles, when Angelique rapped on the door. She took a step back, pushing sunglasses onto her head.

"Oh my God, Ryan, what the hell happened?" she exclaimed.

Ryan did jazz hands at her.

"Finger painting, want to join us?" he asked.

Angelique examined her kid gloves. "Not today thanks, I came to see Joey, spend some time, may be take him out for a ride?" she tried a smile. Ryan looked into her face, checking for signs. She snapped the shades back down. "Please, Ryan." There was a tremble in her voice.

"Come in Angelique, we need to talk." Ryan stood back to let her pass, instinctively stepping outside to check for paparazzi along the lane. No-one there, but he could see Pat MacReady leaning against his taxi in Maguire's car park. It looked like he was talking to somebody but Ryan could not see who. Ryan surmised Angelique's 'driver' was on standby to take Joey for a ride. At his young age the main purpose for putting Joey in a car was to get him to sleep, and besides Innishmahon was a small island, wild and beautiful in the summer, treacherous in the swirling, dampness of autumn – there was nowhere to go for a ride.

Ryan shuddered, pulling the door closed behind him. Angelique was in the kitchen, standing away from the babies on the rug. She watched transfixed as Bridget streaked fistfuls of yellow paint through Joey's hair and he, jiggling around to avoid her, slapped sticky blue hands on the back of her pink pyjamas. Monty, who was wearing a violent green mohican, courtesy of Ryan, was wagging his tail at their antics. He stopped when he saw Angelique, and gave a growl in the back of his throat.

"Still smoking?" Ryan asked her.

"No, I stopped, all part of the program," Angelique eyed Monty.

"It's just that Monty's not keen on smokers. Always grumbles at me when I've had my after-dinner fag."

"I've given up all my vices. The team at the clinic were totally supportive, I've really turned a corner, I'm so clean, I squeak." She gave him that beam again.

Ryan smiled back, trying to seek out her eyes through the ubiquitous black lenses – her face perfectly made-up as usual, the mask sitting on the skin. Ryan knew all the tricks of the trade. But Angelique had been stone-walling the world from behind dark glasses for so long, he wondered if she would ever make it back to normality.

The actress' road to stardom had been a given. The daughter of Franco Rossini's only sister, she told her doting uncle she wanted to be a star, and he said "*so be it*". Remembering how easy it had been to fall for her, Ryan stood and watched her: a stunningly beautiful woman no doubt; an accomplished professional when the mood took her; but a self-obsessed, substance-addicted mess most of the time these days. He tried hard to support her, bringing in professionals, but she refused to be helped, and with her blatant infidelities, he was at the end of his tether when he came to Innishmahon to start afresh. Looking at her now, he felt suddenly sad it had come to this: a marriage of convenience with the complication of a beautiful baby boy.

Ryan made coffee, strong and black, the way she liked it. She sat as close to the babies as Monty would allow. Her hand trembled as she took the mug from Ryan, not taking her eyes off Joey for a second.

"He looks different," she said quietly. She lifted her glasses to look more closely at her son. "Better than I remember. He's truly handsome, beautiful even."

"Shall I clean him up so you can hold him, play with him maybe?" Ryan asked.

"No, don't do that," she swept a hand from head to toe, indicating the camel coat and cream dress beneath. "I don't think I'm much of a player." She bit her lip, Ryan laughed.

"Perhaps not that kind of player," he teased.

She flashed him a look. "I didn't come halfway round the world to trade insults with you, Ryan."

He raised his hands. "I know, I know." He waited for calm to return. She took a deep draught of coffee, then gave him one of her best Hollywood smiles. He was immune; he did a good line in superstar beams himself.

"Sorry, a bit jet-lagged, I guess," she said, looking around the room, "where's er...?"

"Marianne? You know perfectly well what her name is. She's out, so you can stop with the abandoned wife act, we both know it's bullshit. You abandoned me and our relationship long before Marianne came on the scene." Ryan was exasperated. "Anyway, you're not here to be reconciled with a husband you don't need and a son you don't want, so let's cut to the chase, shall we?"

Angelique turned to face him. She took her sunglasses off and placed them on the kitchen table. Reaching into her bag she removed a bulky, envelope and pushed it along the surface towards him. He raised an eyebrow.

"An arrangement: a divorce, custody of our son, with rights for me and maintenance – call it an allowance – paid monthly into a private bank account, in case anything happens to you and I have to take care of Joey – education, college, you know the sort of thing." Her voice had changed, no sultry Texan drawl for this particular speech. Angelique tapped her toe against the quarry tile floor. Monty growled again, hackles raised along his back.

"Put that mutt out back for pity's sake; needs a good horsewhipping if you ask me." She glared at the dog.

Ryan ignored her, indicating with his hand for Monty to back off. Monty reversed and sat down next to the children, ears flat back, not taking his eyes off Angelique. *Mutt indeed!*

Ryan also ignored the envelope.

"Everything was agreed before we married, Angelique, you know that. We made sure the prenup was watertight for all our sakes, especially Joey's. You had your cut of the wedding publicity payoff, a generous settlement, all signed and sealed. Whatever you've dreamed up now, no deal."

Angelique pushed the envelope nearer to Ryan.

"Read it," she snapped. "It all changed when you abducted my son. If you'd read the small print before your pathetic announcement, you'd have known that. You made the prenup null and void when you got on that airplane with my son, *without* my permission."

Joey made a small sound. Ryan lifted him up.

"Keep your voice down, you're upsetting him," he said.

"And you're upsetting me," Angelique flashed back. "Just do as I ask and I'm gone, outta your hair for good," she gathered her gloves and glasses.

"What's changed, Angelique? What's wrong now? What kind of trouble are you really in?" he asked.

"Just do it, Ryan. Sign it and send copies to your lawyer and the money to my account." She rose to leave.

Joey was whining softly under his breath. She glanced at the child.

"I have to go before he starts that...that noise he makes. Christ, it sets my teeth on edge. How can you stand it when he makes that noise?" Her eyes scanned the room for an escape. "How can you live here, all of you?" she admonished. "It's no more than a shack, Joey could burn himself on the fire, there's no yard, no pool, no help – I could easily have him taken from here, into proper care, the care he needs." Her voice was rising. She twisted her gloves in her hands.

Joey was whining louder now, Bridget had started to snivel. Ryan stood to open the door, facing Angelique with Joey in his arms; Joey turned his head into his father's chest.

"Leave now please, Angelique, I won't have the children upset." He indicated the door leading to the hall, as Marianne came in from the garden.

"Oh sorry," she said, and was immediately annoyed for apologising. It was her kitchen. She looked quizzically at Ryan. Monty rushed at her, yapping and wagging his tail in relief. She gathered Bridget into her arms, shaking her head to clear the jangled atmosphere in this, her home, her haven.

"Angelique is just leaving," he said coldly.

"Really, I'm sorry," she apologised *again.* "Won't you stay and have lunch with us, I'm sure Joey would like that."

Angelique turned a strained smile on Marianne. Joey was making a hideous high-pitched whine. Marianne looked at him; she had never heard that sound before.

"I'm afraid I have to go. Maybe we could do lunch tomorrow?" Angelique said.

"We could," Marianne ignored Ryan's glare, "or dinner later?"

"I can't do dinner," Angelique flustered. "I have a da... dangerously, blinding headache coming on. I'll need to lie down until it passes. I should be fine by tomorrow, will you call around one. Is there anywhere to eat around here?"

"We could eat in the pub?" Marianne offered.

"Really," Angelique was incredulous, "What about Joey?"

"That's no problem, he'll come too," Marianne replied. Did Angelique actually wince?

"Just you two then," she called as she left. Joey stopped making the bizarre noise immediately.

"What's in the envelope?" Marianne asked Ryan, as the atmosphere lifted.

"A new deal, she's saying the prenup's out the window because I *abducted* Joey. She wants more money, a big payoff and – get this – a regular allowance in case I'm off the scene and Joey needs looking after."

Marianne frowned. "So Larry was right. Do you want me to read it?"

"Nah, leave it for now. I'm up to here with it. I'll look at it later when I'm in a better frame of mind." Ryan pulled his mouth in a tight smile. "No need for her to spoil the whole day. Do you think it's wise to have lunch with her though, she obviously wants to tie you up in knots to help her get what she wants?" Ryan asked.

"Well, at least if I talk to her woman-to-woman, I might find out what's going on in her head," Marianne told him.

"Good luck with that one," he replied. "What makes you think she'll tell you? She's very good at twisting everything anyone says to her own advantage."

"'Course she'll tell me, I'm an award-winning, investigative journalist, don't forget. She doesn't stand a chance," Marianne told him, wiping Bridget's nose.

"Be careful," Ryan said, kissing her on the forehead before taking the envelope and putting it in a drawer, out of sight.

Chapter Thirteen

All That Glitters

Kathleen MacReady was photocopying paperwork for Oonagh's Project, the young carers' holiday home. She and Marianne had ploughed through acres of forms and spreadsheets, and were relieved that everything the EU, Irish government and it would seem, any passing alien visiting from another planet might require to give the scheme the green light, was now in place.

She was pleased to have a distracting hour with her daughter, because although Marianne appeared to be taking Angelique's surprise appearance in her stride, there were shadows under her eyes, and even when she smiled, a frown lurked between her brows. A mother notices these things, Miss MacReady acknowledged to herself.

She was gathering the last batch of paperwork ready to drop off at the priest's house for his signature, when she heard the bell tinkle in the shop area of the post office. She checked her face in the mirror and, realising she was without earrings, grabbed the diamante drops left on her desk the night before, not quite right with the tweed suit she was wearing but they would do, and made her way to greet her public. It was Larry.

"Ah, Larry, it's yourself, come through. I'll make coffee. I've homemade shortbread too." She lifted the hinged counter-top for him to pass into the inner sanctum.

"Hope I'm not disturbing you, ma'am," Larry said, removing the waxed trilby he had been wearing more or less permanently since his arrival on the island.

"Ah sure, disturb away. What would a crusty old postmistress be doing, she wouldn't love to be disturbed by a handsome young man like yourself?" she beamed at him, but Larry only frowned back, the second anxious visitor she had encountered that morning. Bad vibes, she looked at the Buddhist altar in the corner, the flowers in the vase prematurely wilted.

Larry was quiet while Miss MacReady made coffee. She brought the refreshments through from the kitchen, arranging exquisite china cups on an elegant walnut table. Larry studied the room while she busied herself. One half – the office half – immaculate: everything in its place, files in cabinets, neat stacks of stationery. The other side of the room – mayhem: a large floral sofa, covered in silk throws and cushions, the walls filled with art. The mantel littered with crystal, photos, ceramic figurines, and everywhere candles – on every surface, in every type of holder. When Miss MacReady returned with a jug of cream, she had to dip her head to avoid the chandelier hanging from the ceiling. She was, it had to be acknowledged, wearing the highest platform shoes.

Larry, unable to find anywhere to hang his coat, laid it on the chair at her desk. He was uncomfortable; he had made that side of the room untidy. He placed it on the floral sofa, too piled with things to make any difference. Miss MacReady sat opposite him, perched on an embroidered footstool. She poured coffee.

"Well, what's the gen'?" she asked, shrewd eyes scanning his face. He looked quizzical. "What gives?"

He took a piece of shortbread and snapped it between his fingers. "Miss MacReady..."

"Kathleen, Larry please, aren't we the closest of friends?" she watched as the shortbread hovered before his lips.

"Kathleen. Can I prevail upon you to keep what I'm about to tell you a total and complete secret?" Larry asked.

Miss MacReady looked aghast.

"Larry Leeson, I'm the very soul of discretion, sure don't I have to be, amn't I the postmistress? I'm told more than the priest and he takes Confession." She was incredulous.

Larry was confused, as often happened when he spoke with Miss MacReady, but he surmised she was indeed confirming her trustworthiness.

"Well, all is not as it seems," he said.

"Really, what's not?" Miss MacReady was intrigued.

"Angelique has not been altogether honest and I know more than she's letting on."

"You don't say," Miss MacReady replied, then impatiently, "Ah, stop with the *Agatha Christie* carry-on, Larry, spill the beans as you New Yorkers say in the cop shows."

Larry coughed.

"Although she was on tour with her boyfriend – the rock star guy – she did not leave his suite at a five star hotel to come here." He paused, making sure she was taking it all in. "She was in hospital, and this time not her usual rehab, she was in a secure unit, attached to a penitentiary, at Her Majesty's Pleasure, as you say."

"We don't say, Larry, we're a republic, but I know what you mean, she was in the 'nick', 'clink', 'slammer', call it what you will, gaol anyway. Pray continue," she instructed.

"Not gaol exactly. Angelique was being detained pending an investigation. She'd been arrested at Heathrow and taken in for questioning – a couple of private detectives had been tailing her. The investigators must have been rather naive, because she asked to use the bathroom and took an overdose while she was in there. They found her unconscious and rushed her into the hospital." Larry finally bit into the biscuit.

"Goodness me, that's awful." Miss MacReady was shocked. "What on earth was she being questioned about, drugs?"

"No, these days whatever she takes is usually prescribed," Larry explained. "This time it looks like embezzlement."

"Heavens above!" Miss MacReady gasped. "But what does that mean exactly?"

Larry took another piece of shortbread. "The fraudulent appropriation of funds or property entrusted to someone's care but actually owned by someone else."

"I know what embezzlement means, Larry, but how...what is she embezzling?" Miss MacReady grew impatient.

"Diamonds," Larry said. "I guess you know about the jewellery?"

"Of course I do, that's one of things she's famous for, hasn't she some fabulous pieces belonged to Hollywood legends and royalty and such?" Miss MacReady knew all about this sort of thing, this was right up her street.

Larry nodded again. "The famous collection does not belong to Angelique, it belongs to the film company, the franchise. She's always been a superb ambassador for the brand, a real live mannequin, wearing the jewels and fabulous designer gowns to events all over the world. But I have it on good authority she's been switching the genuine article for copies, good copies, but copies none the less and stashing the cash."

"Ah go on, Larry, you're making it up!" Miss MacReady exclaimed.

"No way, ma'am, I'd never do such a thing," Larry replied, shocked. Miss MacReady smiled. Larry took every word she said so literally. "Here's how it works. Angelique takes a piece of jewellery to a less than reputable jeweller and gets him to swap the real gems for fakes. The piece still looks the same, but instead of being worth hundreds of thousands of dollars, it's just costume."

Miss MacReady refilled his cup. "Go on," she was wide-eyed.

"The jeweller sells the gems on the black market, gets paid a commission and Angelique pockets the rest. She's clever. She only sells one piece at a time and uses a network of crooked diamond merchants all over the world." Larry snapped the shortbread and popped a piece into his mouth.

"My word, that's brilliant." Miss MacReady touched the diamante earring in her left ear. "How long has this been going on?" she was on the edge of her seat.

Larry gave a dry laugh. "Ever since her habit got too expensive to maintain and the acting offers dried up."

"Jesus, Mary and Holy Saint Joseph," Miss MacReady blessed herself. "How on earth did a young woman like that get into this sort of thing? I thought she came from a good family, plenty of money, no need to want for anything."

"That's all true, Kathleen, but Angelique has been indulged all her life, and she's always been attracted to *bad* boys," Larry said.

"Ryan?" Miss MacReady asked, anxiously.

"No, not Ryan, he likes a good time and they had fun together, but Ryan wasn't into the heavy stuff and Angelique always has been. I think the family were hopeful Ryan would be an influence for the better and he was for a while. No, Ryan's clean, he'd never have landed the *Thomas Bentley* role if he'd still been living the 'high life', if you take my meaning." Larry tapped his nose.

Miss MacReady left the table to pour whiskey into cut-glass tumblers.

"Not for me," Larry said. She paid no attention to his instruction.

"Sláinte," she said, knocking hers straight back. "Well, well, well, where does that leave things then I wonder? What you're saying is, technically she escaped from gaol?"

"After a fashion," said Larry, "absconded from detention anyway." Larry stood up and started pacing the room. "The insurance company had a tip-off following her trip to Amsterdam. I have a pal there. He rang to warn me Angelique was going to be questioned, so I could manage the situation if the story hit the press. But news of Ryan quitting the movie broke about the same time Angelique disappeared from hospital. At least that kept the newshounds off her tail at the time. A good day at the office, I don't think." Larry said flatly.

"So I'm right, she's here to do a deal for as much money as she can. She's no interest in the child, above and beyond what he's worth to Ryan and subsequently to her," she poured herself another large one, "and she's hoping she can get things signed and sealed before news of her escape breaks. Will the police be after her?"

"No, the detectives who picked her up work for the insurance company, they're gathering evidence but it's not police business yet.

She's avoided being questioned so she's not even been charged." Larry sat back.

Miss MacReady went to the telephone on her desk. It was an original two-tone trim-phone, it reminded her of *Star Trek*, one of her favourite shows. She lifted the receiver. Larry charged across the room and pulled it out of her hand.

"What are you doing?" he yelled. Miss MacReady nearly jumped out of her skin.

"Why, ringing Marianne to tell her what you've told me. She'll know what to do, she has contacts." She was flabbergasted. Larry replaced the receiver.

"I'm sorry, Kathleen this is *strictly* confidential. We don't know who or what is involved, this information goes no further and I mean that." He stood facing her, she looked into his face – he meant it alright.

"But why tell me?" she was still puzzled.

"Because I need your help." He looked her straight in the eye.

"Really? My help? Why, what do you want me to do, go undercover, hack into someone's emails, tap a few telephones, what?" she joked.

"I want you to rob the post office, or to put it another way, I want you to allow the post office to be robbed," he said firmly.

"Oh, that's perfect, no problem, at your service." Miss MacReady's face broke into a smile – until she realised he was serious. "What? I can't do that – it's more than my job's worth. This is my life's work, this is what I do, who I am. I can't allow..."

Larry took her by the hands and led her to the sofa. He sat down beside her.

"You have no choice Kathleen. The lives of those you hold most dear are at risk. In fact all our lives are." He was staring into her face.

"At risk? All of us?" she said.

He nodded gravely.

"I've said it before, Larry, it's you should have been the actor!" Miss MacReady laughed, unconvincingly.

"I know you've Angelique's jewels in the strongbox here," Larry said, looking around.

"The leather case, yes Padar brought it up from the pub. He has a safe alright but only Oonagh knew the combination so he brought the jewels here. I just locked them away."

Larry raised his eyebrows. "May I see them?"

"Of course." Miss MacReady crossed the room. She took the key from the chain around her neck and went into the darkest corner of the building. She returned with an elegant leather jewel case.

"It's locked," she told him, placing it on the table.

"Hairpin?" he asked. She produced one immediately. Larry picked the lock in a second, the clasp sprung open.

"Larry Leeson, you're a man of many talents," Miss MacReady cooed. Larry blushed. She switched on a lamp as he lifted the top of the case. The brilliance was blinding. Miss MacReady stretched a tentative finger towards the gems. Bang! Larry slammed the top shut. She jumped. He laughed.

"Gotcha!" he grinned.

She gave him a look. *Pretty Woman*? You cheeky thing," she laughed back. He opened the lid again, slowly.

"Ah," she whispered in awe, "that's the most fabulous collection I've ever seen."

"Indeed but which are real and which are fake?" Larry asked in a hushed voice.

Miss MacReady was trying on rings, draping bracelets over her wrist. "If any of these are fake, they're very good." She held a square cut diamond ring up to the light. "Very good indeed," she told him, clearly beguiled.

"And that's why I need you to allow the post office to be robbed. I need this lot stolen, it's an opportunity not to be missed," Larry went on.

"Okay, let me get this straight, you want to set up a heist and steal the jewellery?" Miss MacReady was checking out a tiara in the mirror. "Surely that's very risky Larry, especially if the insurance company is already suspicious."

"We'd need to do it quickly and it has to look genuine, involve the police, make sure everything is reported. You see this is all itemised and insured for millions," he said. "Then we can claim the insurance."

"I get that, but who gets the insurance money?" she asked.

"Rossini, the collection is insured under the franchise operation," he said.

"So you arrange for the collection to be stolen and the insurance claimed but what happens to the jewels?" she asked.

"They disappear for a while, then sold, black market, gone." Larry was grey with seriousness.

"And that money?" she asked.

"Back to the franchise," Larry shrugged. "It costs around a hundred million dollars to make a *Thomas Bentley*. Like all businesses the franchise needs capital, and since the crash, the banks are nervous about the industry, there's just not enough money around to keep the franchise going."

"I see." Miss MacReady toyed with a diamond bracelet she was wearing. "Let me get this straight, Angelique is literally hiving off the family silver and instead of handing her over to the authorities, you've decided to pull a fast one on the insurance company, claim the money for the stolen gems *and* pocket the funds once they've been sold?"

Larry looked uncomfortable.

"When she showed up here with them I couldn't believe it, it was like an opportunity to help out landed right in my lap," Larry said. "Whatever we claw back will certainly pay the interest on the loan until the big bucks from the box office returns start to roll in," Larry said.

"The interest!" Miss MacReady exclaimed. "Good grief, how much has Rossini borrowed, and more to the point, from whom?"

Larry chose to avoid that particular question. He got up and walked back to the desk, collecting the items Miss MacReady had been trying on as he went. He closed the lid of the case and shut the clasp.

"This is all highly irregular," she told him, "I mean, it's criminal, Larry, we could get into serious trouble."

"What's happening to Rossini, the franchise and the movie business in general, that's what's criminal, Kathleen," he said, sternly.

She followed, him and standing very close, looked up into his eyes, she could smell his cologne – woody, expensive. She slipped a ring he had missed from her finger, and placed it lingeringly in his hand, stroking his palm with her nail.

"Well, well, Larry, you're full of surprises. Of course I'll help you, I'll do whatever you want, I've never heard of anything so exciting," she purred, running her tongue across her lips. Larry was beginning to perspire. She handed him the other whiskey. He knocked it straight back.

Chapter Fourteen

The Lynx Effect

Padar pulled a face as he pulled a pint. "Jaysus, what's that smell?" He looked along the bar: a few locals in their usual spots, Sinead Porter in the snug with a glass of wine and one of those gossipy women's magazines. He sniffed again. He looked at Shay, the ganger for the building workers. Shay shrugged. Padar moved along the bar, sniffing.

"Good God Sean, it's you! What are you wearing at all? You stink. You smell like me Auntie Nellie's knicker drawer, mothballs and stale lavender, ugh!"

Sean Grogan looked up from the newspaper he was pretending to read, while keeping an eye on the door.

"I'll have you know I'm wearing the one that fella, David *Beckingham* wears, if it's any of your business," Sean said, haughtily. The main door to the bar swung open, every head turned to see who it was. Father Gregory filled the entrance. The men went back to their pints. Sinead looked up and smiled.

"Ah, Sinead," he said, shaking rainwater off his cap, "do you mind if I join you, a couple of things needed for the project, I thought you might be able to help." She nodded. "Good, I'll get us a drink, so." He went to the bar. "Dear Lord Padar, what are you using to clean the pipes these days? Smells like rotten eggs."

Padar flicked a look along the bar at Sean. The priest stood back.

"Good evening Sean. Something different about you, what is it?" the priest asked.

"Nothing new Father," Sean replied.

"There is. New hairstyle?" Father Gregory referred to Sean's few grey strands, flattened to his head with gel. "A new jacket?" Sean was wearing a purple velvet jacket; it had huge lapels and was well-worn at the elbows.

"I've had this years," he told the priest.

"Aha, a new Holy Medal. Isn't that nice, I haven't seen a Holy Medal the likes of that in a long time," Father Gregory said, eyeing the massive gold medallion on Sean's bare chest.

"I didn't know you could get Saint Christopher in life size. Has that *Beckingham-fella* one of them too?" Padar enquired, hiding his smirk with a glass cloth.

"Ah, can't a man have a bit of a wash and brush up now and again around here?" Sean asked angrily, finishing his pint before stomping off to the gents.

"What's that all about?" Father Gregory asked, paying for his drinks. He looked along the bar, Shay looked highly polished too: designer jeans, sharp shirt, freshly washed hair. The priest raised his eyebrows at Padar.

"You've heard of 'The Lynx effect', well this is the 'movie star-effect'. Your woman, Angelique de Marcos is staying here," Padar said.

"Really, so she's as attractive in real life as she is on screen then?" Father Gregory asked.

Shay overheard, "Attractive? She's red hot, Father, and the shape of her." Shay demonstrated Angelique's womanly curves. "Jaysus, you wouldn't mind having a bounce off that yourself, Father, and we wouldn't say no to you giving us a go too." The men laughed. Father Gregory scowled at Shay and was just about to reprimand him, when the door flew open and Angelique appeared like a vision in the midst of them. A wan-looking Dermot closed the door behind her. All mouths dropped open. Hair wild and flowing, Angelique wore a see-through blouse, leather shorts and thigh-high boots. Her lips and nails were ruby red, perfectly matching the fur draped across her shoulders.

"Well hello boys," she called, sashaying up to the bar. Those who could find their voice mumbled a greeting.

"Parrdaar,"she dragged out Padar's name seductively, "could you be a real sweetie and find me some of that fine French champagne? Put it on ice and bring it over to the fire for me, will you? Dermot gave me the most delicious breakfast..." she licked her lips, and half the men in the bar licked theirs, "...but we ran out of champagne. If there's one thing that little old boat needs, it's a bigger icebox." She turned on her heel and strutted across the room to the fireside chair. Dropping her fur on it, she nestled in, crossing her long legs and smoothing the silk on her thighs with her palms. Dermot stared at the men at the bar, until each and every one of them went back to their beer. He took the champagne bucket and glasses off Padar.

"Celebrating something?" Padar asked, eyes twinkling.

"Yeah, surviving a night with that one!" Dermot replied under his breath.

"No way," Shay overheard, "you lucky dog!"

Dermot shrugged, "One man's meat..." Shay frowned.

"Is another man's poison," Father Gregory finished the quotation for him as he went to join Sinead, and Dermot pulled up a stool at Angelique's feet.

Larry walked with Miss MacReady up as far as the priest's house at the top of the village and turned left towards the coast road, which ran a complete circuit around the island. He had some thinking to do. It was Lena's phone call the previous evening that set the cat among the pigeons and what she had to say was so disturbing Larry had been awake all night.

Lena was aware Angelique was in Europe but only just found out she had been arrested at Heathrow, and following her overdose taken to a special unit awaiting further investigation. News that the movie star had made it to Innishmahon was as much a shock to her, as it had been to everyone else. Realising Angelique had the jewels with her, it was Lena's idea to set up the heist.

"But I can't do that!" Larry barked into the receiver, "it's illegal, we'll all end up in gaol." They were speaking on the landline, as he dusted the hall table in the cottage he was renting from Padar Quinn. But Lena talked him round, explaining Innishmahon was the ideal place to enact the perfect crime. He would be doing them *all* a favour, taking the jewels away from Angelique, preventing her from becoming embroiled in a scandal when it came to light what she had been up to, and by ensuring Rossini received the insurance money, he would also be helping to prop up the franchise and keep them all in business.

Larry had to smile. Lena really was the sharp end of the operation, a real tough cookie, with a heart of gold, however deep she hid it. She always looked out for them and he loved her for that.

Larry stopped dusting and thought for a minute.

"I'll have to get the postmistress on side; the jewels are in the strong box there."

"Do whatever you need to. I'll handle the heist, a couple of professionals, in and out in a flash. You just gotta make sure the cops turn up when it's all over."

"That should be easy, there isn't even a traffic cop on the island, they'll have to come by sea," Larry said.

"Good and you need to be as far away from the action as possible, preferably back here in the US, not a hint of suspicion. We're all squeaky clean, okay?"

Larry's heart was pounding in his chest; he needed one of his pills.

"No-one is to get hurt, Lena. I can't be involved if anyone gets hurt."

"Don't worry, it'll be a slick operation, over and done with, but this is between you, me and whoever else you *have* to involve. Don't let on to Ryan or anyone else. This can't go wrong, okay?" Lena said. "Look, Larry, I have to go, I've a meeting with Rossini's publicity people. Whatever else happens, we still have a movie to make. How is our client by the way?"

"Ryan's good, all things considered. Angelique turning up was a bit of a shock but he and Marianne seem to be dealing with it. He's so grounded here, I see the best of Ryan when he's with Marianne," Larry told her.

"True love," Lena laughed, "a rare and wonderful thing." She hung up, and so did the other person listening on the line.

Pleased he had Miss MacReady on side, Larry was going over

the plan for the heist when he spotted Ryan and Monty running along the beach. It was a mild, bright day and even though the sun, hanging low in the sky, was streaked with the merest trail of cloud, it did little to cheer him; he felt chilled to the bone.

"Morning Larry, out for a walk? Your physician back in New York will think you've had a miracle cure at the shrine at Knock, you look so well," Ryan called as they ran towards him.

Must look better than I feel, Larry thought, forcing a smile. Ryan stopped. Monty greeted Larry with a rub against his legs, Larry bent to scratch his ears.

"It's the air don't you think? It kind of energises you. I feel better here, about everything," Ryan said. Larry could see that, Ryan looked fit: shiny slate-blue eyes, thick black hair with touches of silver, sculpted cheekbones, determined chin.

"I know that look, Larry, my agent checking the stock. Don't worry, I'll be ready when the call comes. No crash dieting or intensive gym programme for me. I'll be there, good to go."

"Glad to hear it." Larry picked up a stick and threw it for Monty. They started to walk back towards the village.

"Decided how long you're staying? Marianne and I wanted to ask you over for dinner," Ryan said.

Larry stopped and looked out to sea. "I'm gonna need to get back pretty soon."

"Shall we invite Kathleen to dinner too? You seem to get along?" Ryan watched Larry's face.

"Aw, come on now, no matchmaking, I ain't her type," Larry blushed.

"A little birdie tells me she thinks you are," Ryan teased.

"Hey, stop with that, don't be making something out of nothing," Larry said.

"I'm not. Think we'll invite her anyway, she's great company, always a yarn or two to spin, not sure how much truth there is in Kathleen's version of things, but for someone who's spent most of her time on the island, she seems to have had an exciting life."

"It's about to get a whole heap more," Larry said, into the collar of his coat.

"What was that?" Ryan asked.

"She certainly ain't no bore," Larry replied, stomach twisting.

Ryan and Monty returned from their run with Larry in tow, who went into spasms of ecstasy because they had pastrami and pickles in the fridge, insisting he made lunch for everyone. He raised an eyebrow when Marianne said she would leave them to it – she and Joey were lunching with Angelique in Maguire's.

Marianne had been in the pub for over an hour and there was still no sign of Angelique. She sat quietly with Joey as locals drifted in and out. Padar made Joey a boiled egg, chopped up with butter for lunch, but Marianne was not hungry. The bar was empty when the vision appeared. She strolled in wearing a perfectly fitted cream trouser suit, ivory polo neck and elegant courts. Her hair was tied and wrapped in a coffee coloured silk scarf, pearl studs in her ears. If anything, the classic simplicity of the ensemble made her appear even more beautiful. She looked disappointed there was no public to greet her and, bringing a glass of clear liquid with her from behind the bar, joined them.

"Hey, really glad you could make it," she said, smiling too brightly. *I live two minutes away, I can easily make it.* Marianne thought, smiling back at Angelique, who clearly had no idea she was remotely late. Marianne was in no mood for feigned niceties.

"Look, we're never going to be in love with each other, so let's not even try," Marianne said. Angelique registered mild surprise. Marianne continued. "But we can be sensible for Joey and Ryan's sake, all our sakes really." Angelique's smile stayed fixed, she pulled up a chair.

"I so totally agree, honey. We both want what's best for Joey, and Ryan's basically a good guy, if a little screwy."

Marianne gave her a look.

"In a nice way screwy, he really thinks he's doing the right thing, dragging my poor child to this god-awful place and setting up home in, well, in nothing more than a cottage." Angelique waved her hand.

"It *is* a cottage," Marianne said.

"Anyways," Angelique continued with the spooky smile, "I'm hoping you'll be the voice of reason and get him to agree to my little package an' all. That way, hey presto it's all done, everyone's gotten what they want and I'm outta here."

Marianne let that go; it was too early in their conversation to begin negotiations. She lifted Joey from the rug where he was playing and looked at Angelique to see if there was even a glimmer of longing to hold her son, feel his skin against hers. Marianne loved to watch the light glint on his eyelashes, stroke the perfect smooth of his cheek, smell his hair. Angelique watched Marianne with her son, but her beautiful, dark eyes remained dark.

Safe in Marianne's arms Joey looked up at his mother – eyes bright, questioning. Angelique touched his hand briefly. He went to grasp her shiny, ruby nails but she snapped her fingers back. She gave a nervous laugh. Marianne folded her hand over Joey's.

"You can probably tell, I'm not that great with kids," Angelique said, "I never planned..."

"That's okay," Marianne was dismayed at the woman, she had just lumped her one and only child in with the rest of the kids on the planet. "I'm not sure I am. I think the best tactic is just to be as natural as you can, they know if you're forcing things."

Angelique gave her head a little shake. "I'm sure you're right honey, but it ain't for me. Of course I'd give anything to have my boy with me the whole time, and I'm looking forward to spending time with him – eventually – but he needs care, a nanny, au pair, you know, professional help."

Marianne frowned. "He's a normal little boy."

"Sure he is," Angelique did not seem convinced, "but you can't take care of him twenty-four seven, it's too big an ask. Neither you nor Ryan really know what you're doing. Be honest honey, this is not a job either of you are qualified to undertake."

"But that's what people do in this part of the world. It's called being a family," Marianne said coldly.

"Don't patronise me, Marianne," Angelique spoke slowly. "If it comes to a custody battle I will win because I will demonstrate how much better my son will be cared for with me. His welfare and education will be paramount and he'll have the best of everything, including the one thing you cannot give him, the love of his mother, because that's me."

Marianne took a deep breath; she would not be bated. She placed Joey back on the rug, moving him out of Angelique's range. "But I thought you wanted him out of your life. I thought you wanted Ryan to take care of him. I thought that was part of the deal," she said.

Angelique rolled her eyes. "Precisely, but it's all or nothing. I do not want one of these flimsy arrangements. Poor Joey needs to know where he stands, so if Ryan is not prepared to agree to every aspect of the arrangement, the deal is *off* and I will go for custody and I will win, hands down!"

She stood to leave. Marianne reached over and caught her by the sleeve. Angelique jumped, as if she had been bitten by a snake. She looked down at Marianne's hand.

"He has told you, hasn't he?" she asked.

"Told me what?" Marianne said.

"Told you what the deal is," Angelique looked into Marianne's eyes. "No, he hasn't. Typical Ryan, head in the sand, hoping it will all go away, somehow everything will sort itself out, so he doesn't have to get his pretty *movie star* hands dirty. Well you ask him what it is I want, and you tell him from me that he has to agree to every single detail and then see if you still want him, because if you do I feel sorry for you, sorry you'd stay with a man who can *never, ever totally* commit."

Angelique shrugged Marianne's hand off and swept out of the room. Joey, who had been silent all the time his mother was present, gave a little sigh. Marianne picked him up. Padar appeared from the cellar.

"Why don't you leave him with me, Marianne? Ryan will drop Bridget off soon enough, I've a great new game for them," he said.

But Marianne was halfway through the door, the little boy clamped tightly to her.

Chapter Fifteen

Ship To Shore

Dermot Finnegan was standing on the deck of the boat he had acquired within days of arriving on the island. He bought it from one of the locals who decided between the weather and EU regulations, he could no longer make a living from the sea and was heading to Australia to join his brother working in IT for a massive conglomerate. Dermot bought it for a good price. It was in pristine condition, kitted out with two well-appointed cabins, galley, good sized heads with a power shower – all very stylish and compact. It was more than comfortable enough to live on, especially in the summer.

He was looking forward to that: long, lazy days with the anchor dropped just off a little bay, fishing line draped over the side, barbecue to cook whatever he caught. He pictured a pretty woman stretched out on the deck, sipping a cold glass of white wine while he prepared lunch. The wind caught the tarpaulin he was folding; it flapped into his face, dissolving his daydreams.

He went below, the debris of the night before splayed about the cabin – an empty champagne bottle, discarded clothing, pasta dishes thrown in the sink. He started tidying, running water into the basin to wash up. He curled his lip at the soggy butt end he found on a plate. The remnants of the weed he and Angelique shared ahead of "getting down and dirty" as she called it. He had been amazed at the energy and variety of his guest's sexual prowess. He thought he knew most of the tricks of the trade, having been seconded to Vice at one stage in his career, but Angelique was *very* imaginative. And when she produced the phials of amyl nitrate, dripping it onto her breasts, before presenting them for him to lick clean, it confirmed what he had suspected: sexual antics such as this were a well-practised hobby for the actress. He remembered the gleam in her eyes as, after he was spent, she brought herself to climax after climax, each orgasm more frenzied and desperate than the last.

Dermot dried his hands, and, replacing a cushion on the couch, found the silk scarf she had tied his hands with while she dug her nails into his throat. He checked in the mirror, the livid marks still evident. He shuddered at the memory. Although aspects of it were far from unpleasant, Dermot had just been doing his job, trying to discover if Angelique, a known substance abuser, knew anything about the shipment destined for the island. If she did, she gave nothing away, and by the time he delivered her back to Maguire's it was Dermot who felt he had been well and truly had.

"Ahoy there, anyone aboard?" a voice cut through his thoughts, bringing him back to the present. Dermot went on deck. A man, he vaguely recognised, in a sailing jacket and cap stood looking up from the quayside.

"Phileas, Phileas Porter," the man said. "Myself and the wife have the pharmacy below in the town."

Dermot broke into a smile. Phileas had served him when he had been in for razors and toothpaste.

"Come aboard. Dermot Finnegan, good to meet you." The men shook hands. "What can I do for you?" Dermot continued in his easy way, checking the other man out: weak handshake, weasel-like face, shifty eyes sweeping over the boat as Dermot watched him.

"It was more me wondering what I could do for you?" the other man said, attempting a smile.

"Really?" Dermot was intrigued, "Listen, I was just about to have a beer, care to join me?"

"No thanks, I don't drink," Phileas replied, "Have you something soft?"

"Sure," answered Dermot, beckoning the man to follow him down below. Funny, Dermot thought, he was sure he could smell alcohol or some sort of chemical on him.

They sat down at the chart table, a can a piece. Phileas was distracted, eyes everywhere.

"You were saying?" Dermot prompted.

"Oh yes, I was wondering if you'll be using the boat the whole time, or whether or not it might be available to hire out now and again," Phileas said.

"Hadn't given it much thought," Dermot replied, looking into the man's face, Phileas did not look the seafaring type – quite wan for an islander. "Why, what would you want it for?"

"Ah, just fishing trips, picnics and such. We don't have much time off, me and the wife, so when we do, we like to make a day of it, head out to sea, maybe swim off one of the bays north of the island. We're from the city, you see. One of the reasons we came here was to enjoy the ocean when we can," he gave Dermot that smile again. "I used to hire this off the fella you bought it from. I was just wondering if we could have the same arrangement. It would help with the running costs, I was thinking, it's not cheap keeping a boat afloat."

Dermot laughed, "Yes, what's that saying, owning a boat in these parts is like standing in a cold shower, peeling off fifty euro notes and flushing them down the plughole."

Phileas nodded in agreement. "That's right enough," he said. "Well ...?" he seemed anxious for an answer.

"Can I have a think about it?" Dermot drained his drink; he had needed a beer after all the champagne. He was planning to live on the boat, weather permitting, while the lifeboat project was underway and there was something about Phileas' request that did not ring true. Dermot decided he might be worth stringing along. "Not sure what I'm doing with it yet, plenty of time. I mean it's October, you wouldn't be thinking about hiring it until the spring at the earliest, am I right?"

Phileas looked surprised.

"Well, maybe a bit before that. The wife's birthday's soon. I was thinking of a little trip then, a candlelight supper, you know the kind of thing," he winked.

Dermot smiled. "Oh I get it," he nodded, "Well, leave it with me Phileas, and I'll see what I can do. When is the lucky lady's birthday, just so I know?"

Phileas got up to go.

"Halloween, the bank holiday weekend, I can close the pharmacy and we can head off." He pulled his cap down over his eyes as he left.

"Fair enough, I'll drop into you below in the shop, so," Dermot called after him, "see ya."

He waited until he heard Phileas clamber down the ladder, and the boat righted itself in the water. Rubbing his hands together he pulled a steel box out from under the berth, clicked the combination lock to release the catch and lifted the lid to reveal a very impressive collection of the latest digital surveillance equipment. Slowly and with relish he unpacked the box piece by piece. There was a selection of the latest cameras, a variety of telephones all with voice recognition, *FaceTime* and *Skype* – he loved the idea of being able to see who you were talking to. Then came his favourite: a range of mini-microphones and sat navs disguised as buttons, earpieces, even jewellery, and to top the lot, a good old-fashioned, two-way radio. He hooked this up first, safer than anything digital and far less likely to be hacked.

"Ship-to-shore, ship-to-shore. Over.*"* he said into the handset. A sharp crackling sound followed and then a voice.

"Is that you Dermot? Speak Irish for God's sake," came the reply.

"Ná bac le hainmneacha, a amadán. Over," Dermot said into the radio.

"What the feck was that?" came the voice again.

"Irish. I said, *don't use names, you idiot,* in Irish. Over," Dermot spoke slowly, fiddling with the controls.

"No, I meant speak normal Irish, like this." The voice sounded a lot clearer now.

"I hate to tell you but we're actually speaking English. Over," Dermot said.

"Ah fuck off, Dermot, you're in Ireland aren't ya? You're speaking fecking Irish when you talk to me anyhow." The connection went dead. Dermot shook his head, not entirely convinced the right man had been commissioned to help with the job at all.

Ryan stuffed the papers into a drawer in the desk when he heard the hall door open. He wanted to read Angelique's proposal with a clear head but every word just fuelled his fury, until he could stand no more, and slung the document aside.

Bridget was in the buggy ready to go. She called to Joey as soon as she saw him. Marianne settled him next to her, clipping him in. They immediately started their chitter-chatter: a giggling gibberish they used all the time. Marianne was convinced they each knew every word the other said, even Monty seemed to understand it.

"How was lunch?" Ryan asked warily.

"Weird," Marianne said flatly. "Angelique seemed spookily calm, serene almost. But she's so detached from Joey – she didn't even pick him up, didn't seem to want to touch him even," she sighed. "She thinks we're incapable of looking after him though, saying he needs professional help, and if you don't agree to the terms and conditions in her new proposal, that's what she'll base her custody claim on. She says she'll win because she actually *is* his mother. But I don't think she wants to win, she doesn't want custody, she doesn't want the responsibility, that's why she keeps spouting on about professional help."

"Bullshit," Ryan spat. "Professional help indeed. She's the one who needs professional help. Where is she now?"

"She took herself off, I don't know where." Marianne was disappointed she had been unable to resolve anything.

Ryan frowned. "Look, I'll take the kids over to Padar as arranged." He put his arms around her; he could see she was frazzled. "Shall I suggest we put off the menu-tasting session at the pub? I'll say you're shattered and I'll cook us a nice romantic supper here, have a bit of time together, what do you say?" he lifted her chin, twinkling eyes looked into hers. Marianne looked quizzical. "You and Padar were going to try some dishes, thinking about having a bit of a hooley for Halloween, remember?"

"I'd completely forgotten," she said, and then smiled. "Your idea sounds better. I didn't have lunch, so can we make it early. I'm flippin' starving."

Taking the buggy, he headed for the door.

"Don't forget the romantic bit; we're having that as well, aren't we?" he gave her a cheeky grin, she laughed as he disappeared but she was feeling far from romantic.

Maguire's was relatively quiet when Ryan arrived with the children. Two of Padar's cousins were behind the bar, stacking glasses and chatting amiably. Ryan went through into the kitchen to find Padar up to his elbows in vegetable peelings.

"One of the recipes for Halloween," he explained to Ryan. "A venison casserole with sour cream sauté potatoes, what do you think?"

"Sounds delicious." Ryan popped a piece of carrot into his mouth. "Look, do you need Marianne tonight, only we've seen so little of each other recently, it would be really nice to spend some time on our own."

"What?" Padar exploded, "I need her here, we've a new menu to produce, people are getting fed up with toasted sandwiches, soup and a bowl of chips – there's only ever anything good on the menu when Marianne's here."

Padar saw his friend's face fall and felt immediately guilty.

"Sorry Ryan, I'm being selfish, youse have a cosy night in, tell her I'll have a practise here on my own and she can have a tasting tomorrow, see what she thinks. Does that sound like a bit of a plan?"

Ryan clapped him on the back.

"Indeed, and it is," he said, and kissing the little ones briefly, made to go. "Have you seen Angelique?"

"Not since this afternoon. She went up to her rooms, didn't have any lunch here anyway. She did send down for another bottle of vodka around five-ish and..."

"She's drinking?" Ryan interrupted.

Padar nodded. "She's wasn't on the wagon for long, started drinking champagne with Dermot yesterday, it's been vodka since. There's not a drop of hot water left in the place if that's any clue as to what she's up to, up there." As if his words had summoned up an incarnation, a swirl of blood-red silk appeared in the doorway. Angelique gave Ryan a lazy smile.

"Well, look who it is, *The Spy who Loved Me!*" she said, exaggerating her Texan drawl, "and you've brought the brood." She pointed at the children, "I just love the way you people have little babies in bars the whole time, what with drinking, and swearing and brawling. It's just the perfect environment for these little ones, and I shall delight in telling the judge precisely that, should I need to." She gave them a beguiling smile.

"They're in the kitchen with their fathers, nothing odd or unusual about that at all," Ryan told her.

"Well, you just think about it long and hard, Ryan, there's plenty that's odd about this whole scenario and plenty that's perfectly sane and sensible about my proposal." She turned to swirl away, "You have *read* my proposal?"

"Of course," he replied.

"Really? Not shared it with the other woman though, have you?" she studied his face.

"I don't know what you mean?" he flew back at her.

"You so do! The bit where it says whatever happens should you marry again, any claim to our son is null and void, custody reverts to me automatically," she sneered, into Ryan's face.

Padar stopped chopping vegetables.

"But that's ludicrous, Angelique, we're getting a divorce. You have a partner, I have a partner, it makes no sense." Ryan was mystified.

She stepped into the room, filling it with fury.

"It makes every sense. You are *not* to marry again. In Joey's eyes, his mother and father are married and always will be, they might not be together but they *are* married, they are his parents." Her voice was rising.

Joey started that strange, intermittent whine he made whenever Angelique was stressing about something.

"Okay, calm down, take it easy." Ryan made soothing gestures with his hands, he reached towards her.

"Don't touch me, you bastard!" she snapped, eyes glittering with tears, and spinning on her heel, swept away.

"Bloody hell," Padar whistled softly, "what was that all about?"

"About herself as usual," Ryan replied, mouth set in a grim line. "Never about anything else except herself."

The door swung open and Ryan and Padar braced themselves for another tirade. The red had turned to blue, equally swirling, but satin not silk.

"Ryan, there you are, excellent. Where's Marianne?" Miss MacReady was in the middle of the room in an instant.

"At home." Ryan blinked, Miss MacReady always made an effort in the style department, but tonight was something else, she had pulled out all the stops. Was that glitter on her eyelashes?

"Are you two free for dinner this evening?" Miss MacReady fluttered the scary eyelashes.

"Er ..."

"Well, it's just that Larry is packing to go back to New York. He's been away from the business far longer than he should have and well, what with it being his last night, I thought it would be lovely for us all to dine together," she said.

"Oh, where?" Ryan could almost feel her twisting his arm.

"Why, here of course." She turned to Padar, "What's that you're making Padar? It smells divine."

"Venison casserole, but ..."

"Sounds perfect, we'll have that then." She smiled at Ryan. "I tried phoning Marianne but no reply, so guessed you were here, where is she?"

"Probably having a lie-down, it's all been a bit ..."

"Indeed," Miss MacReady interrupted, "this is just what she needs, an evening out, with close friends and family, here in the sanctity and safety of the friendliest pub in Ireland. Shall I go and fetch her?"

"No, that's okay, I'll go, but we were planning a night in, what with Padar and Sinead babysitting and all." Ryan gave her a cheeky wink.

Miss MacReady waved her hand, "Ah sure you can do that anytime. No, you must come tonight, we must be here, all together, to say goodbye to Larry and assure him of a warm welcome when he returns. Now, where's Sinead, I wonder if she'll join us once she's settled the children for the evening?"

Ryan knew when he was beaten.

The children were asleep on the sofa with Monty in the middle, looking for all the world like a litter of puppies, arms and legs everywhere, out for the count. Sinead had been unable to stay, telling Padar, "Phileas was not the best" whatever that meant, and Padar had been too busy to enquire further, although he fleetingly thought she looked as if she had been crying again.

Miss MacReady checked on them between courses and with Ryan busy making them all Irish coffees, she and Marianne took the opportunity to transfer them to the nursery created out of the boudoir Oonagh made for herself and Bridget when the Quinn's precious little girl first arrived.

"Funny, Sinead having to go, she adores minding those babies," Miss MacReady commented, gently pulling on Joey's sleep suit. "Mind you, he can be tricky that Phileas and not a bit sociable, while she's so nice and personable."

"I don't think all's well there, do you?" Marianne asked her. "She comes into the pub most nights now and seems so sad too. She's such a hard worker and takes her job very seriously. I wonder if there's something else more than tiredness, what do you think?"

Miss MacReady nodded. "The light's gone out of her alright, such a shame. Maybe she and Phileas are going through a bad patch, it happens to everyone from time to time."

Marianne shrugged, standing at the door waiting for Monty to join them, before switching off the light. Monty snuffled the cots in parting and trotted to where his mistress stood. She closed the door and he sat down on the landing in front of it; he had developed the habit of sleeping outside the nursery whenever the children stayed there.

"I don't know Phileas at all," Marianne said, as they went down the stairs.

"Don't think anyone does, not even Sinead, maybe that's the problem," Miss MacReady replied, sweeping into the bar to rejoin the jollity. As usual, Kathleen MacReady knew far more than she was letting on, thought Marianne, following her as Ryan, full Hollywood smile lighting up the place, handed them each a deliciously creamy Irish coffee.

"Shame we had to put our plans on hold," he smiled at her. "Good night though, I haven't seen Larry this happy in ages." He nodded at his friend, doing a plausible impersonation of a well-known popular singer on Maguire's ancient upright.

Leading the applause, Miss MacReady joined him at the piano for an impromptu rendition of 'The Moon and New York City'. Larry, shirtsleeves rolled up, glasses on top of his head, was having the time of his life, eyes shining, the broadest grin stretched across his face as he tickled the ivories with surprising skill.

"Larry, you look positively glowing, have you lost weight too?" Ryan asked, teasing his portly friend.

"Bound to have," Larry said. "I've walked miles round this island, pushing that buggy-thing whenever Kathleen's been on babysitting duty. I ain't never worked so hard."

Marianne and Ryan exchanged a look.

"Now, now you two," Miss MacReady smiled, reapplying a flash of fuchsia pink to her lips, "your love story is quite enough to be going on with, Larry and I are just good friends." And they all laughed, even Larry, whose blush added to his glow.

Despite all the gaiety at their table, it had not gone unnoticed that Angelique was entertaining Dermot in the snug. Padar was ferrying food and drinks backwards and forwards at an alarming rate, and although Angelique ordered everything on the menu, she seemed to eat nothing. Her sassy laugh and Dermot's deep guffaws gave the impression they were enjoying an evening of unbridled ribaldry until they heard an almighty crash. Angelique jumped up, pushed her chair back so violently it toppled over as she launched herself at Dermot.

"How dare you suggest I've had too much to drink," she snarled. "Who the hell do you think you are? What am I even doing having dinner with you? You're nothing but a peasant, get out of my sight!" She covered her eyes.

Dermot looked across at the others. Ryan turned his hands upwards. Dermot threw his napkin on the table and left.

"Ryan," Angelique wailed.

"Here we go," Larry said.

"You won't believe what the brute said to me." She staggered to where they sat, wild-eyed and trembling.

Miss MacReady looked at Marianne and put a finger to her lips.

"Hey, Angelique, easy now, you're tired, jet lag," Larry tried.

"I am *not* tired or jet-lagged," she screeched. The whole pub fell silent.

"We better deal with this," Ryan whispered to Marianne, "okay?"

She had never seen Larry move so fast. In less than a minute they had scooped the actress up and deposited her in her rooms.

"You've obviously had that little task to perform on more than one occasion," Marianne said, as the gentlemen rejoined them.

"Too often," growled Ryan, then raising his glass, "but she's not going to spoil our evening, oh no, those days are long over."

"Too right," agreed Larry, and they all chinked glasses.

Chapter Sixteen

Engaging The Enemy

With Padar's culinary efforts declared a resounding success and plans for a Halloween Hooley well underway, the two couples were saying their goodbyes as the clock struck midnight. Marianne was just about to go and check upstairs before they left, when Ryan stopped her.

"Finish your coffee, I'll see they're okay," he said.

Music drifted down from the nursery. He stopped. He could hear something else, a high-pitched whining: the noise Joey made when he was with Angelique. Ryan flew up the stairs and burst through the door.

The picture that greeted him would have been one of serene beauty had it not been for the strange sound underpinning the music: Angelique in a nightgown, hair about her shoulders, her child in her arms as they nestled together on a chaise longue; they looked so peaceful sleeping there. But on closer inspection the woman was grey and the child snow-white. Joey's eyes were closed, lips parted, and from deep within his chest the ear-piercing whining noise. Ryan lunged across the room and grabbed Joey. He was cold as ice.

He called his name, shaking him; the little boy's eyes flickered and closed. He placed his hand on the woman's forehead, burning up beneath a film of grey sweat.

"Angelique, wake up," he shouted, taking her by the shoulders. "What have you done? What have you given him?"

Panic rising, Ryan heard footsteps. Marianne and Miss MacReady ran into the room.

"Oh God," Marianne gasped, taking in the scene.

"Phileas, get Phileas, stomach pump, hurry." Ryan tried to shout, his voice strangled in his throat. Miss MacReady kicked off her shoes and fled. Ryan laid Joey on the bed, quickly loosening his clothes. Marianne was examining him for needle marks, bruising, anything. Ryan spotted the plastic beaker and, pulling the top off, smelled it.

"She must have given him this, what is it?" he pushed it at Marianne. Joey had stopped making the noise, his eyes were rolling in his head, spit trickled from the side of his mouth. Marianne pulled him upright.

"Salt water. Now," she barked. Ryan did not want to leave him. "Go!" she shouted. He reappeared in minutes with Larry.

Larry went straight to Angelique. "She's out of it, what the hell happened?" he hauled her to her feet: her knees buckled, head flopped on her chest. "She needs a pump."

"We're here." Sinead arrived with Phileas. Miss MacReady behind them. Phileas checked Joey, then Angelique. He nodded at Sinead.

"Okay, we need him to vomit," she told Marianne. "Get that salt water down him, then make him sick."

"Let's get her in the bathroom and pump her out." Phileas was unpacking his kit as Larry dragged Angelique into the other room.

"And turn that music off," Sinead ordered. Miss MacReady switched off the CD player. At the same time Padar said, "Where's Bridget?"

They scanned the room, no sign. With the music off they could hear whimpering; it sounded like a child, or an animal. They turned to where it came from – the airing cupboard on the landing. Padar flung the door open, Monty growled and Bridget screamed. Padar fell to his knees, taking the terrified little girl in his arms. Monty limped out, tail barely wagging, searching the room for Marianne; there was a large, bloody swelling above his eye. Ryan was holding Joey upright as Sinead continued to force feed him salt water from a baby's bottle; he was gagging and fighting her off, growing more and more upset. Ryan looked desperately at Marianne as she held Joey's hands away from the bottle. She was trying not to cry, trying not to beg Sinead to stop and leave the little boy alone.

"Come on Joey, drink up, that's the way, you can have something lovely to eat once you've had your medicine," Sinead was saying. Joey's body went into spasm. Sinead dropped the bottle, grabbed the boy and turned him over. He made a squawking sound and vomited, and vomited and vomited. All was quiet, and then he started to cry – loudly. Sinead checked all his airways were clear and handed him back to Ryan, smiling grimly.

"He might be sick again but not much. When he's settled we'll give him some sweet tea. We don't want him to fall asleep for a good while." She headed off to the bathroom.

The little boy started to sob softly. Ryan looked at Marianne, relief flooded his face. Marianne was holding an antiseptic wipe against the cut over Monty's eye. He nodded at Monty.

"He's fine, must have got in the way of someone's boot – only doing his job." She cuddled the dog briefly. Monty's tail wagged.

There was a loud moan from the bathroom, a scuffle and a thud. Phileas reappeared.

"She's coming round. She'll need coffee, lots of it. It's a bit of a mess in there, best if we keep her awake for as long as possible. I'm really not sure what we're dealing with." He went over and took Joey's temperature. "Nearly normal," he said.

"Thank God," Miss MacReady said, handing Phileas the beaker. "What did she give him?"

Phileas smelled the creamy liquid. He raised his eyebrows, tasted it.

"That's just milk, what does she be on?" he asked Ryan.

"Lots of things," Ryan replied flatly.

"Prescription? Non-prescription?"

Ryan shrugged, "A bit of both, mainly prescription these days, though, I think." Phileas scowled, he took the beaker and the thermometer over to the basin and washed them.

"I'll have to make out a report," Phileas said.

"You will indeed," said Miss MacReady. "A big fat report, and I'll make sure everyone sees it, and copies go to the right authorities. That woman is dangerous – she could have killed them all."

"And herself," Padar said, bitterly.

"She's tried that more times than I care to remember," Ryan said, "but I never thought she'd hurt Joey. I never thought she would do anything to her own son. I feel such an idiot. How could I have been so naive?"

Marianne squeezed his knee.

"Hey now, enough of that, he's going to be okay, we all are."

"And it's going to be a long night, I'll get the coffee on the go," Miss MacReady said, relieved she could finally be of use.

Phileas put his kit away. "It could have been a lot worse," he said grimly, "I reckon we were only minutes away from them both needing hospitalisation. And how would we have got them there? That's what people don't appreciate. The sooner they get that bridge built, the better."

Larry emerged from the bathroom, dishevelled and sodden. He glanced at Ryan. It was obvious they had been through this before.

"She's gonna be okay, this time. She wants to go home as soon as possible, says she can't remember a thing," he shrugged.

"Really? How convenient," said Marianne going to where Padar held a white-faced, red-eyed Bridget in his arms. "I think we've all had enough excitement for one night. We can keep an eye on Joey at home and Monty needs his own basket, is that okay with you?"

Ryan stood up too. The further Joey was away from Angelique the better.

"I'm so sorry," he said quietly to no-one in particular as they left.

Back at Weathervane Ryan and Marianne switched to autopilot. Joey was washed and changed. Marianne turned back the eiderdown on the big bed, placing Monty's blanket at the foot and Joey's teddy on the pillow. Ryan went through every room, drawing curtains and locking doors. It was a bleak, black night; he needed to keep the blackness out there.

Still silent, they climbed into bed, Monty on lookout in his old position, Joey lying between Marianne and Ryan. Ryan was keeping him awake with a brightly coloured storybook. Marianne entwined her feet in Ryan's legs, resting one hand on Joey's head and the other on her stomach, willing the swirling anxiety inside to stop. Her eyelids grew heavy, Joey gurgled as she drifted off to sleep. It sounded like sweet music.

Marianne heard a noise and was awake in an instant. It was daylight. Monty stirred. She looked at Ryan with Joey asleep on his shoulder – they looked peaceful, normal. She let a breath out and, grabbing a fleece, flew downstairs. She looked out of the window – no-one there. The door rattled again: she opened it a fraction. Miss MacReady stood in the porch, still in last night's ensemble: her only concession to the new day, a headscarf over the curlers pushed hastily into her hair.

"Is everything okay, how's Joey, Monty? Where's Ryan? I couldn't sleep a wink, did you get any sleep at all?" she looked anxiously into her daughter's face.

Marianne beckoned her in, indicating with a finger at her lips to be quiet. They went into the kitchen, Marianne flicked on the kettle. She assured Miss MacReady everyone was fine.

"And you?" she asked the older woman. There was mascara on her face; she had been crying.

"Fine love, fine. It was all such a shock. There we were having a great night, enjoying the craic and there she was...well, doing I don't know what, but nearly killing Joey and herself." She stifled a sob. Marianne gave her a mug of tea. She caught sight of their reflection in the mirror; she could see the resemblance in their strained features. Miss MacReady drank the tea gratefully.

"What happened afterwards?" Marianne asked.

Miss MacReady sniffed. "Padar helped Larry get your woman sobered up and into her rooms. She was making an awful fuss by the time I left, saying she had been drugged and so had Joey, blaming you, Ryan and everyone else she could think of, saying we all wanted them dead and she was going to the police. She'd have won an Oscar for that performance, let me tell you!"

"What do you think happened?" Marianne asked pouring more tea. There was no denying her mother was sharp; she knew stuff.

"Accidental I think, anyone who wanted her dead would have taken a gun and shot her years ago. Should have been drowned at birth that one." Miss MacReady finished her tea and thought for a minute. "Not altogether sure though, Marianne," she said, softly. "I'm sworn to secrecy, but she was in a spot of bother before she turned up here, absconded from a secure unit where she was being detained. She was under investigation."

"No way, what for?" Marianne was shocked.

"Only embezzlement! You know the famous jewellery collection, well it belongs to Rossini, to the franchise and she's been siphoning it off, selling diamonds to dodgy dealers, having them replaced with fake ones and pocketing the cash. Oh, she's a model mother alright. A judge will be rushing to stamp her custody order, I don't think so." Miss MacReady was coming round, she started to take her curlers out.

"Bloody hell!" Marianne sat down.

"This custody thing is a load of shite, bluster. She's using it as a threat to get a more lucrative deal out of Ryan. That's all she's interested in." Now she had spilled the beans, Miss MacReady decided to embellish the story with her take on things. "In my opinion, her career is more or less over. She's been rumbled as a common thief, and I think last night was either an accident or someone else is trying to get her out of the picture."

"Wow." Marianne pushed her hair behind her ears. She really ought to be taking notes. "How do you know all this stuff?"

Miss MacReady shrugged, fluffing her hair out as she walked to the dresser and lifted the whiskey decanter. She looked at Marianne.

"Sure, help yourself," Marianne said. Miss MacReady poured a couple of stiff ones.

"You could do with one too," she said, pushing the glass in front of her daughter. Simultaneously, they lifted the drink to their lips, but Marianne put her glass back down, untouched.

"Does Ryan know any of this?" Marianne watched Miss MacReady carefully.

"Not at all, sure Ryan's head's all over the place, God love him. He wouldn't be aware of anything. I'm led to believe this whole thing is very hush-hush, it's not even hit the news, at least not yet," Miss MacReady assured her.

Marianne thought for a while. It seemed to make sense. Miss MacReady tapped the table with a fingernail.

"Have you actually read the documents detailing what the Angelique-one wants?" she asked.

"No," Marianne replied.

"Why not?" Miss MacReady was incensed.

"Haven't got round to it yet, there's been a bit going on!" Marianne went back at her.

"Bullshit, Ryan hasn't shown them to you." Miss MacReady needed a cigarette, giving up did not suit her one bit. "Why didn't you just read them anyway? It affects your man, your life."

Marianne shrugged. "It's still his business."

"But you're an investigative journalist!" the other woman insisted.

Marianne looked her mother in the eye.

"Yes, and I've always played by the rules, fair and square. No bribes, no hacking, no cheating – call me old-fashioned."

"Where are the papers?" Miss MacReady demanded, exasperated.

Marianne's eyes flicked over to the drawer where she had seen Ryan place the envelope. Miss MacReady was there in a flash.

"Mother, that is not addressed to you," she hissed.

"Marianne, I am the postmistress, the head of communications on this island, it's my job to handle and monitor *all* correspondence." Miss MacReady unfolded the document, holding it far enough away to read. "Pretty much as I thought, she wants a lump sum payoff, more or less to go away and not cause any trouble, then a monthly allowance paid directly into her bank account as maintenance. It increases substantially if Joey is with her at any point, and she wants the majority of Ryan's estate when he dies."

"Nice!" Marianne said.

"Aha, here's another nice twist alright – he's *not* to remarry." Miss MacReady placed the document on the table before Marianne, pointing at the paragraph.

"What? Why?... what's that all about?" Marianne was bemused.

"She's a control freak, clearly. It says 'for the sake of their son's ongoing welfare and security, his father is not to remarry until Joey is over the age of twenty-one; and if Ryan has any more children their allowances and inheritance are to be legally agreed in line with what has already been agreed, on Joey's behalf,'" Miss MacReady stopped reading.

"But Ryan already has a son. I know Mick is an adult and Ryan had very little to do with him growing up, but they're close now and Mick too has a child, what does the arrangement say about that?" Marianne asked.

Miss MacReady examined the small print. "To all intents and purposes anyone claiming to be a benefactor of the estate needs to have had all their rights verified and their legitimacy signed in blood and witnessed by the devil himself."

Marianne frowned at her.

"Meaning, if this sticks, her clever lawyers will have everyone and everything tied up in knots," Miss MacReady concluded, dropping the documents on the table.

"But that's horrendous." Marianne was aghast. "Sounds like she expects Ryan to work his heart out till the end of his days and give whatever he earns to her."

"That's about the size of it and he's not to marry because a wife will have all sorts of claims on him. She doesn't want you or anyone else in the picture at all." Miss MacReady folded the papers away. "Sounds like you have another battle on your hands, I'm afraid."

Marianne was quiet for a minute.

"We've never discussed marriage," she said.

"Really?" Miss MacReady was surprised, "Well, it looks like it's time you did!"

"The mere mention of it seems to put the kibosh on it for me. I prefer things as they are," Marianne said glumly.

"But surely you'll marry. You're perfect together, so in love, so suited. Getting married would be the best thing ever, then you could be a proper family and you would have your *happy ever after.*" Miss MacReady smiled broadly.

"Good grief, I didn't think you of all people would perpetrate that despicable myth. I thought you were a feminist!" Marianne teased.

"Not at all, I'm an equalist, but the sexes are *very* different, we each have to play to our strengths. But if we don't believe in *happy every after*, why bother to fall in love?" Miss MacReady said.

"Like we *have* a choice?" Marianne asked.

"I take your point. If we had a choice I would never have fallen for that spineless bastard, Brian Maguire!" Miss MacReady hissed.

"My father?" Marianne queried.

"The very man, but then I wouldn't have had you, so I was compensated along the way. That's more than most people get who fall for the wrong person," Miss MacReady said, matter-of-factly.

Marianne laughed out loud. "Mother, you're hilarious." She knew Miss MacReady loved her to call her mother, even if it was just when they were on their own.

"Amn't I?" Miss MacReady replied sardonically.

Monty trotted into the kitchen. He looked up at her, his left eye closed from his vicious encounter of the night before.

"Give me that," she said to Miss MacReady, getting to her feet, stuffing the documents in her pocket.

"Where are you going?" Miss MacReady asked.

"To engage the enemy," Marianne replied, dragging on her jacket as she headed out into the dawn.

Marianne climbed over piles of luggage in the hallway, having let herself into the now deserted Maguire's. Angelique's rooms were empty. She wondered what time the poor girl she hired as her maid had been roused from her bed to pack and clear away after the film star's night of overindulgence. She looked around for Monty; he had a way of indicating with a twitch of his nose where something or someone might be. But she had left him at home, telling him not to rub his poorly eye.

She looked out through the landing window, across the pub car park, the street and beyond to the row of shops and the beach. She saw a flash of red, Angelique was at the shore. Marianne took the stairs, two at a time. She looked left and right. Angelique was nowhere to be seen. *Shit*, she thought, *I hope she's not thrown herself into the ocean and I'm the only one around to rescue her. That would be ironic.* She looked left again, catching a glimpse of crimson beyond the rocks. Marianne ran along the beach. Angelique was crouched behind a sand dune, hugging her knees, scarlet fur draped over her. She looked dreadful, smaller, shrunken. Marianne slowed when she saw her, the angry words she had been rehearsing dissolved on her lips.

"Hi," she said, "mind if I?"

Angelique continued to stare ahead. Marianne sat down. They looked out to sea.

"I didn't mean any of that to happen," Angelique said finally.

"Didn't you?" Marianne's tone was light, gently questioning.

"No," Angelique sighed, "I'd had a glass or two yes, but not a huge amount, I just wanted to see him, check he was okay, to see if he was, I don't know, any different with me on our own."

Marianne remained quiet, waiting for Angelique to continue.

"But he wasn't," she said. She turned huge eyes on Marianne. She looked so desperately sad, Marianne almost pitied her. "He got all tensed up and started that god-awful noise. I was only holding him for Chrissakes and then that mutt started growling and the other kid howling. I don't know, I just snapped, put them in the closet till they shutthefuckup – it never hurt me when I was a kid!" She twisted a strand of hair in her fingers. "But Joey kept on, so I gave him a drink to make him sleep and guess I must've passed out. And that's it, that's all that happened." She looked back out to sea. "No harm done, as you say."

Marianne took a deep, calming breath. "Not this time, thank God, but there could have been serious harm done. What did you give Joey?"

"Milk."

"And in the milk?"

"Nothing. Wait, no now I remember, the tiniest drop of vodka."

Marianne bit her lip. "And you Angelique, what had you taken?"

Angelique's head snapped round. "Only a drink. I only drink vodka or champagne. Why? What's it to you?" Angelique pulled the fur more tightly around her shoulders.

Marianne could see perspiration on her upper lip.

"I see you're packed to go," she said.

"As soon as the ferry is ready to leave, I'll be on it. I've had enough of this place. I'm not a bit happy about Joey staying here, but it will have to do, until Ryan gets his act together and my maintenance and Joey's custody arrangements are settled." She flashed Marianne a look. "But in the meantime, I guess you're harmless enough."

Oh do you? Marianne thought to herself, *well think again, lady!* She looked towards the ferry port; lights were coming on.

"Won't be long now. Shall I walk you back to Maguire's? Pat can get the taxi loaded."

Angelique struggled to her feet. Marianne thought she was going to be sick, but taking Marianne's hand, she steadied herself and walked falteringly on.

"Thanks," she said, seemingly grateful for a little kindness.

"Just helping you safely off the island," Marianne said, with a grim smile.

Back at Maguire's, Angelique emerged from the bathroom reading a text. She seemed even more anxious. *Were they on to her,* Marianne wondered, *had the investigators tracked her down?*

"Can I get you a coffee? Would you like something to eat?" Marianne offered.

"No, I'd like to see my son. I need to see Joey, to say goodbye." Angelique pushed her cellphone into her bag. Marianne looked her up and down, slowly.

"Are you completely mad?" she let the question hang in the air for a moment, "There is no way on this planet I'd let you within a hundred miles of that child ever again. You nearly killed him. You put *God knows what* in his drink to stop him crying, and you nearly killed him." Marianne walked across the room and gripped the other woman by the arm. "I've been extremely patient, Angelique, now I suggest you put your bags in the car and get on that ferry before I call the police and you end up back where you came from. 'See my son', indeed!"

Angelique broke free. "How dare you? You two-bit whore! Who do you think you're talking to? Why you ain't even hired help for Chrissakes!"

Marianne continued to glare at her. Angelique's eyes filled with tears, hard to tell whether acting skills were coming into to play or not.

"You have taken everything from me, everything. The man I love, my only child. You've lied and cheated your way into my life and all you wanted was to rob me of my own family. You're a despicable *bitch,* Marianne Coltrane, and I'll never forgive you for what you've done. Why you've killed me stone dead!" *Bit too soap opera to be Oscar-winning* Marianne thought, *but not bad.*

Angelique, hands trembling, reached for her vanity case and, flipping clasps open, began rummaging through its contents, popping pills out of blister packs straight into her mouth. Horrified Marianne pulled the case out of her hand.

"What are you doing? *Stop,* Angelique, for God's sake, you've just had your stomach pumped."

Angelique pushed a pile of pills into her mouth. Marianne slapped her hard behind the shoulder blades, she spat them out.

"*Stop it!*" Marianne shouted.

"I'll make sure he never marries you," Angelique said between sobs.

"I don't care about that," Marianne went back at her. "I only care about them, Ryan and Joey."

"But you have *everything* I want," Angelique cried.

"No, Angelique, you have everything *I* want, everything I have ever wanted, to marry the man I love and to have his child. It's you, Angelique, who has everything!"

Angelique threw herself on the bed. Marianne raised her eyes to heaven.

"But I can't go on, you've ruined my life," she wailed.

"I think you'll find, Angelique, it's *you* who's ruined your life!" Marianne was furious.

"Then I shall end it," she screeched, with all the drama she could muster.

"Then do!" Marianne said, throwing the vanity case and its contents on the bed beside her.

"You'll be sorry for this," Angelique hissed as Marianne left.

"I already am." Marianne collided with Larry on the landing. Her eyes swept over him – belted raincoat, hat, holdall.

"Everything okay?" he asked, nervously.

"Just peachy," she said, giving Larry a crooked smile.

"I'm leaving with Angelique," he told her. "I think it's best I go with her don't you?"

"Good luck," she said, heading down the stairs.

"Is that all you have to say?" Larry asked plaintively.

"You'll need it!" Marianne called back, slamming the door as she left.

Chapter Seventeen

A Place In The Clouds

Larry stood in the doorway. "It's for the best. I can keep an eye on things," he said soothingly.

"I don't need keeping an eye on, thank you," Angelique retorted, snapping the clasp on her case.

"Angelique, please," Larry placed his hands on hers, "you're not well sweetheart, I'll be there if you need me is all, okay?"

She gave him one of her dreamy looks, eyes filled with tears.

"It's not in my nature to cause a fuss, you know that, but if you think it's for the best, okay, I would hate to put you to any trouble." She clicked her fingers at Pat MacReady, smoking nervously in the porch.

The rain was relentless: the wind pushing it round the car park in icy swirls. Larry shivered, tucking his scarf inside his coat. He looked along the lane, hoping for a glimpse of colour, someone coming to say goodbye, someone warm and friendly, who would say she would miss him until they met again, but the street remained grey and empty.

"We'll have to get a move on sur, if we're to make that plane," Pat told him as he put the last of the movie star's bags in the car. Larry helped Angelique into the back. Balancing luggage on his lap, he squashed into the passenger seat. He pulled the sun visor down. *Shit* he thought, *no vanity mirror*, he wanted to keep an eye on her. He shrugged. What harm could she do? Pop a few diazepam, take a swig of vodka from her hip flask. She had been well frisked: anything remotely dangerous removed and flushed away. Pat started the car, the windscreen wipers totally inept against the driving rain.

"You will take it steady now Pat," Larry said as the driver revved the engine, spun the wheel and screeched away. Larry was not the most relaxed passenger in the world. Angelique sighed, closing her eyes behind huge designer sunglasses.

"Driver, you get me as far away from this godforsaken hell hole as fast as you can!" She pulled the fur collar up around her ears.

Larry's cellphone bleeped to life as they left the village, he checked it hopefully. It was only a message from his network. She really was mad with him then. Perhaps just as well, he was growing uncommonly fond of her, he thought grimly, gripping the door as Pat swerved to avoid yet another pothole en route to the ferry and the road to Knock.

Safe within the civilised confines of business class, Larry wrapped himself in a blanket, secured earphones in his ears and pulled the eye-mask down; at last they were on board, next stop New York. Larry loathed flying. He hated being manhandled by security, fawned over by stewardesses and air-conditioned to freezing point. He detested taking off, being suspended in the sky and then plummeting to the ground, but until now he always endured this excruciating discomfort on his own. To have this horrendous experience exacerbated by Angelique's incessant whingeing was almost unbearable.

She was complaining about not being in first class, refusing to accept these were the only seats available, and her constant stream of unrealistic demands – asking loudly why did *she* have to switch her phone off – and general bad behaviour was more than his nerves could stand. When Angelique announced she had spotted an old friend in first class and was going to join them for a glass of champagne, Larry nearly wept with joy.

"Take it easy," he said pointedly, as she reapplied lip gloss, ahead of pouncing on her hapless friend, "the airline is very strict about overindulgence."

"Oh Larry, you're such an old woman," Angelique told him, and with a toss of her hair, flounced up the aisle.

He was dreaming about Innishmahon: he was in Maguire's, it was warm, he could hear sweet music playing...someone tapped him on the shoulder, would he like another drink, a big juicy steak?

"Sir, I'm very sorry sir, but the lady who was with you, she was with you sir, wasn't she?" Larry pushed his eye-mask onto his forehead; he gazed glassily into two pairs of very concerned eyes. The male steward was frowning, the female indicated for Larry to remove his earphones.

"Sir, could you come with me please?" the steward said, gripping Larry's arm. Larry did not want to be released from the comfort of his blanket. He felt warm and safe there; he could tell that wherever they wanted him to go, it would not be warm and it would be far from safe. The steward gave a furtive look around the cabin. "Please sir, I must insist."

Larry grunted, freed himself and stood. Looking down the aeroplane he could see first class was cordoned off, and there were two more stewards on guard at the entrance.

"Oh dear," he winced, "has she been causing trouble?" They started to guide him down the aisle. "Is she drunk, is that it?" The stewards kept walking. "Oh no, it's worse, she's stoned, gee I'm so sorry." The stewards outside first class parted to let them through. Another area had been cordoned off with yellow tape. *How come they always had yellow tape?* Larry thought vaguely. Something bulky lay under the standard-issue airline blanket. Larry could just see a single strand of glossy black hair. He knew immediately that beneath the blanket was one of the world's most famous movie stars. He stopped and put his hand to his mouth.

"Oh my God, is it...is it Angelique?" he said, his voice strangled.

"If you could officially identify the body sir, that would be most helpful," said the steward who had led him through.

"Body?" Larry repeated, horrified.

"I'm afraid your companion is dead sir." The steward waited for the news to sink in. Larry was blinking rapidly. "She locked herself in the bathroom, sir. When we finally gained access, I'm sorry to say she was beyond help." The pretty blonde stewardess looked into his face. Larry staggered a little, turning green.

"Sick bag, quickly," shouted the stewardess; as Larry relieved himself of the contents of his, already queasy, stomach.

"It's a fine boat," Ryan said, having examined below deck, checked out the cabin, the hold, admired the solid in-board engine. He ran his fingers over the wheel. Dermot was fastening large fenders over the side. "You got it for a good price?"

"Yeah, the fella I bought it off couldn't make the repayments, only had it a season, said there was hardly a living in fishing these days. Said he was going to Australia, try his hand at computers?"

Ryan pulled on a sheet, coiling the end neatly on deck.

"History repeating itself. We've always had to leave to make our way in the world, yet something stays behind, pulling us back, pulling at the heart." He looked back at the shore. Dermot laughed.

"Some of us do better than others. I could have stayed in London, trying to be an actor, I suppose, but I needed to eat. Thank goodness my Pa was in the Gardaí and I was young enough to change career." He handed Ryan a can of beer from the icebox, as the purring engine pushed them out to sea.

"You were good though," Ryan said. Dermot shrugged.

"A struggling thespian only, not handsome enough, not well connected enough," he shot Ryan a look.

"I did offer to help, I'd have got you a part in a miniseries, you know that," Ryan told him.

"Ah, America, the land of opportunity," Dermot looked out across the Atlantic. Ryan took a swig from his can, his hands were cold; he rubbed his fingers together.

"Weren't you with a girl at the time?" he reminded his friend.

"Maybe, don't recall," Dermot said.

"Yes, you do. A beautiful girl, well-heeled too, what was her name?" Ryan watched him. Dermot kept his face blank.

"Annabelle Ellingham, that's who it was, the singer. Now I remember! You were smitten, that's why you didn't follow me to the US. You'd fallen in love, that or you were thinking with your dick!" Ryan laughed. Dermot stayed silent. Ryan zipped up his jacket against the breeze, waves were breaking, it was becoming choppy.

"What happened?" he said, more gently.

"The usual," Dermot tried to smile. "She was in love with someone else." Dermot put pressure on the throttle.

"Really? But she was always hanging around with you...us." Ryan said. Dermot looked him up and down.

"You're a right thick culchie at times," Dermot told his friend. "You, ya fecking eejit, she was in love with you. Ah, sure they were all in love with you." He forced a laugh, pushing the throttle harder. The boat lurched; Ryan grabbed a rope to steady himself.

"What's the plan?" the movie star asked the captain as they bounced through the waves.

"Let's go round the island a couple of times. I need to get to know it like the back of my hand if I'm going to make sure the new lifeboat and crew is up to the job," he said.

"Do you need me for crew?" Ryan asked.

"Yeah, I'll give you a job, if you're up to it," Dermot said, then, looking away, "More than you ever gave me."

Ryan did not hear his last comment. "I'm up to it, have to keep myself fit don't I? I'm an international *super-spy* amn't I?" he said, flexing his biceps.

Dermot laughed, more heartily this time.

"No Ryan, you're an actor and not a very good one either. You just got lucky. In fact, you get lucky with everything, you ugly son-of-a-bitch!"

And Ryan laughed with him. He was probably right; the call from the *Royal Shakespeare Company* would not be forthcoming at this stage.

They circumnavigated the island, when Dermot finally slowed the vessel and dropped anchor in a small cove, sheltered from the wind. Ryan went into the hold for the fishing tackle while Dermot heated soup. They sat companionably at the chart table, drinking thick creamy soup out of mugs. Ryan produced a lump of cheese and some fruit soda bread out of his backpack. He chopped it into chunks and they ate it between them, mopping the soup dregs out of the mugs with the sweet, fresh bread.

Dermot opened a cupboard under his seat, pulling out a bottle of whiskey.

"A tot only," he said to Ryan.

Ryan nodded. "Agreed, you have to keep your wits about you handling a vessel like this in unknown waters. Goes like the wind though. We got a fair old speed up out there."

Dermot smiled. "Yeah, I'm pleased. She handles well, turns on a sixpence and powers through the waves like a dream. A good steady vessel, up to the job."

"What job?" Ryan asked.

"Anything I ask of her, I suppose, what more could a man want."

The sun came out. A bank of cloud like spun cotton drifted away to the east; the island shone like an emerald in the sunlight, the cliffs glinting grey. The men shrugged off their sailing jackets and took up position, throwing their lines over the side.

"Be a good spot for lobster pots, I reckon," Ryan said, lighting one of his French cigarettes. The scent of sweet tobacco trickled past Dermot's nose.

"I thought you gave up, you being father to a youngster now? You'll have to be politically correct, environmentally friendly as well as ecologically sound if you don't want your parenting skills lambasted in the tabloids!" Dermot passed him another tot of whiskey. Ryan raised an eyebrow. "Sustainability," Dermot said, downing his drink. Ryan laughed. He had forgotten how much he liked Dermot, how close they had once been.

They were silent for a while, the water gently lapping against the bow, the sun giving the air a soft, heated glow.

"Are you going to be okay?" Dermot asked as Ryan flicked the cigarette butt into the sea. The actor was the most relaxed he had been since his estranged wife's arrival on the island.

"Sure, we'll be grand. We'll all be grand."

"She's some piece of work, Angelique. I mean, I can understand you getting involved, she's absolutely gorgeous, but marrying her, was that a wise move?" Dermot asked.

"No choice, really," Ryan replied. "She was pregnant with Joey, he's my boy, I'd have little or no chance of taking him out of the US if we'd not been married, though he couldn't have stayed with her either, with her issues!"

Dermot nodded. "She is a bit...*demanding.*"

Ryan looked at him. "You've had relations?"

"Well yes, or she's the one who had the *relations* as you so delicately put it. She's very forthright." Dermot had the good grace to look uncomfortable.

"So I believe. Wasn't like that with me though, in the beginning. Very much the lady, maybe because I'm a bit older, I had to do all the running." Ryan looked out to sea, "it was awhile ago now, things hadn't been good for a long time."

"Hey, I wouldn't have gone there if I'd have thought..." Dermot put his hands up.

"I know that. Like I said, a long time ago," Ryan gave his companion a half-smile. Dermot was a red-blooded male, a bachelor, why would he refuse the advances of a stunning, *up-for-it* female.

"And Marianne, where's that going, not just another notch on the bedpost, surely?" Dermot asked, checking his line, no takers.

"No way, she's just great isn't she? Intelligent, gorgeous, funny, she's the best thing that's ever happened to me," Ryan's face broke into a big grin.

"Hope she knows that. Hope you're going to make an honest woman of her then, because she'd be the one for me, no mistake." Dermot slapped Ryan on the shoulder, "Wish she had a sister."

They both laughed. Ryan stopped suddenly. "Sadly, no can do the marriage thing at the moment. I haven't asked her you understand, because even if I did, we can't get married yet."

"What do you mean? You and Angelique get divorced, you and Marianne get married, make a go of it on the island, like you said you would." Dermot was surprised.

"Angelique's managed to get a lawyer to tie me in knots. Not marrying again is one of the *terms and conditions* of the settlement, part of the custody deal." Ryan looked at his hands.

"What? She can't do that, that's inhuman. Ah, she has a screw loose, no-one would expect you to stick to that, it's nonsense." Dermot was incensed.

"Well, I hope you're right, but I need a bloody good lawyer, that's for sure." Ryan shrugged.

"Hey, Marianne's worth all the *terms and conditions* in the world. Ignore them, tear the papers up," Dermot said.

"It's complicated. Don't forget, Angelique's uncle Franco is my boss. There's my contract. I've agreed to honour that at least." Ryan pressed a finger and thumb against his eyelids.

"Jeez, what kind of fucking hold do these guys have over you, it's like the *Mafia*," Dermot said angrily.

Ryan did not need reminding.

"What would you know about it? A friggin' traffic cop from County Dublin!"

But Dermot would not let it go.

"What kind of crap are you involved in at all? Contracts, franchises, big money, drug money, it's all in the mix, it has to be. You know more than you're letting on." Dermot poured himself another tot.

"You do talk a load of shite at times, Dermot." Ryan got up to go below, trying to end the conversation. Dermot followed him.

"Money laundering? Bet you've done a bit of that in your time too, eh? How else can the millions needed to make these movies be raised these days – sure, all the banks are bankrupt, only serious criminals have that sort of money, bet I'm right," Dermot slurred a bit.

Ryan was pouring himself another drink.

"You missed your vocation Dermot. You should have been a friggin' script writer." Ryan offered Dermot the bottle.

"And what about Marianne, does she know any of this, has she any clue what she's getting involved with?"

"Shut your mouth," Ryan snapped.

"Why shouldn't I tell her? Before it's too late, before she makes the biggest mistake of her life?" Dermot sneered.

"You go too far," Ryan spat at him.

"You've always gone too far," Dermot shot back, moving to stand nose-to-nose with one of his oldest friends. Ryan threw his drink in Dermot's face. Dermot leapt on him, they wrestled, the deck was wet, they slipped. Ryan tried to push Dermot back, but Dermot grabbed him in a headlock, twisting him round and clamping him to his chest. Ryan kicked out, smashing the chart table as they both fell backwards. There was a loud thwack and a groan. Dermot's grip loosened. Ryan pushed round, onto his knees. Dermot was flat on his back, eyes closed, a small trickle of blood oozed from the back of his head.

"Jesus, Dermot!" screamed Ryan in panic. Dermot's eyelids fluttered, then opened.

"Ouch, me head," he put his hand to his skull, trying to get up.

"Whoa a minute, you fecking eejit, lie still, you knocked yourself out," Ryan said. Dermot gave Ryan a sideways look.

"Were we fighting?" he asked.

"Ah, not really, just a bit of a skirmish, nothing serious," Ryan smiled with relief.

"That's good," replied Dermot. "I've missed our little dust-ups, what's life without a good mate to have the odd brawl with?" Dermot gave Ryan a wobbly grin.

"Fucking head case," Ryan said, attempting to haul the big man up.

Marianne watched from a short distance as the men off-loaded the boat. It was early evening, the light not quite disappeared, a pale smudge above the marina wall. The breeze caressed her cheek, a cool kiss. She could taste salt on her lips: sea spray or tears she knew not which.

Ryan jumped ashore. Monty spotted him first, rushing to greet him, barking in welcome. He bent to ruffle the dog's fur, looking round for Marianne. She wiped her nose with her hand and stepped out of the shadows into the gangway which led to the boats. He saw immediately something was wrong. He dropped his bag, speeding towards her.

"What is it? Joey? Bridget, what?" he held her shoulders, she looked up into his eyes, glittering black under the lamp light.

"It's Angelique," she said, placing her hands on his. "It's bad news Ryan. There's no other way to say this but she's dead."

He blinked at her, disbelieving.

"What?"

"She's dead Ryan, that's all I know."

Dermot joined them: he too could see something was wrong.

"Marianne?" he stood next to Ryan, sandy hair awry from a day at sea.

"How, what happened?" Ryan was saying. Marianne remembered Angelique and Dermot had been close. *How close?* She wondered what to say to him. Ryan said it for her.

"Angelique's dead." All colour drained from his face.

Dermot looked from one to the other. "Jeez, I'm sorry," he said flatly. "Do you know any details Marianne?"

Marianne looked at them, eyes wide, "Only that Larry's been arrested."

Chapter Eighteen

An Arresting Situation

Ryan was shocked, "*What?*" he gasped, "on what charge?" and releasing Marianne, turned to Dermot. "This is terrible, they can't arrest Larry. My God they can't put Larry in a cell, he'll freak. There's got to be some awful misunderstanding, it has to be mistake."

Dermot nodded grimly. "How did you find out?" he asked Marianne.

"Lena rang Miss MacReady, Larry gave her the post office number, but she didn't make much sense, nor did Miss MacReady when she arrived at Weathervane, but I got the gist of it. Miss MacReady said she'd mind Joey so I could come and tell you as soon as you docked." Marianne looked from one to the other, anger and confusion building behind their eyes, "I didn't want you to see me straight away in case you thought something awful had happened to Joey after the other night and panicked. All I can gather is she was found in the washroom on the plane. They landed at JFK, the medics went on board but she was already dead. She was taken away, presumably for autopsy and Larry was arrested at the same time."

Ryan sucked air through his teeth. "Know anyone in the New York Police Department, Dermot?"

"Certainly, done a bit of training with their anti-terrorist team, good lads too," Dermot told him.

"Can you find out what the hell is going on? Then let me know how I get my buddy out of this mess," Ryan said.

"Leave it with me," Dermot replied. He turned to go, then reached over and shook Ryan's hand. "Larry will be fine. I'm sorry about Angelique, sorry for..."

"Hey," Ryan said flatly, "forget it, never happened." He clapped Dermot on the back, "Meet us back at the cottage when you have something. I'll try to speak to Lena in the meantime."

Marianne was standing with her arms wrapped around herself. Monty was sniffing the mooring posts. Ryan put his arms around her; she looked up at him, narrow eyes, tight mouth. He gave a dry whistle and Monty joined them. The three of them headed back to Weathervane as the night turned totally black behind them.

Dermot shook off his jacket and hung his baseball cap on the hook. He could smell coffee; he would not be waking anyone up anyway.

"Everyone okay?" he asked as he entered the brightly lit kitchen. Monty gave a yap, he liked Dermot.

"Kathleen's reading to Joey upstairs, trying to keep things as normal as possible." Ryan said, though Dermot could tell things were very wrong indeed. Marianne poured another cup. Dermot drank gratefully.

"Larry's being held for questioning, not charged with anything as yet. They're waiting for the results of the autopsy and have taken statements from everyone on the plane. They're holding a steward for questioning and two passengers who were in first class, the singer Gloria Grenston and her personal assistant. Seems they were having drinks with Angelique before she went to the bathroom and passed out. That's as far as I've got. You get anywhere?" Dermot asked Ryan.

"Spoke to Lena, who's calmed down a little, she had Larry's lawyer there, I spoke to him too. He thinks this is all pretty routine, but he did say they would try and keep a cap on it from a media point of view. Anything to do with airlines sends the world into a total tailspin of panic, since 9/11 anyway." Ryan shrugged, "Not much we can do except wait to hear."

Marianne went to stand beside him. She rubbed his shoulders.

"I think you ought to have a bag packed ready to go," she said.

"Go where?" Ryan was surprised.

"New York, of course, when the press get hold of this you'd better be there, dealing with it. Then there'll be the funeral to arrange..."

Ryan put his head in his hands.

A tall, dark figure appeared in the doorway. Startled, they looked up.

"Bad news, I hear," Father Gregory said in his brown, velvet voice. "I came as soon as I heard, the poor woman, God rest her soul." He blessed himself. Dermot followed suit. Marianne stared blankly at the priest. "Such a shock, any idea at all?" he asked.

Ryan shook his head. "Don't know yet. Autopsy, though they don't usually hang about do they, especially as she's famous?"

"Was," Dermot corrected.

"Oh God," Marianne's face crumbled, "I'm sorry, so sorry."

Ryan took her hands. "Hey, come on now, none of this is your fault, none of it." He gave her his lopsided smile. "And what were you just saying about packing bags and all? You're right I need to be there, but not without you." He looked into her eyes. "We can do this together. Can you bear to come with me?"

"Let's not talk about this now, let's see what tomorrow brings." She offered Father Gregory a coffee, but Dermot had found the decanter.

"I'll go and check on Joey," she said, leaving the men to their whiskey and speculations.

Marianne found Miss MacReady and Joey on top of the eiderdown on the spare bed, both fast asleep. She went to wake Miss MacReady but deciding against it moved to cover them up; the postmistress' mobile phone fell from her fingers; the screen lit up, she had been trying to send a text but Weathervane was notorious for poor reception. Marianne read it.

'I've heard. Don't worry. We'll get you out, if I've to turn up with a chainsaw and tear down prison bars. Her death nothing to do with you, know that. She's responsible or someone helped. Can't blame them, dreadful woman. Try not to worry. They'll get to the bottom of it. K. PS sorry we argued. X'

Marianne let the phone fall onto the bed. She was dreading them 'getting to the bottom of it', finding out the truth, that it was she who had given Angelique the wherewithal to kill herself, she had encouraged her to do it, she who wanted her dead. Marianne felt the bile rise in her throat, for as much as she loathed herself for what she did, she dreaded what was coming next, because she knew her already fragile world, was about to be torn apart.

Chapter Nineteen

One Of Our Own

The next day in Maguire's the tension was palpable. Padar was busy behind the bar though distracted, forgetting little details: a slice of lemon here, a mixer there. The television was on, a large, flat slab of colour on the pewter wall, a window on the rest of the planet, a pipeline to the outside world. Padar looked on as the locals gathered in front of it. He wanted to shut it off, but they had come to hear the news.

Sean Grogan was on his usual stool at the end of the bar. Shay was unenthusiastically practising darts in the corner. Father Gregory drank coffee as he scratched a few words in a notebook, some thoughts for tomorrow's sermon, a tricky one. He looked up when he heard Sinead's voice; Phileas was with her, a rare occurrence these days. The priest nodded at the couple, taking their drinks to a table near the TV. Sinead smiled back. Phileas was concentrating on the screen. Father Gregory was relieved to see them together, hoping Sinead's recent threats in the privacy of the Confessional had dissipated, and they were trying to get their marriage back on track.

"Turn it up," said Sean, "here it is."

Padar pointed the remote, the theme tune to the national news programme giving way to the anxious face of the anchor man. He rattled off a few headlines and then:

"News of the death of the actress Angelique de Marcos has shattered the island community of Innishmahon. The American actress was returning to the US following a visit there, when she was taken ill on board a flight en route to John F. Kennedy airport. One local farmer told this programme, 'the islanders had taken the actress to their hearts'."

The screen cut to a shot of the island: a glorious summer's day, golden sand, glittering sea, sails on the horizon. They heard a crackly phone line and then an echoey voice.

"She was a lovely woman, one of our own. She said herself how much she loved it here, how she wanted to stay. She loved it so much."

Padar turned in slow motion to look at Sean, grinning up at the screen; Father Gregory was staring at him too.

"Jaysus Sean, it's you," Padar exclaimed. Those gathered shushed him. The reporter continued.

"Miss De Marcos' son and former husband are living on the island at the moment?"

"Oh yes, though she was only visiting, she made it very clear she would be back. She made lots of friends, good friends here." The echoey voice continued.

Dermot had just arrived. Sean gave him a shifty look.

"There were reports that the actress had not been in the best of health recently, any comment on that?" the reporter pressed a positively gregarious Sean, over the phone.

"She looked very well, beautiful looking woman I have to say.

No, I don't think anyone here would have said she was anything but the picture of health," he confirmed.

"And how will you and the other islanders remember her?" the reporter asked.

"With great fondness, a real star. Sure, we'll probably put up some kind of memorial, a statue or something, she was a very special lady, we're all brokenhearted, I don't think we'll ever get over it."

"Thank you. That was Sean Grogan, a close friend of the actress Angelique de Marcos, whose death was reported in the early hours of this morning."

The picture of the island cut to a stunning shot of Angelique at a red carpet event. *"Her husband, the Irish actor Ryan O'Gorman was unavailable for comment. Cause of death has not yet been confirmed. We'll bring you more news as it breaks."* The presenter looked earnestly into camera and then turned to a guest, waiting patiently to speak about the latest dairy policy.

"Close friend? How did that come about?" Padar glowered at Sean, as the gathering beneath the screen dispersed.

Sean shrugged. "The reporter must have had my number after the last time they were here, reporting on the storm. They only wanted an unbiased comment from someone who knew her," Sean said, folding himself over his pint.

"Who made you the spokesman for the island? Did you even speak to her while she was here?" Dermot asked sharply. Sean did not reply. "Might I suggest that's the first and last time you speak to the press about this, or anything else for that matter."

"Ah, another blow-in giving out orders, telling local people what they should and shouldn't be doing!" he growled into his pint.

"I'm serious," Dermot towered over him. "The last thing we want is a shower of bloody journalists crawling over the island, finding scandal and corruption where there is none and preventing proper work from being done."

Father Gregory was at the bar. "Dermot's right. Sean, if we are going to encounter the media again, we need to present a united front."

"We do," Padar agreed, "We want people to come here to enjoy themselves, not think the place is a mausoleum to a dead actress."

"Oh do we?" said Sean. "Well, some of us, who were born and bred here, would prefer it if people didn't bother coming here at all." He drained his glass and made to leave.

"Just don't speak to the media again," Dermot warned.

"Just fuck off," Sean snapped back. "You might be coxswain of a non-existent lifeboat boyo, but you're no 'cock of the walk' around here." And with surprising agility Sean jumped from his stool and left.

The phone behind the bar rang. Padar spoke into it and then called over to Sinead. Phileas scowled up at her as she left to take the call.

"No problem at all," she repeated into the receiver. Father Gregory stopped her as she came out from behind the bar.

"Okay?" he asked.

"I'm heading over to Weathervane to collect Joey and his things, bring him here to stay with Padar and Bridget for a while. I'm not working at the moment, so I can mind them when Padar's busy." She went back to Phileas.

"Don't you think you should have cleared that with me?" the priest heard him say.

"They need a hand, that child has just lost his mother," Sinead replied.

"And I seem to be losing my wife," Phileas hissed back at her.

Marianne had never been to New York or flown first class but Ryan thought it best. Despite their casual attire and dark glasses, people were staring and commenting. Dermot said he would come along as security but Ryan declined the offer.

"I want our life to be as normal as possible," he told his friend. "I know that's a big ask at the moment, but I want to try and go it alone."

"Cool," Dermot shrugged, but he made sure Ryan had details of his detective friend at NYPD and wished them luck. "How long do you think you'll be gone?" he asked. Ryan pushed his glasses onto his head.

"The results of the autopsy should be tomorrow, funeral arranged the day after. Angelique was Catholic, so a quiet family burial. Then if she can bear it, I'd like to show Marianne a bit of New York. I don't want her only memory of one of the most fabulous cities in the world to be a sad one, but neither of us want to leave Joey for very long."

Dermot punched him on the shoulder.

"He'll be fine. I'll keep an eye on things. Go on, get outta here," he said in his best *Kojak* accent.

He watched as they passed through the doors to departures. There was a hell of a lot to do in a week; Angelique's demise had not been helpful at all. He had wanted to develop their relationship a little more, hoping she would at least hint who her contacts were. He too had been tipped the wink she had absconded from the secure unit at the hospital. The authorities were not coming after her at that point, they were waiting to see what she did next. It could have been a red herring, but Dermot needed to know if she had any information about the drugs shipment, anything that could help him unravel a bit more of the thread.

Her death left him at a dead end, his leads run dry. If he did not come up with something soon, he was worried he would be taken off the case. They might send a big shot down from Dublin, someone with a track record who could handle the pressure of working for the other side. That would be a disaster, a black mark on his otherwise unblemished career. He wanted this job to be his swansong, his glorious finale.

As he climbed into the car, Dermot's phone flashed a text. *Stay overnight at Joyce MacReady's bed and breakfast. Your contact, female, will be there.*

Excellent news, he thought, I'm back on track. He dialled the number of the guesthouse. Joyce was so welcoming she sounded like she had been expecting his call. Dermot scratched his head as he bumped the 4x4 onwards, mildly surprised one of the key players co-ordinating the shipment was a woman. What did she look like? Maybe like one of those glamour-girls that starred in the *Thomas Bentley* films with Ryan. That made him smile. Then he considered Joyce MacReady and wondered if she was as cultured and well-informed as her younger sister, Kathleen. He loved a lively discussion over a glass of port. He had no idea, at this stage, how rewarding that discussion would be, how in fact, it would change his life, forever.

Marianne dressed carefully in a navy suit, tights and chestnut knee high boots. Ryan helped her with the pearls Miss MacReady had thoughtfully placed in her case, texting her they were there. The matching studs with a tiny circle of diamonds, a gift from Ryan, were perfect. She smoothed her hair back and taking her clutch bag and dark glasses, sat patiently in the vestibule of their suite.

She phoned Sinead after breakfast and all was well at home. It crossed Marianne's mind that Sinead was a godsend, to be up early and at Maguire's with breakfast done and dusted, two children washed, dressed and ready to head off to the little kindergarten she and Joan Redmond, newly returned to the island with her young family, had recently set up. She wondered fleetingly if Sinead had stayed the night but dismissed the idea. Phileas would never tolerate Sinead being away from her post at the pharmacy for any length of time. She decided not to ask the question as they said goodbye, Sinead wished her well, it was going to be a difficult day.

Ryan appeared in the hallway: white shirt, black suit and tie, hair gleaming. He gave her a sad smile; he looked tired. They had spent most of the night with Larry and Lena. Larry was deeply disturbed by the whole experience. He had been released the previous day, following the verdict of death by misadventure pronounced by the New York City medical examiner's office.

They had gone straight to Larry's apartment from the airport. Lena greeted Marianne as if they had always known each other. Marianne liked her immediately; she looked like a female version of Larry – larger, with extravagant bouffant hair, perfect make-up and expensive, too tight, clothes.

"Hey you guys, come on in. Good to see you. My gawd, though who would have believed this? I mean, it's just awful, I can't tell you how relieved I am you're here. And Larry, I thought he would just die, I mean, well it's just the pits, what can I say?" Lena led them into Larry's immaculate drawing room. Elegant cream sofas faced each other, before a virtual flame fireplace. Larry was stretched out on one wearing a velvet eye-mask and an ice pack on his forehead. Despite the central heating he was draped in a satin throw.

"I gave him a sedative, he was distraught, he's of a nervous disposition as you know, I've never seen him so stressed out." Lena wrung her hands, then checked her manicure, "well, now you're here I can go to my hotel and prepare for tomorrow. It ain't gonna be easy. It's afterwards though Ryan, after the funeral, we need to meet with Mr Rossini and his lawyers. There's a lot to discuss. Marianne, I've asked Lisa, Ryan's PA if she'll accompany you while we're tied up: shopping, sightseeing, whatever you want to do."

"Thanks Lena, but maybe another time, Marianne and I will hear what Rossini has to say together," Ryan told her. Lena shrugged, although their most successful client, Ryan was far too troublesome to be her favourite.

Larry pushed the eye-mask up and shrugging off the throw, jumped up from the sofa.

"Ryan, Marianne, thank God you're here, it's been hell!" He hugged them both. His face was grey, eyes bloodshot. "I'm so sorry your first visit to my home town is under these circumstances," Larry said to Marianne.

"Are you okay Larry? It must have been a terrible ordeal. Is that the end of it, are they sure there was no foul play?" Marianne asked.

"D'ya think?" Lena asked, searching in her bag for cigarettes. "I'm not so sure, they might have filed the autopsy, but I don't believe Rossini is going to leave it there. He'll call for a private inquest, a full investigation. Don't let's forget, Angelique was all the family he had. Sad but true, anyone related to him don't seem to last no time."

"But she's being buried tomorrow," Ryan said, taking the drink Larry had conjured up from the gleaming bar in the corner of the vast room.

"D'ya think?" Lena said again.

"Oh my," Larry said, gulping back a large slurp of the drink he had prepared for Marianne. "She's probably right," he said to Ryan as the white telephone on the blond sideboard trilled. Larry gripped the handset to his ear.

"Yes, yes, I understand. Yes, we can all make it. It's rather unusual though, isn't it? Not that I know much about these things." Larry went quiet; he was listening intently to the person on the line. "Very well, we'll be there." He replaced the receiver and turned to his three guests.

"Well?" Ryan asked.

"That was Arnie, our lawyer. There's to be an investigation alright but a rather unconventional one. Rossini wants to see us, before the funeral. He wants every detail of his niece's last days and if he's satisfied her death could not have been avoided the funeral will go ahead. If not, well who knows?"

Ryan squeezed Marianne's hand. "More drama," he said.

"Well," Larry gave a hollow laugh, "he is one of the greatest movie producers in the world, what can you expect?"

"I expect some dignity and decorum. Angelique and I may have been separated, but I'm still her next of kin. The autopsy report has been filed, the funeral has been arranged and everything goes ahead as planned. She should be laid to rest in peace and we should be free to get on with our lives." Ryan was firm: he was in no mood to be bullied by Rossini.

"He's right," Lena said, unexpectedly on Ryan's side. "Rossini may be family, but he's only an uncle."

"A powerful one though," Larry said, "who could cause trouble."

"I think it's Angelique who's caused all the trouble," Marianne said quietly.

Lena sighed and then said matter-of-factly, "Let's look at this rationally. Angelique died on the airplane. She had clearly been indulging in some sort of substance abuse and that's highly likely what she died of. It's perfectly acceptable her doting uncle wants to talk to the people she spent her final days with, ahead of her funeral. What's not acceptable is whatever we tell him sends him into a rage and he demands a further investigation and puts our lives not only on hold but back in a rather unwelcome spotlight. Now ..." they were all seated at this stage, "... has anyone got anything to tell, anything at all? So we're prepared and can get this over with as painlessly as possible."

Larry tutted, "Really Lena, you're so, well, clinical about all this."

Lena eyeballed her brother, "Need to be. Rossini can be tricky. We have a contract to fulfil, emotion should play no part. We want him to believe his niece had a happy visit in Ireland with her child, ex-husband and his new partner. All was convivial and non-acrimonious. Her dependency on certain substances her problem. I'm guessing he doesn't know she was far from clean."

"Christ, don't tell him that!" Larry shrieked.

"I will if I have to," Ryan said, steely eyed.

"I'd keep whatever we know to ourselves as much as we can," Larry advised, "We don't know what Rossini knows. We don't know if *he* might be involved in any way, we just don't know is all I'm saying."

Lena gave him a look, then went to her bag for another cigarette, "But no-one did anything to help her take her own life, okay?"

Ryan and Larry drained their drinks simultaneously. Marianne sat staring at her glass; she felt dreadful; she could not decide whether it was jet lag, guilt or both.

"I don't think I can go through tomorrow and not say anything," she said.

"*What?*" Lena strode across the room." What are you talking about Marianne? Come on now, no upsetting the apple cart."

Ryan leaned forward. "What is it, Marie, what's wrong?"

"I did it, it's my fault," she looked into his eyes, "I gave her the drugs."

"*What?*" Ryan's turn to be horrified.

"In her rooms at Maguire's. We had words. She was shoving pills down her throat. I tried to stop her and then I lost it, threw all the stuff at her, told her to do it, kill herself and left her to it. She must have kept popping pills, and during the flight the overdose kicked in, she went into a coma and died." She stifled a sob. "I should have taken everything off her, flushed it down the toilet, but I was so mad with her, I didn't care if she took them. I wanted her dead, so you see it's my fault, *all* my fault really," she looked up at the three pairs of eyes staring back at her.

It was a dark, rainy morning. The doorman held a large umbrella emblazoned with the logo of the five star hotel in gold as they climbed into the waiting limousine. A couple of cameras flashed in their direction; Marianne was getting used to ignoring them. Ryan put his arm around her as they settled into the back seat.

"You look lovely, perfect," he said, softly, "and remember, I don't care about Rossini, Lena, Larry, or all the lawyers in New York put together. Say as much or as little as you want. Tell it like it is. You've done nothing wrong. None of us has."

Marianne squeezed Ryan's knee. "It just doesn't feel like that." Marianne said as she turned to look out at the shiny New York streets, bodies huddled under gleaming umbrellas like a great glossy centipede, as the car slid slowly towards the freeway heading north.

After her outburst the previous evening, Larry took up the story, explaining he arrived as Marianne was leaving. Angelique was in a dreadful state, threatening to take everything and finish it, once and for all. He had talked her round, surreptitiously destroying anything dangerous and leaving her with a couple of diazepam and a flask of vodka to get her through the journey home. Lena and Ryan looked relieved as Larry concluded his summing up. Marianne remained unconvinced; she could not shake the gloomy guilt that enveloped her. The pulse of this most vibrant city seemed to slow, keeping pace with the dull, thud of her heart.

She looked at Ryan staring blankly ahead. Should she reveal what Miss MacReady had told her, about Angelique embezzling the family jewels, that the actress was already in serious trouble when she arrived on the island, or should she let sleeping dogs lie, leave him with one less thing to worry about, let the story die with her. She took his hand in hers.

"Let's get this over with and go home to where we belong," Ryan said, resting his head back, pulling his shades down over his eyes.

Franco Rossini was planning a private burial at the lakeside cemetery near his ranch in upstate New York. It was where most of his nearest and dearest were buried. Two elderly Italian cousins he brought over when the vineyard had been sold after his father's death; his wife's maiden-aunt who had been his cook and housekeeper; his gardener and friend, Roberto, a variety of dogs, cats and even a couple of horses. Franco was sentimental about the people and creatures he loved, and he was at the ranch so rarely these days it was good to be home, even if it was for a funeral.

The largest and most beautiful memorial in the exquisitely maintained garden was to his wife Sophia, cruelly taken from him just after their twenty-fifth wedding anniversary. The pale alabaster angel stood, head bowed over a plain slab of marble bearing an inscription in gold letters, *'Sofia Magdalene Rossini, moglie amata di Franco. Sono soltanto una metà fino a quando ci incontreremo di nuovo e mi renderai intero.'*

He brushed a leaf off the marble and sat down. The spaniel came to join him. Franco loved the way spaniels never noticed the rain; they loved life so much, were so engrossed in just being, the variables of the elements never even registered. He also loved the way they seemed to pick up on every emotion, as the one sitting beside him now turned sorrowful eyes towards his, ears drooped in sympathy. Franco absent-mindedly rubbed the dog's head.

"It's a sad day, Sophia. Angelique, our beautiful, lovely wayward girl is no more, gone. Drugs, alcohol, I dunno what, and what does it matter? Nothing's gonna bring her back, nothing's gonna change anything. I feel so helpless, like we let her down. We were all she had, she was all we had, and now gone." He wiped his eyes with the back of his hand. The dog licked his fingers. Franco did not notice.

"Now there's only the little boy. The only Rossini left on the planet, far away on some godforsaken island somewhere. The only thing we have left." He sniffed loudly. He was beginning to feel cold; the marble was wet, seeping through his jeans. "I think we need him here, home with us, is what I think. I think we need to bring him up and educate him in the old ways. So he knows he's a Rossini and what it means. A guy could get lonely on a big ranch and if he came to stay, I would come back here, spend more time. It would be good, good for both of us, all of us. Family's family

Sophia, I need him here with me, you, all of us." He threw out an arm to encompass the graveyard.

He sat silently for a while and then smiled. He could see her in his mind's eye, hand on hip, wagging her finger at him. She would be saying, "Are you crazy? You want a young child here, out here in the middle of nowhere, with all these dead people?"

Just like when they were married, he would stand his ground, "You're wrong Sophia, it's perfect for him. He needs to grow up knowing who he is."

But she would come back at him with something like, "You're a lonely old man is all, harking back to the old days. Those days have gone. Buy him a pony, send money for his education but let him be."

Franco shook his head to clear the images and rose slowly to his feet. He put his fingers to his lips and pressed a kiss on the marble.

"My Sophia," he told the spaniel. "So beautiful, so wise ...so bossy." He started back towards the house. He needed to prepare. It was a sad occasion; nevertheless he was looking forward to some company.

Chapter Twenty

The High Commander

Joyce MacReady was a wonderful hostess, and in common with most of the MacReady's there was something beguiling about her. Not in the flamboyant way of her younger sister Kathleen, but Joyce had style, shades of nobility, fine pearls, good shoes – the way she always changed for dinner – even if she were dining alone.

There were splashes too of the *big house* about the place: old silver, paintings, a couple of Chinese rugs. Joyce had staff: Milo an elderly gardener cum handyman and a couple of girls from the nearby village who helped with the bed and breakfast, booked solid every summer.

Legend had it that as a young girl Joyce met a celebrated ballerina returning from the United States to retire. The glamorous dancer and the young countrywoman developed a friendship, and Joyce moved into the ballerina's fine Georgian farmhouse to become her companion.

Of course there was a rumour it was more than a platonic arrangement, but such things were not spoken of in polite society in the west of Ireland during the nineteen seventies and the two women lived a happy and fulfilled existence. They bred Labradors; Joyce training them to the gun, bartering the puppies in exchange for shooting and hunting excursions for the many guests she and the ballerina entertained, arriving in a constant stream during the season from every continent. It was said, during their heyday, a couple of earls and even the odd prince made an appearance at the house.

When the ballerina passed away she left the house, furniture, everything to Joyce. And although a couple of relatives crawled out of the woodwork to dispute the Will, nothing came of it, and Joyce became known as 'the heiress', subsidising cash flow by turning the residence into the thriving, first-rate establishment it had become.

Dermot was sitting at the end of a long polished table, his chair towards the fire, watching the peat flames flicking purple and red, reflecting in his glass. Two of the house guests had taken their leave and headed wearily to bed after a punishing day walking. Another guest, an attractive, rather serious looking young woman in a smart suit, remained. She sat beside Joyce at the far end of the table. The women were chatting quietly, their porcelain cups chinking as they drank.

He looked under his eyelids at them: flashes of jewellery at their ears and throats, twinkling in the candlelight. He wanted to speak to the young woman, but did not want to disturb them, thoroughly enjoying this scene of highborn domesticity. A confirmed bachelor, wedded to his career, he had many late and lonely dinners – good food, fine wine and elegant company were a rare treat. He could feel his eyelids drooping, warmed through to his bones, his hand dropped to his lap. He jumped, startling the women.

"I'm sorry," he said, "I'm nearly asleep, you have me so stuffed with delicious food and drink Joyce."

Joyce folded her napkin.

"Your bed is turned down and ready, Dermot," she told him. "I'll get you a nightcap to take up with you, if you'd like." Not waiting for an answer she left the table to find something special to serve as her guest's nightcap. The younger woman stood to leave. Dermot was on his feet.

"I'm sorry we didn't have more conversation," he said to her with a grin. The other guests had insisted on regaling the whole table with every detail of their walk. They had travelled from the Netherlands, so the undulating Irish landscape had them totally bewitched.

"Me too," she smiled back, the smile transformed her face, making her pretty, with twinkly eyes. "But I'm afraid my bed is calling, goodnight to you." She turned as Joyce reappeared bearing a large tray of bottles.

"Were you to meet anyone here?" Dermot tried: he was sure she was his contact.

"No, just a stop-off, on my way in the morning," she was curt.

"A nice drop of malt, Dermot?" Joyce cut in, laying the tray carefully on the sideboard. "This one from Tyrconnell is lovely, light as a feather and rich at the same time." She went through the bottles. "Erin, will you join us? Just the one? Go over to the fire, take that easy chair there, sure we didn't get a chance to even talk to the poor man, that nice couple from Holland were so full of their day out."

The woman hesitated. Dermot wanted her to stay, he liked the look of her.

"Thanks Joyce but I won't stay, if you don't mind. I've had a long journey and I've further to go tomorrow," she said in a warm husky voice, difficult to place the accent: a mixture of Dublin and English.

"Of course," Joyce gave her cheek a little kiss, "goodnight dear."

"Goodnight Erin," Dermot said disappointed, she could have been his contact, she did look like she could be in a *Thomas Bentley* film. She did not reply, just slipped quietly away, leaving a faint scent of jasmine behind her.

Joyce handed Dermot a squat glass of solid crystal. The amber liquid glowed gold in the firelight. She held it up like a jewel, examining each facet.

"The best time of day, sláinte" she said, taking a sip. "Well young man, I'm guessing you're here to receive your orders?"

Dermot blinked at his hostess.

"Well, aren't you?" she said.

Dermot smiled to himself. Of course, Joyce was his contact. She knew why he was there, she was well ahead of the game. He loved working with professionals, even if they were on the other side.

"High Commander," he nodded a salute before he sipped his drink. She waved a hand, dismissing his elevation of her rank. "There's a big shipment on its way, I just need to know when and where to do my bit," he said hoping he did not sound too vague.

Joyce looked at him shrewdly.

"I'm only a messenger Dermot, a go-between, I don't get involved in anything risky, I'm not a criminal, just a supporter. I'm intrigued though, what is it?" she asked.

Dermot decided to share what he knew; a sprat to catch a mackerel.

"We've hived off some standard-issue guns and ammunition from the British Army, on its way to Afghanistan I believe." Dermot said.

"Poor bastards, I wouldn't send a snake out there," Joyce said grimly. "How's it coming in?"

"How much do you need to know ma'am?" Dermot asked, hedging his bets.

Joyce laughed, "Just tell me it's not Pat using that ridiculous section cut out of the chassis of the taxi. Good heavens above, thinks he's *James Bond* completely if he brings a bit of contraband to and from the island in that. He also thinks the local Garda haven't a clue what he's up to, the eejit."

"You mean those two uniforms are clean?" Dermot was surprised.

"Not at all, but they'd never get involved with Pat. He's no discretion at all, though he's a great decoy, if you ever needed one," she said.

"Interesting," Dermot said. "Have you heard if anything else is coming in with the shipment?"

Joyce raised her eyebrows. "Do you mean drugs?"

Dermot nodded.

"No!" She banged her glass down on the table. "No, no, no. I won't have anything to do with drugs. I don't care certain elements of the organisation use them to fund other things, but it's not right. It sullies the campaign, makes it less honourable. I'm a great believer in the old ways," she said.

"I'm sorry?" Dermot asked.

"Donations, that's my department, I try and keep up the pressure on New York. I have good contacts there, still our biggest ally in my opinion." She went silent, staring into the fire.

Dermot used the silence to think things through. So Joyce had no inkling the arms shipment was being used as a decoy for the cocaine. In fact if she did it sounded like she would go and sink the whole lot herself. Dermot was pleased he had played his cards close to his chest.

"What's the plan then?" Dermot asked, bringing her back to the present.

"Well, my niece Marianne has bought the big house on the island. She's going to turn it into a children's home, or something," Joyce said.

Dermot nodded, he knew this.

"It's been empty a long time and we've used it in the past as a safe house, a stock hold. There's good landing for a small, study boat. It can get a bit rough thereabouts, the bay sits in a deep dip, and nothing can be seen from the village or even out to sea – a smugglers' paradise," she told him.

"Maybe in the past but everything's so much more high-tech now, we probably don't need an old smugglers' hideaway." Dermot did not like the idea of any part of the operation being near anything to do with children, Marianne, or civilisation for that matter.

"That's up to you, just giving you a bit of local knowledge" Joyce said, "But you'll need to stash it somewhere until the dust settles, although I doubt the disappearance of a cache on its way to Afghanistan will go public. Even if the press did find out it would be quashed. Very bad PR to admit a consignment of expensive guns and explosives has disappeared off the face of the earth, too embarrassing."

"Which is why this should all be relatively easy," Dermot assured her, and himself. "Now I just need to know what my job is?" Dermot said. This was going well, very well indeed.

Joyce went to the bureau, and retrieved a large, black document wallet from a drawer. She expertly spun the combination lock and handed Dermot a USB stick, a slim, silver case no bigger than a cigarette lighter – a tiny memory stick.

"Everything's on that: files, customs and excise notations, shipping documents, the lot. The goods will land on the coast, south of Westport, in about six weeks' time. It will be aboard a fishing trawler coming from Plymouth. You're to load it straight onto your vessel and get it back to Innishmahon ASAP. The plan is to off-load it and hold it there until we get instructions that C-Division is on its way to collect. The last stage of your involvement is to ensure it's loaded onto their boat and is safely away heading north."

"Seems simple enough," Dermot said, flipping the memory stick in his fingers.

"Not quite. There could be more trouble than just the obvious." Joyce was watching him carefully.

"What do you mean?" Dermot asked.

"There are already rumours an undercover operation is in place. It's highly likely someone is going to try to intervene at some stage, nab the shipment and return it to its rightful owner or, depending on how bribable they are, sell it onto the highest bidder. There's quite a market for what's been acquired out there." Joyce gave the dying fire a gentle poke, the last of the peat glowed.

"Tricky," Dermot scratched his head. Joyce was as sharp as a knife, he had indulged a little too readily in her generous hospitality; he had to be careful not to let anything slip.

"Ah sure, nothing to a man of your calibre, Dermot," Joyce went to refill their glasses. "I'm surprised I never came across you before. Were you active in the organisation while you were in the Gardaí, or is this part of your retirement plan?" she gave a little laugh.

Dermot smiled, "Despite what the newspapers would have you believe, Dublin is *not* the centre of the criminal universe, I've done my stint serving the community, so jumped at the chance of the lifeboat captaincy on Innishmahon, but it's a love job. When the opportunity came along to give the cause I hand, sure I decided to give it a go."

Joyce returned to her chair, handing Dermot his glass.

"I had no warning you were coming but I guessed they'd send someone soon enough. Sure that's often the way, you just have to go with the flow," Joyce told him. "And the movement, how did you get involved with that? Have you always believed the whole of Ireland should belong to the Irish? Or did something happen on your road to Damascus?"

Dermot had never given it much thought; he frowned briefly. "Oh, I see what you mean. I imagine my beliefs are very similar to your own Joyce," he smiled at her warmly.

"Really?" Joyce was intrigued.

"In fact, I was hoping you'd tell me all about it. Your role in the whole thing, vital cog in the wheel, a genuine freedom fighter. I believe you're considered quite the heroine in high places."

Joyce beamed at him and settled into the wing chair to regale this handsome young man with tales of derring-do. What a treat. Dermot sipped his drink; he was in for a long night. As Joyce began, he thought he heard a footstep on the stair. He glanced across the room, a brief shadow, silence. He sat back struggling to keep his eyes open.

Chapter Twenty-One

Nothing To Forgive

Before making Innishmahon her home, Marianne had been an award-winning, investigative journalist. In her former life she mixed with politicians, entertainers and aristocracy; she had seen the homes, yachts and trappings of the wealthy and powerful. Franco Rossini's home in wealthy upstate New York was not going to intimidate her. So she was surprised when the limousine slipped through a large, plain gateway, rolled along a well-maintained but unremarkable drive to the entrance of a smart yet unostentatious ranch-style house.

As the chauffeur opened the door to guide her out, a sprightly gentleman with gunmetal-grey hair and moustache rushed to greet them. Marianne recognised him immediately. He too wore navy. A beautifully cut Italian suit, white shirt, plain navy tie; he had a fresh camellia in his button hole. He pulled a tight smile at Ryan, clamping him in his arms, kissing him on both cheeks.

"My boy, what a time eh?" he said. He turned warm, brown eyes on Marianne. His face softened. "And this is Marianne," he said her name with a flourish. "My dear child, I am so sorry your visit here is for such a sad occasion. Thank you for coming."

"Mr Rossini," she went to shake his hand. He kissed her on both cheeks too. "I'm pleased to meet you, I'm sorry under such circumstances."

He nodded solemnly, "Call me Franco, please." Marianne looked into his face. His welcome was genuine, despite his sadness. The car bearing the siblings, Larry and Lena Leeson with Arnie Cohen, their lawyer drew up behind them.

"Come," Franco opened his arms, guiding his guests into the house. A woman stood at the door. She wore the uniform of hired help, there was no-one else there. Marianne was suddenly sorry for this wealthy, successful elderly gentleman. He had nobody. He was alone.

They gathered in the library off the main hall. The walls were lined with books and paintings of faraway vineyards, cypress trees and sweeping mountain ranges, a fire crackled in the grate. It was the home of a gentleman farmer, a man of the country, with no indication of the glitzy industry that had made Rossini his millions. Seats were arranged before a large desk, coffee served. Another man and woman arrived. Ryan recognised Albert Emmanuel and his wife Nina, old friends of the Rossini's; Albert was also Franco's lawyer. Albert checked his watch.

"Shall we begin Franco?" he asked.

The older man nodded.

"This isn't an inquiry," Albert said, after formal introductions, "rather, Franco's wish to understand the last few days of Angelique's life. They had become estranged and although he was informed of her whereabouts and tried to maintain contact, it was difficult."

Ryan nodded, watching Franco intently.

"So if everyone is in agreement, Mr Rossini would like a few questions answered, just for his own peace of mind and if all is satisfactory we can proceed with the funeral."

The room fell silent. They could hear the grandfather clock ticking in the hall.

"Shall we start with you, Ryan? The last time Mr Rossini spoke to his niece, she told him she was going to Ireland, she was hoping for a reconciliation, she said she was sure you and Joey would be coming home to the US very soon."

"What?" Ryan was on his feet. "She said what?" Larry stood too.

Mr Rossini raised his hands. "He's only saying what she told me the last time we spoke on the phone, that's all."

"But it's not true Franco. That was never going to happen. It was over. We have new partners, I have a new life," he looked at Marianne, she smiled back at him. Mr Rossini motioned Ryan to sit down.

"Let's just look at the facts Ryan. We'll tell it our way, then you tell it your way. It's hard not to get emotional, it's an emotional time, but easy, take it easy," Mr Rossini said in a soothing voice. "Albert, you got the report from the hospital there?"

"Angelique's latest medical report indicated that her treatment was successful and her condition greatly improved – she was no longer substance dependent. She had been clean for six months, including alcohol," Albert was reading from a file now.

Ryan shook his head. "I'm sorry, Franco," he said, "none of this is true."

Arnie coughed. A little man with a shiny bald head, he wore glasses with bottle-end lenses and carried an air of anguished intensity. He opened his briefcase and took out a large wodge of paperwork.

"Mr Rossini, I have all of Miss de Marcos' latest medical reports here but if, as Mr O'Gorman says, these are unsubstantiated, more interestingly I have further, more recent witness statements from hotel staff, airline representatives who all confirm that Miss de Marcos was not clean, shall I go on?"

Franco turned to Albert. "What's all this? Did you know any of this?" he demanded.

Marianne was watching them carefully.

"Has he always had her under surveillance?" she whispered to Ryan.

He shrugged. "Didn't think it was anything as thorough as this."

Arnie's file looked impressive: *what else had he uncovered?* Marianne looked across at Larry. *Surely he was the one who told Miss MacReady that Angelique was embezzling, about the insurance company wanting to question her and her absconding from the secure unit. Would any of this be revealed now?* But Larry looked relatively calm, like he pretty much had things under control.

Albert put his hand over Mr Rossini's clenched fist on the desk.

"Angelique had powerful friends, unscrupulous people, you know that. I have suspected for some time that much of the information, particularly the health reports we receive, is falsified. People paid to say what we wanted to hear, paid to deliver a version of Angelique's life that was not entirely accurate."

"That's putting it mildly," Lena said sharply. They all turned to look at her, "If you want the truth, Mr Rossini I think you should have it. Marianne, will you tell Mr Rossini what you told us last night, then Larry can fill in the gaps right up to where he was arrested and nearly had a nervous breakdown over Angelique and her condition." She waved a hand at Arnie, "We've paid a fortune and spent frantic days pulling this evidence together and I'm sorry, Mr Rossini, but it's time to stop pulling punches, then maybe we can lay that poor girl to rest, and get on with our lives. There, it had to be said."

Everyone in the room blinked at her. Mr Rossini reached across the desk and closed the lawyer's file.

"Very well," he said, taking in the whole room with his glance, "let's hear the truth, it will be quite a refreshing experience for me, I get given so much crap these days." And he shot Albert a look.

Two hours later, Marianne and Ryan were in the limousine, heading south towards New York City. Franco had listened intently to their accounts of Angelique's final days. Arnie even showed a video of Sean Grogan's bizarre interview to those gathered. Rossini sat quietly throughout, staring out of the window at a most remarkable view; rows and rows of thriving vines, standing like soldiers across the hillside, sweeping down to Canandaigua, a sprawling, dark lake; Rossini's *little Italy* in upstate New York.

"That bit was true, wasn't it? She was a beautiful woman, and the people did take her to their hearts." His eyes were filled with tears. They mumbled agreement before he called an end to the proceedings and led the way to the little chapel at the entrance of the private graveyard. A young priest gave a short service before the burial. Marianne watched as the ivory coffin, borne aloft by Ryan, Rossini, Albert and Larry, was taken to the plot beside Sophia's angel and lowered slowly into the ground. She stayed a little way back, as Franco gave each of the guests a lily to toss into the grave – a final goodbye. The others were chatting. She was reading Sophia's inscription when Rossini appeared beside her beneath a cypress tree.

"What does it mean?" she asked him.

"Sophia Magdalene Rossini, beloved wife of Franco. I am only half until we meet again and you make me whole," he gave her a sad smile. "I think you know what that feels like." He offered her a lily. "Will you go and make peace with Angelique, tell her you forgive her, give her space to forgive you," he said, looking into her eyes.

"There's nothing to forgive," she said.

"Well, that's a good place to start," he replied. Marianne took the lily and went with him to the grave, to say a final goodbye to her lover's wife.

The most haunting aspect of the whole event for Marianne was Mr Rossini – he and his solitary spaniel. She watched them out of the rear window as they drove away; a lonely old man and his dog, standing in the rain. She turned back and looked at Ryan, white-faced, fists clenched in his lap. It had been a tough day.

"Let's just go home, Ryan," she said quietly, 'let's get home as soon as we can."

He squeezed her hand, too drained to speak.

Dermot was disappointed to find Erin had left before breakfast. He looked down into the drive to find only a pile of leaves where her neat little car had been. Joyce was outside in wellingtons and a wax jacket, sweeping the porch. She talked long into the night, reminiscing about her time in Donegal, when she realised she had a 'calling' to support the campaign for the reunification of Ireland, heavily influenced by her mother and the enigmatic men who used to visit their cottage on the island, using it as a halfway house during the volatile nineteen seventies. She and Kathleen were only teenagers at the time. Dermot knew of their mother, the charismatic

Bridie MacReady, a 'dyed in the wool' revolutionary, but he had no idea how important Joyce was until last night. Now he knew this neat, little countrywoman was highly respected and as active as ever. Would he mention her in his report? He was not sure, the authorities already knew about her, how else would he have been given the connection? But Joyce had never been arrested, questioned even, she must have friends in very high places, he mused as he shaved.

He flicked on the TV. The breakfast news flashed up a report of the small private funeral of the actress Angelique de Marcos in upstate New York. Ryan and Marianne were getting into a black limousine. Larry held an umbrella, shiny with rain, over them. They all wore the same, strained expression. He watched, razor poised, as a reporter pushed a microphone at Ryan.

"What will happen to the franchise now, Mr O'Gorman? Will Mr Rossini continue to make the movies?"

"This has been a very sad and difficult time for us, the whole family, but I'm sure, once we've had time to grieve and reflect, it'll be business as usual. Angelique was devoted to her uncle and a huge fan of his work. It's what she would have wanted," Ryan said, matter-of-factly.

Dermot shrugged at the screen, wondering vaguely if Marianne had any idea the type of business certain members of *her* family were involved in. Any clue of what was part of her, until recently, unknown heritage. He remembered Joyce proudly showing him photos of her mother with members of the organisation, a couple of American supporters and a still good-looking crooner from the nineteen fifties. He had been struck by how like Marianne, Bridie MacReady was, sparkling eyes, determined chin, chestnut curls tumbling past her shoulders. And how the men acquiesced towards her, flanking her protectively, leaning in, trying to gain her attention. She was a looker alright. In one photograph, at a grand event, she wore a fabulous purple dress; it showed off her figure perfectly, her bronze, bare shoulders gleamed. It was nineteen seventy-six, the year of the heat wave, everyone was tanned and happy.

"A well-known photographer took that picture of mother. All the magazines ran it. She was quite a celebrity," Joyce had told him, proudly.

It could have been Marianne; Dermot was stunned by the likeness.

"What happened to your mother, Joyce?" he asked, as they made to leave the fireside.

"She died," Joyce said sharply, gathering up the pictures sprawled across the table. "Sleep well," she called from the stairs, shutting off the lights, leaving him in the darkness with his thoughts.

A loud gong brought Dermot back to the present – breakfast. He shaved speedily and headed downstairs. He had a busy day ahead and needed to get back to the island. Now he knew how and where the arms were coming in, he had to make arrangements. With the guns and explosives just a ruse, a decoy for the biggest shipment of pure cocaine Europe had ever seen, it was going to be doubly dangerous, live ammunition could be unpredictable at the best of times. He loved working undercover. Sitting at the breakfast table alone, he popped the memory stick into his laptop.

Poor Joyce, he thought, living in the past, she genuinely thought she was helping old-style freedom fighters, she had no idea what was really going on, but she had provided him with vital information. He hoped when the whole thing blew wide open, the authorities would go easy on her. Women like Joyce built empires, fed armies and ruled the waves, she was a true queen in her own way, republican or not.

Dermot felt a frisson of excitement as he tucked into his full Irish breakfast but he knew, in his heart of hearts, he could not pull off something as big as this easily. These were ruthless people; it was going to be a tough job.

He was paying the bill when a screech of tyres signalled Pat MacReady's arrival at the front of the house. He heard raised voices. Joyce and another woman, the dark velvety tones he recognised from last night. He pushed open the large Georgian door. Erin Brennan was standing beside Pat's taxi. She looked completely different, faded jeans, turquoise sailing jacket, hair flying in the wind.

"Dermot, there you are, thank goodness. Erin's car's broken down. Pat spotted her on the road. He's to go to the airport for a pickup. Are you able to give her a lift at all? I'll phone the boys at the garage below in the village, they can sort the car out, but she needs to be on her way."

I've to be on my way, myself. Dermot forced a smile, he could never refuse a damsel in distress.

"No problem, no problem at all. Where are you headed, Erin?" he asked, striding across the gravel.

"Thanks, I'm really sorry to put you to any bother," she said, pushing the hair out of her eyes. "Joyce, I'll wait till the car is ready, it's not a problem."

"Not at all, sure I can have it delivered to you once it's fixed, Dermot can give you a lift, you'll be company for each other." Joyce said.

"Where are you headed?" Dermot asked.

"The island, Innishmahon – do you know it? If you could just drop me at the ferry, that would be brilliant." Erin said.

"Innishmahon? No bother at all, sure I'm going there myself."

"Really?" she seemed surprised.

"Yes, I'm the coxswain of the lifeboat, I live there," he smiled broadly now.

"We have a lifeboat?" she was incredulous.

"Not yet," he grinned, "but it's on its way, we're building the lifeboat station as part of the redevelopment, the new bridge, marina and all."

"Oh yes, the bridge has gone," she said.

"Been gone awhile," Dermot replied, taking her bag as Pat sped away. "So have you by the sounds of things."

"A very long time," she said quietly, "a very long time indeed."

Chapter Twenty-Two

The Lost Babies

Marianne slept fitfully on the plane home; she was dreaming about Miss MacReady and Monty. They were on the beach digging for treasure, a pirate ship was anchored just off the bay. They dug a huge hole and found an old-fashioned pram full of photographs. Photos of babies: tiny black and white shots of infants, hundreds of them, and when Miss MacReady flipped them over in her hand, there was a large, red question mark on the back. Somebody asked her the name of her mother. She opened her eyes.

"I wondered if you'd like another drink?" Ryan looked down at her huddled beneath the blanket in the seat. "You were murmuring. Your lips are dry." He smoothed her hair back.

"Just some water please," she said.

"It won't be long now," he reassured her. She gave him a weak smile.

"I've never felt so far away," she whispered.

"I know what you mean," he told her.

She struggled up to sit beside him. He looked pinched and weary. She took his hand and kissed it.

"Did Mr Rossini mention Joey? When you two went off for a chat, I wondered ..."

Ryan rubbed his chin.

"Yes, he did. He asked me how we were going to break the news to him, were we going to keep Angelique's memory alive for him, how we were going to educate him, care for him, even what religion we were going to enforce on him!" His eyes flashed at her, "Too many questions, too much detail, too soon, I told him." He fell quiet.

"We've all that to decide in time but Mr Rossini is always welcome to visit, spend some time with his great nephew. He seems quite alone in the world, despite all the glitz and glamour of his career. I can see how he loves the ranch and vineyard, how he would love Joey to enjoy it when he's older." She kept her tone conciliatory, she wondered what had been said to make the memory of the conversation with Rossini cause Ryan's temperature to rise.

"That's all well and good, and as usual, Marianne, you have everyone's best interests at heart but I don't trust Franco. I love him, he's like family to me, he and I go way back, but as much as I love him, I don't trust him." Ryan sounded disappointed.

"You don't think he'd do anything to harm Joey, surely?" Marianne asked in hushed tones.

"No way, nothing like that, but I wouldn't put other stuff past him, he can be quite controlling in his own way. I can see him trying to lay the law down where Joey's concerned. What religion, I ask you?" Ryan sat back.

"Well, it's a valid question, from where he's standing, trying to cling to the old ways." Marianne responded.

"Ah, that's a load of crap, Marianne. Joey can make his own mind up, in his own time. That was one of the problems with Franco and Angelique's relationship: he was wildly generous, giving her gifts, money, but there were conditions, strings attached, almost like he was jealous she might enjoy herself too much from what he had given her, so he *always* gave with a condition, she had to do something to deserve it, whatever it was."

"How do you mean?" Marianne was wide-awake now.

"For instance, the apartment in Manhattan. He gave it to her, but there were certain friends of his she had to entertain and bring other guests there too, entertainers, movie stars, well-known people Franco wanted his friends to meet and socialise with," Ryan said.

"And who were these friends, where were they from?" she asked.

"Mainly men. Mainly Russian." Ryan was watching her now; he could almost see the cogs whirring in that journalistic brain of hers.

"Backers?" Marianne looked around to make sure no-one was listening.

"Franco's always played that very close to his chest. In the olden days it was said the business was built on Mafia money, that Franco laundered funds all over the world. With the type of movies he makes he could easily do that, locations on every continent. But that sort of money dried up and although the movies made profits, Franco spent lavishly, especially after Sophia died. And then the recession, it affected everything." Ryan told her.

"But surely everything Mr Rossini does is legal and above board. He's too high profile for anything underhand, isn't he?" she asked him.

Ryan folded away the copy of the *New York Times* he had been reading.

"When I resigned from the franchise and flew out to New York to see him that time, he took me to lunch at one of his favourite restaurants. He had two guys with him, like he needed protection. He told me I had to do the movies, complete the contract for his sake. He had to borrow a lot of money and the conventional routes to finance had been closed to him. He said the interest rate was crippling and to have to start all over again with a new, unknown leading man after our success was one pressure, one chance he couldn't afford to take. He begged me to finish the contract for his sake, for the sake of the family business. That's why I agreed. I had no choice."

Marianne nodded, "I know that. It'll be fine, I know it will. Hey, some of it could even be fun. Remember what that was like, *FUN*! We could do with a bit of that, couldn't we?" she poked him in the chest and pushed her hands under his jacket to tickle him.

"Hey stop," he laughed, "stop, I can't bear it." He grabbed her hands.

She looked up at him; she made those slate-blue eyes twinkle anyway. He smiled down and kissed her.

"You're right. It certainly feels like we should be having some fun. It's just ..."

"It's just not right yet, it'll take a bit of time. I've lost people in my life too, remember, and whatever you felt at the end, if there has been love and good times, there will be happy memories too. Hold onto those, hey?"

He nodded and kissed her again. A deep, warm kiss, that melded them together. Marianne released her arms from beneath the blanket and wrapped them around his broad shoulders, pulling him tight to her. No-one kissed like Ryan. It still made her nose tingle.

The cottage smelled of baking – Ryan was learning how to make bread like his grandmother. Marianne was busy on her laptop, lining up tradesmen for Oonagh's Project, whilst co-ordinating correspondents looking for their families via the *Lost Babies* website she set up. It never ceased to amaze her how the constant stream of enquiries did not let up, especially after a number of well-known celebrities revealed they too were victims of this insidious practice.

Ryan kept an eye on her when she was working on this particular project. Sometimes it upset her so much she would slam the laptop shut, grab a jacket and march off to the beach with Monty, reappearing hours later with red eyes and a runny nose, Monty trotting solemnly by her side.

"Want to talk?" he would ask, taking her favourite glass from the dresser, fixing her a whiskey with a couple of chunks of ice and that weird Irish concoction, Red Lemonade. Red lemons, who knew! She would shrug, collapse on the rug before the hearth, pulling Joey and Bridget to her if they were there. If not, she would just sit staring into the gold and purple flames, until the fire and the whiskey had warmed her through and smoothed the brittleness away.

This was such a night. Having returned from New York drained, Padar and Sinead scooped the children up and left the lovers to an evening of peace. Ryan was in charge of supper but was so carried away making soda bread for the grilled garlic king prawns, it looked like it was going to be a very late meal. The kitchen was a bombsite, as he prepared a salad of watercress and cherry tomatoes, with yoghurt ice cream and mangoes for dessert. A typical O'Gorman eclectic mix, and with the evening to themselves, it did not matter when they ate.

He joined Marianne and Monty on the rug, slinging a couple of lumps of peat on the fire.

"Hey," he said, tugging her unruly pony tail, "what's up?"

She took a sip of her drink and pulled her knees up to her chest. Monty nestled into her legs.

"I was wondering," she said, staring into the flames, "if with everything else, we're taking a bit too much on."

Ryan pushed a strand of hair out of her eyes.

"Go on," he said.

"Well, most people would find setting up home together, not to mention having one and a half children to look after," she gave him a smile, "quite daunting and enough to be going on with. But we've all the other stuff to deal with as well. I was just thinking that maybe my idea of the holiday home in Oonagh's memory was rash. Maybe I haven't thought it through enough, it's going to take shedloads of money to set up and an inordinate amount of time to run, and I wonder if I've overstepped the mark and maybe I should call it all off for a while and just spend time with you, and Joey and Bridget, being, ...well ... being a mom." She turned to look at him, "I was just thinking. What do you think?"

It was Ryan's turn to gaze, into the fire. He was trying to prevent his mouth from twitching into a smile.

"I think you're probably right," he said after a while.

"Right about what, which bit?" she asked him.

"All of it," he said.

"All of what?" she was trying to catch his eye, he turned away.

"Everything you've just said. I'm sure you're probably right."

"Ryan, did you hear what I said? Are you taking me seriously at all? I want to know what you think." She was annoyed. He looked back at her, trying not to grin.

"Marie, you always ask me what I think about things, and I love you for thinking you take my opinion on board, but ninety per cent of the time you've made your decision anyway," he gave her his beaming Hollywood smile to show he was not remotely offended, "so it doesn't really matter what I think."

"What're you on about? I ask your opinion about everything the whole time. You know exactly where you stand with me. We agree everything jointly." She went to pour more drinks. Supper was still a long way off; Ryan had only just put the bread in the oven.

"Look, Marianne, I'm your biggest supporter. Anything you want to do, I'm right behind you. You take things on, some of the scariest projects I've ever heard of, because you care. You want to make a difference. That's one of the reasons I love you. And although those two little ones love you too, and need you, they're not your responsibility."

"What?" she exclaimed. "Joey's my partner's son and I'm Bridget's godmother. Her own mother, my best friend is dead." Tears pricked the corners of her eyes.

"I know," he made calming gestures with his hands, "but the children are ultimately the responsibility of their parents and both Joey and Bridget each have a perfectly good father. There's no reason why fathers can't be excellent single parents. The majority of children of single parents, male or female, turn out just fine." He watched anger and dismay flicker behind her eyes. She put her glass down.

"Exactly what're you saying?" she asked.

"I'm saying, no-one expects you to give up any aspects of your work, to be a mother to ..."

"Children who aren't mine, who are nothing to do with me, is that what you're saying," her voice was rising, Monty had taken himself off to his basket under the stairs; he had been aware of tension building all evening.

"No, of course not," Ryan said, keeping his tone even. "I'm saying you must do what you have to. Don't use Joey and Bridget as excuses to change tack. You have dreams, plans, ambitions to fulfil. I don't want you ending up resenting us for preventing you from doing what you believe you've been brought here to do."

"Have you spoken to Padar about this?" she was standing, arms folded.

"About what?" he was confused.

"About me not being involved in the children's lives, in how they're brought up," she spat her words at him.

"That's not what I'm saying." He pushed his hands through his hair.

"No wonder Sinead's been cosying up to him, trying to get her feet under the table; stepping into Oonagh's shoes when I'm out of the way."

"Whoa, where's this coming from? Sinead is one of our best friends, she's not cosying up to anyone, she's a great girl, what would we have done without her?" Ryan watched as Marianne picked up her glass and took a deep draught.

"Precisely, making herself indispensable," she was snippy.

"How many of those have you had?" he asked, gently.

"None of your bloody business," she replied and turned to leave.

He crossed the room, gripping her by the elbows.

"Don't be like this. All I wanted to do was show you that you have the freedom to choose. Your work is important, it's part of what makes you who you are. I don't want to turn up with all my baggage and dump everything on you. I want to be with you, I want a relationship with *you* first. You decide whether you want the baggage or not, but *when* you've decided about me, whether I'm the one you want to spend the rest of your life with."

There was a long silence. She turned to face him, looking up at him with sorrowful watery eyes. She blinked, two large tears slid down her cheeks.

"There's something else?" he asked.

She nodded. "The *Lost Babies*. Someone came on the website today who said her baby sons had been taken, taken by their father, her own husband, and he's sold them. Sold them to feed and clothe their other children because their business has failed, they've lost their home and he can't provide for them." Tears splashed onto Ryan's hands as he held hers. She took a deep breath.

"No wonder you're upset. Do you know when this was, where it happened?" he squeezed her fingers, trying to take the pain away.

"That's the most upsetting part. It happened only recently, here in Ireland," she said in a dead voice.

"Is that one of the reasons you thought it might be a good idea to become a full-time mom?" he asked.

She nodded.

"And because you're so worn out and exhausted with everything that's going on, you don't feel as if you can continue with your work. You don't want to run the *Lost Babies* website anymore, and you want to stop the project to turn the big house into a holiday home for kids who don't get a holiday? Christ, I've been so selfish!" he said. She frowned at him. "Making things in my life a priority, when my priority in life should be you," he smoothed her hair back and kissed her forehead. She sniffed loudly. "Now all that's off your chest, how about a nice cup of tea?"

She nodded.

"Come on, we'll eat in bed, I'll bring up a tray. You get nice and cosy and we can talk everything through tomorrow. You always say things look better in the morning, especially on Innishmahon."

"They always do." She gave him a weak smile.

"I love you," he told her. "I won't let anything happen to hurt you ever. That's my job in life now, you do know that don't you?"

"Yes Ryan, I know that," she agreed, smiling now. "I also know Sinead is up to something. Much as I like her, she's definitely up to something." She started upstairs, albeit a trifle wobbly.

"You're so suspicious Marianne. It must be the journalistic training. Is there no-one you trust?" he said, disappearing into the kitchen.

She stood on the stairs, swaying a little. "I trust you, you and Monty." Monty thumped his tail at the mention of his name. She turned and wagged her finger at him. "Don't you two ever let me down is all I'm saying. Whatever happens, I have you two, right?" she tried to climb upwards but stood on her slipper, tripped and landed with a thud on her arse on the landing – the drink in her hand, aloft.

"Ha, ha," she said, as Ryan's head reappeared. Monty was on the first step, poised to fly to her aid. "Didn't spill a drop. Look not one drop. Not pissed you see, not pissed at all," she started giggling to herself.

Ryan raised an eyebrow at Monty. Monty gave his nose a twitch and trotted back to his basket. *I'll leave that one with you,* he seemed to say as he settled under his blanket. Marianne was still fully dressed and out-for-the-count by the time Ryan arrived with the tray. He ate his prawns and toast as quietly as he could, watching her sleep.

Chapter Twenty-Three

The Prodigal Daughter

Autumn was refusing to give way to winter as the last days of October burned streaky bronze sunsets across the bay and a gentle ripple of sea flicked lazily on the sand. The air was pungent with the scent of peat fires as Miss MacReady, slipping off her suede gilet to serve as a groundsheet, pushed the faded gold cap back from her eyes and sat down. She was halfway up the cliff on a broad ledge, sitting sideways on. If she turned left she looked directly to the Atlantic and, with a bit of imagination, America; to her right, the sweep of Horseshoe Bay, the lane beyond and the village. She could just make out the pub sign, with the roof of Weathervane nestling behind. She had been coming to this spot all her life. It was a magical place, allowing her wildest dreams to twist and soar high above the waves and yet it kept her grounded, anchored to the island shore, while her fantasies ran free.

She fiddled with the glittering bracelet on her wrist, stretched out her long fingers to admire how the jewels in her rings flashed in the sunlight and, taking her mobile out of her pocket, dialled his number. The phone gave the long steady ring tone signalling she was dialling foreign parts.

"It's me," she said in hushed tones, though no-one was around to hear her high on her Irish cliff. "What's the plan?" she listened intently to the response. "Okay, I get it. A couple of guys turn up, make a bit of a mess, break into the safe, yes? I'm to hide the jewellery somewhere else, okay. We've to report the burglary to the police, make a fuss ...the newspapers, TV and so forth ...yes got all that." She went quiet while she listened. "Okay, I understand, but we don't really know what's genuine and what's fake. Any idea what the value could be if say half of it is the real deal?" she waited. "What? Five million dollars! Are you serious? That's in the post office, sitting in my safe? Dear Lord, why didn't you say? Good God, man, I could have been robbed, murdered in my bed!" she squawked down the phone. The voice on the other end was trying to calm her.

"Alright, okay, but get the job organised as soon as you can. I'd no idea there was that amount on the premises, I'm quite overcome." She fanned her face with her hand and half a million in diamonds twinkled in the sun. "Keep me posted. Goodbye now." She flipped the phone shut and shivered. Dragging on the gilet, she pulled her hat over her ears and climbed nimbly down to the shore. It she had not been wearing so many of the gems in question she would have called into Maguire's for a much-needed Bloody Mary. She started off towards the post office, then changed her mind. Sure, no-one in Maguire's paid any attention to anything she was wearing, ever. She turned back and headed for the pub.

Marianne had been up at the post office looking for her mother. After a good 'let's clear the air talk' with Ryan that morning, they agreed she was to continue with her work and could be as involved with Joey and Bridget as she wished. Ryan, Padar, Sinead and Miss MacReady could all muck in with childcare as and when, just a like a real family, because that is what they were.

As Marianne and Monty took the long way up to the post office, she thought it through again. She had a good network of friends around her and nothing to reproach herself about. Everyone was in full support of the *Lost Babies* website campaign *and* setting up the holiday home for young carers. Well, Padar was not too keen on Oonagh's Project, but they would win him round eventually. Joan Redmond's little nursery was a godsend, the children loved it, and on top of all that, Ryan did not have to go back to the day job for six whole months. Anything could happen in six months, she knew that well enough.

She smiled, thinking about Ryan. He had given her a lecture about not sharing things that upset her, and after a few tears and some sweet, gentle lovemaking in their big, warm bed before breakfast, everything looked and felt a whole lot better.

Now walking briskly along the main street, she wanted to find Miss MacReady and organise a meeting. They needed to rota out the work to be done on the big house sooner rather than later. When she arrived at the post office the 'Back in ten minutes' sign was on the door. She laughed. Everyone on Innishmahon had one of these signs and used them regularly. Most locals knew it rarely meant ten minutes, and if you headed to Maguire's you usually found whoever you were looking for there.

It was a beautiful morning so she took the beach walk back, and not five minutes later ran into the postmistress about to cross to the pub. Miss MacReady hugged her and lifted Monty to be kissed on the snout. It made him sneeze, but he loved the exotic cocktail that was Miss MacReady, so did not mind at all.

"I haven't seen a bit of you since you returned from New York. Was it awful? Did the press tear into you over there?" Miss MacReady asked, looking with concern into her face.

Marianne shrugged. "They weren't too bad. The funeral was sad though. I felt so sorry for Mr Rossini – big house, farm, vineyards, all the money and success in the world and so terribly lonely," she said.

Larry had not painted a particularly flattering portrait of Ryan's boss. Miss MacReady was surprised at Marianne's empathy towards this man who controlled so much of her world from afar.

"Did he not have a phalanx of lawyers and all sorts bombarding ye with questions and suspicions? I believe he's a terrible tyrant." Miss MacReady could not resist.

"Maybe on the set of a movie, but no, he was charming. He wanted to hear the truth about Angelique, so we told him. She led him to believe rehab had worked, but he knew the truth, you could tell. It was heartbreaking really." She shoved her hands in her pockets, looking out to sea.

"And Ryan, how was he about it all?" Miss MacReady asked looking into her face.

"Sad and a little bit angry too. He's the one who'll have to tell Joey about his mother when he's old enough to understand. That's not going to be easy," Marianne said. Miss MacReady took her arm.

"She was a very selfish woman, and they make bad mothers, he's better off without her," she said sharply, "I should know."

Marianne wanted to ask Miss MacReady what she meant. She had been disparaging about her own mother on more than one occasion but Miss MacReady spotted someone going into Maguire's and gripped Marianne's arm.

"Well, I ..." she said watching the figure disappear. "Come on." She marched Marianne and Monty across the road.

Padar was in the porch putting up a large poster. *Halloween Hooley – Saturday Night – Dress to Distress!* it said in gaudy, blood-dripping writing, with a gaggle of ghouls and ghosties floating off it on little wire springs.

"Work of art, don't you think?" he said as they stopped to read it. "Sinead and I did it the other night, the kids helped." He beamed at the two women. Marianne laughed. She was pleased the Halloween party they were planning was going ahead. She loved Halloween: mystical stories and magical tales, traditional games like apples bobbing in a barrel and delicious food made with all the richness of autumn. An old-fashioned evening of story-telling, game-playing and a bit of a boogie to some appropriately spooky songs, sounded excellent.

"I have the Finnegan Twins booked and I thought we'd start early so people can bring the whole family. Those coming by boat can get back in the daylight. Sure, we can dress the place up with pumpkins and candles," Padar told them.

"If we put black paper at the windows, no-one will know it's not night. It's great idea Padar," Marianne agreed, as they pushed through the doors.

Miss MacReady, taking in the whole place with a glance, seemed disappointed. She bustled up to join Father Gregory and Sean Grogan, seated in their usual places. She tapped the polished surface impatiently. Padar had disappeared into the gents, and as he ran the place on his own during the week, she would have to be unusually patient.

"Typical," she said loudly, "he could have waited until we at least had our drinks."

"No bother," said Marianne, well used to Miss MacReady's weird concoctions. Taking a glass from a shelf, she went to ask Miss MacReady what she wanted, when the cellar door opened and a voice called up.

"If that's you giving out, Kathleen MacReady, I'll be up in a minute and I'll make you one of my specials. You haven't had one of them in a long time."

Marianne dropped the glass to the floor with a loud crash. Wide-eyed, she stepped away from the door, staring at it in horror. Father Gregory and Sean looked at each other.

"What was that?" called the voice. Marianne started to tremble.

"Who's that?" Miss MacReady shouted back, but she knew who it was. "Come up here and show yourself!" she called. They heard footfall and a young woman with pale skin and a cloud of dark hair stepped through the cellar door into the bar.

"Erin Brennan, as I live and breathe," exclaimed Miss MacReady, rushing around the bar to embrace the newcomer. "Where did you spring from? What on earth are you doing here?"

The woman hugged Miss MacReady warmly.

"Always with the questions," she said, in a deep, husky voice; Oonagh's voice. She turned and noticed Marianne standing silently beside her. She extended her hand – the same chunky, farmer's wife fingers. Marianne looked into familiar, grey eyes.

"Hiya, I'm Erin," she said.

"Hiya," Marianne said back, flatly.

"Erin, this is my daughter, Marianne," said Miss MacReady. Erin raised her eyebrows at the postmistress. "Long story," Miss

MacReady continued. "Marianne, this is Erin Brennan, native islander like myself, took off to the bright lights of the city years ago. And here she is back among us. Have you landed just this minute?" Miss MacReady smiled broadly.

"I arrived yesterday," Erin said, with an arm around the postmistress' shoulders. "Not quite got my bearings yet, but so far very little has changed."

"Sorry about that, ladies," Padar clattered into the bar. "Aha, I see my surprise is spoiled, so you've seen who's back, Kathleen." He grinned at them, "herself!"

Marianne continued to look askance. Had she just entered a time-slip, a remake of *Sliding Doors*? She could hear whooshing in her ears as she gripped the bar for balance. Father Gregory noticed.

"Perhaps we should have mentioned, Marianne," the priest said softly. "Erin is Oonagh's younger sister. You can probably see the likeness."

Marianne's mouth was dry; she struggled to find her voice.

"I didn't know, I can't remember Oonagh ever mentioning she had a sister. I'm sorry."

Erin smiled, but her eyes stayed hard.

"Don't apologise. I'm sure she never did, we weren't what you'd call close."

"Oh," was all Marianne could manage, looking at the glass on the floor, "I'll go and fetch the dustpan."

As she left, she heard Miss MacReady declare this was surely something to celebrate, the return of the *prodigal daughter*. But Father Gregory could not stay, he had some calls to make before the *Stations of the Cross* and despite the likelihood of at least one free drink, Sean decided he too needed to be elsewhere. He passed Marianne coming back.

"Perfect timing, I reckon," he said, flicking a look back at the bar.

"What is?" she asked, still in shock.

"Erin Brennan, back for Halloween," he said. "Hope she hasn't left her fecking broomstick in Padar's disabled entrance or there'll be hell to pay." He left laughing at his own joke.

"Did you ever hear of anyone called Erin Brennan?" Marianne asked Sinead later that day, as they sat on the little sofas Joan Redmond arranged in the kindergarten, for grownups to enjoy a coffee while the children played. Sinead looked at her over her cup.

"You've met her then?" she said.

Marianne nodded. "I'd no idea Oonagh had a sister, she never mentioned her *ever*!" Marianne had not stayed to have a drink with Miss MacReady celebrating the return of the *prodigal daughter* as she called her, she was so badly shaken. She left the pub on the pretext of an urgent email, leaving Miss MacReady and Erin chatting like long-lost friends.

"Apparently they fell out badly years ago. Oonagh, as you know, left the island in her late teens, Erin's a bit younger, she took up where Oonagh left off." Sinead spoke in hushed tones but only the children laughing in the ball pool were there.

"Took up what?" Marianne asked.

"With Padar. You know Oonagh was engaged to Padar when they were only teenagers. She met someone holidaying on the island and followed him back to Dublin, leaving Padar brokenhearted. Erin stepped in and she and Padar became an item." Sinead explained.

Marianne's eyes widened. This had clearly all happened a very long time ago. Padar and Oonagh were the type of couple you imagined had always been together.

"Anyway, the fella up in Dublin, one of those rich, *Hooray Henry* types, dumped Oonagh for the girl his parents wanted him to marry. She came running back to surprise Padar, only to burst in on himself and Erin at it like rabbits in the cellar of the pub." Sinead put her cup down.

Marianne blinked, "No way!"

"Well, that's what I was told," Sinead said.

"Who told you?" Marianne asked.

"Sean Grogan, but Joan confirmed it ... Didn't you Joan?" Sinead said to Joan as she arrived back with a couple of large brack loaves: delicious dark sticky fruit cake the Irish love to eat at Halloween, and all through the winter if the truth be told.

"What have you involved me in now, Sinead Porter?" Joan laughed. Joan and her family had recently returned to the Innishmahon, she was small, with *Brillo Pad* hair, bright-blue eyes and, despite five young children, a big, bruiser of a husband and a full menagerie to care for, was always smiling. She had grown up on the island and knew the Brennan sisters well.

Joan was slicing the cake and slavering it with rich yellow butter. Sinead went to make drinks for the children.

"What happened then?" Marianne asked the two women. Joan was arranging little pieces of brack on plastic plates. She stopped what she was doing and wiped her hands on a tea towel.

"It was awful, the most terrible row. Oonagh had no idea about the other two. Padar never mentioned he was seeing Erin," Joan said.

"But to be fair to him, why would he? Oonagh had left him for someone else, a fly-by-night in off a fancy yacht. Her head was easily turned, what was he supposed to do?" Sinead said.

"Oonagh always did love a bit of glamour." Marianne defended her friend.

Joan shrugged. "Well anyway, Oonagh left cursing the pair of them and took herself back to Dublin, not to be seen here again for nearly twenty years after that."

Marianne took the cake Joan offered her, "And Erin and Padar?"

"History repeated itself. They had a whirlwind affair, got engaged, and then within, what was it now ...about six months in, she met another fella here for the summer, and took off with him."

"Crikey." Marianne was agog.

"Padar vowed never to get involved with another woman. He'd had enough and kept himself to himself, until Oonagh reappeared. Oonagh and Padar reconciled their differences and married, needless to say Erin wasn't invited to the wedding." Joan popped a large piece of buttered brack in her mouth.

"They were so well-suited those two, didn't you think, Marianne?" Sinead asked.

"Oh completely, a real love story I would have said," Marianne agreed.

"You know baby Bridget was IVF? They were desperate to have a family. It was so unfair for things to end the way they did, they had so little time together," Sinead said sadly. Marianne's eyes filled with tears, she missed Oonagh every single day. She coughed, hardly able to swallow the cake.

"And now Erin's back, I wonder what that's all about?" Sinead asked of no-one in particular.

"Who knows?" said Joan, hauling the little ones out of the ball pool to eat. "Maybe she needs a change of scene. There's been loads of people made redundant. Dublin's an expensive city with no job."

"What did she do there?" Marianne asked, feeding Joey cake from her plate.

"Not sure," said Joan. "I heard she had a very good job, something to with the government or the Garda or something."

"Really?" said Sinead, incredulous, "I heard she was a retired pole dancer and ran a high class brothel in Ballsbridge."

Marianne and Joan burst out laughing.

"You've been listening to that fecking Sean Grogan again," grinned Joan. "You couldn't believe his version of the ten commandments."

Ryan was stomping sand off his boots when Marianne returned with Bridget and Joey. Monty bringing up the rear. He swept as many of them as he could into his arms, rubbing his wet, salty face in their hair making them giggle. He had spent most of the day out on the boat with Dermot, supervising Shay and the building team from the water, working on pilings for the slipway for the new lifeboat. Marianne left him grappling with hoods and gloves while she lit the fire. The glorious autumn day had suddenly turned damp and cold.

"Well, what about all the latest excitement," he called from the hall, "have you heard?"

"Do you mean Oonagh's long-lost sister?" she called back, drawing the curtains against the encroaching night. Ryan brought them all in to cosy up on the rug. The children were sleepy.

"Yeah, Dermot told me all about her. Met her at Joyce MacReady's by all accounts. Her car broke down, and he gave her a lift." Ryan said, matter-of-factly.

"Oh." Marianne was disappointed Ryan already knew about Erin. Even ex-journalists like the idea of a scoop.

"Took Padar completely by surprise, he was moved to tears

at the sight of her. She told Dermot she had been planning to arrive unexpectedly for Halloween. It was a special time for them apparently," he said.

Marianne was further disappointed, "Oh, you know they were an item then?"

"Back in the day. I think it's nice she's come to check on her brother-in-law, make sure he's coping and stuff." Ryan threw a couple of lumps of peat on the fire.

Marianne remained unimpressed. "Is that what she's doing here?"

"So Dermot says. Bit of a looker too according to him, but Dermot's taste in women has always been dodgy." Ryan gave her a grin.

Marianne threw a cushion at him. "Typical man, if she's a bit of a looker that's alright then."

Ryan laughed and threw the cushion back.

"Aw, come on Marianne. Padar's been brokenhearted since Oonagh died. It's a good thing Erin has come to visit, see how he's doing," he said.

"He *should* be brokenhearted, I'm brokenhearted. Whatever-her-name-is turning up out of the blue is not going to change that, let me tell you!" She pushed past into the conservatory and the decanter.

"And there's Bridget, don't forget." Ryan smiled at the bundle on the floor in front of the fire. "She's Erin's niece and blood's thicker than water, after all." *Ouch*, Ryan wished he had not said that.

"Do want a drink or would you like it pouring over your head?" Marianne called back.

"Given half a chance you might even become friends, you never know," Ryan said brightly, hoping to lift things a little.

"I don't think so." Marianne returned with their drinks. She sipped hers delicately. "I believe she's a retired pole dancer," she said, hoping to shock.

"Oh no, really?" he exclaimed. "I was hoping she hadn't retired, we could do with a change from the Finnegan Twins over in Maguire's from time to time." And, taking his drink, disappeared quickly before it was tipped over his head.

Chapter Twenty-Four

Trick Or Treat?

The excitement leading up to Halloween was building. Lots of regulars who had drifted away over time, texted or telephoned Padar to say they were delighted he was having a hooley at last and they would be there.

It was early on October thirty-first. Marianne, having fixed a date for a meeting of the board to get things moving on Oonagh's Project, put her files away, switched off her laptop and donned chef's whites to organise Maguire's kitchen ahead of the arrival of, hopefully, hungry hoards. Padar had seconded a couple of cousins to help and with entire families invited, no-one had to miss out because they had to stay home babysitting.

Resourceful as ever, Sinead set up a crèche in one of the ante rooms off the main bar so sleepy heads could rest undisturbed and others, who wanted to play with *GameBoys* and the like, could do so in peace. Miss MacReady volunteered to read ghost stories to the older children, and with everyone else kicking up their heels to the legendary Finnegan Twins in the bar, it was going to be a proper, old-fashioned Halloween Hooley, except for the proviso that it would be happening in the middle of the day.

Taking a detour to pick up sheaves of black paper, Marianne was surprised when she arrived at Maguire's to find most of the windows already blacked out. The door to the kitchen opened and Erin Brennan appeared. A coloured bandana covered her hair; she was in paint-spattered overalls and there was a smudge on her nose. Marianne recognised the bandana, it was Oonagh's.

"Hiya," she said, and set the paint down on a stepladder in the corner to continue her work.

"I thought we were going to use this?" Marianne said, waving the paper at her.

"Oh, I didn't know, so just grabbed what was handiest." Erin continued working.

"That'll take ages to get off," Marianne told her.

Erin shrugged. "It'll take as long as it takes, I suppose," and carried on blacking out the panes of glass.

Miss MacReady arrived with a large sack containing every kind of candle and holder she could lay her hands on.

"Good work, Erin," she said, setting candles in holders on tables and tea lights in every nook and cranny she could find. Marianne slammed down the pile of paper on a nearby table.

"Oh, there you are Marianne; need a hand in the kitchen when I've finished this?" Miss MacReady called across the room.

"No thanks, Padar will muck in if I need anything," Marianne said. "Where is he?" she cast about.

"He's gone to the ferry to pick up a few boxes of pumpkins. Sure, we only had a couple in the kitchen," Erin told her.

"I'm making pumpkin and parsnip soup. I won't need loads," Marianne said sharply.

"I thought we could do with them scooped out and lit up all over the place, you know – get the atmosphere right," Erin said, slapping the paint on with abandonment.

"Who's going to scoop them out? It's a very time-consuming job," Marianne replied tersely. Erin gave one of her now familiar shrugs.

Marianne stomped into the kitchen, surveying the clutter in dismay. Erin's influence was already in evidence. She sighed. She and Padar had a well-practised routine; they ran Maguire's efficiently and effectively. She did not know how long Erin was staying or what she seemed to think her role was while she was here, but Marianne was unimpressed thus far. She would have to make her feelings known, but not yet. Ryan had asked her to be patient and accept that Erin was Padar's sister-in-law and Bridget's aunt and they needed time together.

Marianne cleared a space and started to wipe down for prep. The kitchen door swung open and Padar staggered in bearing aloft three boxes of pumpkins; he promptly dumped them on her newly cleaned surface.

"Padar!" she shouted.

"Sorry," Padar replied, realising what he had done.

"Padar!" called Erin from the bar.

"Sorry," Padar said again to Marianne, leaving her alone with the unwanted pumpkins.

Twelve noon, October thirty-first, and there was standing room only in Maguire's. *Purveyors of Fine Wines and Ales and Quality Provisions*, as the sign outside emphatically stated. People had arrived by car, truck, quad bike and tractor, with still more making the trip by boat, chugging purposefully across the little stretch of water between the mainland and the island. Suddenly there was any amount of vampires, zombies, witches and warlocks piling into the pub.

Bridget wanted to be a fairy princess, and Joey, who really only wanted to be Joey, gave in to an eye patch and a terrifyingly realistic cutlass to appease her. Ryan transformed himself into a classic *Count Dracula* complete with purple-lined cape courtesy of Miss MacReady, and Marianne was going as *Morticia* from *The Addams Family*, again with Miss MacReady coming to the rescue producing a waist-length black wig, featuring the trademark white streak. Marianne was sure she had seen her wearing it on more than one occasion but kept her counsel. Miss MacReady was insistent all this paraphernalia had been unearthed from a childhood dressing-up box.

Marianne complemented the wig, with a full-length backless number she had bought for formal business events and certainly had no call to wear on the island. Ryan went straight into character attempting to bite her every time she passed him as she did her make-up, fixed her hair, sought out her shoes. As she slid on long black gloves, he leapt out from behind the bathroom door and, wrapping his cloak around her started to gnaw at her neck. She beat him back with her single-stemmed, plastic lily.

He held her close, spitting onto her chin. "Sorry," he said, whipping out the false fangs, "but I really fancy you in that get-up, you look amazing." She smiled up at him as he crushed her in an embrace, breasts pressed against his chest. He placed a hand on her bottom pulling her to him, so she could feel he was turned on.

"Hmmm," she murmured, enjoying him against her, "*Count* you are naughty, I shall see you in your coffin later, you bad boy," she teased in her best Transylvanian accent, smoothing his hair back, as he dropped a kiss on her throat. Monty rolling around on the floor dissolved the moment. He was growling gently, fighting with the ruffled collar and unicorn horn Bridget was making him wear. Marianne released herself from the *Count* and Monty from his costume.

"I know, why don't you come as a West Highland Terrier?" she told him. He wagged his tail in relief; he was sure he could give that a go.

Miss MacReady was seated on a red velvet throne, wearing a gold lamé evening gown and a huge witches' hat decorated with glittering stars. She was reading from a large tome, and carried a sparkling wand that played the *Harry Potter* theme tune every time she waved it. Children of all ages were enthralled.

Sean Grogan was on his stool at the bar, grumbling like mad. Padar was the happiest he had been in an age, rushing out and greeting his patrons dressed as a sort of *Shrek*, with a battered crown on his head to add gravitas. Even Father Gregory had entered into the spirit of things with a ripped and bloodied T-shirt and a couple of bolts in his neck.

As the team behind the bar went into overdrive, pulling pints and pouring drinks, a little queue was forming to the right of the bar leading into the snug. En route to see how things were shaping up in the kitchen, Marianne stopped to see what ghoulish attraction was engaging so much male attention.

It was Erin Brennan, busy serving *Love Potion Number Nine* the sign said, a smouldering cauldron of a cocktail she was pouring into phials and selling at five euro a pop.

"Guaranteed to make you strong as a bull," she laughed, looking at Dermot under her lashes as she handed him a shot.

"What's in it?" he asked.

"It's a secret recipe, handed down by the *Queen of the White Witches*," she told him darkly. She looked up and spotted Marianne "Hiya," she said, "Nice rigout."

Marianne's heart sank. She and Erin were dressed identically – long streaky wig, masses of black eyeliner and stick-on shiny red talons. Erin's dress was more frontless than backless though, displaying her cleavage to full advantage.

"What's that?" Marianne asked sharply.

"Just a shot of vodka with purple food colouring and dry ice – makes it look spooky – want to try one?" Erin replied.

"No thanks, I've work to do," Marianne said, heading to the kitchen.

Dermot was lingering but Erin had a queue of zombies to attend to, and she knew how demanding zombies can be, especially when a decent love potion is on special offer.

As soon as the Finnegan Twins started up with the instantly recognisable introduction to Michael Jackson's *'Thriller'* the place was hopping and patrons of every shape, size and infirmity were interpreting the video's dance routines enthusiastically.

'Werewolves of London' followed, the whole place howling like mad at the chorus and with *'The Monster Mash'* next on the set list, Halloween had well and truly begun.

During the break, while venison casserole and large plates of delicious sticky skinned sausages with jacket potatoes were being served, Dermot found Marianne doling out apple and oat crumble in the kitchen.

"I thought you might be tuning up, getting ready to join the rest of the Finnegan family on stage?" she joked.

"We're probably related somewhere down the line, sure everyone is around these parts but they're far more talented than I ever was. Need a hand here?" he smiled through fangs and werewolf facial hair.

"Can you dollop ice cream on each of these, school-dinner style please," she said, without looking up. Dermot took zealously to the job, flinging ice cream into bowls with abandonment.

"Yum, what is that?" he asked, licking his fingers.

"My home-made yoghurt ice-cream," she said, "good isn't it?"

Dermot, finally catching her eye, moved swiftly across the room to hold the scoop before her lips.

"Try some," he tempted.

Marianne looked up into his grey-green eyes, twinkling playfully back. He was flirting outrageously, but she liked Dermot, he was too nice to be dangerous.

"I know what it tastes like, I made it!" she laughed, pushing him away.

"Go on, just a little taste," he teased, making a growling noise.

"I don't take sweeties from werewolves, you never know what might happen," she said sternly, "now stop it!"

"Please," he said in a sweet voice. The ice-cream was beginning to melt; it would slide off the scoop onto the floor any second. "Go on, just for Dermot, just for your little werewolf."

Marianne leaned forward to lick the scoop. The werewolf grabbed her and with a huge roar, buried his face in her neck. Marianne nearly jumped out of her skin. She screamed, trying to release herself, but Dermot would not let go, turning his savaging into a lingering kiss. The door swung open and Ryan came in backwards carrying armfuls of dirty dishes. He turned just as the werewolf sprang away from his quarry.

"Hey you guys," he said cheerily, then pulling a face at Marianne, "you look a bit flustered, you okay?"

She swallowed, "Yep, nearly done, just need these desserts out there and that's the whole lot fed."

"Good." He dumped the dishes. "I'd like a dance with my lovely *Morticia* then, it's no fun being a blood-sucking vampire with no-one to suck. I haven't had a pint all night."

The door swung open again.

"I wondered where all the best looking monsters were hiding," Erin said, flashing looks at Ryan and Dermot. "Not having a blood-curdling orgy without me I hope?"

Marianne blushed. The men looked at each other; clearly enjoying the image Erin's comment had conjured up. Marianne untied her apron and took Ryan's hand.

"Come on, I've done enough in here, let's go and have some fun," she said. "No attacking any innocent young virgins now," she wagged a finger at Dermot as she left, "stick to your own kind." She glanced at Erin, pulling the *Count* and his flapping cloak behind her.

The rest of the afternoon went by in a flash. Everyone joined in the games: apples in a barrel, carrot on a string and a riotous version of spin the bottle, where instead of being kissed, the hapless victims were savagely plastered with large, blood-red gorges. The one with the most wounds won. The teenagers particularly enjoyed this.

It was late afternoon when the Finnegan Twins announced their last number, *'Time Warp'* from the *Rocky Horror Picture Show,* and everyone shuffled into position to give the festivities literally a final fling.

Ryan and Marianne were side by side.

"I love this one, do you know it?" she said over the noise, as people pushed tables and chairs to one side.

"Know it? Sure I was in it. I played *Frankenfurter* in a tour of the east coast back in the day," he grinned, licking his lips in character. She burst out laughing.

"I sometimes forget you're from another time-zone," she teased.

"Another planet," he said. "That's why I need you, to keep me grounded." His eyes glittered at her. "Besides, I'm a vampire that makes me hundreds of years old." He pulled her to him, draping her in his cloak. "But there's plenty of life in the old *Count* yet." He wiggled his pelvis against her, making her laugh again.

"Better make sure you have another pint of blood then, keep your strength up for later," she grinned, beating him off with her lily, as he tried to bite her neck.

Chapter Twenty-Five

To Catch A Thief

Dusk was bringing the last day of October to a close in spectacular style. Orange embers of sunlight splashed against charcoal clouds, draping the cliffs like a backdrop, the sea glimmered inkily below. The remnants of Maguire's Halloween revellers – a family of ghouls, a fairy princess and a few bats were wending their weary way home.

Miss MacReady, exhausted from her zealous storytelling, followed by a couple of jigs and reels, and some serious jiving with Father Gregory, was going through her evening routine, rather earlier than usual.

She locked the back door, clicking along the hallway in mules to check the main area of the post office. Turning off the light, she tried to remember if the front door was bolted, when she caught sight of her reflection in the mirror and took fright. She had forgotten her hair was already wrapped in the huge spongy curlers she favoured when sleeping alone – far too frequent an occurrence these days, she thought ruefully. She was sure she had bolted it, so flicked the switch, plunging the entire shop into darkness.

A loud crash – blast of cold air – footsteps and muffled grunts – stopped her in her tracks. She stood frozen to the spot. Flashes of light criss-crossed the gloom, then turned upwards to shine on grotesque faces. Wild eyes glinted at her. She closed her eyes and screamed. When she opened them again, the monsters were still staring at her. She swallowed, then laughed. It was a silly Halloween prank, even in their garish masks she was sure she recognised them.

"My word, you nearly gave me a heart attack." She touched her chest. Rough hands grabbed her shoulders, spinning her round, as something smooth and sticky was slapped across her mouth. Her arms were pulled behind her back and she felt a savage twisting and tightening around her wrists. She kicked out – a grunt – she made contact.

"Take it easy," a male voice hissed in her ear. She could smell alcohol and cigarette smoke. "The more you struggle the worse it'll be. Stay calm, be quiet."

She tried to free herself from his grip, then something was tied tightly over her eyes and she was pushed to the floor. She fell awkwardly, crying out, but the tape around her mouth prevented any sound escaping. Struggling to sit upright, she heard hushed voices and shuffling around her, she pushed herself backwards against the wall. Winded and shocked, she sat in the pitch-black, trying to think rationally, trying to recall her last conversation with Larry. She remembered he said the post office would be raided, but she could not remember if he told her *when*. Surely he would have given some warning of this? No, this was it alright – the robbery to steal the jewels – so they could claim the insurance.

It's okay, she told herself, *these aren't real thieves, these are the guys Larry has set up to do the robbery*. She tried taking some deep breaths, difficult with the tape over her mouth. If she had warning she could have cleared the safe out properly, leaving the jewellery but removing the valuables that islanders left in her care. She tried to picture what was in there: a Holy Relic Mrs Molloy had been given by an African priest; a Georgian candelabra left to Joan Redmond, and a plain leather document wallet with a brass lock. She could not remember where that came from, nor could she open it, but it would remain in her care until whoever had left it claimed it.

Then another thought: *what if these were not Larry's burglars, what if these were real thieves?* She hoped the robbers, whoever they were, would take only the jewellery. She would be heartbroken if the belongings left for her to mind were stolen too.

A clatter and a blast of cold air brought Miss MacReady back to the present.

"Hey, what's going on?" shouted a loud, strong voice, followed by a scuffle, clunk and a groan.

"Let's go, get out of here, *now!*" Another voice, one she thought she recognised.

"Not so fast," said the first voice. She could tell the lights were back on.

"Good God, Kathleen," Father Gregory cried out. He pulled the blindfold off and she squinted in the glare, casting her eyes backwards, grunting at him. He looked behind her and untied her hands.

Then Sinead ran up the steps and in through the door. Miss MacReady blinked. She had not seen her all day.

"Don't pull that tape," Sinead ordered. "I'll need solvent and antiseptic gel. That stuff will rip her lips off." She crossed the room to where the postmistress sat huddled with the priest beside her.

Sinead had brought the doctor's bag and was already applying liberal amounts of lubricant to the ducting tape over Miss MacReady's mouth.

There was another scuffle in the corner. Dermot Finnegan had a zombie in a headlock; a ghoul was spread-eagled on the floor. Father Gregory leapt away from Miss MacReady and in one movement plonked himself heavily on the ghoul's back, as Ryan burst through the open door.

"You were right," Ryan said, handing his friend the handcuffs he produced from his pocket, "they were on the wall." Dermot expertly snapped the cuffs on.

Erin Brennan was next up the post office steps.

"Is everyone okay? Is this a prank gone wrong or something?"

"Sadly not," Father Gregory remarked. Miss MacReady grunted in agreement.

Erin went to help the postmistress to her feet. Ryan, hands on hips, stood before Dermot and his now restrained captive.

"Time to reveal?" he nodded at the masked intruder.

"Okay," said Dermot, his arms clamped tightly around the man. Ryan pulled the ghoulish mask off the prisoner. There was an intake of breath. It was Pat MacReady.

"Pat!" Miss MacReady shrilled, finally able to speak, "what are you at?"

Pat blinked at his sister. "Had to be done, Kathleen," he shrugged at her. "Didn't mean you any harm, hope we didn't hurt you."

Ryan helped Father Gregory haul the other assailant to his feet. They each held an arm. Ryan yanked the mask off.

"For feck's sake," Miss MacReady exclaimed again. "Phileas what on earth?"

Sinead turned away; there were tears in her eyes.

"What do we do now?" Ryan asked Dermot grimly.

"We need the guards, these boys are in big trouble."

"Well, now I am confused," Miss MacReady said, "they were supposed to be professionals, in and out in a flash and *then* I call the police. I can't believe he sent these two eejits in fecking Halloween masks."

The room fell silent.

"Or is this all part of the set up?" she asked quietly, scanning their faces.

"What set up?" Ryan was intrigued.

"You weren't tipped off about a robbery?" Miss MacReady replied. They looked at each other.

"Dermot, surely you knew?" Miss MacReady insisted.

"What was I supposed to know? I was walking back with Gregory from the pub, when we noticed the post office door was wide open," Dermot replied.

Miss MacReady turned to Ryan.

"Same here, out for a stroll. Dermot rang me, said there's a suspected intruder up at the post office, I nipped back, grabbed the old handcuffs off the wall of the pub," Ryan told her.

"Ah Ryan, they're part of the historical display, the Black and Tans," Miss MacReady exclaimed, dismayed.

"Doubt there'll be a key, so he won't be going anywhere soon," Erin said in her usual matter-of-fact style. "I've called the Gardaí anyway, they're on their way." She put her phone away.

Phileas and Pat just stood there, eyes averted.

Father Gregory put his arm around Miss MacReady.

"Sinead, will you fetch Kathleen a tot of brandy?" he asked gently. Sinead disappeared into Miss MacReady's inner sanctum. Father Gregory gave the postmistress a hug.

"You might be a little delirious, Kathleen, huge shock, understandable. Take a few deep breaths now," he said.

"Ah feck off, Gregory, I know what's what," she snapped, taking the glass from Sinead, knocking the brandy straight back. She looked up at Pat and Phileas. Huddled together like naughty schoolboys, they looked pathetic. She was starting to think more clearly. This was not the professional team Larry had lined up, they looked just like the couple of chancers they were. "You're probably right, Gregory, I'm not myself," she acquiesced, "I certainly would not have a house full, and still be in my curlers, if I was."

Father Gregory nodded solemnly and patted her hand.

"I can't believe you two would actually do something like this to one of our own, in your own village. You've done some stupid things in your time, Pat, but Phileas?" the priest glared at the men.

"I don't have to answer to you or anyone else, priest," he hissed.

"No, of course you don't, Phileas, you're only a ghoul having a bit of fun on Halloween, you've not broken into the post office, or attacked Kathleen here, you're not even a real burglar!" Ryan was angry.

Erin scowled at them both. "He's right, this is a very serious matter."

Pat was just about to protest, when the roar of engines, sirens and blue flashing lights signalled the arrival of the police. Within minutes Sergeant Brody and Garda O'Riordan were charging up the steps and into the shop. Miss MacReady sighed. She knew it was necessary but the boys did love an excuse to switch that fecking siren on.

"Aha, I see the suspects are restrained. Everyone okay here?" Sergeant Brody asked giving Dermot a half-salute, then, spotting Erin widened his eyes. She frowned back at him. Miss MacReady had not missed a trick. She gave them all a stern look, before heading off to her living quarters for more brandy. It was going to be another long night.

Sergeant Brody and Garda O'Riordan did not seem a bit surprised to find Phileas Porter and Pat MacReady sitting back to back on two kitchen chairs in the main area of the post office. Sergeant Brody thought the handcuffs on Pat were a bit over the top but Dermot Finnegan was a tough cookie and both Father Gregory and Ryan the *actor-fella* were fit men, so the villains of the piece were not going anywhere in a hurry.

Miss MacReady, now standing by the safe, arms folded, was scowling at them, as Sinead packed away her doctor's bag unable to even look at her husband.

"I thought some eejit would have a go at lifting the film star's jewels, right enough, once we heard she'd left without them, God rest her soul." Sergeant Brody blessed himself.

Miss MacReady remembered that morning well. She had been on the phone to Larry when the sergeant arrived at the post office for his weekly chat over a cup of coffee. She had been having second thoughts about the whole robbery idea, and when she heard Angelique was leaving, asked Larry to come and take the jewellery and return it to the actress. Larry said Angelique would be expecting him to deal with things, so to leave the jewels where they were and give him time to think things through. They argued and she slammed the phone down on him.

Sergeant Brody was still talking. "I'd have given these two losers credit for a bit more intelligence." His shrewd eyes swept over the pair, shifting in their seats. "What are ya got up like at all?" he asked, acknowledging the Halloween costumes the would-be jewel thieves had donned as disguises.

"I'm disgusted," Miss MacReady had rallied, "my own brother

and Phileas Porter, supposed to be a stalwart of the community, what on earth were you thinking?" Silence. Dermot walked across the room to the Gardaí.

"If it wasn't so serious, it would be funny," he said.

Sergeant Brody opened a new pack of *Silvermints* and offered them round, ignoring the hapless prisoners. "Are we charging them so?" he looked at Miss MacReady. They were cousins; he did not like the idea of charging one of their own.

"This is the post office Sergeant, it's a crime against the State!" she was emphatic.

"An attempted crime," the officer corrected.

"A pretty violent attempt," Father Gregory said. "It's a good job we got here when we did. Miss MacReady had been attacked."

"Ah no," squawked Pat, "we'd never have harmed her, I swear to you."

"The shock alone could have killed me," Miss MacReady told him. Pat shrank back into his chair.

"Did they break in?" Garda O'Riordan asked her.

"Burst in through the door while I was locking up, doing my last rounds, frightened the life out of me, dressed up like a pair of monsters, the fools!" Miss MacReady told him.

"Better take statements from everyone, then we'll get *Frankenstein* and *Shaun of the Dead* here down to the station and charge them. Youse can call your lawyers from there," he told the accused.

Ryan checked his watch. "I'll ring Marianne and tell her what's gone on."

"How much will you tell her?" Dermot asked.

"Why, everything of course, any reason why not?" Ryan replied.

"Will she tell the press, do a story?" Miss MacReady was enthusiastic.

Ryan shrugged. "Not sure about that, she's not in that game anymore."

"Mightn't be wise involving the media," Dermot offered, "couldn't be good for tourism, criminal activity on the island."

Miss MacReady laughed. "There's always been criminal activity on this island. Demonstrates the extent of it when your own family turns against you, tries to rob you in your home." She was not letting it go.

"Ah, Kathleen," Pat pleaded.

"Shut up, I'm finished with you. I never want to see you or speak to you again. Wait till I tell Joyce about this stunt. You've done some stupid things in the past Pat, but this takes the biscuit." Pat looked more fearful at the mention of Joyce's name, than from anything the Gardaí had said. He glanced across at them, taking statements from Sinead and Father Gregory. The priest was holding Sinead's hand, she was trembling.

"I don't want to go home," she said quietly, flashing a look at Phileas sitting with his head bowed. Father Gregory smoothed a hand over her shoulders.

"He won't be there. It's likely he'll spend the night in the cells," the priest told her.

"I still don't want to go home." She said, plaintively.

"There's no way you can go back there, no way," interjected the radar-eared Miss MacReady. "You stay here with me, love. You'll be nice and safe with me, no hassle and no men!"

Ryan came out of Miss MacReady's inner sanctum.

"Marianne reckons it'll hit the papers anyway. It's a big story for a small island."

"Was she shocked? What did she say?" Miss MacReady was anxious.

"Concerned about you, obviously, but she didn't seem surprised someone tried to steal the jewellery. It was general knowledge Angelique left a pile of stuff here. She did describe Pat and Phileas as a pair of shits though." Ryan threw them a look. "Quite mild for Marianne." He gave Miss MacReady a smile, the colour was coming back to her cheeks. "I'll head back, if you don't need me." Ryan touched Dermot's arm briefly as he left, "Good work," he said.

The other man winked, "Sure, we were always a great team."

Dermot helped the guards bundle the unfortunate burglars into the secure cabin on the launch.

"What do *you* think?" he asked the sergeant as they prepared to cast off.

"It won't be good for them, when all's said, although they didn't get away with anything. It's serious and Pat already has a record. Not sure about Phileas though, thought he had a bit more about him."

"Do you think his wife knew what he was planning? She seemed very shook by the whole thing." Dermot observed.

"I think it was all spur of the moment, probably a result of a night on the gargle. Seemed like a good idea at the time, sort of thing." The Sergeant gave a grim smile.

Dermot nodded, then said, "I didn't think Phileas drank?"

"Maybe not in the pub," was all the Sergeant replied.

The engine started as the boat slipped away, turning towards the mainland winking in the distance. The wail of the siren made Dermot jump as the blue lights flipped on, flashing urgently into the night, blotting the blackness of the sea and sky with colour.

Chapter Twenty-Six

Ring A Ding Ding

Marianne was pacing the kitchen when Ryan returned. The house was quiet, the children sound asleep after their first Halloween. Marianne was desperate to see Ryan and be assured everyone was unharmed and she was furious something so despicable had spoiled such a great day.

She threw a lump of peat on the fire and went to make drinks. He stopped her on the way to the kitchen, catching her from behind, wrapping his arms around her, nuzzling her neck.

"You took your costume off," he said.

"You've been gone hours," she told him.

"I really fancied you in that," he said.

"Thanks, I look better as one of the undead!" she laughed.

"No," he grinned back, "I'd fancy you in anything, even your grubby old robe, with those huge curlers in your hair, you know that."

"How dare you?" she whacked him with a tea towel. "My robe may be grubby but it's not old!" He kissed her before she squirmed away.

"Sit down and tell me all about it," she said, bringing through drinks. When he finished the blow-by-blow account of the would-be thieves' apprehension, Marianne was interested to know what was going to happen to the jewellery. Ryan took a sip of whiskey, stretched his legs towards the fire and shrugged.

"Don't know. Don't really care, do you?" he said, eyes half-closed. She sat down beside him; she could smell peat in his hair. She pressed her lips against the soft skin of his neck, massaging his temples gently. He gave a murmur of pleasure.

"I saw Miss MacReady wearing the most spectacular emerald and diamond ring the other day. I wondered at the time if it might go astray, conveniently ending up in her jewellery box." Marianne smiled.

"Hmm, quite a radical thought. How did you come to that conclusion?" he asked.

"Something she said recently. *'Don't be surprised if I'm robbed in my bed, now Larry's told the world there's a collection of jewels worth millions in the Innishmahon post office strongbox.'* Almost flagging it up. Did she seem truly shocked about it all?"

Ryan thought for a moment.

"She seemed genuinely shocked it was Pat and Phileas alright, though she did babble on a bit, but she was delirious, bound to be, they'd been a bit rough with her, if truth be told."

"The bastards, a pair of chancers it sounds like to me," she said in a quiet voice, suddenly feeling tired and velvety from the fire and whiskey.

"You could be right." He slid his arms around her, pushing his hands up her top, caressing her breasts gently. It was her turn to murmur with pleasure. He knelt before her, pulling the soft fabric over her head, freeing her breasts and then drew her to him in an embrace. He pushed his fingers through her hair, kissing her mouth, his tongue darting in and out of her lips. He stopped suddenly, stood up and dragged off his sweatshirt. She watched as he unbuckled his belt, sliding the fabric down his strong thighs, stepping out of his jeans. The light from the fire made his still-tanned skin gleam; shadows shaded the contours of the muscles of his arms, his hard, flat stomach.

She could see his growing arousal as he looked at her, she stood before him, longing to feel her breasts crushed against his chest. He held her tantalisingly at arm's length, looking directly into her eyes. The slate-blue glittered with heat; she could feel his gaze burning into her. He bent to kiss her mouth and then ran his tongue from her chin, down her throat, along her collarbone and past the space between her breasts. She watched as his mouth pressed kisses against her stomach, drawing down her pants with his teeth. He nipped at the flesh at the inside of her thighs, she could feel his hot breath between her legs. Weak with desire, she dropped to the floor and, wrapping her legs around him, pulled him on top of her. He lifted his chin and grinned at her, a wicked flicker of lust in his eyes.

"Take me *Count*," she whispered in her dreadful Transylvanian accent, "I vont you inside me, all of you inside me, now!" The *Count* did not need asking twice, he lifted her hips and pushed himself gently inside her, as deep as he could go. She shuddered with pleasure and kissing his mouth, held onto him as he started to move rhythmically, making love to her, filling her with himself, right there on the rug, in front of the fire, the way they had, the very first time he had totally and completely seduced her, in what seemed a lifetime ago.

Later, snuggled together before the fire, he toyed with the replica weathervane at her throat – the exquisite platinum and diamond pendant he had commissioned for her – to remind her that whenever he was away, scattered to the four corners of the earth, she was his rock, his anchor and whatever life threw at them, he would be coming home, to Weathervane, Innishmahon and to her, his true love. Pulling her to him, he kissed her as she dozed.

"And would you like a beautiful emerald and diamond ring my darling, more precious than anything anyone has ever seen?" he whispered.

She was half asleep. She murmured, turning to nestle beneath his chin.

"Would you? Shall I buy you a beautiful ring, a symbol of my love. Would you like that?" he said into her ear.

She stirred, placing her fingers on his lips to quieten him.

"Would you, my love?" he pressed.

"I have plenty of jewels." She tried to sound blasé, but he felt her tense.

"Really? I thought all women loved jewels, especially spectacular ones, bought for them by their men." He was curious.

"Not me thanks." She touched the pendant at her throat. "I love my weathervane, it's very special. No, I've enough jewels to last a girl a lifetime."

"Not even a wedding band?" he asked. She squirmed away, wriggling free of the throw.

"Ha," she forced a laugh. "If that was a proposal O'Gorman, it lacked your usual dramatic flair, I have to say." She pulled herself up, arranging the fabric around her, hiding her nakedness. "Anyway, you know my track record. Mention marriage and everything falls apart, enough said."

"But," he caught her by the wrist, "surely it's something we should discuss at some point?" She turned away.

"Not now though Ryan, the very word holds bad memories for me. Claude was a mistake. I thought we'd marry, but that ended in disaster and then, getting engaged to George, everything arranged just before ... " She let her shoulders droop, avoiding his eyes: they had both loved George.

"Third time lucky?" he offered, squeezing her hand, giving her his lopsided grin.

She looked at him, willing her eyes not to betray her heart. "It's too soon to talk about marriage. I'm not sure it's for me, can we just leave it there for now?"

He pulled a face, then hugged her. She waited for him to mention the 'no marriage' clause in Angelique's custody deal, wondering if something had come to light. She already felt guilty about reading his private papers, maybe he knew. But he made no other comment, just put some more peat on the fire and settled down beside her. She was soon fast asleep.

Ryan was restless. He pulled up the collar of his jacket as he walked along the coast road. It was pitch-black, a good hour before the first glimmer of dawn would be visible on the eastern horizon. He crossed the familiar track of sand down to the beach, found a clump of grass and sat down. He was exhausted and in seriously bad humour to boot. *Why had he mentioned a ring? What was he thinking?* He knew how anti-marriage Marianne was. He knew neither of them had particularly good track records where relationships were concerned, but he did know, deep down in his heart of hearts, how much he wanted things to work out with Marianne, always to be there for her and she for him. He wanted to bow out of his hugely successful career and return to make his life on Innishmahon with his son and yes, Marianne Coltrane his wife. He bounced the heel of his hand off his forehead.

"Why do I never think anything through, why do I just open my big Irish gob and say whatever comes into my head? No wonder I need a script to do the fecking day job," he told himself wryly as he wriggled down into the sand, zipping his jacket up. Now the sea air had hit him, was so tired he could barely keep his eyes open.

Further along the beach, Dermot Finnegan was talking into a handset. "So, looks like it's going to be the week after next? You can't give me anything more definite than that? Over."

"Not yet, but it's definitely on its way. Over," came the crackly reply.

Dermot sighed, exasperated, he would never work with this fella again, talk about unprofessional.

Dermot flicked the switch. "And how will I know it, any word on that? Over."

"It's a fishing boat, I know that much. Over."

Great, thought Dermot, *that narrows it down then, fishing is the main occupation of the entire area.*

"Will it be flying *the skull and cross bones*? Over." He was in no humour for ditherers.

"No, she won't be flying anything and *Captain Hook's* not on board either. Over." His contact sounded tetchy.

"Look," Dermot barked, "I need firm details, co-ordinates, timescales and, you know, something a bit more specific if I'm to intercept a vessel and arrest those on board, which is what I've been tasked to do. Over."

"On your own?" squeaked the other voice.

"No, aren't you supposed to be helping me? OVER." Dermot was *really* frazzled now.

"Ah no, sorry about that, I can't make it."

"WHAT?" Dermot roared, "What do you mean you can't make it? I thought you were supposed to be working with me?"

"I am, but I'm on annual leave that week. I have to take it or I'll lose it and I can't do that, I need a break, this job is very stressful."

"GIVE ME STRENGTH!" Dermot yelled, "OVER!"

Ryan stirred. He pushed himself up on his elbows. The merest slice of light across the bay had turned the beach to grey, he could see a dark figure striding towards him. It looked like Dermot. Ryan fumbled in his pocket, pulled out a lighter and a pack of cigarettes. He lit one.

"Hey, who's there?" came his friend's gruff voice across the sand.

"*Count Dracula*, who do you think?" Ryan responded. Dermot was beside him in a couple of strides.

"What are you doing sleeping rough? Trouble 'ut Mill?" Dermot asked in a perfect Lancashire accent; he had always been good at dialect.

"Nah, just needed a breath of fresh air," Ryan said, indicating the cigarette. "Everyone's asleep. Yourself?"

"Couldn't sleep, mad day, weird ole night, what with one thing and another. Fancy a jar?" Dermot asked.

"I'd love a good cup of coffee. Marianne never makes it strong enough." He smiled, offering his friend a hand to haul him up.

"She's not perfect then?" Dermot asked cheekily.

"Oh yes she is," Ryan replied.

"Isn't she though?" Dermot said under his breath, letting go of Ryan's hand at the crucial moment, so he fell back, landing on his arse. "Gotcha! You always fall for that one," he said laughing.

As they clattered up the gangplank Ryan noticed the lettering picked out in navy edged with gold on the side. Dermot had named the boat *Dream Isle.*

"Nice one," he said, "a play on words. Dream I'll, I'll Dream, is that it?"

Dermot smiled. "Yeah, that's right. Good isn't it? Suits her?"

"It does, certainly. Hope it turns out to be a dream isle for you, we all need one." Ryan said.

"Well, it has for you," Dermot replied.

"Still in the planning stages it would seem," Ryan told him and then, "getting there though."

They were sitting down below, a mug of fresh coffee apiece.

"Who were you shouting at over the radio back there?" Ryan asked. He had seen Dermot push the handset into his sailing jacket, when he came upon him on the beach.

"Ah, someone I'm doing a bit of a job with." Dermot stirred his drink.

"Not going well?" Ryan asked.

"It's a two man job and he just told me he's on *annual leave* so can't make it. *Annual leave* – why doesn't anyone take holidays anymore?"

"Is this police business? I thought you'd taken early retirement?" Ryan asked him.

"Sort of," Dermot was serious. "This is my last job."

"Well, if you need a hand, I'm your man. I'm not required back at the studio for a few months, and as soon as Marianne starts on the holiday home project we won't get a minute's peace, believe me." Ryan told him.

Dermot frowned. "It's very hush-hush, totally undercover. If I tell you I'll have to kill you."

"No change there then." Ryan looked him in the eye, "I *am* an *international super-spy,* you know, it really is an offer you can't refuse."

Dermot took a deep breath. He knew Ryan. He trusted Ryan. They had been through a lot together.

"Okay, here's the scenario, purely fictional of course but here it is anyway." And Dermot explained to one of his oldest friends, how his latest job was to intercept a consignment of cocaine disguised as a shipment of arms, destined for a drugs cartel masquerading as a breakaway gang of Freedom Fighters.

"Wow," Ryan exclaimed, "a classic double bluff, designed to totally confuse the authorities no doubt."

Dermot nodded. "And of course no-one is acknowledging the arms have even gone missing. The entire investigation is undercover, so much so I wonder myself at times if anyone knows who anyone else is and precisely what the hell is going on."

"And does this purely *fictional* scenario have any basis in reality at all? Anything to do with the fact that you've always wanted to work undercover and this could be your big chance?" Ryan pushed him.

Dermot shook his head, "Nah."

"And you'll need a hand with this imaginary job when?"

"Probably the week after next, when I get the intelligence I need," Dermot said.

"Is that the real week after next or a fictional one?" Ryan responded.

"Pretty real, I think." Dermot replied.

"Well, I'll probably be around to help if I'm not showjumping my unicorn or having the moat dug around my fairy-tale castle," Ryan told him with a grin.

"Cool," Dermot said. They chinked mugs. "That's good, coz you might be needed, you know how dreams come true from time to time."

"And nightmares," said Ryan, drinking back his coffee as he made to go.

The two men clambered down the ladder and onto the marina. Dermot wanted to walk Ryan back to Weathervane, apart from filling him in on some details regarding the forthcoming job, he was also hoping Marianne might prove to be the angel he fantasised she was and have a full Irish breakfast on the go by the time they arrived at the cottage. He was over-optimistic; it was not yet seven on the first day of November and the day before had been very long indeed.

They were striding purposefully down Main Street when something or someone scuttled across the road. Ryan looked at Dermot.

"Anyone we know?"

Dermot shrugged. "I couldn't see, could you?"

"No," Ryan replied.

"Not someone else after the jewels?" Dermot asked. The post office was next door to the pharmacy.

"I hope not," he replied, "besides I wouldn't take on Miss MacReady and Sinead after the night they've had, would you?"

Dermot smiled. "No way!"

They carried on; the morning growing brighter as they walked. A cat meowed as a light came on above the pharmacy – the village was awakening.

There was no home-cooked breakfast waiting for them in Weathervane. Marianne was still asleep on the sofa with Monty wrapped in her arms and was far from impressed at being disturbed.

"Thought I'd make us all a decent breakfast," Ryan announced as she opened a bloodshot eye.

Dermot lifted a hand in silent greeting. "I'll make the toast," he offered, as she slumped back on the sofa, pulling the throw over her face.

The men retreated to the kitchen and, having decided everything in the fridge needed eating, were cooking up a storm. Dermot took down one of Marianne's antique meat platters and started piling it with food. Rashers, sausages, white and black pudding, mushrooms, grilled tomatoes and the essential ingredient no self-respecting male breakfast can be without – baked beans. Ryan was just finishing off the scrambled eggs, when Marianne, fully dressed with her hair scraped back in a cap appeared in the kitchen. Monty, who had been the happy recipient of two overdone rashers and half a sausage, pricked his ears, wagging his tail at her.

"Not staying for breakfast?" Dermot asked, laying the table. Ryan was frying bread in a large iron pan.

"No thanks." She went to where Ryan was cooking and put her arms around his waist. "Smells good but oh dear, the cholesterol!" She took Monty's lead from behind the door.

Ryan looked up; she had her serious walking boots on.

"Will you be gone long?" he asked.

"I need a good walk," she said, "still groggy."

"Ah stay and have a decent breakfast first," he waved the spatula, "we've done loads."

"I'll take the healthy option," she said, spotting yesterday's barn brack on the dresser. She took a knife, and sliced a piece off, putting it in her mouth. She bit on something hard; it was a parcel of greaseproof paper. She unfolded it to reveal a small brass ring;

one of the secret ingredients stirred into the cake mixture during baking. Traditionally the ring foretold of a wedding before a year was out. She looked at it glinting teasingly up at her from the palm of her hand, then pushed it into her pocket, fastening her coat. She popped the remainder of the cake into her mouth and left the men to their feast.

The early November morning was remarkably still. A soft sea mist trailed tendrils across the cliffs as Marianne and Monty walked briskly towards the beach and up the track. They climbed steadily, the lights of the village twinkling in the distance as they went. The ground was moist. Marianne slipped. Dislodged sand and shale tumbled downwards. She gripped a clump of grass and pulled herself upright, checking in her pockets for her flashlight and phone. Monty stopped sniffing the undergrowth and looked up at her, they had been caught out on the cliffs before, he hoped history was not about to repeat itself. But the further they climbed the clearer it became, until nearing the summit and the cliff road, Marianne slipped off her jacket, tying the sleeves around her waist as they pushed on to the top.

Reaching the picnic bench just beyond the lay-by, Marianne sat down gratefully. It was where she and Oonagh had spent many happy afternoons, baby Bridget sharing her lunch with Monty and the women dividing whatever delights Oonagh had secreted in her backpack ahead of their excursion. Even when Oonagh was too tired to manage the cliff walk, Marianne would load them all into the 4x4 and take the long shiny black road up to their special place.

She lifted Monty up for a cuddle as they sat gazing out to sea, the autumn sun chasing the mist away as the Atlantic glimmered below. She took a deep, cleansing breath of air which became a sigh, and before she knew it, tears burned her eyes, rolling down her cheeks and dripping into Monty's fur. Despite the heart-lifting beauty all about her, she was suddenly, inexplicably sad. She missed Oonagh desperately. Her blunt, wise-beyond-her-years chubby chum was probably the closest friend she ever had.

She could have told Oonagh all about Angelique's unreasonable divorce settlement, the weird 'non-marriage' clause in the custody arrangements and Ryan's half-hearted proposal. Oonagh would have tutted and sympathised and then told her she needed to do *less* thinking and *more* talking. Meaning, tell Ryan how she felt. Oonagh was a great one for telling people, to tell other people all about their feelings. She always said women put far too much pressure on men, expecting them to be able to guess what a female was thinking. Just tell a man what you want, then put on your sexiest outfit and seduce him so thoroughly he will think it was all his idea anyway, was Oonagh's advice. Marianne laughed, burying her face in Monty's fur. Oonagh thought that was the best course of action whatever the situation, it usually worked too.

She decided to take the road home, calling into the post office to see how Miss MacReady was after her ordeal. She imagined her mother would be less than fazed by the attempted burglary, yet still furious with the perpetrators. When news of Pat's involvement reached his other sister Joyce, he would probably be better off staying in gaol for as long as he could.

Kathleen MacReady was on the phone to Joyce as she let them in. She pointed at the coffee pot for Marianne to help herself.

"Well, I don't know what's got into him, he's always erred on the dodgy side, bringing God knows what across in the *secret* compartment in that old cab. *Secret*, there's a laugh, sure one of the reasons the guards leave him alone is because he's so blatant with it, thinking he's just a fecking simpleton. Anyway Marianne's arrived, so I'll go and fill her in on the details. You know journalists, they want everything from the horse's mouth." Assuring her sister she was unharmed, Miss MacReady replaced the receiver and swished through the beaded curtain to join her daughter.

Marianne hugged the other woman, who was pale with dark blotches under her usually sparkly shrewd eyes.

"Eejits," she fed Monty a biscuit, "frightened the life out of me." She rubbed her wrists where they had been bound.

"What's the latest?" Marianne asked, handing her a cup. Miss MacReady's hand trembled as she took it.

"Ah sure, it's Sunday, can't see anyone's lawyer leaving the golf course and a decent lunch for that pair. They'll be left cooling their heels until at least tomorrow." She scowled into the mirror at herself.

"You okay really?" Marianne asked. Miss MacReady gave a small smile.

"I'm not surprised there was an attempt at robbing the jewels, Larry warned me that might happen, but never in a million years would I have imagined the perpetrators would be my own people. That's upset me, I can't stop thinking about it. They deserve everything they get."

Marianne gave her a quizzical look; there was something in her tone.

"Well, what did you imagine?" she asked.

Miss MacReady fiddled with the cuff of her kimono.

"Ah, you know yourself," she said, vaguely.

"No, I don't know myself. What do you know though?"

There was a silence.

"Mother, I asked you a question?" Marianne pushed.

The phone rang. The post office was also the telephone exchange. The old analogue system was heavily relied upon on the island. Miss MacReady answered it.

"Oh, it's you. You heard did you? No, not at the moment, I'll call you later?" she put the phone down.

Marianne folded her arms.

"Larry?" she asked.

Miss MacReady nodded. She hated deceit.

"He heard about the robbery. Wanted to know if everything was okay?"

"That's good of him." Marianne felt sure Miss MacReady was expecting Larry's call. "I bet Larry knows who would benefit if the robbery had been successful and a very large insurance claim was paid out."

Miss MacReady busied herself at her desk, putting post into piles.

"No doubt." She was taciturn.

"But it's all still here isn't it? All safely locked up in the strongbox?"

Miss MacReady nodded.

"So what happens now?" Marianne asked, prompting Miss MacReady to tell her the plan, because she was sure there was one.

"I'll have a chat with Larry later, but I think it's best a security firm be commissioned to take the jewellery away, return it to its rightful owner." Miss MacReady waved a hand, dismissing the subject.

"Who is?" Marianne was not letting it go, "who *is*?"

"Why, the film company of course, you know that." Miss MacReady said.

"Just making sure you do," Marianne said. "Commissioning a security firm to ship the collection back seems a good idea to me."

But Marianne remained unconvinced this was going to happen. She was sure the bungled attempt by Pat MacReady and Phileas Porter had been purely opportunistic, but some sort of heist had been expected, planned even, and she was sure her mother and Larry were at the back of it somehow, and it was not over yet.

The phone rang again.

"Okay thanks for the warning. Marianne's here, she'll know what to do." Miss MacReady replaced the receiver. "A reporter and cameraman just boarded the ferry." Marianne checked her watch; it was the first trip of the day. "I'll have to go and get ready. Will you stay and handle the PR?"

"Course I will," Marianne smiled. There was already a twinkle in the other woman's eyes; she loved a bit of drama.

"Will you contact the others? I'm sure they'll want to talk to them too," Miss MacReady said.

Marianne was not convinced the rest of them, barring Ryan of course, would be keen to be on camera.

"You get changed, I'll find out what they want to do," Marianne said. "What about Sinead? Will you wake her?"

Miss MacReady was disrobing as she left.

"You'll have to ring her, she didn't stay here after all. Said she'd be better off in her own bed. She was so upset by it all," Miss MacReady called from the bathroom.

Marianne sat down at the postmistress' desk and started to dial Weathervane's number. She wanted to tell Ryan first. The jewels were his late wife's, they belonged to his employer and he and Dermot had foiled the burglary. The media would definitely want to talk to him. The fact he was also a *world-famous movie star* was a bonus as far as any newshound was concerned.

Ryan said he would be up to the post office as soon as he had given the children breakfast.

"And Dermot?" she asked. There was a mumble in the background.

"Dermot says he'll babysit. He hates being on camera with me, I always make him look so damn ugly," Ryan joked.

"Fine, make it snappy then," she told him, going into professional media-mode. She rang Father Gregory next.

The first reporter and cameraman were followed quickly by a well-known presenter, who had been holidaying on the mainland and then a freelance journalist reporting for both a quality broadsheet and a salacious gossip magazine. Any mention of Ryan O'Gorman had that effect on the media; they came crawling out of the woodwork, especially as the star's glamorous lifestyle contrasted so starkly with the island he had chosen to make his home.

Marianne thoroughly enjoyed her morning back in the media mix: setting up shots outside the post office; reminding Father Gregory to go back and fetch his dog collar, he looked far too cavalier, with a view of the sea behind him, in a navy Arran sweater, turquoise eyes glinting in the sunlight.

"Good grief, they'll think there's only drop-dead hunks here and the ferry will be loaded with lovelorn fans desperate for a glimpse of yourself and Ryan." She pushed him across the road playfully. Dermot hoved into view. Not another one, she thought, painting on a smile, as the big man strode up the main street. Dermot made her uncomfortable, especially since his shenanigans in Maguire's kitchen on Halloween. He had really caught her off-guard and she had no desire to encourage him, yet she liked him, despite herself.

"All the TV stuff finished?" he asked.

"Not quite, just a quick interview with Gregory, but I sent him back because he'd no dog collar and I thought the piece needed gravitas. You know, the village priest putting things into perspective, rounding the report off by saying how such activity is a rare occurrence on Innishmahon, and how it's a fine island community with lots for tourists to enjoy, that sort of thing."

Dermot agreed, "Will they bugger off then? Last thing we want is the place swarming with media."

"I think the freelance journo over there," she nodded at the young man working for the broadsheet and the tabloid, "wants a chat with a few locals, get their take on it. Wouldn't be surprised if he did a follow-up on Angelique too, the story of how the jewellery collection was amassed. It would make a great feature for one of the Sunday supplements."

"Thought you'd retired?" he remarked.

"Not necessarily, just changed direction. Bowed out of the rat race, you know how it is?" she looked down at her clipboard.

"Guess so," Dermot said, desperately trying to catch her eye.

Miss MacReady reappeared as the camera crew were wrapping up. She fed them coffee and brack, chatting easily with them. She was wearing a green chiffon tea dress, reminiscent of *The Great Gatsby,* complemented with a huge straw hat, fastened under her chin with a silk polka dot scarf. The wind had got up and her jade and turquoise earrings jangled about her bare shoulders. Marianne was relieved her mother was back on form. It may have been an unusual ensemble for late autumn, but it really suited her. Waving the crew farewell, she joined Marianne as they walked down Main Street, Dermot and Gregory bringing up the rear.

"Dying to see what we all look like on the telly, aren't you Marianne? We haven't had this much drama since the storm." Miss MacReady was as excited as a puppy.

"I think everyone gave a good account of the incident, some more colourful than others," she gave Miss MacReady a look, "but I hope they don't edit it too much."

"Shame you missed it, Dermot," Miss MacReady called back to the big man.

"Ah, there was enough of you telling the tale. I like to keep myself to myself."

"And no Sinead either. Sure we'd have been lost without her, she certainly has a gift where anything medical is concerned," Miss MacReady told them. "Anyone seen her at all today?"

"Did she not stay with you?" Dermot asked.

"No, went home to her own bed when she knew those two fecking eejits were being kept in the cells overnight. Good riddance if they throw away the key, that's what I say." Miss MacReady stopped. "Someone ought to check on her, see if she's alright."

Marianne turned to go back.

"I'll go," Father Gregory said, "see if she wants to come down to Maguire's for an hour, watch us all making headlines. No point in sitting up there worrying."

Marianne touched his arm. "Go easy Gregory, I'm sure she's totally mortified Phileas was involved. Assure her the reporters are only saying two men have been arrested in connection with the robbery. Let her know that much."

Father Gregory nodded as he left. Miss MacReady pulled her purple shawl tighter against the breeze.

"Sure the reporters don't have to name names in this place. It'll be all around the island in a flash."

"Well, I haven't said anything about who was involved," Dermot remarked.

"Nor I," said Marianne. "Only a straightforward news report, no names given," She lifted her chin at Miss MacReady.

Miss MacReady's hand flew to her mouth. "Damn, I rang Joyce and told her it was Pat and Phileas. She's my sister, I tell her everything."

Marianne and Dermot declined to comment.

By Sunday lunchtime it was the talk of the island, as Maguire's regulars were joined by other villagers, astonished to learn the flashing blue lights and sirens of the night before were not the Gardaí on an impromptu test-run, but an attempted robbery at the post office. They crowded in front of the large television screen to watch news reports of a major incident which had taken place only a few hundred yards away.

Once inside the packed pub, Miss MacReady was feted as a heroine, and after kisses and congratulations, took herself off to the snug with a trendy fruit cider and the journalist, who was indeed planning a series of articles about the jewellery collection, featuring the provenance of the rarer pieces.

Ryan waved over at Marianne, passing her a glass of wine through the crowd. Padar was wearing his 'isn't this great for business' smile and Erin was busy helping him pull pints. She was wearing Oonagh's bandana again Marianne noticed. Another one getting her feet under the table, she thought, uncharitably, then looking up, saw Ryan standing beside her. He bent and kissed her nose.

"How's my award-winning, stunningly gorgeous journalist then, happy with your morning's work? Did I look good on camera?" he turned to give her a view of his profile.

She sipped her wine.

"Yes, I am as it happens. Has there been a bulletin yet?" she stood on tiptoe trying to see the screen.

"No just a trailer saying they were bringing the latest on an attempted robbery at the *top of the hour*," he said.

She looked at her watch, half an hour to go till noon. "The children?"

"At kindergarten. Dermot got them ready and down there in time for the morning session. Joan said Sinead had not shown though, and she was supposed to be on duty, probably overslept," Ryan told her.

"Can't say I blame her," Marianne replied. "You and Dermot couldn't have got much sleep either?"

"No, I met Dermot on the beach and went back to the boat for a coffee – been a long night," he said.

"Dermot was on the beach at that hour?"

"Yeah, he was ..." Ryan stopped himself.

"Was what?" Marianne asked.

"Do you know what, I think I'll go and help Padar, give Erin a break. It was a long night for her too."

Marianne looked up into his eyes.

"Dermot was doing what?" she asked.

"What? Oh, walking on the beach, taking a breath of air, like I said ..."

"I know, it had been a long night," she finished his sentence.

"Some of it was fantastic too," he smiled, twinkling down at her.

"Ouch! Ryan O'Gorman, did you just *pinch* my arse?" she demanded, as he weaved through the crowd to the bar to relieve Erin as he promised.

Marianne found herself standing next to Erin as the news came on. Erin was in sweatbands and tracksuit but these were *not* Oonagh's. Erin was much slimmer than her sister; this looked like serious training kit. Marianne wondered if Erin was the jogger she noticed from time to time on her morning walk.

Erin was staring at the screen. Marianne felt immediately guilty she had not included her in the report.

"I'm sorry, I didn't send word to you when the TV crew showed up," she said to the other woman.

"No bother," said Erin, staring at the screen. "Ryan called in on his way and asked me to come along. But I said I rather not, if it was all the same."

"Oh," was all Marianne could muster, annoyed with Ryan for including Erin and annoyed with herself for not. The newsreader broke the awkward silence.

"... it is believed the attempt was to steal the actress' fabulous jewellery collection which was in the post office safe following her recent visit to the island. Our reporter was on Innishmahon earlier today to speak to Kathleen MacReady, the postmistress, who was brutally attacked during the raid. A number of locals were instrumental in foiling the attempted heist, including the actor Ryan O'Gorman, the late actress' ex-husband ..."

The camera panned to the island's magnificent coastline, a shot of the post office sign and then Miss MacReady's beautifully made-up face filled the screen. She answered the journalist's questions quite succinctly, then going into grisly detail about her attackers and their methods of restraint, giving a blow-by-blow account and showing the marks on her wrists to the camera. Marianne would have preferred that bit to have been edited out, but none of it was untrue.

The reporter introduced Ryan, who skilfully avoided any questions about his ex-wife and the jewellery collection, saying simply that it was in the safest place on the island and the foiled burglary confirmed that. The jewels would be returned to Angelique's family to be disposed of, along with the rest of her estate at the appropriate time. Marianne nodded. She had briefed him on that bit. *Good work, Ryan,* she thought.

Father Gregory was spot-on with his summing up, mentioning Dermot, Erin and Sinead and saying this was typical of what a tight-knit community like theirs was capable of and why tourists and visitors would always be welcome and safe on the island.

"We all agree with you there, Father." Padar told the television screen.

"And finally, Miss MacReady, how safe are the Innishmahon jewels at this point?" asked the reporter.

Miss MacReady glared into the lens.

"Totally and utterly safe, as is anything else left in my care. Let me tell you something, the Innishmahon post office and indeed the postmistress herself are no pushover for any old bowzies who think it's worth giving it a go." Miss MacReady blinked, pushing her sleeves up at the elbows and adopting a prize fighter's stance at the camera.

The whole pub burst into loud cheering and rapturous applause, as Miss MacReady took her bow.

"The two men involved were arrested and taken by the police to the mainland where they are being held in custody. It is likely they will be charged with aggravated burglary tomorrow," the newsreader concluded. *"And now the weather ..."*

More cheers and applause as Padar, totally overwhelmed by the occasion, produced an ice bucket and champagne, filling the glass Miss MacReady held aloft with aplomb. Relieved it had gone well, Marianne left her to bask in glory and slipped out of Maguire's and across to Weathervane where Monty was waiting for her. She bent to give him a huge cuddle and was nearly knocked flying as Ryan opened the door behind her. Apologising, he picked them both up, kissing her mouth and rubbing his chin on Monty's head.

"Not in the mood to celebrate?" he asked her.

She shrugged. "I understand why everyone else is, but it's a happy and sad occasion really. Sad someone thought Miss MacReady and the post office were fair game and sad it was Pat and Phileas."

He put Monty down, and looking into her eyes, drew her to him.

"Don't be too hard on them. They're only human, we all are."

He gave her a hug.

She ferreted around in her pocket to put her keys back on the hook, when a flash of gold flew past them and landed with a gentle ping on the table. It was the brass ring from the barn brack. He looked at her.

"It was in the cake. It's supposed to mean there'll be a wedding before a year's out," she told him.

"Really?" Sometimes the island's legends and superstitions left him bemused.

"This marriage stuff won't leave me alone at the moment." She pulled a face at herself in the mirror.

"What marriage stuff won't leave you alone?" he took her by the shoulders and sat her down.

Marianne put her head in her hands as Monty snuffled at her knees. She patted him absent-mindedly.

"I know about Angelique's proposal. The 'no marriage' clause, the bit that said she would only agree to you having custody of Joey if you never married again." She picked up the brass ring and spun it on the table.

"Well, that's academic at this stage, given everything that's happened. But how do you know about that? I deliberately never told you, thought you had enough on your plate, what with her just showing up and everything."

Marianne had the good grace to look shamefaced.

"I read the papers. Well, I didn't read the papers, someone else did and told me what was in them."

There was a silence; the clock chimed the hour.

"You shouldn't have done that. I'd have told you what you needed to know in the fullness of time, those papers were private," he said coolly.

"But we were worried, we wanted to help," she offered.

"We? You and Kathleen I suppose. The investigative journalist and her busybody mother, nice one." He turned to look out of the window. It was still a gloriously bright day, his mood suddenly black.

"Well, it doesn't make any difference any way. You know how I feel about marriage. It's not for me. Angelique's clause was irrelevant." Marianne was desperately trying to dig herself out of a gaping hole.

"Only irrelevant if we stay together and not getting married suits us, what if we split up? What if we meet other people and I want to marry and keep my son."

"Oh, I hadn't thought, but ..." she burbled.

"I *hope* it's irrelevant now Angelique is dead but what if Rossini decides to go for custody instead or as the executor of her Will, attempts to impose the conditions of Angelique's proposal on me. What then?" he said sternly.

"No, surely not." She was befuddled by the concept of them splitting up, meeting other people.

"It could still all go horribly wrong. Who can I trust when someone I thought was on my side is not on my side at all," he said.

"No!" she spun round, "that's not true!"

"Then why are you sneaking around reading my private papers and trying to decide the future for us without even consulting me?" he turned back to face her, eyes burning.

She was not letting him get away with that.

"You're a fine one to talk about deciding our future without consultation. You're the one who turned up here with all your baggage, more or less moving yourself and your son in without being invited!" she barked at him.

"What? Are you serious? Whoa," he held up his hands, "whoa right there madam. We discussed it, agreed to give it a go, we're supposed to be in love for God's sakes!"

"We only discussed it *after* you showed up," she retorted.

"I couldn't discuss it before, I couldn't reach you." His voice was rising.

"Ha," she threw back, "what absolute bollocks!"

"And the love thing? Is that absolute bollocks too?" he was mad now.

"What do you think?" she snapped back.

"Oh great, just great!" He stomped to where his jacket lay and dragged it on.

"Look at you, do what you always do when you're losing an argument. Storm off in a huff. Why don't you go and see your new best friend, Dermot? Or better still Erin? See Sinead too, tell them all about it!" she said, now furious with herself for going on the attack because she had been in the wrong. *Why could she not just apologise?* She was hopeless at saying sorry, even Oonagh told her off about that.

Ryan sighed. "It's time to collect the kids, in case you hadn't noticed. Anyway, you're probably right. I probably did rush things, I usually do, never think things through. So yes, let's take a step back, give everyone some air, some thinking time," he was calmer now. "We'll go and stay in Maguire's for a while. I'll pick up what we need tomorrow. Okay?" he looked into her face.

"But ..." she started to say as he made to go. He gave her a look. "Okay," she said in a small voice, and he left.

Monty eyed his mistress from his basket, where he had deposited himself as soon as voices were raised. He watched her get up, say "Agh!" very loudly and fling the hapless circle of metal across the room. It pinged off the sink, hit the back of a chair and landed with a slight thud in his basket. He sniffed it, then buried it under his blanket with his other treasures: a plastic bone, a rubber ball and a very shiny worm.

Chapter Twenty-Seven

Absence Makes The Heart Grow Fonder

Ryan came upon Padar and Sinead in the kitchen of the pub. Sinead was sitting at the table, Padar had his arm around her. She blew into a tissue as Ryan bumped the double-buggy over the step and into the room. Erin came in carrying a couple of glasses of wine. Sinead ran straight to the children, smothering them with kisses and fussing with belts and coats. Padar gave Ryan a look.

"Sinead's going to stay here for a while, till the other thing is settled," he explained.

"Makes sense," Ryan replied.

"I'll be glad of a bit of female company," Erin said in her deadpan way, "You're all a bit bloke-ish around here, even you and you're an actor."

Ryan took Joey out of the pushchair into his arms.

"I am not bloke-ish, I'm very in touch with my feminine side I'll have you know!" He gave her a glare of exaggerated effrontery.

"Oh really?" asked Erin. "Why is it then, that when you, or the other *Father of the Year* over there," she tossed a nod at Padar, "have those two poor children for longer than an hour, we need an entire army of females to sort out the devastation you've left in your wake."

"Here now," Padar exclaimed, "I take exception to that remark!"

"Excepting it's true," said Ryan, smiling at Erin, who laughed and took a good sip of wine.

"Is it?" asked Padar. "I didn't think we did too badly." He was genuinely perplexed. Sinead came to his defence.

"I think Erin's being a little harsh. You both do very well considering, you just need a little more practise," she smiled at Bridget as she put her in the highchair.

"Yeah, you'll be grand by the time these two are ready to go off to university." Erin looked at the children, then at Sinead. "You shouldn't be patronising them with 'you do very well considering' Sinead. Tell it like it is, they're both barely competent and need to brace up. It's a big responsibility having children, I wouldn't leave a Labrador with these two!"

Padar was just about to retort, when Sinead put her arm around him.

"Don't mind her, Padar, she's only trying to wind you up. You're a marvellous father, you both are." She smiled at Ryan. "You just need a bit of help from a female from time to time. Like I always say, the sexes are equal but different."

Erin laughed and drained her glass.

"Well, why don't they do their fair share of the work then?" she asked Sinead as she went back out to the bar.

"Ouch, she's a bit tetchy," Ryan said after she had gone.

"She's always like that, she doesn't mean any harm," Sinead said, "just speaks her mind, that's all, don't you think, Padar?"

Padar was still scowling after Erin.

"True enough, she was always blunt speaking, made Oonagh look like a charm offensive and she could slice you in two with her tongue when she had a mind to. That's why they were always falling out."

"They never meant it though, I'm sure," Sinead said, leaving her wine untouched as she went to prepare the children's meal.

Padar noticed Ryan was very quiet.

"Fancy a pint?" he asked him.

"Maybe later," Ryan replied. "I was just wondering Padar, if you had any spare rooms."

Padar went to the booking diary, which was neither use nor ornament since Oonagh was no longer around. He rarely remembered to fill it in and relied heavily on Sinead, who might have heard him taking a booking over the phone, reminding him to put the dates in. Padar flicked a couple of pages.

"Looks okay at the moment, I'll have the building lads back after the long weekend, but that shouldn't be a problem. For how many and how long?"

"The two of us, Joey and myself, indefinitely," Ryan said.

Padar and Sinead exchanged a look. Erin shouted in from the bar.

"Ryan do you want a pint? The other caveman is here and wants to know if you'll come through and share a few grunts with him."

Ryan placed Joey carefully in the other highchair as Sinead dished out the babies' food.

"Go ahead," she said, her eyes still pink and a new worried look on her face. "I'd rather be busy, honest I would."

Ruffling his son's dark hair, Ryan went to see what Dermot wanted.

The men took their pints into the empty snug.

"Alright?" Dermot asked his friend. Ryan did not look in the best of form. He just nodded, taking a grateful swig of stout.

"I'm about to finish lunches, do youse two want anything to eat – sandwiches or a burger obviously – wouldn't give you anything requiring cutlery, being as you don't know how to use a knife and fork!" Erin called to them.

"What's she like?" Dermot asked, keeping one eye on her shapely bottom as she moved along the optics, dusting as she went.

"Bit of a handful, I'd say," Ryan said, flatly.

"Aren't they all?" Dermot replied. "Anyway," he pulled his gaze away from Erin's rear, "I've had word, the job."

"It's real now is it?" said Ryan without enthusiasm.

"Yes, but there's a slight set back. It seems the lads down to do it have been unavoidably detained." Well, that was how Joyce MacReady described it when she spoke to him on the mobile earlier. "So it's been put back a few weeks while they find a couple of replacements to get the shipment from England to here."

"It's a bit of a voyage that, isn't it? What if it gets intercepted along the way? What if one of the other forces get lucky and nab the shipment en route?" Ryan asked him.

"As soon as we know which vessel it's on, there'll be an *all-points bulletin* to the entire force, lifeboats, helicopters the lot, ordering them to leave well alone. That's where we come in," Dermot explained.

"But why not let the other fella's nab it on the way? It would be a lot easier and a lot less risky," Ryan said.

"No, far too risky on three counts," Dermot replied. "There's a risk that someone in one of the other forces could be bent, and the arms and the cocaine would disappear, ending up somewhere else entirely. Then there's the risk that an unscheduled interception could go badly wrong, meaning it could be both unsuccessful and result in loss of life; and thirdly, the even bigger risk, that if intercepted by those, how shall I put it, less able than myself, we may never find out who *Mister Big* is and we'll be no nearer catching the real criminals involved. And that Ryan, is priority number one, that's what I've been tasked to do. Nope, no-one is to come in and give us a hand until I send for them, then they'll be there in a flash, no worries."

Ryan gave Dermot a smile.

"Sounds exciting." Then he looked at him squarely, "You're not joking are you? This is a real job, this could be dangerous?"

"Not half as dangerous as what would happen if this cargo goes undetected and hits the streets. Think of all the lives it would ruin," Dermot said.

"Won't those lives be ruined anyway?" Ryan asked him. "If not from this source, won't they get it from somewhere else?"

"Not if supplies dry up," Dermot said.

"But will supplies ever dry up?" Ryan persisted.

"We've got to pray they do, hope there'll be an end to it and no more babies will be born addicted to crack cocaine," Dermot said.

An image of Angelique healthy and heavily pregnant flashed into Ryan's mind. Thank goodness they managed to get her into a clinic and clean before Joey was born, before such a dreadful fate could have befallen their beautiful little boy.

"You're right," Ryan agreed, grimly.

Erin appeared at the entrance to the snug. She was holding a tray bearing plates of sandwiches and a bowl of Maguire's famous chunky chips. She placed it before the men, her black T-shirt with the words *Born to Bitch* emblazoned across her bosom was cut fetchingly low, revealing a tantalising flash of décolletage. Dermot watched her, fascinated. Ryan was miles away.

"I know you didn't order anything, but being two lonely old bachelors, I guessed you'd need something to keep your strength up." She arched an eyebrow at them, giving a faint wiggle as she left. Dermot fell on the food.

"What *is* she like?" Dermot asked his friend.

"She's like a woman," Ryan replied unenthusiastically.

"And what did she mean about the bachelor thing? You're hardly single," Dermot said, pushing chips into his mouth.

"Ah well, I might be a bit single," replied Ryan, picking at the corner of a beef sandwich.

How Marianne and Ryan managed to avoid each other for a whole week was nothing short of a miracle, bearing in mind Maguire's side entrance opened directly onto the lane-way which led to Weathervane's front door. If either of them had spotted the other during that time, they each must have turned and fled, being careful not to run directly into each other's arms, the island being so small they could have met themselves coming backwards.

Of course each was desolate without the other. Marianne insisting on doing a rota with the children so she would not miss them too much and Ryan, via a message from Padar, taking Monty for runs on the beach when Marianne had the children. Everyone else thought the situation was either hilarious or heartbreakingly sad. Ryan nearly had an argument with Father Gregory when the priest suggested he acted as unbiased counsellor, so they could discuss their issues, and

Marianne sent Miss MacReady away with a flea in her ear when she arrived bearing cake and whiskey in an effort to talk some sense into her stubborn and clearly brokenhearted daughter.

"Mother, don't even start!" she said as she opened the door and Miss MacReady, dressed from head to toe in sombre grey flannel, clicked into the hallway. Miss MacReady said nothing, just opened her arms for an embrace. Marianne ignored her and banged on the kettle instead. Miss MacReady lifted Monty for a cuddle, eyeing her daughter shrewdly.

Marianne turned to her.

"Look, I don't want to talk about it to you or anyone else, no offence," Marianne was snippy. Miss MacReady made no comment. "The truth is, mother, we just don't get on. We're okay for a while, and then, we clash. He drives me mad. He more or less accused me of snooping on him because we read those papers. I mean, we were *trying* to help! He's so full of himself, working out all the time, and chauvinistic, thinks the world revolves around him. I'm sorry, but I can't live like that. Life was so uncomplicated before he came along. Him and his child – who I love completely, Joey is just gorgeous, and his ex-wife – killing herself all over the place, and his *OCD* agent, Larry *hand me a wipe* Leeson – mind you I really like Larry, he's a great bloke – and all the other stuff, it's too much, it's all *too* much!" She plonked herself down at the kitchen table.

"I didn't come to talk to you about Ryan, your situation is your business," Miss MacReady told her.

"Really?" asked Marianne disbelieving, *this is a first.*

"You're adults, nothing to do with me. I bring exciting news."

Marianne noticed Miss MacReady was wearing red patent stilettos beneath the long grey skirt. *Not all bad then?*

"I'm going on a trip, to New York. I'm going to stay with Larry, see the sights – *Breakfast at Tiffany's* – you know the sort of thing." Miss MacReady was alight.

"What? How did that come about?" Marianne was surprised.

"Well, Larry had the most brilliant idea. Now that Phileas and Pat – I'm sure he was adopted you know – have been charged and things have quietened down on the media front, he thought it would be a good idea if I brought the jewels back to New York, back to Mr Rossini. Far more practical than hiring a security firm and much more fun." She gave a little twirl.

"Are you mad?" Marianne asked aghast. "It's too risky, what if you're mugged, murdered? No way."

Miss MacReady frowned at her daughter. "God you can be a pain-in-the-arse killjoy when you want to be, Marianne! It's not remotely dangerous, I take the jewels in a locked case, check them into the hold, where they stay throughout the flight. I collect them at the other end. Larry and one of Rossini's men meet me. I hand the case over and hit the town in celebration of a job well done."

Marianne scowled back at her. "I see you have it all figured out."

"Yep, the week after next. Flight's booked, the lot!" Miss MacReady told her.

"Thanks for consulting me." Marianne was grumpy.

"Why would I consult you? I'm a grown woman, going on a trip." Miss MacReady beamed.

"What about us, with all that's going on here?" Marianne said.

Miss MacReady shrugged. "Leave you to it. You'll do what you want to do whatever anyone else says. As for Ryan, he's as bad. Now, are we having a whiskey and piece of cake or not?"

Marianne was incensed, "Well thanks Mother, thanks for all your support, thanks a bunch!"

"I'll take that as a no then," Miss MacReady replied, scooping the goodies into her basket and sweeping from the room in her red high heels.

Ryan was sitting at the table in the kitchen of Maguire's attempting to do some work on his latest script. The children were sleeping soundly, having spent most of the day with Marianne at the kindergarten. Sinead had taken them for their bath hours ago, saying she wanted an early night herself. Padar was serving a few late-night stragglers in the bar when Erin appeared in the doorway, having been dismissed for the evening.

"You okay?" Erin asked, flipping the tea towel over her shoulder, "you haven't said more than a sentence in days, and you're losing weight, they won't want you back in that film if you look like a seven-stone weakling."

Ryan gave her a half-smile. Erin went to the fridge, grabbed a bottle of vodka and poured them both a shot. Ryan raised his hand, "I don't ..."

"Drink? Jeez, have you taken the *pledge* as well?" Erin asked.

"No, I don't drink vodka, it makes me drunk," he told her.

Erin burst out laughing. "I see, and it's only vodka that does that, the stout or the whiskey or the wine has no effect?"

"You know what I mean," he nodded at the glass, "you go ahead."

"I've every intention," she said haughtily, "don't need your permission."

Ryan started to gather up his papers.

"Don't go, I was only joking," she told him.

"Can I be frank, Erin," he asked.

"Be anyone you like Frank," she smiled.

"I'm not in the best of form and you're just a bit too much like hard work." He stood to go.

She held up her hands. "Sorry, know where you're coming from. Tell you what – I'll get you a nightcap, we'll put some music on and just chill for half an hour. I won't even talk, okay?" she seemed genuinely sorry for him. He thought about it.

"Okay," he said, quietly.

By the time Erin returned Ryan had packed his work away and *Roxy Music's 'Avalon'* was on the radio. He was standing at the window, gazing into the dark. She handed him a drink.

"You guys'll work it out. You're in love, it'll be grand," she said, knocking back the shot, "Christ, that's rough," she said, shaking her head, then smiling at Ryan. "You've just had a bit of a crap time – Angelique's death and everything. Where did it happen?"

Ryan turned back into the room. "On the plane," he said.

"Was she okay when she left, not out of it, not in a coma or anything?" Erin asked.

"They wouldn't have let her on the plane in a coma now would they?" Ryan gave her a quizzical look.

"I just wondered if you thought there was any, what do they say, 'foul play'?"

"No I do *not*," he continued "Marianne saw her on the beach, she was already packed and ready to go. They came back here, Larry arrived to go with her to the airport and home. Why do you ask?"

Erin was swaying to the music.

"Just curious, you know. Do you think she killed herself?" she asked. Ryan had not touched his drink.

"Yes, there's no doubt Angelique killed herself, Erin. She had been killing herself for a long time. Whether she deliberately decided to kill herself on the flight home, who knows? I doubt it. I think she just died, from what, who knows? The autopsy said death by misadventure, the toxicology report showed high levels of alcohol in her system. *My* opinion, cause of death – lifestyle – simple as that."

Erin moved to face him, still swaying.

"Yeah, I suppose that could be true of so many," she said.

"Nearly everyone really," Ryan said, dryly.

"Dance?" she asked, holding out her arms. She lost her balance. He lunged to save her, holding her up.

"Phew, this stuff is strong," she smiled crookedly.

"How many have you had?" he asked.

"Just a few. I can drink vodka. I have a quick nip while I'm helping out, numbs the brain," she hiccoughed.

"And everything else," he laughed. She had turned to jelly in his arms.

"You laugh. First time you laugh since you came here. Ah, poor sadly Ryan, love Marianne so much, she loves you too, go back and say you love her. She'sha great girl." She wobbled again. It was easier if Ryan just held her up, while they swayed.

"She is," he agreed, "a great girl. I didn't think you two were mad about each other though?"

"Ah, Padar told me she and Oonagh were very close. She probably thinks I wasn't much of a sister, not around when Oonagh needed me. She's entitled to her opinion. Bit stuffy though but hey, s'up to her. But you be a good movie star and go back to her, she's as miserable as hell too. Do us all a flavour, eh?" She slurred.

"I'm hoping absence makes the heart grow fonder," he said, but it was too late, Erin had flaked out, wrapped around him with her head on his shoulder. He gripped her tightly, trying to steer her towards the stairs and bed. He did not see Dermot staring wide-eyed through the window, on his way in for a late one. Dermot scowled, changed his mind and headed onto Weathervane where a light still shone.

"Hey," Dermot Finnegan filled the doorway.

"Hey," Marianne replied listlessly. He eyed the hair in a topknot on her head. She was wearing one of Ryan's skanky sweatshirts and jogging bottoms covered in dog hair. She looked good enough to eat as far as Dermot was concerned.

"How's it going?" he asked.

"So, so," she said.

"Mind if I come in?" he took a step closer.

"I'm not really very good company at the moment," she told him.

"That's okay nor am I," he smiled. A big brash, Dermot Finnegan smile, and Marianne let big brash Dermot Finnegan in. He sat down. There was an empty whiskey tumbler on the table. He picked it up; it looked like a glass thimble in his huge hand.

"A nightcap, perfect," he said to her.

Marianne took another glass off the dresser and poured them each a large one.

"Is everything okay?" she asked him, "you know, over there." She nodded towards Maguire's.

"Sort of," he replied. "I'm more concerned about you, how you're getting on?" There was a file beside him on the table; he turned it to read the words on the front.

"*Lost Babies Case Studies.*" The file was huge. "Are there really this many?" he ran his thumb down the paperwork. "There must be hundreds here."

She nodded solemnly, her eyes were sad, the corners of her mouth turned down.

"I've just reunited my thousandth baby with his long-lost mother. He's thirty, so not a baby anymore, and she's spent the last three decades mourning him. I can't help feeling someone should be punished for that." She sounded deflated.

Dermot agreed, "I suppose the trail has gone cold at this stage, no way of tracing back who was actually responsible for taking the baby and telling the mother he died."

Marianne sighed, "Usually more than one person involved, a team, deceitful and despicable each and every one of them."

He looked up at the dresser, a couple of her trophies in among the delph. "I'd no idea you're *Marianne Coltrane – the famous award-winning journalist*, I'm full of admiration, I really am," he said.

"There's no reason you would know that," she shrugged, blushing.

"But you set it all up, run the charity, the website, it's all voluntary too. I think it's amazing work." He lifted his glass, he noticed she was not drinking. "Here's to you."

She took the file from the table and put it in her desk.

"It chimes with me, you see," he went on. "I was a *Lost Baby*. In one sense anyway, abandoned as an infant and adopted by the Garda who found me. Luckily he and his wife didn't have children so I fitted the bill perfectly. They spoiled me rotten, only family I've ever known or needed."

"I didn't know," she gave him a small smile, "worked out well for you, that's good."

"My mum was convinced the angels sent me. That was always good enough for me too. A simple soul, me." His eyes softened. "What's your story then?"

She was tired. She wished Dermot would just drink up and go. She felt lonely, isolated this past week. She was hoping he would bring news of Ryan, maybe a message of some kind and then leave.

"I was adopted too," she said putting papers away, tidying around him. "The discovery of my birth mother is relatively new and with both my parents passed on, that's fine."

"I know all about it. Miss MacReady collared me in Maguire's one night when she found out I was the only person on the island who didn't know the story. Your father sounded a right bastard abandoning her like that, especially when her own family had disowned her."

Marianne did not want this conversation now.

"We only have one side of the story to be fair," she said brusquely. Dermot speaking about her father like that made her uncomfortable, but Dermot always made her uncomfortable one way or another. "I'm sorry Dermot. I've a busy day tomorrow."

"I won't stay long," he said not moving. "I just wondered would you show me the website, explain it to me. I'm fascinated and you never know I might be able to help in some way. I'm quite a good detective."

The cynic in Marianne gave him a look. *Was he serious?*

"Okay, but just briefly," she said. "Come through." She went into the cosy sitting room, the last of the peat glowed in the hearth, the curtains were drawn against the night.

"This is nice," Dermot said, bringing with him two replenished whiskey glasses. "Nothing makes a house as welcoming as a peat fire, bowl of stew and a good woman."

Marianne laughed. "Are you a nineteen fifties ad for *Bord na Móna* or what?"

"Aha, she laughs," he grinned back at her, "a smile suits you."

She laughed again. "Dermot, you're too cheesy for words."

"Amn't I?" he said, handing her a drink. "Now don't show me the sad stuff. Have you a happy page, one with thank-yous and grinning pictures of people reunited?"

"That's what I've been working on," she flicked on the computer. "Some brilliant success stories, look," and her mood lifted, the passion for her project making her eyes shine and words sparkle. An hour later they were jabbering away like the oldest friends.

"So, being adopted, not an issue for you?" he asked. They were on the sofa now, pictures from albums strewn between them as Marianne described different boats she sailed with her parents.

"Not sure, now you ask." She looked at him. "I always felt as if I was surplus to requirements where my parents were concerned. I often wondered if they thought adopting me made them complete, when they were already complete."

Dermot shrugged. "Why was that then?"

"They were highly organised, everything compartmentalised, the only thing they were passionate about was their research and each other," she told him.

"Maybe that was just their way. Did they love you?" he moved closer to her.

"Yes, I'm sure of that." She smiled at him. He was a little bit out of focus – he was either too close, or that last whiskey had been too large.

"How could they not?" he said dreamily. She felt his hot breath on her cheek.

"Dermot, I think you might be a tinky-winky bit drunk."

"No way, snot at all," he gave a wobbly smile. "Ah maybe a tiddle bit,"

"Come on," she said, putting her glass down, standing up, a slight sway, that whiskey was a *very* large one. "Off you go, home now."

"Aw, do I have to go? Just one more little nightcap," he drawled.

"Home Dermot, and go steady. If you fall in the sea getting onto the boat you're a gonna, no-one to save you round here. Lifeboat's not ready yet you know," she said sternly.

"You can't send me home like this surely? I'll fall in the sea and be a gonna, no bloody lifeboat or anythin'." He started to giggle.

"Come on." She grabbed his arm and tried to hoist him up.

"Ryan doesn't deserve you, you know. Won't stay, he'll go back to all the glitz and glamour, addicted to it, always has been," Dermot said, trying to focus on her. *Here we go,* she thought. "Thinks he wants a quiet life, but he dusn't, he's so vain, can't cope without his adoring fans, honestest. You need a proper bloke, someone who'll mind you, stay on the highland, someone like me," he slurred. He tried to get off the sofa twice, gave up and slumped back.

"Now, now," she wagged a finger at him, "none of that talk, I love Ryan, he loves me, we'll be fine."

"Really?" Dermot was bemused. "Ah shite, don't say that, I'm mad about you meself."

"That's very nice, Dermot, and I'm sure that's not entirely true. You're just feeling a bit sentimental and you need to go home." She tried to pull him up but he fell back. She took his arm and hauled at it, but he was a dead weight.

"I hope he's true to you, had a trebbible reputation when we were ...when we were ..." his eyes were closing.

"Dermot, Dermot, wake up! You can't say here, Dermot!" She slapped his cheeks. His head slumped forward, he started to snore.

"Shit!" she said loudly. No response. Monty scraped at the door, she let him in. He sniffed Dermot and trotted back into the kitchen. He looked at his mistress.

"Nothing to do with me," she told him. "Can't take his drink!" And kissing his snout bade him goodnight, leaving Dermot out for the count on the sofa.

Ryan was letting himself in, as Dermot let himself out.

"What – the –?" Ryan said, giving Dermot the once-over: dishevelled hair, stubbly chin, red-rimmed eyes.

Dermot held up his hands, "Not what you're thinking, mate."

"You don't know what I'm thinking! What are you doing here?" Ryan asked sharply.

"What are *you* doing here?" Dermot hated being challenged, particularly with a crick in his neck and a thumping great hangover.

"Come to take Monty for a run. Anyway I don't have to explain myself to you! Where's Marianne?" Ryan snapped.

"In bed," Dermot replied, "where I left her."

"What?"

"Only joking. We had a few drinks, I fell asleep on the sofa, not that *I* have to explain myself to you. Anyway you were looking pretty cosy with Erin last time I saw you." Dermot glared at his friend, "Who put *her* to bed I wonder?"

"I did, but I'm ..."

"Ahem." Marianne was at the top of the stairs, eyes blazing down at the pair of them. "Do you two want to take this discussion elsewhere?" she said coolly.

"Marianne, I ..." Ryan looked up at her.

"Now!" she barked, turning on her heel and slamming the bedroom door.

"Thanks," he said to Dermot, as Monty joined them out in the rain.

Marianne did not go back to sleep, she lay there fuming. She was annoyed with herself for not being firmer with Dermot and sending him home early last night and cross with Ryan for just turning up, assuming he had the right to let himself into her home, when he had been the one to take himself and Joey off to Maguire's anyway. And what was that about getting cosy with Erin? *What was going on there*, she would like to know. *In fact, what the hell **was** going on?*

She threw back the covers and jumped out of bed. She showered, dressed and was pulling the hall door closed behind her in less than fifteen minutes. It was nearly nine o'clock when she let herself into a very orderly and unusually empty Maguire's kitchen. She walked around the table a couple of times, no sign of breakfast, the children's highchairs side by side in the alcove by the door. She opened the fridge, everything cling-filmed, sealed and put away. She heard the chink of glass coming from the pantry. She went to the door and just as she put her fingers to the handle, it opened and Erin appeared. Face scrubbed of make-up and hair tied back in a bun, she looked younger and less like Oonagh than usual.

"Can I help?" she asked Marianne, closing the door quickly behind her. Marianne looked her up and down. She was wearing faded blue jeans, white T-shirt and a long navy and white striped apron over her clothes.

"I do work here you know," Marianne responded.

"Haven't seen you in a while," Erin said, in her usual manner.

"I've had some time off, family stuff," Marianne said.

"Really? Most of your family seemed to have moved in here," Erin reminded her, taking a mixing bowl and ingredients from cupboards.

"What are you doing?" Marianne asked her.

"Making steak and ale pie. We're a bit low on stuff for lunch, and with the weather turning stormy later, I'm guessing the building lads will be in for the afternoon." She busied herself at the table.

Marianne fetched her apron from the back of the door. She tied her hair up and put on a catering cap. Erin gave her a look.

"Give you a hand?" Marianne said and started seasoning the beef ahead of browning it in the large pan. "Where is everyone?"

"Sinead had the whole lot up, dressed and out early, she's amazing that one. Padar's gone to the wholesaler on the mainland. Don't know where Ryan is." She carried on chopping vegetables.

"He came to take my dog for a run," Marianne said.

"Youse are speaking then?" Erin sounded hopeful.

"Who said we're not speaking?" Marianne asked sharply.

"No-one, but I thought ..."

"Thought what?" Marianne said.

"Thought you were having a break. Things aren't going that well between you, that's why he's moved in here isn't it?"

Marianne felt the words ping off her like tacks.

"We'll be fine," she told Erin, sorry she mentioned Ryan.

"I hope so." Erin sounded genuine. "He's been through a lot, seems a nice guy, nice kid too."

"What do you know about it?" Marianne asked, avoiding Erin's eyes.

"Not a lot. Only I can see how sad he is, how much he loves the kid, and you. People imagine that kind of lifestyle is amazing – movie star, travelling the world, fame, money – but looks like nothing but pressure and hassle from where I'm standing, poor bloke."

Marianne turned to face her new workmate. "Does it seem like that to you?"

Erin nodded, wiping her hands on her apron. Marianne eyed the table. Erin had ingredients everywhere; Marianne hated working in a mess.

"Any idea how long you're staying?" she asked.

Erin shrugged, "As long as it takes. Don't want to be here any longer than I have to. This place never changes, it's the pits."

"You think so?" Marianne was wiping around Erin's workspace.

"Don't you? Anyone with a business works their fingers to the bone for nothing, and those who don't work just moan about those who do. Then there's the gossip, everyone just talks about everyone else and the weather, gawd all it does is rain."

"I love it here," Marianne said emphatically.

"Ah, you haven't been here five minutes, what would you know?" Erin replied. "No, I'm off as soon as."

"I thought you'd come back because of Padar, because Oonagh had died," Marianne said coldly.

"No, I'm here on a job. Pure coincidence this happens to be my home town." Erin kneaded the pastry dough.

"Job? What kind of job?" Erin ignored the question, Marianne continued, "But you were engaged to Padar, now he's single again ...and then there's Bridget."

"Yep, that's what everyone's supposed to think." Erin's floury hands pushed a strand of hair behind her ear.

"Sorry, I don't get it?" Marianne was snarky.

"Thought you were supposed to be vaguely intelligent?" Erin was snarky back. "I'm working undercover. Even you journos do it, I believe."

"Oh, I hadn't realised. Undercover what?" Marianne asked coolly.

Erin waved the rolling pin at her.

"That wouldn't make me undercover anymore, now would it?" she raised a patronising eyebrow at Marianne. Marianne scowled at her across the table.

"You don't like me very much, do you, Marianne?" Erin said, matter-of-factly.

Marianne felt the colour rush to her throat. "I was very close to Oonagh."

"So was I, once," Erin came back at her.

"I believe the estrangement was down to your behaviour," Marianne was sniffy.

"I believe you should mind your own damn business," Erin shot back at her. Marianne turned pink. She glared at the other woman.

"Well, if you dislike it so much here, the sooner you go back to where you bloody well came from the better," she sniped at Erin.

"And so should you!" Erin said.

"So should I what?" Marianne's voice was rising.

"Go back to where you bloody well came from!" Erin's decibel level rose to match her opponent. Marianne was confused.

"Actually, this *is* where I come from," she said triumphantly, thumping the table with her fist.

"And so do I!" hissed Erin, facing her adversary across the table. Stalemate. Silence.

They could smell burning.

"The beef!" squawked Marianne. She pulled the pan off the range. "Ow, that's HOT!" She shook her hand away from her.

"Ah shite, that's all we had too," Erin said, taking Marianne by the arm over to the sink. She turned on the cold tap and pushed the bright pink flesh under it. Marianne was pale with shock.

"Bet that hurts," said Erin. "Keep it there, I'll get you a painkiller." She returned with a couple of white capsules and a glass of clear liquid, "Knock them back." Marianne gagged. "Padar's vodka, foul isn't it? But it deadens the lips, so it's bound to numb that burn," Erin advised.

"Thanks, I think," Marianne said, eventually.

Erin gave her a smile.

"Fancy a nice drop of wine to take away the taste?"

"Drink, with you?" Marianne was incredulous.

"No-one else here," Erin replied. The vodka hit Marianne in the chest, burning down to her stomach. She started to laugh. Erin looked at her in surprise.

"Probably long overdue – a glass of wine and a good chat," Marianne said, checking her throbbing hand. She sat down at the table. "What about the builders' pie?"

"Ah, feck them and their pie, they can have toasted sandwiches and be glad of it. You're right we're long overdue a bit of downtime. Do you mind if we don't talk about Oonagh though? Padar's been over it time and again, blames himself entirely for what was an accident, a terrible accident but that's what it was. And I'm sorry we weren't closer, but we weren't and that's that," Erin told her.

"Fine by me," Marianne said as Erin brought a good bottle of Sauvignon Blanc, cheese and fruit to the table, helpfully slicing an apple and serving Marianne.

"Do you have any sisters, Marianne?" Erin asked, pouring the wine. Marianne shook her head, mouth full of cheese and grapes. "Not all they're cracked up to be you know, especially if they go and die on you before you can tell them how you really feel." And Marianne watched as a very large tear rolled down Erin's cheek, splashing onto the table before she had a chance to wipe it away.

Chapter Twenty-Eight

Big Girlie Wuss

By the time Sinead returned from kindergarten with the little ones Marianne and Erin had shared the best part of a bottle of wine and were chatting amicably. Despite not wanting to talk about Oonagh, Erin did confirm they had once been close and yes, Joan Redmond's version of those long ago events was true.

"Padar never stopped loving her, Marianne," Erin explained, "I was a poor substitute and only fooling myself. She was my big sister. I was furious she left me, so I wanted what she had, her man, her lifestyle but it wasn't to be. I know Padar was thinking of Oonagh every time he made love to me. He'd drop me like a stone if she ever came back on the scene. She was livid with me for taking up with Padar but he was a free man when we got together. She left him, she had no cause for complaint. We had the biggest row, never spoke to each other again. Padar should have made her see reason, but he didn't. Anyway, all water under what was a pretty rickety bridge to begin with when you look at it."

Marianne touched Erin's hand, "I'm sorry."

Erin gave her head a small shake. "One of the reasons I'm so direct, some say blunt. Misunderstandings cause half the world's problems if you ask me. Say what you think, then at least people know where they stand. Pussyfooting around for the sake of people's feelings causes a lot more damage."

If Sinead was surprised to see them sitting amid vegetable peelings and spilled flour, she did not let on, she just kissed Marianne and went off to fetch her medical bag. Marianne welcomed the opportunity to spend some time with Bridget and Joey. Avoiding Ryan for over a week had left her bereft of Bridget's giggling antics and Joey's clingy cuddles.

"Any news?" Marianne asked, referring to Phileas and Pat, when Sinead returned.

Sinead shot her a look. "He's dead to me now, Marianne, not interested."

"They'll be in custody for months, I reckon." Erin told them. "They've been charged with aggravated burglary, but who knows when the trial will come up?"

"A bad business," Marianne said.

"Has Kathleen mentioned what's happening with the jewels?" Erin asked casually, combing Bridget's hair into ringlets.

"Only that they need a special courier to get them back to the States," Marianne did not know how much of Miss MacReady's latest revelation should be public knowledge. Or indeed how much of it was fanciful.

Once Sinead was happy the wound was clean and dressed, she suggested Marianne go home to rest, it was a nasty shock and Sinead thought she looked exhausted. Erin whipped her apron off saying she would walk Marianne back to Weathervane before going for her run. Outside the pub she took Marianne's arm and steered her towards the beach.

"What is it?" Marianne asked.

"How well do you know Mrs Porter?" Erin asked.

"Quite well, she's a good sort, always there if you need her, works like a Trojan, why?" Marianne replied. She wished she was wearing another layer; the wind was whipping at the water, strands of scrub grass blown flat.

"Bit too zealous in the arse-wiping department in my opinion, *Dettol* wipes anything that moves. She's finished with her husband, there's no doubt about that and she definitely has another fella on the go, but I can't quite work out who though," Erin told her.

"Really?" Marianne said. They were walking arm in arm with their backs to the breeze along the shoreline. "She sometimes chats to Shay, the builder."

"Yeah, true and she always has a drink with the priest and seems close to Padar," Erin commented, checking them off. "Her and Phileas been married long?"

Marianne nodded, "A good while, why?"

"No kids? None planned?" Erin asked.

"Never discussed it with her. She loves children though. I'm guessing it would only have been a matter of time. She's all for the holiday home for young carers, the one I'm planning in Oonagh's memory, I don't suppose you ...?"

"Nah, I won't be around anyway," Erin said, breaking into a run. She turned back to wave goodbye, pointing behind her.

"Your fella's coming up behind you," she called above the wind. "Remember what I said about pussyfooting and people's feelings." And she turned away, running off towards the cliff and the ravine which led to Horseshoe Bay.

Marianne waited for Ryan to catch up. Monty brought her a nice clump of seaweed as a gift.

"Hey," he said and fell into step beside her. They walked in silence. He kept looking at her, willing her to turn her face to his, hoping he could break the mask with a smile.

"Miss you," he tried.

"You too," she said, staring straight ahead.

"Ready to talk about it?" he asked.

"I've always been willing to talk, you're the one who flounced off in a huff like a big girlie wuss," she said, keeping the smile out of her voice.

"Only because I'm an actor dahling," he said. He took her hand, turning her to face him, hair blowing wildly, eyes glittering. He gave her his sad, lopsided smile and suddenly she longed to kiss him, be crushed against his old leather jacket that smelled of sea and musk and him.

"I don't mean to keep things from you, but there are things you don't need to know. My life and career is complicated, you don't need to know every detail. You won't fully appreciate what worth's worrying about and what isn't," he told her.

She clung to his hand, wrapping her fingers around his tightly. "I'm a big girl you know."

"Indeed, with more than enough on your plate. I want to make things easier for you, us. I want us to have a nice life together, so there are certain elements of mine I have to deal with myself, my way, okay?" he took her by the shoulders, looking straight into her eyes, holding her chin in his hand. "I love you, I love you, I love you." A gull screeched overhead.

"When I, we, read those documents, it was with the best of

intentions, but it was wrong, I'm sorry." She gave him a watery smile.

"Forgiven, never to be mentioned again," he confirmed.

"But you *must* promise you'll tell me everything from now on, everything you're involved with, everything you've been asked to do. Let's make decisions together from now on, yes?" she moved closer, her lips brushed his mouth as she spoke. "No more secrets!"

Erin had told her she was undercover. Marianne dismissed it, not really a secret, nothing to tell. Miss MacReady told her Angelique was arrested for embezzlement, but Angelique was dead, no need to resurrect that particular piece of intelligence; nothing to do with Ryan. Miss MacReady was taking the jewels to New York, who needed to know?

"Of course, whatever you say, I totally and utterly agree," and even as he pulled her into his arms, pressing his lips against hers in a strong, hungry kiss, the secret assignation with Dermot flashed into his mind, his promise to help his friend intervene and counter the importation of illegal drugs and munitions. The sort of thing he could not tell Marianne about, precisely the sort of thing that would worry her to distraction. He pushed the thought from his mind, as he pushed his tongue into her mouth and she melted against him. It was a good feeling, his woman, back in his arms.

A few days later Marianne was helping Miss MacReady pack, or rather she was helping Miss MacReady unpack.

"Crikey, how long are you going for?" she eyed the pile of clothes on the bed and the mismatch of trunks, suitcases and bags strewn across the floor.

"Only a week," Miss MacReady replied. "Don't you think I have enough?"

"A *week*?! You have enough here for three changes a day for a month!" Marianne told her.

"But it's New York, Marianne, the city that never sleeps!" Miss MacReady was already buzzing with excitement, draping satin-covered hangers with evening gowns, cocktail dresses and negligees on every conceivable surface.

Erin came in from the post office. She was carrying a small black case made from titanium, with a neat combination lock and a chain attached to the handle.

"I've checked everything. All matches the inventory, all good to go," she told the postmistress. Marianne looked up in surprise.

"Private detective, working for the insurance company. I was sent here when they found out Angelique went back to the States without the collection," Erin explained. "Told you, I'm undercover."

"You knew about the burglary in advance?" Marianne asked.

"No, but it was a foregone conclusion someone would try it on and we had been tipped off. It's my job to ensure the jewels get off the island safely, so I suggested Miss MacReady for special courier, saves me going to New York, I hate the place." Erin explained.

Marianne raised her eyebrows at her mother.

"Larry knew the insurance company would send somebody to protect their interests, particularly when word got out about the robbery," Miss MacReady said, holding an emerald gown up in the mirror, swishing the fishtail from side to side.

"Surprised Larry didn't consider setting up a heist himself," said Erin, trying on a turquoise trilby. "People often have valuables 'stolen' so they can claim the insurance money and then sell them on the black market, it's a very lucrative scam if you can get away with it."

Miss MacReady turned pink, clashing with the dress.

"I'll make us some tea," Miss MacReady offered, dropping the gown. "Marianne can you start sorting out some sensible footwear? I want to do lots of walking while I'm there, see as much as I can," Her voice trailed off down the stairs.

Erin placed the trilby over one eye.

"Here's looking at you kid," she told her reflection in the mirror.

"And here's looking at you," said Marianne. "Good work, how did you get into it?"

"Police force, then Special Branch, then I was made an offer I couldn't refuse. The insurance companies pay well if you're successful. With my connections to the island, no-one was going to suspect why I was here. Sometimes it can be dangerous though. South America is vast and the Russians very tricky."

Marianne sat down on the bed fascinated. What a brilliant interview Erin would make, even if she had to stay undercover for the story.

Miss MacReady returned, composed, offering tea and cake.

"There are quite a few boudoir ensembles here, Mother dear," Marianne said teasing. "I assume you're staying with Larry? Any idea what the sleeping arrangements are?"

Miss MacReady put her cup down. "Well, I didn't like to ask. I know Larry lives alone and no mention of a partner, but I wouldn't like to assume a romantic assignation where there's none intended."

"You're a bit old for him aren't you?" asked Erin taking a slice of cake.

"Nonsense, look at Fliss Alridge the actress, her husband is thirty two years her junior and Trula de Ville, the singer, her beau is sixteen years younger than her, so with only a few years between us

I'd say *not* in this day and age," Miss MacReady replied haughtily, checking her temples for greys at the same time.

Marianne hid a grin beneath a blouse she was folding.

"I may be wrong, but I never got the impression Larry is particularly interested in sex, he doesn't give off any vibe really."

"I disagree," Miss MacReady retorted. "He has a lovely mouth and have you seen him dance? Shades of the gorgeous Ricky Divine, make no mistake." The other women looked at each other. "Check him out on *YouTube*, sex on legs," Miss MacReady confirmed. They burst out laughing.

"Your generation really needs to get a grip," she wagged a finger at them. "You totally understand the concept of a *dirty old man* but think older women stay home and knit. Grow up. We're the ones who invented vibrators don't you know!"

"Stop!" shouted Marianne, throwing a slipper at her.

"Well, you started it," laughed Miss MacReady, throwing it back. "And if I have intentions on Larry, that's our business, so I'd keep this conversation between ourselves if you don't mind."

Erin opened a bedside drawer and took out an instantly recognisable sex toy. She waved it at the postmistress.

"Well if you're not taking this with you, can I borrow it while you're away? I left mine in Dublin!" And the three of them roared their heads off.

"What's the plan?" Ryan spoke into the phone.

"I've had an idea if you don't mind staying in Maguire's for a bit longer. I want to decorate the spare room for Joey, so when you come back for good he has his own space, what do you think?" Marianne sounded excited.

"Great idea. He's never really had his own room, can I help?"

"Of course I want you to help. It's going to be our home, our proper home, yes?"

"And in the meantime we have sex in lots of random places, yes?" Ryan used his pseudo-weirdo voice.

"Stop it," she laughed. "Okay then, but the quicker we get it done the sooner we'll be together again as a family."

She sounded happier than she had for ages. He loved her like this, practical as ever, making plans, giving them all even more work to do. "See you for dinner?" he asked.

"Yes, an early one though, we have a board meeting and site visit tomorrow for the project, then we're taking Miss MacReady to the airport. *New York, New York,* don't forget."

"Yeah, Larry's really excited about it."

"Her visit or getting the jewels back?" Marianne was unsure.

"Both, don't be cynical." Ryan said.

"Question – has Larry ever had a girlfriend?" Marianne could not help but ask.

"Not to my knowledge." Ryan replied.

"Boyfriend?" she tested.

"No, why do you ask?" Ryan laughed.

"Love you," she said, blowing kisses as she put the phone down.

There was a lot of work to be done before Ophiuchus, the fading Georgian mansion standing proud above the village, could be turned into the *Oonagh Quinn Foundation,* Marianne's dream holiday retreat for young people, whose daily lives were filled with the stress of being full-time carers.

The board, as Miss MacReady insisted they call themselves, were poring over plans in the back room of the post office, the paperwork spread across a large table. Sinead was making tea in the kitchen. Marianne pushed the papers aside, making way for refreshments. Miss MacReady was deep in thought, halfway through yet another list.

"We'll need a couple of working parties," Marianne said, once everyone was settled again. "Ryan and I had a good scout round last weekend and though there isn't any major work needs doing, the cellars and the attic rooms are vast, running the length of the place top and bottom and there are cupboards and chests full of stuff from the Maguire days."

Miss MacReady took her glasses off.

"I'd love a good dig about in some of those big chests," she said, eyes wide in anticipation. "They had some very good silver, a fine art collection and a super library back in the day."

"I doubt there's anything of any value left. The agents acting for the stockbroker were very thorough, they cleared the place out, even took the garden furniture." Marianne said, between bites of cake. Miss MacReady looked pensive.

"Well, we can make a start can't we? And if there's anything too heavy for myself and Ryan to shift, we'll have to call upon Padar and a few of the lads," said Father Gregory.

Marianne started folding the plans away.

"You'll be wasting your time with Padar. He won't have anything to do with the project."

"Even though it's in Oonagh's memory?" Sinead was put out.

"He's not keen on roughnecks coming here from the towns, as he put it." Marianne shrugged, "We'll win him round eventually."

"I'll ask him to come and give me hand if you like. When he

sees how amazing it's going to be, I'm sure he'll change his mind."
Sinead was adamant.

"And the building lads are full-on working on the new bridge,
thank goodness." Miss MacReady cut in. "What about Dermot and
the lifeboat boys? I'll supervise their shift, if we can get them to
help. I'd like to watch them work up a bit of sweat."

"Now, now, Kathleen," laughed Father Gregory, "not in front of
the clergy."

"If we need more labour, I can leave the recruitment to you then,
Mother." Marianne flashed Miss MacReady a look.

"My pleasure," she beamed, lifting a china cup to crimson lips.
She loved it when Marianne called her mother, even if it was in
chastisement. "I'll see to it when I get back from New York if you
like. Did you know I was going to New York?" she asked Father
Gregory and Sinead, who had no choice but be regaled with every
detail.

They were in the largest cellar room, at the very end of the long
corridor which ran from the bottom of the stairs the length of the
house. The windows were high, small but plenty of them. Painted
white instead of gloomy mustard brown, it would transform the
place, Sinead thought, placing her clipboard on a chest.

"Great breakout area, don't you think? Perfect for a pool table,
some sofas, a bit of music," She said to Padar, hoping he was
impressed. He strode to the far end of the room, pushing back a
screen on squeaky wheels.

"Hey, what's this?"

She looked up. Half a dozen steps led to a pair of narrow doors.
The doors were paned with glass but the glass had been blacked out.
He tried them.

"Stuck, or locked or both." He took a crowbar from the tool bag, easing it into the gap. It made a loud crack, and as he pushed the doors open, beetles and moths scrabbled for cover. He brushed cobwebs away. The doors led onto a patch of overgrown gravel, a lower lawn, a slice of beach and then the shore.

"Come and see," he called to her, amazed the house, so high above the village, secretly slid down to the water once you were inside. He looked up. "I've found a balcony, a tiny Juliet balcony." He pulled at the strands of ivy, trailing down. "Romantic."

"There hasn't been much romance here in a long time," Sinead said, beating dust off the drapes with her clipboard.

"Come out here," he demanded, taking her hand, pulling her outside to stand on the gravel looking down to the secret beach.

"Oh," she said, surprised. "It's like a smuggler's cove."

The sun was sliding towards the horizon, the sky cloudless and bleached blue. They stood side by side, arms touching. They could feel the heat. She dropped his hand and stepped back inside.

"Okay, you win, I'll help. Do you want to make a start on the painting, or have we other stuff to do?" Padar called after her.

"The first coat's not dry yet, tomorrow's job. Let's get stuck into these chests, see what we can sling or recycle," she told him.

"Good plan," he agreed, not moving from his lookout post, the bewitching promise of a glorious sunset rooted him to the spot. "Look at this."

She was poking through a pile of files.

"There's so much should have been thrown away, medical records from years ago."

"Just bin them," he advised. "Come and look at the sunset *woman*."

She had a headache, her feet hurt. She dropped the bin bag and, kicking off her shoes, went to join him.

"At last," he smiled into her face. A light breeze was coming off the water, the air sweet and clean. They stood shoulder to shoulder looking out. It stretched before them, a smooth of green, a rustle of blond and then the sea, deep, dark and glistening. She shivered. He put an arm around her. She inhaled deeply and nestled into him, his scent mixing pleasingly with the salt air. She put her head on his shoulder. He leaned down to her, rubbing his cheek briefly on her hair, breathing her in. She lifted her chin to speak, her lips almost touching the small, soft space of skin beneath his ear. The sun had turned into a huge, orange orb.

"This is stunning," he whispered, staring straight ahead. "I could stay here like this forever."

"Me too," she replied, the breath from her words tickled his skin. He wrapped his arms around her, pulling her close. She looked up at him, his eyes were soft, kind, loving. She was suddenly tearful.

"Hey, hey," he said cupping her chin in his hand. "You're too beautiful to be always so sad."

She blinked the tears away, then standing on tiptoe she kissed him, the lightest kiss, her mouth just brushing his lips.

"And you, all the sadness you've had, I wish I could kiss it all away," she told him.

Releasing herself, she went back into the house. He pushed his hands into his pockets, frowning out to sea, breathing deeply, willing the desire away. He watched the sun start to sink.

"Come inside," she called out to him. "I've something to show you."

The room was gloomy now, the sun nearly gone. He went to switch on the lights.

"Don't, come here," she said softly, her voice coming from behind the screen near the drapes. He followed her voice, his foot caught in something soft, he kicked it aside.

"Are you hiding?" he asked, with a smile in his voice. He pulled the drapes aside. She stood there in the half-light, hair loose around her shoulders, blouse open to the waist, her breasts barely covered by a sheer vest top. She had taken off her long chambray skirt and her smooth legs shone like marble against the dark, full-length curtains. She raised her arms above her head, leaning back against the wall so he could see her, every inch of her from head to toe. She was smiling, a low sweet smile, lips parted.

He was stunned, too shocked to speak. His eyes flickered as his gaze swept over her, her glistening lips, the curve of her breast, the nipples raised, her softly rounded belly, thighs slightly apart. He tried to look away but his body was responding in a way he had not felt for a long time. Seeing him struggle, she gasped and pulled her blouse closed, stooping to collect her skirt.

"I'm so sorry," she whispered, her voice a rasp in her throat.

"Oh God, don't be," he begged, taking her hand, letting the skirt fall. He took her face in his fingers and with one piercing look of hungry desire, pressed her mouth with a kiss. She sank into his arms as his tongue darted thrillingly in her mouth, eating her with passion. He pulled the blouse from her shoulders, pushing down the thin satin straps of her top to reveal her breasts. She moaned with pleasure as he cupped the soft flesh in his hands and burying her fingers in his hair, she pressed him into her skin, every inch of her tingling with longing.

He stopped.

"Did you hear something?"

Her heart was pounding in her ears.

"No, don't stop," she begged.

"I heard something."

"Please don't stop," she started to unbutton his shirt, desperate to feel his warm, hard chest against her naked breasts. He undid his belt. She ran her fingers across the hardness in his pants. She let out a gasp as he released himself.

There was a muffled clunk behind them. He looked backwards.

"Ignore it," she whispered, parting her legs, ready for him, taking him inside her.

Voices. Another clunk – closer.

"I thought they were here," someone said.

A door banged, another opened. A key slipped into the lock.

"Here, it's open," a voice said.

The door swung wide, the lights flicked on.

"*Don't,*" she called out, pulling the drapes around them, "stop."

"Sinead?" a woman's voice asked, "Sinead is that you?" Another figure stepped through the doorway, a man.

"And Padar," he whispered, taking Marianne by the shoulders, turning her quickly away. Ryan switched off the light and pushed her out into the corridor, closing the door behind them. "Well, that's them found anyway."

"Ryan, what ... the ..?" she burbled. "Was that what I think it was?"

"Haven't a clue. I'll be honest, Marianne, I've no idea what you're thinking, ever," he replied, walking stoutly on. "Now come on, we've work to do."

Marianne was in what would have been the kitchen of the old house. As part of the refurbishment programme carried out by the previous owner, the former kitchen had been turned into a highly organised utility room, with washing machines, tumble dryers, large built-in airing cupboards and masses of storage. Whatever hobby or pastime the former incumbents or their guests may have wished to indulge in, every conceivable piece of equipment was to hand.

Marianne was determined to put any uncharitable thoughts regarding Sinead and Padar out of her head. She was merrily opening doors and enjoying the elegant swish as they closed when Sinead appeared, her pretty face slightly pink, hair smoothed back into its customary clip. She stood in the doorway, nodding appreciatively at the smooth, clean lines of the room, its fitments appealing to the clinician in her.

"Fantastically equipped," she said, running her hands along the work surface.

"Yes," said Marianne, straightening up to look her companion in the eye, "more than fit for purpose."

"It's such a shame it's never been used to its full potential. Used for what it was designed for," Sinead said.

"Indeed." Marianne folded her arms. "But we never could have been able to buy the property and carry out refurbishment anywhere near to this standard, it's a gift really."

The door from the kitchen opened. Padar and Ryan clattered down the stone steps to the utility room. Sinead turned away as they entered, reaching up to a cupboard, to see what was stored there.

"Look, life jackets and sea boots, we'll have enough for all the activities we could ever dream of." She pulled on a piece of fabric and a pile of clothing tumbled down. Padar took the length of the room in two strides, reaching over to catch the equipment before it landed on her.

"Careful," he said, arms extended, hands full of kit.

"I'll try to be," she answered, looking up at him, brushing her fingers against his as they laid the contents of the cupboard on the worktop. Marianne turned to Ryan, who was flicking switches and turning dials in the laundry.

"It's amazing, it's almost as if the English stockbroker, had kitted it out for you. All you could need to run a small five star hotel, anyway," Ryan said.

"Not so small," said Padar, "Sinead and I counted two forty-piece dinner services and the same amount of breakfast things. Fair play to you Marianne, you knew what you were about."

Marianne laughed.

"A happy accident, like so much of my life," she said, kicking Ryan playfully on the ankle.

"Accident or not, there's still an awful lot to do before we can open this place for business," Ryan said, marvelling at the broom cupboard filled with water-skis and fishing rods.

"Miss MacReady is on the final lap with the official stuff. She'll get everything as near as she can, then if we've to go to Dublin for meetings, we'll go as a team, with roles and responsibilities agreed," Marianne said. She looked at Sinead. "Do you think you'll be able to join us, Sinead? It will be full-time, especially in the summer when our guests are here."

Marianne was acutely aware Sinead had a heap of responsibilities, her part-time job as a midwife on the mainland, her role helping Joan at the kindergarten, and what was going to happen to the pharmacy with Phileas in prison; the chemist's was particularly busy in the tourist season, with no GP surgery on the island.

"I'll sort something out one way or the other. It's time to do what I want with my life," Sinead said sharply. They looked at her in surprise, "time marches on, doesn't it? Now, I'm off to do an inventory of the kitchen."

Marianne turned to Padar.

"She seems troubled lately, only smiles when she's with the children. I think Phileas let her down very badly and it's tearing her apart inside, it's heartbreaking to watch," she said quietly. "What do you know of it Padar?"

"I think Phileas is a fucking eejit and Sinead one of the most wonderful women I've ever met in my life," Padar said, and followed the wonderful woman out the door.

Chapter Twenty-Nine

New York, New York

L arry watched the doors anxiously. JFK Airport was buzzing as usual: friends and families who could not be together for Thanksgiving, making trips to celebrate ahead of the event; keen Christmas shoppers arriving to take advantage of the city's many department stores; and lovers, hundreds of lovers making the most of the romance New York oozes out of every crack in every sidewalk.

Another surge of newly arrived passengers pushed into the arrivals hall. His eyes darted to and fro, seeking her out, his pulse racing, a thin line of perspiration on his upper lip. There she was, a splash of yellow, sunshine breaking through the cloud. She saw him, waved her hand, the hand chained to the case. He raised his in response, smiling back; she lifted his heart whenever he saw her.

A scuffle, a scream, the crowd parted. A man was running, grey hoodie, black trainers. He grabbed her hand, a flash of metal, she shouted, took a swing at him and he was gone, darting through the crowd, scampering like a rat in a sewer. A whistle blew, more shouts, then hammering, the sound of boots running. Larry broke free from behind the barrier. He threw his arms around Kathleen MacReady. She clung to him.

"Larry, the case," she gasped.

"I know, are you okay? That's the main thing," he said.

She looked up at him, eyes bright with fear. "He had a pair of pliers – just clipped through the chain and was gone."

"You sure you're okay?" he asked again. She showed him her wrist; what remained of the security chain swung free.

"Fine, he didn't touch me but the case, the jewels ..." She turned to watch the stream of blue snake through the crowd; the police were trying to pick up the trail, follow the thief. People gathered around, other passengers, checking pockets for wallets, holding handbags and purses closer, tighter. Two police officers appeared beside them.

"Will you come with us ma'am. We'll need a statement, you can tell us exactly what happened." A handsome officer smiled at her.

Larry took her arm. "I'll come too officer. This lady is my guest, it's her first visit to New York."

"I'm sorry ma'am. We'll deal with this as quickly as possible and get you on your way. Where are you travelling on to?" the nice officer asked.

"The nearest bar if I have anything to do with it." She flashed him a smile. There was something about a man in a uniform.

Later, in Larry's immaculate nineteenth floor apartment, Miss MacReady was relieved to kick off her heels and remove her hat, letting her hair down. She sat at the large glass and chrome dressing table in Larry's spotless guest suite, examining her reflection in the mirror. *Not bad,* she thought, after an eight and a half hour flight across the Atlantic, an airport mugging, a police interrogation and a taxi ride downtown. She took off her jacket, undid a couple of buttons on her blouse, sprayed cologne on her throat and wandered into the sitting room where Larry was mixing a stiff gin and tonic at the bar.

"I heard you on the phone earlier?" she said, arranging herself on a large cream sofa.

"I called Lena, to tell her what happened. She's going to let Mr Rossini know the score. The jewellery belongs to him, he'll have to deal with the insurance company, not our responsibility anymore. The method of transportation – by that I mean you and the airline – was all agreed. We're in the clear." He handed her a glass. She took a grateful sip.

"That's good to know. They'll pay out then?" she asked.

"They'll have to, eventually." He came to join her on the sofa. He looked cool and elegant like the room: soft turtleneck sweater, pale grey slacks.

"And if the jewellery turns up?" Miss MacReady was impressed by how relaxed Larry appeared.

"It won't, not in its current form anyway." He checked his watch. "No, that's long gone by now and good riddance."

Miss MacReady watched his mouth as he drank. She moved a little closer; he gave her a smile.

"I can't help feeling I was set up, part of a *sting*. Call me a *romantic* but it was like a bad thing happened for all the right reasons." She gazed into his eyes.

"You're a romantic," he said, looking back at her.

"Then kiss me," she whispered, her lips nearly touching his.

"With pleasure, ma'am," he replied and at last she tasted that warm, sweet mouth full-on.

They arrived at the bar between 46th and 45[th.] The archetypal Irish pub, a proper New York tradition, with huge semicircle windows, olive green paintwork and gleaming brassware at the entrance. A welcome mat stretched the width of the pavement, emblazoned with a shamrock and the words 'Maguire's Bar and Grill'; a massive gold and green striped awning ran the length of the building. Larry stepped out of the cab, taking her lavender-gloved hand and guided her to the building, opening his arms to encompass the impressive frontage.

"Well, what d'ya think?" he said. "One of my best pals has had this joint forever, inherited from his grandfather. It does well, works damn hard though."

Miss MacReady smiled, Larry and his 'work ethic', she stood on the sidewalk and took in the building. A feeling passed through her, like a ghost.

"Have I done the wrong thing? Is this the last place an Irishwoman visiting New York wants to go, an Irish bar?" he looked askance.

"Not at all, same name as the pub on the island, I'll feel instantly at home." Miss MacReady beamed at him, tipping her matching lavender trilby over one eye. She would have preferred a visit to *Tiffany's* of course, but Larry had been stressing about her visit ever since they had agreed she would take the jewellery back. He had gone to a lot of trouble and she wanted him to enjoy it as much as she did.

They swung through the doors; every surface gleamed and shone, crisp white table cloths, sparkling glassware, gleaming cutlery. A doorman in green livery raised his hat.

"This is Malachy, Kathleen, or Sergeant Malachy should I say," Larry grinned.

"Long retired," laughed the big man. "Is this guy bothering you ma'am?" he asked, winking at the glamorous female on Larry's arm.

"Ah sure, bother away, I'm delighted to be bothered at all!" She smiled up at the broad, fair-skinned face.

"No way, you're Irish, heavens above, you're the real deal." The ex-policeman looked down at her. "Where are you from ma'am?" But before she could answer, Larry whisked her away.

"Pushy, ain't they, these Irish?" he said nodding back at the doorman, as an elegant maître d' swivelled into view.

"Mr Leeson, madam, your table is ready, follow me." Another Irish accent, this time cultured, with a hint of the north. A young cloakroom attendant appeared to take Miss MacReady's coat and hat. Larry shrugged out of his sheepskin jacket and they followed the maître d' through the glistening tables to a window booth, a few steps from a small dance floor and shiny, baby grand piano. Miss MacReady took her seat. A napkin was placed on her lap, water poured, breadsticks and butter served. She squeezed Larry's hand on the table.

"This is lovely." Her gaze swept the room, laughing young couples on weekend breaks, well-heeled middle-aged women on shopping trips, friends, families, lovers. *Sunday brunch in New York* – a glorious, time-honoured tradition.

The waiter indicated the buffet table: fresh fruit; pancakes; syrup; eggs of every description; hash browns; ham; steaks, the menu inexhaustible.

"Ma'am if you would like to help yourself, I'll bring drinks, what's it to be?" the waiter asked.

Larry nodded at her, "Well Kathleen, it's nearly Monday, Sunday anyway, what about one of your favourite cocktails?"

"Oh yes," she grinned up at the nice looking young man, "a Bloody Mary please, good and spicy. Will you join me Larry?"

Larry raised an eyebrow, "Why not, it's a special occasion after all."

They enjoyed a sumptuous meal and two hefty Bloody Mary's apiece when Miss MacReady decided it was time to help the pianist out with a song. Larry was about to protest. He knew she could sing, but a singalong in a country pub was a far cry from a classy joint in uptown New York; he did not want Miss MacReady to embarrass him, or herself. He need not have worried. Miss MacReady was nothing if not surprising, she could sing alright. Her rendition of *'Wind Beneath My Wings'* brought diners to their feet and, because her public demanded it, Miss MacReady finished her set with a swinging version of *'You Make Me Feel So Young'*, one of her mother's favourites.

"Do you bring all your young ladies here?" Miss MacReady asked, twirling the stirrer with the bar's logo in her drink.

"Every last one!" Larry teased, "Funnily enough it was Ryan who discovered the place. He knew Mac, the owner, who of course has Irish roots. Mac was good to us when we were struggling actors off-Broadway, fed us, gave us free drinks. Now this is my patch, office across the street, apartment a few blocks away. You could say it's my local."

"I can see why you love it, New York, your life here. It's so, well alive." Miss MacReady sat back to survey the surroundings yet again: the huge floor to ceiling mirror behind the slick, marble bar, brass lamps standing tall along the length of it, the waiters in their crisp white aprons bustling to and fro, traffic humming outside.

The door swung open and Larry raised a hand in recognition.

"Ah, here's Mac now, I'd like you to meet him," Larry said.

The man, tall, broad-shouldered, about Miss MacReady's age,

saluted back, indicating he would be right over. He removed his coat, gave it to the cloakroom attendant, chatted briefly with the maître d', then nodding at tables, walked through the room towards them. He looked relaxed, in control.

"Well Larry, haven't seen you in a while, someone said you were in Ireland," the man said warmly, a hint of accent only, "and who is your charming companion?"

Larry stood up to shake his hand.

"Great to see you Mac. Allow me to introduce Kathleen MacReady, a very good friend of mine, all the way from *the old country.*"

Mac held out his hand. Miss MacReady did not take it; she just looked up into his face.

"We've met," she said. "Hello, Brian."

"Kathleen MacReady, I, I can't believe it," the man stammered.

"You know each other?" Larry was surprised, pleased. Miss MacReady remained seated. She took her napkin from her lap and folded it neatly, placing it on the table.

"Larry, would you mind if we left now," she said quietly. "I feel rather tired."

"Don't go!" Mac, or Brian, or whatever his name was, said loudly. People looked over at them. "Please don't go," he said more quietly. "I'll just die if you go."

She could not bear to look at him. "And I'll just die if I stay," she whispered, getting unsteadily to her feet. Larry rushed to take her arm.

"Kathleen?" he was bemused.

The other man reached out towards her, "Please don't let me spoil your brunch."

"Spoil my brunch, are you joking? You, who has spoiled my entire life." She shrugged him away. The man waved a hand. Waiters appeared pulling out chairs. The cloakroom attendant arrived with their outer garments.

"A cab for my friends," he said to the maître d'. Miss MacReady walked the length of the restaurant head held high. She took her seat in the cab, Larry beside her. Mac or Brian shut the door.

"Is that who I think it is?" Larry asked, holding her hand.

"You mean is that the piece of shit who fathered my child? Yes, Larry it is."

"Ah," Larry sat back as the cab pulled away. "I'd better cancel the booking for dinner then, I thought we'd go there on your last night, you were such a hit!"

"It'll be his last night if I ever see him again," she said, glaring out of the window at the city streets, pink spots of anger stinging her cheeks.

Now Brian Maguire had Kathleen MacReady back in his life, he was not prepared to let her go easily. By the time the florist had made four deliveries, Larry's apartment was filled with flowers – white roses, her favourite. Every card the same message. *'Meet me, we have to talk, Brian'.* She was tearing up yet another into tiny shreds when Larry appeared with tea and toasted bagels. He sat beside her, taking her hands in his. She had not slept a wink. "Won't you even contemplate seeing him?" Larry tried. She shook her head. "It was all such a long time ago, surely you could at least talk?"

She turned tear-filled eyes on him.

"He's been here all this time, not dead, not lost. Living and working in New York. Never a word, no hint, nothing." She pulled her negligee around her. She seemed suddenly small, birdlike. "I want to go home now, Larry. I can't even stay in the same city, I'm sorry."

Larry sighed, he had never seen such a change in a person; the frivolous flirt he had been escorting around town vanished.

"Sleep on it?" he offered.

"But that's the whole point Larry. I won't. I can't sleep, eat, Christ, I can barely talk." And she left the room. Later, he heard her crying in the bathroom, the door locked. Larry phoned Mimi and asked her to change Miss MacReady's flight; she would be going back to Ireland that very day.

When the man sat down beside her, clicking his seatbelt shut, she did not look up. She closed her eyes ahead of take-off. She did not open them again until the refreshment trolley was at her side. She licked her lips; she could do with a drink.

"What can I get you ma'am?" the pretty stewardess asked.

"Have a cocktail Kathleen, it's Monday," the man beside her whispered in her ear.

"I'll need a fecking large one if I've to sit next to you all the way back," she told Brian Maguire fiercely.

"Better make that two," he said to the stewardess, "I'll have whatever the lady's having. I always do."

Marianne was itemising the contents of some of the boxes they had discovered in the attic at the big house. One in particular would appeal to her mother, crammed full with furs, gowns and bags of accessories, and not all of it moth-eaten. One dress in particular had caught Marianne's eye, a swirling purple satin, lined with lavender silk, as new as the day it was made.

She and the team had been hard at work all day, but they were getting there. She was exhausted. She laid her pen down, and was just about to drift off to sleep when the shrill ring of the telephone woke her with a start.

"It's me Marianne, your mother." Miss MacReady sounded tense, yet excited. Marianne wondered why she was telephoning from New York. More news on the mugging? Had the jewels re-appeared?

"Can you come over?" Miss MacReady asked.

"To New York?" Marianne was sluggish.

"No, I'm home, can you come up to the post office?"

"Now?" Marianne's stomach rumbled. When had she eaten last?

"It's important, I need to see you first before anyone knows I'm back."

Miss MacReady replaced the receiver. "She's on her way," she told the man standing beside her.

"Okay, if you're sure the shock won't kill her," he said, running his fingers through his hair.

Careful to avoid the tins of paint on the landing in the half-light, Marianne told Monty to stay and headed out into the early evening.

The revelation that the handsome man standing next to the postmistress in her inner sanctum was her father rendered Marianne speechless. She heard a loud whooshing in her ears and her throat started to burn, eyes darting from one to the other. Miss MacReady took her by the hand and sat her down on the large, floral sofa. The whole room appeared in black and white except for that garish piece of furniture. Marianne's mind whirred blankly.

"Anyway, I wanted you to know first, meet in private, take it from there," Miss MacReady was saying. The man was pouring a drink; he handed it to Marianne. She looked up into his face. *Why was it so familiar?* She had never seen him before in her life. She took a sip.

"I'm sorry," she whispered.

"I'm the one who's sorry," he said, a warm, soft voice, a hint of the island, shades of New York. "Yet thrilled, delighted beyond my wildest dreams to meet you Marianne, my daughter, finally."

"It's a lot to take in, probably best not to even try," Miss MacReady said, lighting candles all over the place.

"Was it planned for you two to meet up? Did you know he was there, in New York?" she asked when she eventually found her voice. The man was sitting quite close to her, a strange look in his eyes.

"Ah, when fate decides to lend a hand," Miss MacReady said, staring at them both. The man shook his head.

"Could someone start at the beginning?" Marianne said, her heart-beat nowhere near normal.

"Good plan," Miss MacReady said, drawing up a footstool to sit as close to them as she could. "Let me take you back, right back to a little girl on a boat. It's only a small boat and her mother is sailing it. She's a good sailor and the little girl loves it. It's a summer's day and they've just landed on a tiny shale beach, which leads to a formal lawn, with a tall, elegant building in the background.

"There's a little boy playing on the beach, building a very lavish sand castle. He's singing to himself, the breeze blowing his dark curls like a black halo around his head. He sees the mother and little girl and stands up, politely waiting for them to reach him. He extends his hand to the little girl and says, 'My name is Brian Maguire, what's your name?' 'I'm Kathleen MacReady,' says the girl and promptly falls in love with him, and from that day on, despite coming from very different backgrounds, the two are inseparable and will love each other until the day they die."

Marianne blinked at Miss MacReady.

"But I'm guessing you'd like a bit more of the practical detail," Brian said, smiling at Marianne.

"Only tell me what I need to know," Marianne replied. "Mother can be either vaguely ethereal or brazenly graphic depending on her mood."

He laughed out loud, making the women jump.

"Mother. I like that, suits her doesn't it?" he said, and Miss MacReady gave a sparkling smile as Brian Maguire told his side of a very typical 'girl gets pregnant, family disowns her, boy is sent away by his parents' story and Marianne listened in awe as she watched the years between them fall away and this long-time, brokenhearted couple weep fresh tears for the child they thought they had lost and a life together they never shared.

"But, you didn't stay in touch," Marianne said eventually in a small voice.

"I wrote every week, the only message I received was 'The baby died, Kathleen never wants to see you again'. The postmistress at the time ..."

"My aunt, Dolly," Miss MacReady interjected.

"Destroyed each and every one of them," Brian said. "She was under strict instructions from our parents to prevent us ever communicating with each other again."

"So they made sure you could never be together, never marry, never have any more children?" Marianne asked, shocked by all she had heard.

"That's the truth of it," Brian looked up at Miss MacReady. "And now we've found each other again."

Miss MacReady's face was wet with tears.

"How cruel, our own parents, it was obvious we were in love, we were young, it wasn't even a mistake, you were a gift, a precious gift." She blinked at Marianne. "My own mother did this despicable thing to her own child." Miss MacReady put her hand to her throat, where a rash of anger burned.

"Now Kathleen, don't talk like that," Brian said, trying to mollify her.

"I will talk like that, ruined my life that bloody bitch did," she flashed at him.

"At least it's not my fault anymore," Brian said smiling at Marianne, who liked him more and more the longer she spent with him.

"Well, well, well, there's a turn-up, as they say," Ryan was tearing lumps of ham off a joint Marianne was resting ahead of carving it for the 'Ham & Egg' special on Maguire's lunchtime menu. He had just had a pint with his old pal Brian Maguire or Mac, as he called him and was filling Marianne in, on how the island connection had meant Mac instantly took to him, and his buddy Larry, when they were young, out-of-work actors in New York.

"He was a bit like a kindly uncle to both of us," Ryan explained, disappointed they could not spend more time together, before Miss MacReady took Brian to the airport and he headed home to New York.

"I bet those who remember him were surprised to see him?" Marianne said, putting mustard into little pots.

"Sean was his usual happy self about the whole thing, asking was it still Halloween, seeing as the dead had come back to haunt us!" Ryan was smiling.

"Surprised we've any tourist trade at all with charming locals like him waiting to greet everybody." Marianne was not amused.

"I think Kathleen has made him welcome though," Ryan twinkled at her.

"Suit each other don't they?" Marianne said, moving the ham out of his way.

"Yes, they do, but she's left Larry brokenhearted," Ryan told her. "He's emailing me every hour with script amendments, schedules, dates for costume fittings, all sorts of crap, clearly throwing himself into his work, now she's taken up with her old flame."

Marianne tutted at him. "Shame Brian couldn't stay longer, I'd like to get to know him, seems a nice guy." She was wistful.

"Said he had some business to attend to, appointments and such, I think he'll be back though, they still seem pretty crazy about each other," Ryan said.

She sidled up to him, "Do you think we'll be like that?" she blew hot breath on his neck. He grabbed her wrist, pulling her to him.

"Oh yes, I'll always be hot for you, especially if you feed me a bit more of that ham, it's delicious." The baby alarm shrilled to life; Joey was teething and cranky.

"Go and see to your son, I'll make you a ..." but before she could finish her sentence Sinead swept through the room and up the stairs.

"I'll see to him, don't want him to set Bridget off," she said as she passed.

Erin came through from the bar; there was a speaker there too.

"It's okay," Marianne told her.

"Sinead?" Erin asked. Marianne nodded.

"She's obsessed with those kids," Erin said.

"Is she?" Ryan asked.

"She is a bit," Marianne agreed, "and she's not looking at all well lately, very pasty."

"I know what she needs, what we all need – a day out at sea!" Erin declared.

"It's November," Marianne reminded her.

"Sure you can get a gorgeous day this time of year. Head out early, pack a good hearty picnic, take a turn around the bay and home in time for tea. Come on, it'll be great, and I'd love to get out on the water before I have to go back to the *rat race.*" Erin said.

They both looked up. Despite rocky beginnings Marianne did not want Erin to leave and Ryan liked her, hoping she and Dermot might hit it off, and Dermot would give up making *puppy-dog-eyes* at Marianne.

"Have you a boat in mind?" Ryan asked her. "Ouch!" Marianne slapped his hand wandering towards the ham.

"Padar," Erin called down the cellar, "will you give me and Marianne a loan of that old boat you have for a turn around the bay?"

"What?" Padar called back, amid clunking.

"Your boat, give us a go of it, will you?"

"Sure, if it keeps you out of my hair for a few hours. One of the building lads hired it for the weekend, you'll have to get it back off him," Padar told her.

Erin shrugged, "I saw it back on its mooring this morning. I know where the keys are, I'll check the weather and we'll make a plan, say Wednesday or Thursday this week. Are you on?" she looked at Marianne.

"Can you skipper her?" Marianne asked.

"No bother," Erin replied, "what about you?"

"Incompetent crew," Marianne smiled.

Sinead appeared with Joey on her hip, he was sucking a banana covered in *Bonjela.*

"Fancy a girlie day out this week?" Erin asked.

"Not sure, the children, you know," Sinead replied.

"We'll bring them with us," Erin smiled at Marianne, "and Monty too. We'll all go, we could do with a nice restful day on the water, a bit of sea air."

"I'd better warn the coastguard," Ryan said, stuffing more ham into his mouth as he fled the kitchen.

"Goodness me, to what do I owe this honour? You haven't been on the island since, let me see, when was it, Bridget's christening? And only then because we had you carried over the water in five star luxury, on one of those superstars' yachts. We've always been a bit rough and ready for you, haven't we, Joyce?" Miss MacReady said, hugging and kissing her sister repeatedly during the diatribe. Joyce waved her away.

"Stop fussing Kathleen, I don't think that at all, but I do think you need a decent bridge to the mainland and the sooner the better. Good men and women fought long and hard to get that bridge built back in the day. It's a disgrace that shower up in Dublin didn't declare it a national priority and send the boys down by the lorry load to get the job done!"

She dropped her bag in the doorway and walked through the spangly curtain into the kitchen. It was *gismo central,* everything coloured, mainly purple. Very appetising, Joyce surmised. She would love a cup of tea, but where to start, was there even a kettle in amongst all the paraphernalia?

"A drink Joyce?" Miss MacReady eyed Joyce's overnight bag uncertainly.

"Yes please Kathleen. I don't enjoy travelling as you know." Joyce re-emerged, beaten.

Miss MacReady disappeared into the kitchen and returned almost immediately with an ice cold sherry for her sister and a large whiskey for herself.

"Well," Miss MacReady asked, settling herself on the sofa, while her guest took the merest sip of her drink, pacing around the room in sensible shoes.

"I'm all ears," Miss MacReady tried again, although she was pretty sure she knew what had brought her well-meaning sister to her door.

"It's a surprise!" Joyce said.

"What's a surprise?" asked Miss MacReady.

"Well, I am, obviously," Joyce replied, lifting her arms and twirling a bit.

"Okay I get that, but why, why are you surprising me?"

Joyce thought about this briefly. "For your birthday."

"Thanks, but you're either six months late, or six months early, depends on how you want to approach it."

Joyce looked a little uncomfortable. "Do I need a reason?"

"Of course you do, I've never known you do anything without a reason," Miss MacReady smiled at her sister to take the sting out of her words. Joyce fiddled with the collar of her neat tweed.

"Well, I haven't seen you for ages, you being in America and all, I just thought ..." Joyce surveyed Miss MacReady's inner sanctum in dismay. If she were to stay, where would she even sit. "... ah sure, I needed a break."

Miss MacReady cut to the chase.

"You know who I saw in New York don't you?" There was a short silence.

"I believe so," Joyce did not meet her sister's eye.

"And you believe so because he told you so, because you have always known he was in America, right there in downtown New York!" She threw her drink down her throat.

"Now Kathleen," Joyce said, crossing the room to where her sister sat, "it's not what you think. I wasn't doing anything behind your back."

"What, for over twenty years you stayed in touch with him and never mentioned or even hinted at it. Did you not think you should tell me, your own sister, for God's sake! That treacherous, spineless, two-faced bastard ruined my life and you're pen pals?" Miss MacReady was livid.

"Ah, Kathleen," Joyce made soothing gestures as her sister's voice rose.

"Ah nothing, it's unbelievable, and then our child, the daughter I was told was dead, is here and still you didn't think I should know about him and he about her. What are you, the Secret *fecking* Service?" Miss MacReady stormed into the kitchen.

"Kathleen, you're angry, I can see that, I understand why, but it's not what you think, it was pure coincidence. Brian and I were put in touch by accident. I didn't know it was him for years, we both operated under code names," Joyce tried to explain.

"Heavens above! Don't tell me you're still at that, playing bloody *freedom fighters* in this day and age, at your time of life. I've heard everything now." Miss MacReady flung herself back on the sofa.

Joyce arched an eyebrow. She may have been lax, insensitive even in the communication department as far as her sister and her estranged lover were concerned, but she would not have her political beliefs, indeed her life's work, mocked!

"Kathleen, you have no idea what you're talking about, the

movement is strong, gaining momentum, there's work to be done, there's a new dawn on the horizon," Joyce refrained from putting her clenched fist to her breast.

"New horizon, my arse! About time you losers got a grip and concentrated on making today's reality work, instead of clinging to a past that never did have a lot going for it in the first place," Miss MacReady scoffed.

"You're a fine one to talk about clinging to the past," Joyce said. Then, when she saw her sister's eyes fill with tears, she ran to kneel beside her. "I'm sorry Kathleen, I didn't mean that."

Miss MacReady looked away. Joyce continued.

"I didn't know who my contact was, I'm not supposed to, but a few years ago I was sorting out some new IDs for the 'couriers' and I recognised him. He's not changed at all really, goes under the name of Mac now I believe."

Miss MacReady wiped her eyes and nodded, "Runs a very smart bar in uptown New York, a pillar of the establishment. Don't tell me that's all a front for your crowd?"

Joyce shook her head, "Not that I'm aware of. Brian was a negotiator, a go-between, I can't say anymore than that."

Miss MacReady sniffed.

"Oh, so he's not actually a mass murderer on top of everything else. That makes me feel a lot better." She stood up. Joyce sat down.

"Kathleen, this is about you and Brian now. When I did find out it was him I had many sleepless nights about whether I should tell you or not. Why stir all that up again, you both had your own lives, we'd no idea Marianne even existed, he could have been married, had a family, so I thought the best thing to do was let sleeping dogs lie."

"You were protecting him, siding with the enemy, that's what you were doing." Miss MacReady headed back to the kitchen for a refill.

"I was protecting you. I couldn't bear to see your heart broken again."

"But can't you see Joyce," Miss MacReady reappeared, eyes blazing, "my heart is still broken. Your betraying me has not made an ounce of difference."

Joyce stood up and sighed, "And now you've seen him, he's been here and met Marianne, are you not reconciled? Is there hope?"

"Hope? How can there be hope, I'm here, he's in New York, so much time has passed. We could have been together. We could have had a life, instead of two, separated, broken hearts." Miss MacReady continued to glare at her sister.

"I can see you're very upset Kathleen and very annoyed with me and I apologise if you think I did wrong, but I did what I did for the right reasons. And as to your heart still being broken, maybe it is, but many of us carry a broken heart, deep down, for most of our lives, wearing yours on your sleeve could be viewed as attention seeking." Joyce went to the hallway and picked up her bag. "From where I'm standing, you have a lot to be grateful for, a lot to bring joy to any heart, broken or not." And she opened the door of the post office, letting herself out into the street. The bell made a hollow ring as she left.

Joyce MacReady cut a lonely figure, walking from the post office along Main Street towards Maguire's. She carried her overnight bag in one hand, securing her hat with the other. It was a bright blustery day. The Atlantic, glimpsed between the buildings, was glittering and playful. Marianne was in Weathervane's little garden, hanging out washing. Monty was helping by taking pegs out of the basket on the patio. Marianne picked him up to retrieve the last peg, when she spotted the woman coming along the street. She thought it looked like her mother's sister Joyce, but she was not striding out the way Joyce did, she looked weary. As she drew closer Marianne saw it *was* Joyce. She let herself and Monty out of the gate to greet her.

"Joyce," she called, waving. The woman looked up, startled. Marianne could see she was crying. She ran to her.

"What is it? What's wrong?" she took Joyce's bag from her. Joyce rummaged in her pocket for a handkerchief and blew her nose.

"Oh nothing, just me being a silly old woman," she gave Marianne a watery smile. Marianne considered Joyce neither silly nor old.

"Haven't seen you for ages Joyce, would you not come over to the cottage and have a cup of tea with me? I was just about to put the kettle on." Marianne looked into the other woman's face. Joyce brightened.

"Thank you Marianne. It's a long way to come and turn straight back," Joyce said. Marianne frowned. Joyce looked as if she had been coming from the post office. It was early. The postmistress would have been at her work.

"Was Miss MacReady not in?" she asked, as they walked the short distance along the lane to Weathervane, Monty trotting between them.

"Oh, she was in alright!" Joyce said, sniffing back her tears. "I probably shouldn't have surprised her."

Marianne cut a slice of porter cake as Joyce sipped her tea. She had removed her hat and fixed her hair and looked a bit more like the fastidiously neat and solid little countrywoman she was.

"Your home is lovely, Marianne. I like the way you've brought the colours of the island into it, and the textures too, very cleverly executed." Her gaze swept approvingly around the sitting room: walls stained the colour of sand; the floor strewn with knotted wool rugs in sea-green and teal; chunky knit throws in ochre and slate; tweedy cushions reflecting the greys and browns of the cliffs.

"Thank you," Marianne handed her a plate. She could see Joyce was not going to tell why she had been crying. "Didn't take much thinking about, just seemed to evolve."

Joyce pointed at the painting, unframed and propped on the mantelpiece; a magnificent stag in silhouette, looking out across a lake, hazy mountains in the distance.

"Who's the artist?" she asked.

"Ryan, actually." Marianne smiled, she loved the picture. She had found quite a few in Ryan's jumble of luggage. All landscapes, echoes of his homeland. She was planning to sort through them, have them framed and hung about the place.

"I didn't know he was a painter as well as an actor and now a writer," Joyce said.

"Neither did I," said Marianne. "He's full of surprises." And she turned away to hide a blush, remembering her early morning wake-up call, as Ryan, letting himself into the house, slipped into the shower, to recreate the lovemaking of their first glorious weekend together, when he had surprised her with a sumptuous scene of seduction she had not even tried to resist. She shuddered with pleasure. Joyce laid her cup on her saucer; the chink broke Marianne's reverie.

"I'm pleased you're making your home here. It must be so nice for Kathleen. Not only to be reunited with the child she thought had died, but to have you here, right beside her and now with your family too. She's become a mother and a grandmother in one fell swoop, from a spinster of this parish to this." Joyce smiled warmly at her niece but there was something behind her eyes. "And you've heard the latest, who she met in New York and was here briefly?"

Marianne was unsure how much Miss MacReady would have told Joyce.

"Yes, I've met him too," she said.

"And how do you feel about it all?" Joyce asked.

"A bit overwhelmed, if I'm honest. Suddenly so much family, when I had none." Joyce was her aunt and Marianne knew nothing about her. "Were you born on the island, Joyce?"

"Yes, we all were. Six of us; I'm the eldest, then Kathleen, John and James, no longer with us," she blessed herself, "Agatha in Australia and then Patrick, the baby."

"And your parents?"

Joyce finished her tea. "Long story," she said, getting up. "Perhaps for another time, but you're the image of our mother, Bridie. I know Kathleen won't have it but you are. She was a beauty, no doubt about that."

"I'd love to hear more, maybe see some photos if you have any?" Marianne said. "Miss MacReady, I mean, my mother, has said so little about her."

Joyce was at the door, about to leave, when it burst open and Miss MacReady appeared. Marianne noticed she was dressed demurely, also in tweed, perhaps in deference to her sister, a full-length heather skirt, matching nipped-in jacket, purple silk scarf, pearls at her throat. She rushed in.

"You're here, thank goodness. I thought I might have missed you," she said to Joyce. Joyce stiffened. "I'm sorry," Miss MacReady continued, staring at her sister, eyes brimming with tears. Marianne looked from one to the other. Joyce waved her hand dismissively.

"Marianne and I had a lovely chat. I was glad of the opportunity to get to know her," she said.

"I'm truly sorry," Miss MacReady said again.

Joyce was putting her hat on. "Marianne, do you know when the next ferry is?" she asked, ignoring Miss MacReady.

"Oh Joyce stay. Don't go off in a huff," Miss MacReady said, moving to put her arms around her sister. Joyce turned to look at her. "Joyce, I said I'm sorry. Come and have lunch with me, see if I can persuade you to spend some time on the island. I see so little of you, please."

Joyce gave her a wan smile, "We always end up disagreeing."

"We don't," Miss MacReady exclaimed, hugging her.

Joyce patted her back, "You're always so emotional about everything."

"I'm not, I'm tired, that's all," Miss MacReady told her.

"Come on then," Joyce said, reaching for her bag. "Where shall we eat?"

"Shall we go to the pub? They do a nice 'special' on Tuesdays and I could do with a drink myself."

"You spend too much time in the pub Kathleen, always have," Joyce said.

"No I don't. You don't have to drink alcohol you know," Miss MacReady reminded her.

"Nor do you!" Joyce said.

They bustled towards the door. It was the first time Marianne had notice a likeness.

"Will you join us Marianne?" Miss MacReady called back.

"Maybe later," Marianne said, smiling as the two women made their way down the path, still in dispute.

Chapter Thirty

A Leap Of Faith

They were sitting on board the deck of *Dream Isle.*
"It's tomorrow or Thursday, depends on the weather. Still haven't got the exact details of the vessel or its whereabouts, but the cargo's on board and they're getting ready to ship it out." Dermot told him.

"And we just have to intercept it, yeah? Tell them they're under arrest and we take charge of the boat and tow them in – no heroics, no funny business," Ryan said.

"Precisely. A case of 'you're nabbed lads'. We'll take them totally unawares – a couple of fellas out fishing is all we'll be." Dermot was swabbing down the deck, making sure everything was shipshape.

That's alright then, Ryan thought, *because if Marianne is out sailing with Erin and Sinead, she will be none the wiser if I just give Dermot a hand bringing these blokes in.* He was treading carefully. She had gone into a complete rant about deceit ruining people's lives, when Brian Maguire had shown up, saying she could not believe he and Miss MacReady had been unnecessarily separated all those years, each still holding a torch for the other. And was it not strange Ryan had known him all along? Ryan told her Innishmahon was like that, weaving its charm around its people, keeping them close no matter how far away. *No, the least said the better where any extracurricular activity was concerned*, he told himself.

"Okay, sounds like a plan," Ryan agreed.

"Good, do you want to go down below and make sure anything we need is nice and handy," Dermot told him. Ryan started down below. "And make sure the firearms are somewhere dry, no use to us if they're damp."

Ryan laughed, "Oh yes, the pistols." But Dermot was not joking.

Thursday dawned bright and blustery, a steady south-easterly forecast, very little cloud, no rain and a gentle swell. Erin stood on the quayside looking at the boat. It was a fine yacht and although it made her sad to think of how Oonagh had been lost, she was hoping taking the boat out might somehow bring them closer, give her a chance to say her goodbyes. It was the last place her sister had laughed with friends and loved ones, a proud provenance. Erin wanted a little of that too.

By the time Marianne and Sinead and everything needed to give three adults, two children and a West Highland terrier a terrific day out on the water had been loaded, Erin wondered if it might sink, they were lying pretty low in the water.

"Does she usually sit like this?" she asked Padar, who was fussing with the engine, squirting things at random with WD40 and rubbing mildew off with his sleeve.

"I think so," he said unconvincingly. "Well it's used regularly and those lads who had it last time said they'd leave it back as they found it." He kissed the children briefly; he did not want to be aboard any longer than necessary.

"What time will you be back?" he asked Erin, stern line in his hand. Erin checked her watch.

"It's ten now – four-ish?" she said.

"No later," Padar told her, "it'll be getting dark, get back nearer to three if you can."

"We're only going to drop anchor and have our picnic the other side of the island, over by the Marine Research Unit. Sure, you'll be able to see us from every lookout point," Erin assured him.

"So you say, but it's treacherous enough, you know that."

"Ah, Padar, I was sailing round this island before I could walk," Erin snapped, holding her hand out for the line. Padar threw it to her. Marianne was at the wheel.

"Take it steady," Padar shouted at Marianne. "Don't make Sinead seasick," he teased. Sinead had nearly cried off. She felt poorly that morning, but everyone was so looking forward to the trip, she splashed cold water on her face and told them she would come anyway.

Padar could not help the lump in his throat as Bridget waved goodbye from the deck, a real islander, the broadest smile on her face, loving the wind in her hair.

Marianne guided the boat safely out of the marina with Erin at her shoulder, and as soon as they were clear of the other boats, she powered on, cutting through the blue, leaving bright white sparkles in her wake. They pushed into the bay, the island behind, the ocean smooth and welcoming, calling them out. Erin took the helm, guiding them beyond the buoys warning of rocks and then swung the boat west, up towards the top of the island, heading around the promontory of coastline that formed a point on the map.

"We'll get round *Widows Peak* and head into *Cloudy Bay*. It'll shelter us from the wind, we can drop anchor there, and if it's nice enough have a little sail after lunch and then head back," Erin said.

"Good plan," Marianne agreed, smiling at the tinkling laughter of the little ones, watching the yacht sending out spray as it cut through the water, Monty looking over the side, tail wagging.

To all intents and purposes Cloudy Bay looked like a small and very welcoming harbour, but any sailor worth his salt knew the silky smooth surface belied a craggy underbelly that could rip the guts out of a vessel in the merest of moments. Erin had checked the charts the night before and the sonar system on board was state-of-the-art, but she steered stealthily through, finding a clear deep pool to drop anchor and switch off the engine.

The sumptuous picnic of seafood chowder, soda bread, cheese and fruit was soon devoured, followed by one of Marianne's favourites – thick hot chocolate with clotted cream ice cream and home-made shortbread fingers for dunking. She laced the grownups mugs with a splash of rum but Sinead said her stomach could not take it and sipped water instead.

"Is Miss MacReady recovered after being mugged in New York?" Sinead asked Marianne as they sat in the lower deck, the boat rocking gently. The village had been stunned by the news the postmistress had been robbed in the middle of JFK Airport, right in front of Larry.

"Seems quite sanguine about it all," Marianne told her.

"I'm sure it paled into insignificance once she discovered Brian Maguire was alive and well and running the very bar she and Larry were sitting in," Erin said, licking chocolate off a biscuit.

Marianne gave Erin a look.

"It seems everyone is pretty nonplussed about the mugging, almost as if it were bound to happen."

Erin avoided her eyes.

"All's well that ends well. The insurance company is going to pay up, Rossini will get his millions, the jewels will be fenced, goodness knows where they'll end up, and that will be the end of it, my job's done. I'll be heading home soon enough."

Sinead settled the children in a bunk; the sway of the boat would lull them to sleep in no time.

"Where's home?" Sinead asked.

Erin shrugged, "Here and there."

"Would you not stay awhile?" Marianne suggested.

"What for? This place is hardly the centre of the universe, not a lot happens here," Erin said. "I mean, when is there even any news, for God's sake, same old, same old."

"I have news," Sinead said, and a dreamy look came over her, 'lovely news if you'd care to hear it."

They both looked at her, then at each other. "You're pregnant!" They said together.

"No wonder you've been a bit green around the gills," Marianne said, smiling at her. "Are you delighted?"

Sinead nodded, her cheeks turning pink.

"That's crap though isn't it?" Erin said in her usual manner, "with your husband, what's his name Phileas, in the slammer."

Marianne raised her eyes upwards. Sinead shrugged.

"Not really, it's not his."

Marianne's mind flashed back to the scene in the big house, when she and Ryan stumbled upon a couple in a compromising situation. She willed the image away.

"So you're finished with Phileas?" Marianne asked.

Sinead nodded. "I tried to make it work, but things haven't been right between us for a long time. Phileas never wanted children. I thought I could win him over, but no. I can't remember the last time we slept together and then he got involved with a bad crowd. I told him I didn't want anything to do with them, and now with the robbery and everything, I've had enough. I just want a normal life." She gave them a sad smile.

"And the father, does he know yet?" Marianne asked.

Sinead's eyes widened. "No, it's very early, you're the only people who know. I'd like to keep it that way for a while, till it's time to tell him."

Marianne lifted her mug, "Congratulations then, your secret is safe with me."

"And me," Erin smiled at her, "but who'd want to bring a child into this hell hole called Planet Earth is beyond me,"

"Just as well the continuation of the human race doesn't rest in your hands then, Erin." Marianne said, clearing things away.

"Too right," Erin replied, then "what's that?"

They could hear an engine, voices, then clattering feet running down the deck towards them. Monty started to bark. Erin jumped up, heading for the stairs, when two pairs of boots appeared above.

"Hey ...who are ...?"

A man pushed her back down below. Another man followed. They were dressed the same, all in black, balaclavas pulled over their heads.

"Stay calm and no-one will get hurt," one of them said, his voice muffled by the fabric. The other man started to move around the salon, as if looking for something. Monty was barking wildly, he went for the man's ankle. The man kicked him away. Marianne was on her feet.

"Stop! What are you doing? What do you want?" she demanded.

"Shut that thing up, or I will," the man said, taking a gun out of his belt and pointing it at Monty.

"Oh God!" Sinead blessed herself.

Erin jumped on the first man, twisting his arm expertly behind his back. He screamed in pain. The man with the gun turned it from Monty to Erin but she pushed her prisoner in front of her.

"Put the gun down," she said.

"Let him go," the man replied. Marianne was straining her ears, trying to hear an accent, trying to identify the voice.

"What do you want?" Marianne asked as coldly as she could, willing the fear out of her.

"We want you to quietly and calmly get on our boat and go back to wherever you came from," the man with the gun said.

"Put that gun down or I'm going to break his arm, I mean it," Erin said, as her captive moaned in agony. He nodded at his partner. The man put the gun back in his belt.

"There are children with us," Sinead said, appealing to the man with the gun.

"We won't harm them or you, just take our boat and go. Now, as quickly as you can," he spoke more softly to her. Marianne looked at Sinead, *did she recognise him?*

"No way," Erin said fiercely,

"Let's do as they say," Sinead replied, getting up. Marianne had Monty in her arms, he was trembling. She looked at the man Erin had in an armlock.

"If she lets you go, you're not to hurt her. We'll go quietly but you're not to hurt anyone," Sinead glared at him.

"Come on, move it, go, *now!*" The man with the gun said.

"I'll get the children," Sinead disappeared.

"I'm not letting him go until everyone's safe on the other boat." Erin gave her captive's arm another tweak to show she meant it.

"What can you see?" Ryan asked Dermot. Dermot was looking through binoculars at a yacht in the bay, Padar's yacht.

"There's a tender alongside I don't recognise. No-one around though, wait a minute, I can see Sinead and Marianne. There's a man on deck, looks like they're getting in the other boat," Dermot handed the glasses to Ryan.

"They're offloading them. Bloody hell, they're hijacking the boat!" Ryan said.

Dermot nodded, eyes fixed on the vessel ahead. "Yep, looks like Padar's boat is the one the cargo's on, bet those bastards got a shock when they went to sail it away this morning and the mooring was empty. Bet they've been going mad looking for it." Dermot was powering towards the yacht now.

"What's the plan?" Ryan looked through the binoculars.

"Have they cast the women adrift?" Dermot asked.

"Erin's just getting on. She's remonstrating though, looks like she's giving them a right mouthful," Ryan said. "They all look okay though, as far as I can tell."

"I hope so, those bastards will be armed." Dermot replied.

"I was afraid they might be." Ryan put the glasses down. Dermot was travelling so fast, the lenses were covered in spray.

As soon as Erin was on board, Marianne started the engine.

"Fecking pirates," Erin shouted up at the men as they pulled off. "You won't get away with this!"

Sinead was in the stern with Bridget and Joey, rugs over their life jackets, she was singing to them. Marianne tried to keep the little boat steady as they bounced across the water, heading back, following the coastline to her right, up along the bay to swing back over Widow's Peak towards Innishmahon and the harbour. Erin spotted the other boat first.

"Look, it's Dermot!" she said. *Dream Isle* was speeding towards them. Once alongside, Ryan ran to the rail, throwing his leg over. Dermot stopped him, "Wait."

"Everyone okay?" he asked Marianne, looking in the stern for Joey.

She nodded, "No-one's hurt."

"Gave us a bloody fright though," Erin said, holding onto a fender to keep them alongside, "one of them has a gun."

"Just two of them?" Dermot asked. Erin nodded. "I'm sure they're both armed."

"What's it all about?" she asked.

"Notice anything, cargo, boxes?" Dermot said.

"Yes," Sinead said, "in the hold, under the sails, I was looking for blankets. Metal boxes, big ones." She opened her arms wide, demonstrating the size.

Dermot looked at Ryan. "That's it!"

"Smugglers?" Marianne asked.

"Erin, can you get Sinead and the kids safely back in that?" Dermot asked.

"Sure," Erin said, moving towards the wheel.

"Marianne, are you able to keep *Dream Isle* alongside Padar's yacht if Ryan and I go aboard and arrest those men?" Dermot was preparing to go.

"No," Ryan said, "no way, she needs to go with the others, it's not safe."

"We've no choice," Dermot looked at the yacht disappearing. "They've seen us, Erin's the best sailor, she'll get the others back. Marianne will be okay with us, but we need another pair of hands."

Marianne was already climbing on board. Reluctantly, Ryan held out a hand to help her. Monty followed, waiting for the bigger boat to dip in the water so he could jump easily aboard.

"Okay?" Dermot shouted above the roar of the engine. "Let's get this job done!"

Marianne lifted an eyebrow at Ryan.

"Thinks he's *Miami Vice*," he offered. A blue light flicked on, sirens started to wail. Marianne could hear Dermot giving precise co-ordinates over the radio.

"Don't tell me, another *undercover* operation?" she said, strapping on the buoyancy aid he passed her.

"You know of another one?" Ryan asked.

"Island's swarming with undercover agents, pretending they're going on innocent fishing trips and the like." She gave him a half-smile, "what's on the yacht?"

"Arms and cocaine destined for the north, a double whammy. The arms are a decoy for the drugs, seems gun-running is a fairly common occurrence around these parts, left well alone by the authorities." Ryan was wiping the binoculars, watching the smaller boat heading back towards Innishmahon.

"So if drugs are travelling with guns they'll get to their destination unchallenged," Marianne said, impressed.

"Unless of course you give the job to Dermot Finnegan, ex-shining light of Dublin's Gardaí, masquerading as the island's new lifeboat boss." Ryan indicated for her to hold on tight.

"And what are *you* doing here?" she had to shout above the noise.

"Just fishing," Ryan smiled grimly as Dermot spun the boat round in front of the yacht. A wave flipped over the side, just missing him. He cut the engine.

Dermot came out of the wheelhouse and tossed Ryan a gun. Marianne's eyes widened.

"She's in neutral, hold her steady," Dermot told her. "Ahoy there, it's the police," Dermot shouted through a megaphone. The yacht started to pull away. "Swing her round, Marianne, block him," Dermot shouted back, as Marianne pushed the gears forward, turning the boat smoothly, accelerating and positioning it expertly at the bow of the yacht.

She looked up and gasped. Phileas was at the wheel. No wonder they were let go unharmed. He looked down at her, waving his arms, telling her to back off. She shook her head. He tried to ram the smaller boat with the yacht.

"Hang on," Marianne roared at her passengers and blasted away, taking a circle turn back to the yacht once they were clear.

"You're under arrest, turn the engine off and come quietly," Dermot said into the megaphone as they came alongside again.

A man appeared on deck. It was Shay, the ganger for the building lads. Shay who had rented the boat off Padar the previous weekend. Phileas appeared at his side. Dermot registered no surprise.

"Heard he'd escaped via the police network this morning," he told Ryan under his breath. "Thought we might see him today."

Ryan was amazed. "Any word on Pat?"

"If he's any sense he'll stay put, sure he already has a record." Dermot looked up at the men, "Come quietly now."

"Fuck off, Dermot," Shay replied. "You're out of your depth." He and Phileas started to laugh.

"I guessed you'd gone over to the dark side, sergeant, or is this what you call *annual leave?*" Dermot asked. Ryan gave Dermot a look. Dermot nodded at Shay, "That's the arse who was supposed to be my partner on this one."

"Undercover?" Marianne and Ryan said together.

Recognising the man from his earlier vicious encounter, Monty had surreptitiously climbed aboard the yacht.

"Come on now lads, don't make it any worse for yourselves." Dermot was standing at the rail, Ryan beside him, their guns out of sight. Phileas just glared back.

"Dermot, I'm telling you one last time, you and fucking *Tonto* get out while you can. If this shipment doesn't end up where it's supposed to, there'll be trouble, big trouble for everyone," Shay said.

"Yeah, yeah," Dermot replied, just as Monty launched himself at Phileas' ankle, sinking his teeth in as far as the bone. Phileas screamed, Shay lifted his boot and kicked Monty the length of the deck.

"Bastard!" Marianne shouted, and in a flash she too was aboard the yacht. She pushed Shay to the floor, then slithered along the deck on her knees to where Monty lay in a ball. He shook himself and gave his tail a wag, he was fine.

With Marianne in danger and Shay on the deck, Ryan leapt onto the yacht. He grabbed Phileas, pulling his hands behind his back. Shay got to his feet, smacking Ryan between the shoulder blades with the anchor chain. Ryan's knees buckled.

"Enough!" shouted Dermot, standing on the cabin roof, now level with the yacht's deck. He pointed a pistol at Phileas. "Final warning, come quietly."

Phileas swung round, a shot rang out. Dermot dropped to the floor. Phileas had shot him in the foot. Dermot's gun went off. *Bang*, a soft thud as a bullet pierced the yacht's hull. Silence, then a low boom.

"What's that?" Shay shouted at Phileas. "What the fuck did you start shooting for, we could've just sailed away."

"He started it," Phileas screamed back.

Ryan was on his feet. He climbed up the steps to the wheelhouse, crouching beneath smoke billowing up from below. Shay spotted him, lunged, pulling his legs from under him. Ryan twisted in his grip, punching him squarely in the face. Shay fell back. Ryan jumped on top of him, pinning him down. Shay reached back, grabbed a boathook and smashed it across Ryan's chest. Ryan rolled off, winded. Marianne grabbed the boathook, she threw it like a javelin to Ryan, who caught it just as Shay wrapped a line round his ankle, hauling him downwards. The line released a chain uncoiling rapidly like an angry snake. The anchor landed on Ryan's elbow, bones cracked apart.

"Noooo!" screamed Marianne, running to reach Ryan.

Phileas caught her from behind, pinning her arms to her sides.

"Now back off," he shouted at Dermot, who, still armed had dragged himself upright, holding onto the rail of the other boat. Phileas held the gun at her temple.

Snarling and baring his teeth Monty ran along the tarpaulin covering the tender and took a flying leap at the man holding his mistress captive. Phileas spun round, took aim and fired. The little dog took the bullet. He let out an ear-piercing yelp and dropped to the deck like a stone. Seizing his chance, Dermot fired one shot. Phileas took it in the chest, the force of it sending him flailing off the steps and into the sea.

Dermot turned the pistol on Shay. "What's it to be?" Without looking back, Shay dived off the yacht.

Marianne ran to Monty. Finding it hard to grip, the deck wet with oil and water, she dropped to her knees and pushed herself along, sliding up to him, taking him up in her arms. The bright brown eyes flickered at her.

"It's okay, it's okay, Mont, nothing to worry about." She held his head, pressing her thumb over the hole where the bullet had pierced the white fur, not noticing her fingers, hand, sleeve suddenly seeped in blood – Monty's blood.

Ryan dragged off his jacket, wincing with pain as he pulled the sleeve off his useless, broken arm. Sliding along the deck on his knees towards her, he went to wrap Monty in his jacket, reaching out.

"*Don't touch him!*" Marianne screeched. "Don't touch him," she whispered, "he's going to be fine. We'll get the nice vet to take the bullet out and he'll be fine, good as new." She buried her nose in the space between Monty's ears. The blood seeped like ink into his bright white fur. She cradled him to her; his eyes were closing now.

"Monty, no, no Monty," She shook him, he opened his eyes again. "Stay with me, Monty, come on stay, we've been through worse than this, this is nothing, come on now, Monty, try harder." She gritted her teeth. "Try, *try* for God's sake."

The beautiful brown eyes looked into hers, glazed over and closed, very slowly. The little dog's head flopped to one side. Marianne let out a sound as if she had been stabbed. She could not breathe. There was a deep thud below, another explosion.

"Marianne, we have to go," Ryan said.

Wrapping the little animal up in her arms, she squeezed him to her as tightly as she could. She started to rock to and fro.

"Marie, listen to me, we have to get out of here, the whole place is going to blow," Ryan said, reaching out to her, as she sat with the bundle of fur, huddled in a corner of the stern. She stared at him as if she did not know who he was. A loud crack splintered some of the deck between them, smoke filled the air.

"Marianne, we have to go," Ryan said firmly. He reached out his good hand, *"Now!"*

She shook her head, "I can't leave him."

"Monty's not going to make it love. He'll be in heaven with George and Oonagh. Come with me now, we have to get back before the boat blows up." Ryan tried to keep his voice steady.

"He's still warm, I can feel a heartbeat. If I leave him, he'll get cold," Marianne said desperately.

"Marianne, he's been hit." Ryan swallowed.

She glared at him, wild-eyed. "He comes too." Another explosion, closer, they were taking a lot of water, the boat listed to one side.

"Okay, but move *now,* out of here before we *all* die." He dragged her to her feet, wrapping his jacket around the dog. He gave her back the bundle, and taking her hand led her towards where they could see *Dream Isle* in the water. Dermot gave one wave of recognition, easing as stealthily as he could towards the steps.

"We're going home now, baby." Marianne said to the bundle in her arms, as Ryan guided her down the steps to take the leap of faith onto Dermot's waiting vessel. Marianne, still clutching her bundle, just made it, when a huge boom rang out, and the yacht, turning gracefully on her side, slid beneath the surface. As the deck began to disappear, Ryan took a dive into the water.

In the nick of time, Dermot skilfully swung *Dream Isle* round and out into the ocean, before the wash from the sinking yacht dragged them down with it. Marianne looked up to see the boat disappear as Ryan hit the water.

"No, Dermot, where are you going? You're going away. Go back, go back for Ryan," she roared at him.

"It's okay," Dermot tried to assure the stricken woman, "he'll find us. We need to get as far away from the wreck as possible." He pushed the boat on. No sign of Ryan. Marianne thought she was going to die, there on the spot. She sat in the boat, the still warm bundle in her arms, staring at the flat ocean.

Bubbles broke the surface. There was a splash and Ryan appeared. Dermot had a fix on him and, powering the boat on, headed straight to him. He hauled his friend out of the water. Ryan's shattered left arm swung uselessly by his side.

"Shit, how did that happen?" Dermot asked.

"Ran into a little trouble my stunt double couldn't handle," Ryan quipped through white lips, before turning green and puking over the side. Marianne started to weep. Dermot looked at his battered cargo.

"Hold on, it's gonna be a bumpy ride," he said, giving the boat all the welly he could, trying to balance on one leg.

As they rounded Widow's Peak blue flashing lights appeared in the distance.

"The cavalry's late," Ryan said.

"Yeah, guess they were told not to show until it was all over," Dermot said, grimly.

Chapter Thirty-One

May The Road Rise Up

Sinead had a busy night ahead and was much relieved Doctor Brian Maguire was back on the island, having returned from New York that very day.

As soon as the message came through, they set up a temporary surgery in the back room of the pharmacy and he and Sinead had everything prepared by the time the walking wounded arrived.

Dermot, in the meantime, insisting his was only a fleshwound, had been airlifted to hospital on the mainland and because of the pressure on the emergency services – out looking for any survivors – Brian assured the police they would handle the casualties on the island as best they could, and would make a full report.

The doctor took a look at Ryan's shattered arm and gave him a shot of painkiller. He would have to wait to be treated. Monty was the main cause of concern. The little dog had slipped into a coma, his pulse very faint. He was dying.

Laying him out on the table, Sinead cleaned the wounds just above his left eye and to the right of his ear. Brian ordered Marianne to go and drink some hot sweet tea; he wanted to see what they were dealing with before giving his distraught daughter the prognosis.

"The good news is the bullet went in here and came out here, hence the two wounds," he showed her. "What we don't know is, how much damage it caused as it passed through. Brain damage possibly, his hearing almost definitely, but beyond that, I don't know."

Marianne held her hand out to the limp little scrap of fur, willing the gaping holes to close up and heal, imagining she had the superpowers to do it.

"Can't we do anything? Have him airlifted to a vet?" she whispered.

"I've spoken to a friend of mine, a brilliant veterinary surgeon, one of New York's finest. His advice is, clean the wounds, stop the bleeding and if Monty's body has gone into a voluntary coma, leave well alone. It might be doing stuff on the inside first. It's like everything has closed down while Monty's dealing with what's happened," he spoke slowly as if to a child. "We've done all we can for now, we're just going to have to give this some time."

Sinead was hooking up a drip. Marianne dampened some cotton wool, wiping Monty's eyes, mouth, nose.

"We're going to see to Ryan now, get his arm strapped up, okay?" she said.

Marianne turned to look at Ryan, her heart clamped in a vice, he looked so broken. He tried to give her a reassuring smile but the pain was sickening now.

"Stay with Monty," he said, "I'll be fine."

Dawn was breaking when Sinead slipped back into the surgery to find Marianne still sitting, staring at Monty.

"Any change?" she asked.

Marianne shook her head.

"Why don't you go home for a while, you're exhausted," Sinead told her. "I'll keep an eye on him, he seems stable enough for now." Sinead checked his pulse and temperature.

Marianne did not want to go home to Weathervane, empty without Monty. By now Ryan and Joey were tucked up in Maguire's. How she longed for one of Joey's clingy cuddles, smelling of talcum powder and rusks. Bridget and Erin would be sound asleep too, Padar would have seen to that, she recalled the ravaged worry in his eyes, standing at the seawall, watching anxiously as the police launch guided them back to the marina.

Sinead sensed her reluctance.

"Just go and get some air then, no point in you making yourself ill too." Sinead showed her out. Marianne stopped in the doorway.

"I'm really pleased for you, about the baby, and sorry about Phileas too, a terrible loss."

Sinead shrugged. "I lost Phileas a long time ago, Marianne, he's been dead to me these many years." She squeezed her friend's hand. "When you know what you want you have to go for it, don't you?"

Marianne nodded, "Sure you do," she said, distractedly.

"Hey," he said softly, crouching down beside her in the sand, trying to keep his balance with his left arm in a sling. The sea was a sliver of silk along the beach.

"Hey," she said back, not taking her eyes off the ocean, arms clasped about her knees, holding herself together. The breeze was gentle, a pale moon hung above, too dull to shine, too bright to fade away.

"You must be chilled, Marie, you've been out here for hours, come home now," he said. She did not answer. He waited a while. "Want anything?" he reached out, letting his fingers fall away before he touched her.

"I want Monty back," she said. He let the words hang there.

"I know you do. I want him back too." He joined her, looking out to sea, the waves barely breaking, hushing to a soft ripple on the beach. He turned to look at her: pert nose, determined chin, auburn hair rammed up in an old tweed cap. She looked down. He saw her take a tiny breath, fighting tears. How could there be any more tears? She looked back out to sea.

"What were we even doing there, Ryan? You were supposed to be out fishing with Dermot. I was on a day out with the girls and the children. There was danger out there. You knew about it, yet you let us go."

"We'd no idea the stuff was on Padar's boat. Do you think I'd let you, Joey, any of you, anywhere there was danger, where you could get hurt?" he asked.

She sighed, "I know you wouldn't but you shouldn't have got involved. Life's not a movie, people get hurt, guns kill, there is no *happy ever after.*"

He had never known her like this. She *always* saw the upside, she was his shining light, she made everything right, she was his *happy ever after.*

"There will be a *happy ever after,* you see. Everything's going to be fine, just fine." He stood, brushing sand off his jeans. "See you later?"

"Not if I see you first," she said. Their joke, one of the first things he ever said to her.

"Too late. I love you," he replied, walking briskly away.

Monty had not moved all night. No change in his breathing, no flutter of eyelids, no flicker of life. Marianne was back at his side, having picked up his blanket and favourite toys, when Erin and Miss MacReady appeared. Her mother threw her arms around her, clutching her tightly.

"Erin's after telling me all about it. What a terrifying experience. God forbid, you could have all been killed," she said tight-lipped.

"We're fine, all fine, except ..."she turned to Monty, her voice caught in her throat. Miss MacReady blessed herself.

"Poor lamb. I believe he was defending you when he took the bullet, such a brave little chap," Miss MacReady's eyes filled with tears. "Thank goodness Brian's here, at least he knew what to do."

"Not much help though is he? Look at the state of it?" Erin pointed at the dog.

"Maybe if there'd been a vet on the island," Marianne shook her head.

"It's not a vet he needs, it's a fecking miracle," Erin said in her frank way. She and Miss MacReady locked eyes.

"That's an idea, we could take him to Knock, the shrine, it's famous for its healing powers, it might do the trick," Miss MacReady offered.

"Good plan," Erin agreed, "Come on, Marianne unhook him off that drip, wrap him up. We'll get him there as fast as we can."

Marianne blinked at them. She looked at the lifeless scrap on the table. He needed a miracle alright.

"I appreciate you trying to help, ladies, but have you two lost the plot altogether?" she asked, surmising they had been going over yesterday's events with a bottle or two between them.

"It's worth a try, isn't it?" asked Erin.

Brian appeared at the door; he had overheard the madcap suggestion.

"I appreciate things look a bit desperate from here, but more time is needed I think. Some peace and quiet and a bit more time." He nodded for the ladies to leave. Suitably admonished, Miss MacReady and Erin withdrew.

"We'll keep lighting candles anyway. I'll have the place ablaze, every deity known to man will be called upon." Miss MacReady said as they left. "Do you know any spells, Erin?"

Brian put his arm around the young woman he now knew to be his daughter, he looked into her face, etched with anxiety, terrified she was going to lose this little soul, her closest companion; she turned huge eyes on him.

"Don't let him die, Brian. Maybe that's why you came back to us, so Monty won't die. Maybe you're the miracle."

Brian patted her shoulder and pulled up a chair beside her. They would stay with the dog through the day and the night, and if things got worse, a lot worse, he might do something he had not done since he had last been on Innishmahon, he just might pray too.

She must have slept, because when she opened her eyes Brian was bent over the table and Ryan was holding something at Monty's mouth. She got up.

"What is it? What are you doing?" she whispered.

"Ryan's been on the internet. He seems to think if you give someone in a coma something they like and will remember, it can stimulate the brain, helps bring them back."

Ryan was holding a pork scratching under Monty's nose. The little dog's nose twitched.

"No way," Marianne bent down to him. Ryan did it again, the tip of a pink tongue popped out and licked the treat.

"Monty, it's me, look, open your eyes, come back, come back to me," Marianne said. Monty's eyelids fluttered, flickered again and opened. Marianne let out a cry. Monty tried to focus; he looked from one to the other.

"Ha, ha, there he is, bet you've got one hell of a headache, haven't you boy?" Ryan asked him, holding a paw in his hand. Monty's tail gave one thump against the table.

"Thank you, thank you," Marianne repeated, dropping her head on Ryan's chest with relief.

Ryan tried to wrap his arms around them both, forgetting his arm was still in a sling. "Ow!" he winced.

"Don't start looking for attention now Monty's on the mend, your arm's only broken, don't make a big deal out of it," she teased, squeezing his good arm affectionately, her smile brighter than the sun shining through the windows onto them.

The excitement in Maguire's that evening was building to a crescendo. Not only had Monty come round enough to attempt a wobbly sit-up on Marianne's knee, Brian had proposed to Miss MacReady in the village gift shop that very afternoon, buying her a souvenir sliver Claddagh ring with a moonstone in the heart of it, promising to replace it with a diamond from Tiffany's as soon as he could.

"Don't you dare!" She told him. She was flashing it at Marianne while concocting an extravagant punch to serve guests at their impromptu engagement party.

"I'm sure it's not legal," Marianne said, watching the weird and wonderful mixture of spirits and wine her mother was sloshing into the punchbowl.

"There's no age limit on love you know," Miss MacReady grinned.

Marianne laughed, "That punch, not the engagement."

"The wedding's going to be fabulous, we'll get everyone together, say our vows, ask Gregory to bless our union, have a helluva hooley and that'll be the job done." Her eyes were sparkling.

"I'm delighted, thrilled for you, my parents married at last," Marianne laughed.

"I told you to believe. Miracles happen all the time," Miss MacReady confirmed. "When Brian went back, he rang me from New York and asked me if I minded if he came home, saying he always wanted to come back to Innishmahon to die. I said, don't come home to die, Brian, come home to live, come home right now, we're here waiting for you. So he put the bar up for sale, bought a one-way ticket and now we're getting married. A lot to look forward to, and I'm certainly not going to let him get away from me again." And she tweaked Monty's nose. "We're all coming into our second wind, aren't we boy?" she said.

Brian turned and gave her the biggest smile and Monty, sensing their joy, wagged his tail three times, Marianne knew this, because she was counting.

With Monty well on the way to a full recovery, Ryan and Joey moving back into Weathervane permanently, and work on the holiday home project going full steam ahead, Miss MacReady announced her wedding to Brian Maguire would take place on

December the eighth, the *Feast of the Immaculate Conception,* a highly appropriate choice in her opinion.

She asked Marianne to help with the arrangements, an informal ceremony high on Croghan, the mountain overlooking the sea, where they would say their vows to one another, Marianne would recite a poem and Father Gregory would bless them. They would invite the whole village to a proper hooley in the pub to celebrate their union in style. Ryan and Padar were working on the menu and drinks, and Erin, Sinead and Marianne were consulted over every detail of Miss MacReady's ensemble and bridal trousseau. The happy couple planned to honeymoon in Dublin, returning to the glamorous hotel where their love affair had flourished all those years ago.

The news that Phileas' and Shay's bodies had been washed up a few miles along the mainland coast had a startling effect on the newly widowed Sinead, who was suddenly thrilled to tell everyone she was pregnant, with many assuming the child was her late husband's and others aware of rumours Sinead had been sleeping over in Maguire's when she was babysitting. The official announcement had not yet been made.

Sinead and Marianne were bathing the children, Marianne put a towel on her knees and lifted Joey onto it, he was giggling back at Bridget, who was flicking water up at him, when Padar appeared in the doorway.

"My turn to put these guys to bed," he smiled at the children. "You've told her then?" he said to Sinead.

"Told me what?" Marianne asked.

"No, you better had but it's best if Marianne hears first, being Bridget's godmother and all," Sinead said. "I'll put these two to bed."

"Okay," Padar said and touched Marianne on the shoulder. "Let's go down and have a drink, we haven't had a drink together in a long time."

Now what? Marianne thought, barely able to swallow, her mouth was so dry.

"This is hopeless, I can barely make ends meet. I haven't a clue what I'm doing where Bridget is concerned, and I'm lonely as hell. Now the funding for the bridge has run out, what hope do we have? Nothing's ever going to be the same again." Padar was near to tears, as he picked at the corner of a beer mat on the table.

"When did you hear about the bridge?" Marianne asked. They had all heard rumours the funding was going to be cut.

"On the news, they just announced it," he told her.

"That is bad news," Marianne confirmed. "But nothing's ever going to be the same anyway, Padar, with or without the bridge," she told him.

"I know," he sniffed a bit, "but this was once what I loved – my home, my business, my life and it's gone, all gone. I've grown to dread every night turning into a new day, dreading what that day will bring. I'm sorry, Marianne, I used to love the place but all the good memories have been washed away. I want a fresh start, a new life for me and Bridget. You have to see that's for the best."

Marianne nodded, her heart breaking for the crumpled heap of a man before her.

"I know it's hard, Padar, but you can't give in, you have to go on." She took a sip of whiskey.

Padar lifted his chin and looked her in the eye.

"I'm *not* giving in. I'm going on, but somewhere else, with someone else."

Marianne looked up, "Really?"

Padar nodded solemnly, "With Sinead, the baby's mine, we're going away together to make a fresh start. It's only fair we told you first."

"Oh," Marianne said in a very small voice, "I see."

It was not until the *For Sale* sign went up over Maguire's that Marianne accepted Padar, Bridget and Sinead were really leaving. She ran to Weathervane to tell Ryan.

"The sign, it's up, they're leaving, they're really leaving," she called up the stairs. He poked his head out of the door, he had been painting, despite the sling.

"You knew that, love," he gave her a sad smile. She flew up the stairs and threw her arms around him.

"I didn't want to believe it. How can we survive without Maguire's? And Erin, she's off too. They'll all go together. You'll be away filming before we know it, there'll be no-one left, it will be awful. Poor Joey," she looked at the little boy playing on the rug with Monty, "he loves Bridget, she's like a sister to him."

"I know," Ryan said, "but I also know why they're leaving. I understand, don't you?"

"I do," she said quietly, "but that doesn't make it any easier."

By supper time her mood had really darkened. She spent the afternoon going over the plans and projections for the holiday home project. Without the bridge bringing tourists and trade to the island it was not stacking up, the ferry could not cope at the height of the summer as it is, potential visitors would just go elsewhere. Innishmahon might as well drop off the map.

She had her head in her hands at her desk when Ryan arrived with Joey and Bridget. It was to be their last supper together. Ryan wanted to make it a bit of a party. Marianne just wanted to go to her room and cry.

"Thought you were going to tidy up a bit, you know, put up a few balloons and stuff?" he said. "They'll be here soon."

"Who?" she said putting her files away.

"All of them. I asked them round for a bit of farewell bash, are you okay with that?" he looked into her eyes.

"Ah, Ryan, I'm in bad form," she said moodily.

"I know, that's why I asked them, to get you out of yourself," he gave her his best Hollywood smile. She pretended to swoon and they laughed.

Before she knew it, the tiny cottage was full. Sinead and Padar were in the sitting room with Miss MacReady and Brian, the children with them. Dermot, on a walking stick, was in the kitchen helping Ryan – left-arm still in a sling – with supper. Marianne and Erin were chatting, as they laid the table in the conservatory. Father Gregory brought peat in for the fire.

"Are you okay?" Erin asked, counting the places.

"No, my heart is breaking, losing all of you at once, but I'll cope, I'll have to," Marianne told her.

"Give it time, might not be as bad as you think," Erin said kindly as Ryan announced supper was ready.

They all piled in. It was still light enough to see across the garden, to the road and the ocean beyond. It was warm with them all in there. Ryan folded back the doors, opening the room to the outside. The sea air came rushing in mixed with the aroma of a good old-fashioned Irish stew. It all smelled delicious.

They sat down. Padar between Erin and Sinead, Marianne between Ryan and Dermot, Miss MacReady and Brian each at the head of the table, with Father Gregory perched on a stool at the end.

Marianne looked around the table at the faces, trying to memorise each and every last detail, searing the memory on her brain, trying to hold them all together for as long as possible. All she loved brought together to say goodbye: her mismatched family, some leaving the island, some staying behind, bereft. She tried to smile, join in the banter, but she could not, her heart was too full with love and pain to speak.

Ryan squeezed her hand, proposing a toast – bon voyage to their guests. Miss MacReady, who had clearly had a cocktail or two, kept interrupting.

"Brian, tell them, tell them," she was saying.

"You had better tell us," Marianne forced a laugh.

"Very well," said Brian, grinning broadly at all those gathered, who were grinning broadly back. Marianne could not help feeling she was the only one who did not know what the news was.

"My fiancée and I ..."

Everyone made woo-woo noises and banged the table.

Brian tapped a wine glass with a spoon. Silence descended.

"My fiancée and I have noticed a fine property for sale in the parish, and as I've experience of such an establishment, we consider it wholly viable to make purchase of said property," Brian said in his most pompous voice.

There was much hooraying and laughter.

"What is he on about?" Marianne asked her mother.

"Maguire's," grinned Miss MacReady, "we're going to buy the pub."

"Really?" squeaked Marianne, jumping up to hug her father, delighted.

"Yes and no need to change the sign either," laughed Padar, thrilled he had found a purchaser so easily.

"More news, more news," said Erin, getting to her feet. "I've been offered a most fantastic opportunity, with no choice but to take the position up with immediate effect."

"Oh," Marianne said, deflated.

"Yep, I'm the new manageress of Maguire's!" Erin exclaimed to more woo-woos and table banging.

"What? I'm delighted, I really am, that's great news." Marianne poked Ryan in the ribs. "Did you know any of this?"

"Kind of," he laughed.

"I've told you about keeping things from me," she pulled a face at him.

"Yeah, yeah," he kissed her on the nose.

Marianne could hear Monty ferreting in his basket, Ryan had given him one of the lamb chops out of the stew, but since his near-death experience his sight and sense of smell had not fully returned, he lost things and grumbled for Marianne to come and help him find whatever he was looking for. She excused herself and left the table.

Erin followed her out in search of more wine. "Not too bad then?" she said, smiling at her hostess.

"Well, you're a dark horse, I thought you hated the island, you have a good job, places to go, people to see."

"Made redundant," Erin told her.

"No way!" Marianne exclaimed.

"Yep, a couple of irregularities regarding my last case helped them make the decision, but I got a good payout. It was time for a change, and the scenery around here has improved a bit, anyway," and she left with the wine.

Monty was scuffling in his basket.

"Have you lost your bone again, monster?" Marianne said,

pulling out his blankets, arranging his toys by his bowl. She noticed something glitter in the bottom, it was the brass ring from the brack. She smiled. So the prediction was correct, there was going to be a wedding before the year was out – her own mother and father. She pocketed the ring. There was still something shining in the corner. Thinking it might be glass or a paperclip, she picked at the wicker it was twisted through and pulled it out. Monty yapped at her. There it was, his shiny worm, he thought he lost it, not seen it for ages.

"Wow!" Marianne let out a low whistle, turning the sparkling necklace in her fingers, holding it up to the light. She went back to the doorway.

"Erin, give us a hand in here will you?"

Erin came through. She could tell by Marianne's expression something had happened.

"What's up?"

Marianne held the necklace out to her.

"Where was that?" Erin asked.

"In Monty's basket, he must have pinched it at some point. What do you think, is it the real deal?"

Erin took the necklace and looked at it closely. She checked the back, the clasp, held it up to the light. "It's the real deal alright. Jeez Marianne, it could be worth millions."

Marianne snatched it back.

"God, Erin, what am I going to do with it? I suppose I'll have to declare it, give it back?"

"Who to? Rossini has the insurance money. Anything turning up now would only complicate things. Forget it, keep it," Erin said.

"I can't keep a million dollar necklace, what would I want with it?" Marianne gasped.

Erin shrugged, "Not many occasions to wear it round here I grant you, wouldn't half help towards the funding for that fecking bridge though!"

Marianne felt the ground move. She gripped the worktop.

"Erin, you're a genius!" she exclaimed, kissing her.

"Amn't I?" said Erin, finding the bone and handing it to Monty. "Good work boy," she told him.

They returned to find Miss MacReady on her feet, glass aloft, tears in her eyes.

"Before it gets too late and I may have had a little drink too many, I'm going to give you all an Irish blessing whether you want one or not."

They quietened to listen...

"May the road rise up to meet you, may the wind be always at your back, may the sun shine warm upon your face, may the rain fall soft upon your field, and until we meet again, may God hold you in the palm of his hand."

"Amen to that," said Father Gregory as they raised their glasses.

Marianne lifted hers and glanced around the table before she drank, taking it all in, this happy sad scene, full of family, full of love and, although in some ways tonight was an ending, it felt like a beginning too. Ryan caught her eye.

"Happy ever after," he smiled.

"I'll drink to that," she said.

THE END

Secrets of the Heart

the final book in The Heartfelt Series is available from Amazon now.

Acknowledgements

There is no '**I**' in team, as my team of readers, writers, colleagues, family and friends has clearly demonstrated. Your encouragement and support has moved me to tears at times, I cannot **thank** you all enough, really, I can't.

If there's one very special thing this writing lark has done, it's forged new friendships and rekindled old ones. Sincere thanks to the teams at The Bell, **Burton Overy**; The Cock Inn, Peatling Magna; The Falcon Hotel, Uppingham and The Octagon, Leicester for book launches. To **Deirdre Cotter Daly** and Barbara Nolan, for hosting my first-ever book club appearances in Dublin, and The Belmont Hotel in Leicester, who took the chance on a literary lunch and it worked! And further afield, thanks to my 'pushers-on' **Joan Cringle** and Val Stowe in Lanzarote, and Rita Swan in Boston.

I am indebted to **June Tate**, my mentor and earth-angel, and **Lizzie Lamb**, my dear and formidable friend. For research and soundings, thanks go to Richard Bell, our vet; Frank J. Edwards, stateside; Darina and Rachel Allen, for helping to inspire menus; Rosin Meaney and **Micheal Meaney** for the Irish and Luisa Travers and **Nadia DiNiro** for the Italian. Lorraine Kelly for encouragement and **Sir Terry Wogan**, a very special valentine. Not forgetting Nick from the Island Cruising Club, Salcombe who taught me to handle a powerboat like a Bond girl!

Thanks also, to writing chums the **New Romantics 4**, June Kearns and Mags Cullingford, and colleagues in the Romantic Novelists' Association, always there, rooting for me.

A big 'Yo!' to my 'homies' **Natalie Thew, David Burton**, Michelle Tayton and Madeline Poole, your faith and support is priceless; my family, the Wrafters, **Marion** – the best PR girl on the planet – **Harry, Reta** and my new brother-in-law **John Reddy**; the **Vaughans**, for unerring support; the **aunts**, uncles and cousins, thanks to my huge **Irish** family, all right behind me, sláinte.

And most importantly of all, thanks to my love story, my husband, **Jonathan**, who constantly supports and inspires. His belief in me is truly amazing.

I cannot let this book be published without acknowledging the passing of three people who have each touched my life in a very positive way. The vibrant and talented **Suzie Milton**; the quintessential newshound **Roger Bushby** and the indomitable matriarch **Ethel Hall** ...*the stars will remember.*

Praise for Adrienne Vaughan

For a début novel this was simply astounding, fantastic descriptions of Ireland, warmth and hospitality, the characters were believable and friendships were the kind you wished you had. A tale full of love and laughter.

F. Keegan, Northern Ireland.

Beautifully written, the characters are so well drawn, the descriptions are vivid and colourful, and the Irish background shines through. I loved it!

June Tate, author.

There is romance, drama, heartache and trauma, you will be wiping a tear away one minute and smiling the next.

Elaine G, Top 50 Reviewer.

I absolutely loved this – with beautifully crafted characters, it's an emotional roller-coaster of a read. I really didn't want it to end and can't wait to get my hands on the next book in the series.

Jennie Findley, journalist.

I only put The Hollow Heart down to sleep and go to work.

K.Wyatt, Amazon Review.

I absolutely loved everything about this book – the quirky characters, the humour and the romance. Cleverly written, full of surprises and hugely enjoyable. The twist at the end was the icing on the cake.

Rosy Dickinson, Amazon Review.

I was hooked from the first chapter and by the end of the book felt like I actually knew these people. The story made me smile, lifted my heart and even brought a tear to my eye. I've never been to Ireland but I could feel the pull on my heartstrings to be part of such a place. I hope the sequel follows quickly.

Linda Bensberg, Sidcup, Kent.

Other books by Adrienne Vaughan

The Hollow Heart

Secrets of the Heart

Fur Coat & No Knickers – a collection of short stories & poetry

Check out these great novels published by The New Romantics4

Boot Camp Bride by Lizzie Lamb

20's Girl, the Ghost & All that Jazz! by June Kearns

Twins of a Gazelle by Margaret Cullingford

An indie publishing group: www.newromantics4.com

Available from Amazon for download and in paperback.

About the Author

Adrienne Vaughan is a born storyteller and as soon as she could pick up a pen she started writing them down. It came as no surprise she wanted to be a journalist and dived headfirst into her career after graduating from the Dublin College of Journalism.

Today, she is an acclaimed novelist and poet, and is always writing, editing or thinking about her next book.

Adrienne lives in rural Leicestershire in the middle of England, with her husband Jonathan, two cocker spaniels and a rescue cat called Agatha Christie.

She still, and always will, harbour a burning ambition to be a Bond Girl!

www.adriennevaughan.com
@adrienneauthor

Printed in Great Britain
by Amazon

44842936R00229